# HOW FLEETING IS FAME?

What would our present-day world be like if many of our cultural icons and political movers and shakers had chosen other careers than those we know them for? Would we still be living in the Middle Ages? Would our government be filled with people from Central Casting? Would we already have colonized distant worlds? Would we have world peace or World War III? Would yesterday's film star be today's used car salesman? Would Mickey Mouse have achieved worldwide fame?

Find out all about the might-have-beens and should-have-beens for yourself as you watch today's top tale spinners send our most famous and infamous celebrities down those paths not actually taken to futures not quite our own.

## BY ANY OTHER FAME

## Other imagination-capturing anthologies from DAW Books:

**WHATDUNITS** and **MORE WHATDUNITS** *Edited by Mike Resnick.* In these two challenging volumes of all-original stories, Mike Resnick has created a series of science fiction mystery scenarios and set such inventive sleuths as Pat Cadigan, Judith Tarr, Jack Haldeman, Esther Friesner, Jane Yolen, Stanley Schmidt, Kristine Kathryn Rusch, Jody Lynn Nye, and David Gerrold to solving them. Can you match wits with the masters to make the perpetrators fit the crime?

**DINOSAUR FANTASTIC** *Edited by Mike Resnick and Martin H. Greenberg.* From their native Jurassic landscape to your own backyard, from the earth-shaking tyrannosaur to the sky-soaring pterodactyl, here are unforgettable, all-original tales, some poignant, some humorous, some offering answers to the greatest puzzle of prehistory, but all certain to capture the hearts and imaginations of dinosaur lovers of all ages.

**CHRISTMAS GHOSTS** *Edited by Mike Resnick and Martin H. Greenberg.* Everyone knows the Christmas season has truly arrived when A Christmas Christmas center stage in both amateur and professional productions. Now, Mike Resnick and Martin H. Greenberg have challenged such creative talents as Mercedes Lackey, Frank M. Robinson, Judith Tarr, and Kristine Kathryn Rusch to tell readers exactly what those Christmas ghosts are up to when they're not scaring a stingy old man into self-reformation.

# BY ANY OTHER FAME

### EDITED BY
## Mike Resnick
## and Martin H. Greenberg

## D A W   B O O K S ,   I N C .
**DONALD   A.   WOLLHEIM,   FOUNDER**
375 Hudson Street. New York, NY 10014

**ELIZABETH R. WOLLHEIM
SHEILA E. GILBERT
PUBLISHERS**

First Printing, January 1994

1  2  3  4  5  6  7  8  9

DAW TRADEMARK REGISTERED
U.S. PAT OFF. AND FOREIGN COUNTRIES
—MARCA REGISTRADA
HECHO EN U.S.A.

PRINTED IN THE U.S.A.

ACKNOWLEDGMENTS

# CONTENTS

# INTRODUCTION

Celebrities fascinate us.

We want to know more about them: where they come from, what they think, what they feel, what makes them tick. Why else would Elvis Presley, Marilyn Monroe, James Dean, Humphrey Bogart and others of their ilk be even more famous, more talked about, more written about today than during their lifetimes?

Well, science fiction writers are not immune from sharing that fascination—but science fiction writers are also in the business of asking *What If?* for a livelihood, and so I turned 23 of the best of them loose on their favorite celebrities and told them to go to work. Their speculations await you in the pages up ahead.

What if Elvis had been elected President?

What if Bogey had been a real-life detective?

What if James Dean had become a race-car driver (complete with girlfriend Natalie Wood and best pal Sal Mineo)?

What if Marilyn had become one of the great feminist leaders?

What if Groucho Marx had been given the role of Rhett Butler?

And, of course, fame isn't confined solely to actors, so you'll also be encountering such diverse celebrities as Golda Meier, Helen Keller, Bonnie and Clyde, Franklin Delano Roosevelt, and even the ill-fated filly, Ruffian.

Some of them go on to even greater celebrity; some of them don't. Some have whatever it takes to succeed in these alternate lives; some can't quite get their acts together. But all of them are here for one reason: because during their lives, they fascinated us, and this curtain call is our way of thanking them.

—Mike Resnick

# FAREWELL, MY BUDDY

## by Barbara Delaplace

*To most movie fans, Humphrey Bogart is Sam Spade and Philip Marlowe. But did you ever wonder what Dashiell Hammett or Raymond Chandler thought when they saw Bogey portraying their creations in the movies?*

*Campbell nominee Barbara Delaplace wondered about it— and, in a bizarre twist, she gives us private eye Humphrey Bogart, who is becoming obsessed with actor Ray Chandler's depiction of his hard-boiled profession on the silver screen.*

"Movie stars!" he growls, and hurls the magazine across the office.

*"Betty!"* His voice rises to a shout. "Quit bringing those movie magazines into the office! And quit standing there staring at me like you've never seen me before!"

The blonde woman standing in the connecting doorway once had a beauty as striking as it was unusual, but now it's hard to tell. Worry has lived on her face too long. She responds quietly to the man's outburst. "Okay, I'll make sure I take them home tonight."

He subsides, glaring as she picks up the fallen magazine. He's sick of movie stars, of fakes, of phony detectives who drive expensive cars and charge three-hundred-dollar fees to rich clients. That's not what it's like. "Why don't they check with a *real* detective and find out? I'd be happy to tell 'em."

"I know you would. But it's just the movies. People don't expect them to be realistic. After all, it's just for fun."

"It's not fun to me. This is how I make my living—and they're screwing it up!"

"I think maybe you're overreacting a bit. They've never even heard of Humphrey Bogart, private investigator."

"Oh, get lost!" he snarls, and with a last worried glance, she goes back to her desk.

He's changed. He's not the man she fell in love with and married eight years ago. That much she's sure of. What she's not sure of is *why* he's changed.

Business hasn't been good, which hasn't helped, she muses. Of course, you don't become wealthy in this game, no matter what Hollywood thinks. Matrimonial work, insurance cases, missing persons, none of it is glamorous, none of it pays much, and all of it takes a lot of hard, tedious work. The clients that came through the door of Bogart Investigations, Inc. were never rich, and sometimes they couldn't (or wouldn't) pay up—something else that never seemed to happen to the movie detectives.

But would a business slump explain his mood swings, his increasing bitterness? She doesn't think so.

Betty sighs, looking at her worn suede pumps. Real-life secretaries never seem to look as glamorous as the ones in the movies, either.

But she does have one thing in common with movie secretaries: she doesn't seem to do much secretarying, at least not nowadays. She picks up the movie magazine again and begins to read the article about Ray Chandler, her favorite actor. He's going to be making an appearance on a popular evening radio show in a couple of weeks, after which he'll begin filming *The High Window,* another in the popular series of Philip Marlowe movies.

It's a week later, and the clients are coming through the door with the same frequency they have for the past month: not at all. Bogart sits at his desk, brooding. He doesn't notice Betty poking her head in and quietly retiring again. She's all too familiar with the danger signs, and knows to stay out of the way.

The office clock ticks loudly, and the sounds of the traffic seep in through the open window. Bogart stares through the grimy glass, past the buildings and the streets and the cars, to the peaceful hills in the distance. He'd rather be out there, not sitting here waiting for someone's problem to come walking in the door. But he can't afford a home in the hills, only a shabby apartment in an aging section of town.

Always problems. People can't seem to handle their own lives and when they fail, they expect others to pick up the pieces for them. Nobody ever picked up the pieces when *he* had problems. He tries to remember why he ever went into this business in the first place.

Clients. He's tired of them, too. The last one complained it took too long for him to show results. "As if I could conjure up his missing nephew out of thin air," he mutters aloud. Sure, two hundred bucks is a lot of money, and he doesn't blame the guy for squawking. It's a legitimate beef. But tracing someone who's done a flit takes time. The client seemed to think Bogart should have been able to track him down in short order.

"I mean, geez, Mr. Bogart, I've seen those detective movies. It only takes them a coupla days to find a missing person. So how come you can't find my nephew? You've had a whole week now."

Bogart grits his teeth for a moment, then replies, "Look, Mr. Wells, I've already found out he had a habit of betting on the ponies, a habit he couldn't afford. Maybe he's in too deep to one of the major players and did a bunk."

"What good's knowing that to me? If he's gone, I won't get my money back. He's my sister's favorite boy, so I don't want to call the cops. But why should I pay *you* for no results? Maybe you oughta learn how Philip Marlowe does it."

He supposes it was just as well Betty had been there

to calm him down. Otherwise he might have punched the guy's lights out.

His hands clench into fists. Maybe it would have helped if he *had* flattened him. At least then there'd be one client who'd know the difference between real detectives and movie heroes like Marlowe.

The dingy office depresses him even more than usual, and suddenly it's too much. He stands up, grabs his hat from the stand, and walks through the door to the outer office. "I'm going out," he says to Betty.

"When'll you be back?" she asks.

"When I get here, okay?" he replies sharply.

"And if a client asks for you?"

"Don't kid yourself. How many have we had in the last four weeks?"

She says, "There's always a chance."

"Sure," he says bitterly. "And there's a Santa Claus, too. I'll see you later."

It's a relief to get out of the office and onto the street. He always feels better when he's on the street. As the light turns red, he dodges through the traffic to the newsstand. There he hands the newsie a dime and accepts a paper and seven cents in return. Folding it and tucking it under his arm, he strides down the street to the coffee shop, and is about to enter when a skinny little man in shabby clothes sidles up to him. "Hey, Bogey," he says in a low voice.

"Yeah, Willie, what d'ya want?"

"You're looking for Jack Huston, right?"

"About a month ago I was. You got a good memory, Willie, but a lousy sense of timing."

"He was out of town. Is that my fault?" whines the man.

"Okay, so it wasn't your fault. Feel better now?"

"I try to do you a favor and you give me a hard time. Some people don't have no sense of gratitude. I hear Jack Huston's back in town, and I say to myself, Willie, here's a chance to help out your old pal Bogey. So I come to you and what thanks do I get?" Willie pauses.

"You get a thanks from me and nothing more. Like

I said, I wanted him a month ago," says Bogart. "Now beat it."

"See if I do you any more favors, Bogey. See if I try to help you out again," grouses Willie. "Who cares about you, anyhow? You're a loser—everyone knows about the Goulet case and how you muffed—"

His wind is cut off as Bogart grabs him by the throat and slams him against the side of the building. "Now you listen to me, you little punk!" Bogart grates, his voice low and menacing. "What happened in the Goulet business wasn't my fault. If I hear you've been telling anyone that it was, I'll come after you and you'll wish you'd used that flapping mouth of yours for guzzling rotgut instead of for talking. Do we understand each other?"

Willie can only croak his agreement. Bogart releases him and he slumps against the wall, his hand massaging his throat. "Sure, Bogey, sure," he quavers, "I'll keep my mouth shut, you can count on me. Gee, I don't know why everyone thinks I can't keep quiet. I'm the quietest guy you ever saw. It's just not fair that ..." His voice trails away, the rest of his complaint lost as Bogart ignores him, pushing through the coffee shop door and letting it swing shut behind him.

He sits down at the counter and orders his usual cup of java, black. When it arrives, he sips it and reconsiders what Willie the snitch told him. Maybe he should go see Huston after all. Huston knows most of the pony players. Even though his month-old client has probably given up on his nephew by now, maybe there's an outside chance he'd pay a little money to know where he's been. Bogart's face twitches into a humorless grin—he knows how far he's reaching for this one.

But almost any action is better than just sitting around behind his desk watching the office spiders hard at work. He drops a nickel on the counter, gets up, and goes out the door.

Jack Huston holds court in one of the more garish downtown bars. Bogart finds a parking spot not far away from the neon-festooned entrance, unlit at this time of day. After making sure the car is locked, he goes into the bar. He takes off his hat, and pauses a moment to let his eyes adjust to the darkened room. Yes, Huston's there as usual at his favorite table, accompanied, also as usual, by a couple of burly hangers-on. Bogart walks toward them.

"Well, shamus, how's business?" says Huston. "I heard you were looking for me."

Bogart sighs inwardly. Willie had a habit of trying to make money from both sides of an exchange. "Yeah, I was," he replies casually.

"Sit down and have a drink, and we'll talk about it."

"No, thanks. I prefer to do my drinking on my own time," answers Bogart. But he sits down, his hat balanced on his knee.

"From what I hear, you been doing entirely too much drinking on your own time."

"What the hell are you talking about?" Bogart's suddenly furious, but he keeps his voice even.

"You lost your touch, the way I hear it. Business is bad. Folks don't want to hire you any more. They say you're too unpredictable. Can't count on you."

"They can count on me as long as they don't play me for a chump."

Huston continues as if he hasn't heard. ". . . and you blew the Goulet case, too. You gotta straighten out and fly right, shamus."

*That little weasel. I'll deal with him and his big mouth later.*

So he's been drinking some. So what? If Huston had *his* problems, he'd be trying to drown his sorrows, too. What business is it of his, anyhow? But he controls his temper. It never pays to pick a fight with Huston, particularly when he has a couple of beefy pals to back him up. "I'll see about taking the cure after I finish up the job I'm working on," says Bogart. "But right now, I could use a little information."

"Seems to me you can always use information, pal. Why should I share the wealth with you this time, huh?"

"Look, Huston, you know the racket I'm in: information's part of my job. And you know I can keep my mouth shut."

"You got a point there," says the gangster. Unspoken between them is a race-track incident involving a ringer that Huston cleaned up with.

"And what I'm after isn't that earth-shaking: there's a pony-player named Eli Cooke who ran off while owing his uncle a little money. I'll bet you've never even heard of the guy, that's how unimportant he is."

There's a pause while Huston eyes Bogart speculatively. At last he says "Yeah, I heard of him. He owed a friend of mine two hundred bucks and was a little slow about paying up."

*And I'll bet the friend's initials were "Jack Huston."*

Huston continues, "The friend had some pals who persuaded him to pay what he owed. I dunno what happened to him after that."

"Did the 'persuasion' involve any damage?"

Huston is insulted. "Hey, what kind of a question is that? My friend doesn't work like that. He's not that kind of guy."

"Okay, okay, your pal's a model citizen. You sure you have no idea where Cooke might be now?"

One of the brawny men sitting at the table with Huston leans over and whispers to him. "He mentioned something about San Francisco. Said his uncle was after him and wouldn't understand if he tried to explain."

Bogart nods, satisfied. It fitted with what the uncle had told him. "Okay, thanks. I appreciate your help." He stands up, his hat in his hand.

"Don't do me no favors or anything, shamus," says Huston, and turns back to his companions.

Bogart puts on his hat and goes out the door.

Back on the street, he considers which is more urgent, visiting Wells with the information Huston's given him, or finding Willie to teach him a lesson about loose lips. Though the latter would be more satisfying, he figures the former will do more for his bank account.

He drives back uptown to Wells' place of business. ("I don't want you coming to my home—my wife's upset enough about this as it is," he'd said.)

"Wells' Quality Meats" says the sign over the door. He walks into the butcher shop. The client is there, dressed in the bloody apron of his profession, deep in conversation with a customer over the relative merits of chuck steak and pot roast. Bogart waits patiently until they're finished and the customer has left. The butcher seems surprised to see him. "What can I do for you, Mr. Bogart?"

"Can we talk for a few minutes?" he asks.

"Okay, sure," Wells replies.

"I know it's been quite a while, but I have some news about your nephew. . . ."

He's in a foul mood when he gets back to the office—Betty can see that at once. "So much for leg work," he mutters.

"What did you say?" Betty asks.

Bogart rips off his hat and throws it down on her desk. "Just that our last client decided I didn't do enough to find his ex-tenant and went and hired another private eye. Only he didn't bother to tell me, and when I went over there just now to tell him I've got a line on the guy and how about paying me a little expense money, he laughed in my face and told me to get lost. 'Philip Marlowe'd do a better job than you did, and he's not even a real detective,' he says to me. I should've flattened the bastard!"

Betty's face mirrors her disappointment, but she tries to smooth it over. "It *did* take a while, though. I guess you can't blame him for wanting fast results; not everyone understands detective work, Bogey."

He scowls at her and paces around the office without replying.

"It's not as though we're any worse off than we were this morning," she offers.

"We're not any *better* off, either." His pacing continues.

She gropes for a safer topic of conversation. "Look,

we need a break from the routine. Why don't we go out on Friday night?"

"And do what? In case you hadn't noticed, we can't afford Symphony Hall. Or even the Odeon."

Her eyes fall on the movie magazine on her desk, and she remembers the article she read earlier. "I know! Why don't we go to the Radio Theater broadcast? It's on Friday, and it's free. We just have to be there a little early and get in line." Bogart stops pacing, mild interest on his face, so she keeps talking, saying whatever comes to mind—anything to distract him from his worries. "I'd love to go, Bogey! The special guest star this week's one of my favorites. I've always wanted to see him in person: Ray Chandler." It's an unfortunate choice of topic, and she regrets it a moment later.

*"Chandler!"* Bogart explodes. "That two-bit phony! *He's* half my problem! Everyone expects me to be like *him!* Yeah, I'd like to go to that radio show. I'd like to talk to him. I'd tell him to quit playing that bogus shamus eye and do it the way it *ought* to be done. You don't see *me* driving around in a new Packard, do you? Or making three-hundred-dollar fees on top of expenses? Hell, I can barely *make* expenses, let alone fees!"

Betty listens to him rant on, and her heart aches for him. All the worries about the business—no wonder silly little things are getting to him. Though he does seem to be preoccupied with Chandler. Oh, well, she decides, it'll pass as soon as the clients start coming in again.

She hopes it's soon. She's so weary of spirit, exhausted from trying to soothe him and keep him in good temper. It seems like months since he's smiled or cracked a joke or hugged her. She could use a little solace herself.

But she doesn't think she'll be getting it from Bogey anytime soon.

The next morning Bogart is walking toward the office after parking the car when he spots Willie the

Snitch on the opposite side of the street. Willie doesn't see him, which is his bad luck. Bogart weaves through the traffic and sneaks up behind him.

"Hello, bigmouth," he whispers in Willie's ear. Willie tries to make a run for it, but it's already too late. One of Bogart's hands is clamped around his right arm, and his other hand is an iron band around his throat. He slams Willie against the wall. Hard. "So you figured you could tell Huston a little story about me, could you? About how I was losing my touch? You ought to know better than that."

Willie's frightened eyes stare at him. "What do you suppose I should do about you, Willie? Huh? Maybe make sure you can't spread gossip around for a while? Sounds a like good idea to me." Bogart's fist crashes into Willie's jaw, and Willie is stunned by the pain and shock. He swings again, and this time his target is Willie's belly. The little man doubles over.

Bogart likes it. He likes the feeling of power, of being in control. He keeps slugging Willie, and somehow, in his mind, the snitch's face transforms into Chandler's. Chandler's face, smiling and joking and accepting big checks. Bogart hits Willie again and again, blind with rage, ignoring the shocked cries of the passersby, ignoring everything around him until the cop on the beat pulls him off Willie's unconscious body.

Willie is a shady character on the edge of the law, but that certainly doesn't justify an unprovoked attack which almost kills him, they tell Bogart at the station. Charges will be made as soon as Willie is conscious and able to cooperate.

Betty comes to the station to pick him up. She's afraid to say anything to him, and the drive home is silent.

Life has to go on, even after that. They continue to keep regular office hours. Maybe business will improve. And when the intercom clicks on, Bogart allows himself a moment to hope his effort has been justified.

"Phone call, Bogey," says Betty's voice, sounding metallic on the intercom.

"Who is it? Not a client?" he asks.

"I'm afraid not. It's the building manager."

*Damn!* He already knows how this conversation is going to go. "Okay, put him on," he sighs.

"Mr. Bogart? You're three weeks behind on the rent. I expect you to pay it by tomorrow. I will brook no further excuses."

"Look, Mr. Greenstreet, business has been bad. You know I'm good for it."

"I know no such thing, Mr. Bogart. A lease is a lease. You *do* remember signing one, don't you? That piece of paper which states that you promise to pay the rent by the first of the month? Of course you do."

"Mr. Greenstreet—"

"This isn't the first time this has happened, Mr. Bogart."

"I know that—"

"But I assure you that it's going to be the *last* time. If I do not have your check on my desk tomorrow morning—and it had better be for the entire amount—you'll be evicted within a week. Do I make myself clear? Good." And the phone clicks before Bogart can get in another word.

*"Godammit!"* he bellows.

He grabs his hat and storms out of his office. Betty glances up from her desk, startled by his sudden appearance. His mood isn't improved by the movie magazine in front of her.

"Mr. Greenstreet was asking about the rent, wasn't he?" she says.

"No. Mr. Greenstreet was *demanding* the rent. He wants it now and he wants in full. By tomorrow morning, or else we're out. You think he'd have a little understanding, for god sakes! He probably thinks we have so many rich clients that this Chandler jerk handles our overflow." Bogart points at the glossy photograph on the magazine's cover. "I'm sick of seeing his face every time I turn around. You're obsessed with that actor!"

"I'm not obsessed—if anyone's obsessed around here, it's *you!*" she shouts back. Suddenly her fears

come boiling up and she gives voice to them reck-
lessly. "You're not the same any more! You've
changed. You're not the man I married."

"What d'you mean by that? I'm the same as I've always been. Don't give me that sentimental romantic
crap."

She gets to her feet. "Don't give *me* that 'I haven't
changed' crap!" she shouts. "Look at what you did to
Willie. The man I married would *never* have done
that!"

Bogart yells, "He *deserved* it! He gave me a hard
time and I had to show him who's boss!"

There is a long pause, and Betty simply looks at
him. He shifts slightly under her gaze, uncomfortable.
"I'm going to the bank to transfer some money from
our personal account," he says at last. "It'll just about
clean us out, but it'll pay what we owe." Feeling helpless, she sits down again and watches him go out the
door.

The Bogey she loved had never worried about proving he was king of the hill. And particularly not to an
insignificant little snitch like Willie. Something is seriously wrong. And she has no idea of how to fix it. But
she intends to try.


The moonlight streams in the half-curtained bedroom window. The only sounds are of breathing. Betty
lies next to Bogart, trying to choose the right words,
now that things have gone so horribly wrong.

She'd wanted to comfort him, regain the closeness
they'd lost. So she cleaned the shabby apartment until
it glistened. She made a brave show with the one good
linen tablecloth they owned, the earthenware dishes,
stainless steel cutlery and everyday glasses; they
couldn't afford silver or crystal. And candles. Those,
they could afford. It wasn't much, but it was the best
she could do.

They couldn't afford steak either, but she prepared
the casserole and salad as if she were the head chef at
the swankiest restaurant in town.

She bathed, and put on a little of her carefully

hoarded perfume. She brushed her hair until it shone golden in the light, and dressed in her prettiest dress.

Then she waited for her Bogey to return.

But *her* Bogey never did.

Oh, he came home, all right, after she'd finally given up waiting and had eaten a solitary supper. She heard his footsteps on the stairs and went to the door and opened it, and he came in, a smell of liquor wafting in the air in his wake. That concerned her, but she was determined to make the effort to mend the gap between them, so she said nothing.

Instead, she put her arms around him and kissed him. And he responded, slowly at first, as if a little uncertain. She whispered "I love you, my darling," and kissed him again. This time, he was eager and responded hungrily.

Their embrace lasted for an endless instant of passion, and he finally broke away to lead her to the bedroom. He guided her down onto the bed, and she followed his guiding hands with mounting excitement. The part of her mind that still could think was filled with happiness, grateful that the breach between them would be healed.

But it wasn't. He couldn't fulfill his part, and now he has rolled away from her in shame.

She tries to comfort him. "Love, you're tired and worried and I should've realized it wasn't a good time."

He doesn't say anything.

"When you've had a good night's sleep and aren't so worried about things, we'll make love again."

He's still motionless, still silent.

"My darling, I understand." She reaches out, caresses his shoulder. "Please, I want to help you any way I can."

He turns toward her. "Get away from me, you bitch!" he snarls, and slaps her across the face. The force of the blow sends her tumbling to the floor. She looks at him in shock. "You don't want to help me. It's Chandler and his looks and his money and his cars that you want! You're always mooning over him. No wonder I can't compete—no man could!"

A chill runs down her spine. She has watched him change and wept inside as the man she loved seemed to vanish bit by bit. But now there's nothing left at all of the Bogey she knew. Her Bogey never came home tonight. Only a hate-filled, bitter man with eyes that frighten her. She slowly gets to her feet and backs away from him, out of the room. His shouts and curses follow her.

"Well I'm sorry I'm not Ray The-Great-Detective Chandler! I know he's the one you'd rather be screwing. Isn't he? *Isn't he?*"

Her sorrow burns, but she knows that now there's no choice. She can't help him fight the demons that are tormenting him; he won't let her. Instead she must, finally, think of saving herself. She can't stay with him any longer.

In the morning, in the midst of a ferocious hangover, he finds the brief note she left, reads it once, then rips it to shreds.

"Damn you!" he shouts, and can't say whether it's Betty or himself he's cursing.

Maybe it's Chandler. Chandler, who started all this with his glamorous private-eye movies. With his rugged appeal and his jokes, his expensive clothes and his lemon-yellow Packard. His rich clients and his high fees.

Bogart broods, his rage growing. Chandler should know that's not how it is. If he was a *really* good actor, he'd *want* to know what being a private eye is really like. Someone ought to tell him for his own good. Tell him for the good of all the genuine detectives who work their asses off trying to make a living at this game. So they don't have to keep running up against clients who figure they're hiring super-detective Philip Marlowe, and hassling them when they turn out to be merely human.

Yeah, someone ought to tell him, teach him a lesson.

Bogart smiles an ugly smile. He knows who the someone's going to be.

He takes his time. Nothing will happen until evening. He showers, then takes it easy, ministering to his hangover with aspirin and tomato juice. By the afternoon, he feels more like himself. He shaves and dresses carefully in his best suit, and drives to work.

On his way into his office, he picks up the movie magazine from Betty's desk, and checks the feature article. It not only mentions the time of the radio show broadcast, it names the hotel Chandler is staying at. The premier hotel in the city, of course; nothing but the best for the great Ray Chandler.

It's all so easy. It doesn't take much detective work. Following a cheating husband is harder. Nailing a kidnapper is tougher.

He takes out his gun and cleans it with meticulous care, then loads it, flicks on the safety, and tucks it back into its holster.

There's time to kill, so he decides to go for a drive. It leaves him relaxed and at ease. Nothing bothers him now, not the money problems, not the pending assault charges, not the fact that Betty has left him. He's made his decision, and he's strangely content.

It's time now. He drives to the radio studio, where he parks the car and locks it—he doesn't expect to need it again. Then he waits outside by the studio entrance, with a few autograph hounds.

He expects Chandler to arrive in style and he's not disappointed. The sleek, expensive Dusenberg purrs up and halts. The well-dressed man steps out and waves to the waiting fans, a friendly grin on his face, then turns and speaks to the chauffeur for a moment. The fans gather around him, and he patiently signs all the autographs with a smile and a quip for each person. Bogart joins the group and waits until there's only the two of them left.

"Hi, buddy. Nice of you to come out and welcome me," says Chandler. "I'm afraid, though, I have to go now—the show starts soon."

Bogart replies, "Sure, I understand, you have to go," and pulls out his gun. The shocked surprise on the star's face is worth it all, he decides.

"Farewell, my buddy," he says softly, and pulls his trigger six times. He's surprised at how easy it is to kill a phony detective named Chandler. It takes almost no effort at all.

He'd hoped to have a cell to himself, but his luck runs like it always does, and he's stuck with two hulking cellmates who have primitive ideas of humor. Once they learn his name, they can't seem to restrain themselves. They've never met anyone called "Humphrey" before.

"So how's little Humphrey today? Was he a good boy?"

"Lay off!"

"Ooh, Humphrey-Wumphrey's mad. I'm shaking in my boots."

Since they're each a few inches over six feet tall, there's not much he can do to shut them up; he's still nursing the bruises and black eye from the last time he tried. So he pretends he doesn't hear them—but that only seems to drive them to greater heights of creativity, and the jeers go on and on.

He tries to block them out by thinking about the weekly movie they saw in the mess hall last night. The prison official who selects the films is a Jimmy Cagney fan, and once again, it was a flick in which Cagney plays—as he so often does—a tough, unrepentant jailbird. Nobody pushes *him* around. The other prisoners respect him. The guards respect him. Even the warden respects him.

Bogart broods. Hollywood again. Screwing it all up again. That's not what it's *really* like. Nobody respects you in the slammer. You just get picked on and harassed and beaten up. If Cagney were here now, he'd tell him what it's like being a real convict in a real prison.

Cagney *ought* to know what it's really like. If he really cared about doing an honest job of acting, he'd do some research, find out for himself. Damn that Cagney! It's his own fault for not finding out.

Bogart's mouth twitches into a secret smile. His sentence isn't so very long, and if he continues being a model prisoner (another thing his cellmates torment him for), he'll be out in just a handful of years.

Cagney's address will be easy to get, just like finding Chandler was easy. After all, that sort of thing is just what a private eye is good at.

Then he'll pay a certain actor a visit, and show him the error of his ways.

Just like Chandler.

"Farewell, my buddy," he says softly to himself.

# A NIGHT
# ON THE PLANTATION

## by Brian M. Thomsen

*It is generally conceded that while it took David O. Selznick two years to find the right actress to portray Scarlett O'Hara in* Gone With the Wind, *the obvious choice for Rhett Butler was always Clark Gable.*

*Well, it's not all that obvious to Brian Thomsen, editor/ founder of Questar Books and currently editor of TSR Books. But then, Brian has always had a Marxian view of life.*

### Hollywood, March 1936

Goldwyn, Mayer, and Zanuck could not rightly be called friends or even cordial acquaintances. They were rivals involved in a cutthroat business where one's success often rested on another's failure. This did not, however, preclude these three from occasionally meeting for an informal lunch, far away from the prying eyes and ears of their studio backlots.

On this occasion they had chosen Goldwyn's beachfront bungalow to chew the fat and gloat.

"Actors are like children," Goldwyn said. "They're consistently getting themselves in trouble, and expecting us to bail them out. Then they ask for a reward for keeping their names in the headlines."

"Yeah, why can't they be more like writers?" added Mayer. "At least they know their place. Never met a writer yet who didn't see my way of thinking once his bread and butter was threatened. By the way, read any good books lately?"

"Not since *Anthony Adverse*," said Zanuck. "Imagine forty thousand for the film rights to that first novel.

It made a helluva of a picture, though. How about you?"

Mayer leaned back in his chair and took another sip from his drink. "Well, speaking of first novels, I managed to get my hands on a galley of that new first novel that everyone seems to be talking about."

"You mean *Gone With the Wind*," chimed Goldwyn. "Latham sent me a copy, too. I turned it down in two days flat."

"Yeah, so did I," continued Mayer. "Initially I was interested. It was a great read, after all, but then Irv Thalberg brought me to my senses. He said, 'Forget it, Louie. No Civil War picture ever made a nickel.' And you know Irv is always right."

"I heard that Doris Warner offered forty for it as a vehicle for Bette Davis, who's threatening to walk. Jack is just trying to appease her," added Zanuck.

Goldwyn nodded and added sagely, "The only thing more juvenile than an actor is an actress. Give them an inch and they'll take a mile."

"What do you expect?" concluded Mayer. "They're women."

*The Office of David O. Selznick*
*Selznick International Pictures, July 1936*

Selznick made it a habit of never getting flustered, nor appearing to give an inch, even when he had to.

"You tell Miss Mitchell," he said into the phone, "that script approval is out of the question. We're paying her fifty thousand dollars for the rights to her book, and that should entitle us to at least a little leeway in the storytelling. Hasn't she seen my versions of *A Tale of Two Cities, David Copperfield*, and *Anna Karenina?* None of those authors had any complaints."

"Sir," the meek voice on the other end of the line interrupted. "Those authors were all dead when you made the films."

"Besides," Selznick blustered, "who's gonna remember Margaret Mitchell? She's a writer, and a female one at that. Besides, Cukor wants to direct, and he wants Sidney Howard to do the screenplay. Time is money. Do we have a deal or what?"

"But sir," the meek voice continued, "Miss Mitchell wants to have some approval in the filming of her book. Perhaps casting?"

"My dear boy, part of my plan for the pre-promotion of this film is in the casting. Imagine it—an international search for the actress to play Scarlett: It will be on page one in all of the papers."

"Well, sir," the voice offered, "maybe she can pick the actor to play Rhett Butler?"

"If that will clinch the deal," he blustered. "Done. Now get her to sign those papers. I have a film to make." He slammed the phone back into its receiver.

"Sir," asked Selznick's secretary, "did I hear you say that you were going to cede Miss Mitchell casting choice on the role of Rhett Butler?"

"Miss Winston, you are a very good secretary but you really shouldn't listen in on my phone conversations," Selznick responded sternly.

"Sir, you told me to take notes on the deal," she answered. "I just thought that you had already promised the part of Rhett to Clark Gable."

"Miss Winston, do you really think there is a woman in all America who would turn down Clark Gable? I'm sure she'll see things my way. She'll come around."


*Atlanta, December 1936*

Margaret Mitchell had finally begun to enjoy her new-found fame.

Originally the interviews with the press had been a bother, and the business deals unnecessarily complicated, but now she was unquestionably the belle of Atlanta, a celebrity to be invited to all grande premieres, balls, and socials. She particularly enjoyed going to the movies, especially the comedies. It took a special kind of talent to keep an audience laughing.

Open auditions were being held for the role of

Scarlett, and she had been encouraging all of her friends to try out, all along reminding them that she had no influence concerning the role of Scarlett.

The hour for high tea was approaching when she was informed by her maid Daisy that Mr. Cukor had arrived to discuss some matters concerning the film.

"Fiddle-dee-dee. I bet he is going to try to talk me into that big-eared Mr. Gable again. Well, I've never met a man yet who I couldn't bring around to my way of thinking. I'm sure he'll see things my way. He'll come around."

### The Office of David O. Selznick
### Selznick International Pictures (the next day)

"I don't care what she says, Cukor," Selznick blustered. "Charles Boyer is out of the question. His accent is all wrong. Miss Mitchell is going to have to be reasonable. Tell her that Rhett Butler has to be an American, and he has to have a proven track record in film. We can't afford to have more than one unknown as a lead, given the price we've paid. And also tell her he has to have *savoir faire* . . . and a mustache. Yeah. A *real* mustache. That's how she described him in the book, and that's what we want to see on the screen. I don't care that you feel uncomfortable around her. For God's sake—she's only a writer! Make her see that Gable is the only logical choice. C'mon! Who has more sex appeal than Clark Gable? Now do it! Time is money!" he finished, slamming the receiver back into the cradle.

### Hollywood, June 1937

Nothing brings competitors together for a good laugh better than another competitor's misfortune. This time Goldwyn, Mayer, and Zanuck had chosen Zanuck's private getaway.

"Can you believe that Mitchell broad wrapping Selznick around her finger like that?" said Zanuck, staring off at the ocean, enjoying the view he knew he was paying through the nose for.

"He should have given her script approval," said Mayer, "and then made the changes in the cutting room. Script approval isn't final cut, after all."

"Well, he blew it. Now Gable's mad at him, and wouldn't do the part for a million dollars," continued Zanuck.

"What could you expect?" offered Goldwyn. "Mitchell took her argument to the press. She had it in writing. She got to pick Rhett Butler by contract. Case closed."

"Yeah, but did she really have to say that she thought Gable was a better choice for that new Walt Disney picture they have in the works?"

"You mean *Dumbo?*" Mayer asked.

"Yeah," said Zanuck. "No wonder Gable is furious. And now Selznick is stuck with her choice."

"Well, he fits Selznick's profile," Mayer conceded. "He's an American with a proven track record in film, and on the stage. He has *savoire faire,* and a mustache."

Zanuck agreed, but still shook his head in disbelief saying, "Yeah, sure he fits the profile but who can believe Groucho Marx in the role of Rhett Butler."

*The Office of David O. Selznick*
*Selznick International Pictures, December 1937*

"George, be reasonable," said a very conciliatory Selznick into his battered phone receiver. "Work with Marx. Face it, we're stuck with him. Make the changes he wants. It could work. At least we don't have to worry about Mitchell having script approval. I'm sure Margaret Dumont will be fine as Mammy. So what if she's white? So was Jolson, and nobody cared. Now, George, we're supposed to start filming next month. Well, I'm sorry that you feel that way."

Selznick hung up the phone, and buzzed for his secretary, Miss Winston, who entered his domain promptly.

"Well, Miss Winston, it appears that we just lost Cukor. Do you have that list of alternate directors I asked you to draw up?"

"Yes, sir," she said primly.

"Who's first on the list?" he asked, realizing the February first start date for principal photography was quickly approaching.

"Victor Fleming," she answered.

"Nah. He's tied up with that Gable and Garland project everyone is so hush-hush about. Who's next?"

"I hate to bring this up, Mr. Selznick, but you must remember that in order to get Mr. Marx to accept the role, you had to promise him approval on any new director in the event that Mr. Cukor left the project. So I took the liberty of having your list sent over to his agent so that Groucho could voice his approval up front in order to save time," replied Miss Winston, trying not to incur her boss's wrath.

"Well done, I think, Miss Winston," he replied. "So read me back his approved list."

"Well, sir," she answered, crossing her legs out of nervousness, "there's only one name on the list."

"Well, who is it?" he blustered, about to lose his patience.

"Sam Wood."

"Sam Wood?" he screamed.

### Atlanta, September 1938

Margaret Mitchell had promised the studio that now she had had her way on the casting of Rhett, she would avoid making any more statements to the press without first consulting the studio's press office. This, of course, did not prevent her from talking to her friends, who could then leak it to the press as they saw fit.

After all, wasn't that what friends were for?

"Hello, Julia," she said into her handsomely-styled bedroom phone, "It's Peggy . . . Fine, thanks . . . Remember when I told you that I was a little nervous about the movie after Cukor left? Well, it turns out that my fears were unfounded. Dear George was a sensitive soul, but he probably wasn't the right kindred spirit to bring *Gone With the Wind* to the screen. Julius stopped by the other day and ... Julius ... oh, I guess it's Groucho to you ... well he stopped by the other day to let me know that filming went along fantastically, embracing the true merits of the South that my novel so richly depicted. His words, not mine. When I asked him a little about George's replacement, this Mr. Sam Wood, he quickly put my mind at ease, telling me about the two previous films they made together. The first was about opera of all things, and the second was about the equestrian set. Honestly, can you ask for a better training ground to prepare a director to capture the glory of the old South? Oh, fiddle-dee-dee, I just can't wait to see it on the big screen! ... Me, too ... Well, not much else, except that Macmillan keeps on bothering me about writing a sequel ... Of course not. If there is any book that doesn't need a sequel, *Gone With the Wind* is definitely it."

## Hollywood, February 1940

Sometimes competitors just get together to lick their wounds and bask in the misery of someone else's success. Goldwyn and Zanuck had decided to stop by Louie Mayer's mansion for their usual meeting of the minds, since Louie had been bedridden all week.

"Who'd have thought it would work?" said Mayer, smiling for the first time in a week. "At least he got even with that writer."

"That's right," said Zanuck. "I hear she was livid when she heard that a new subtitle had been added."

"Well, you have to admit," added Goldwyn, "*Gone With the Wind, or A Night On the Plantation* has a certain ring to it."

"I'd like to know how they kept from her that all of

Scarlett's husbands were being played by Groucho's brothers?" said Mayer.

"Or that Ashley was being played by Harpo with his usual silent freneticism?" added Goldwyn.

"Now that you mention it, don't you think his stunning rendition of 'Dixie' on the harp added a new dimension to the character?" offered Zanuck.

"There wasn't a dry eye in the house when I saw it," said Mayer, adding, "Everyone was laughing too hard."

"Mitchell claims that her book has been defamed, and that all of the best parts were left out," said Mayer. "But if you ask me, who needs the burning of Atlanta anyway? Besides, they had to downplay the Civil War parts because you know what Irv Thalberg said. . . ."

Zanuck and Goldwyn chimed in with, "No Civil War picture ever made a nickel."

The three friendly competitors all laughed at their little joke, temporarily forgetting their sadness over Selznick's success.

"I understand that Mitchell now wants to write a sequel to 'restore' *Gone With the Wind* to its former literary prominence," added Mayer.

"What's she going to call it—*Breaking the Wind?*" offered Goldwyn.

"Or maybe *Back With the Breeze,*" added Zanuck.

"Well you can be sure of one thing," said Mayer, clearing his slightly congested throat. "Some damned fool will publish it."

"Yeah. Mitchell got what she deserved, and Selznick definitely managed to take a lemon and make a ton of lemonade," interrupted Goldwyn.

"And a ton of money, too," added Mayer.

"And a ton of money, too," agreed Goldwyn, "but do you really think it deserved all of those Academy Awards?"

"Well, Vivian Leigh deserved one for just managing to keep a straight face. And Larry Parks was excellent doing his serenades of Margaret Dumont. I'll always think of him whenever I think of 'Mammy.' "

"Yeah, those I can agree with," Goldwyn assented, "but what about Groucho for Best Actor?"

"Why not?" said Zanuck. "And he wants to be called Julius now, in keeping with his new image. You're just ticked off that Clark Gable didn't get it."

"Maybe you're right," Goldwyn agreed. "But I really thought he was a shoo-in. It's funny. Do you know he borrowed his most famous line in the picture from Howard's original script on *Gone With the Wind,* and from the book as well, I think?"

"You mean . . .?" interrupted Mayer.

"That's right," said Goldwyn, regaining control of the story. "In the Oz farewell scene, Judy as Dorothy says to him 'Scarecrow, I'll miss you most of all,' " and he replies, " 'Frankly, my dear, I don't give a damn!' "

# ALLEGRO MARCATO

## by Barry N. Malzberg

*When you were a kid, being forced to practice your piano lessons, did you ever wish you were a major league baseball player?*

*Sure you did.*

*Well, Barry Malzberg, one of the true giants of science fiction, author of such classics as* Beyond Apollo, Galaxies, *and* The Gamesman, *has imagined a world in which the great maestro, Arturo Toscanini, is just simple Art Tosca, the manager of the New York Yankees and the man whose job depends on an overgrown adolescent by the name of Babe Ruth.*

Sooner or later it had to come down to this confrontation. Art Tosca knew it, had battled it for months as best he could, but the big fellow was outrageous, impossible now, and there was a point past which you could not tolerate this. You would lose support, lose the club all the way down the line. Even Gehrig was giving Tosca strange glances in the dugout now, shaking his head. When Gehrig gave that look, the end was near. *Basta,* Tosca thought. He had not changed his name from Arturo Toscanini to Art Tosca, struggled his way out of Genoa, Parma, taken the long way boat to the docks at California, fought through the wretched years toting fruit and taking shit from longshoremen, spent those endless years in the minors coming in to find curses lettered on his locker and his uniform tied in knots on the floor, so that he could end up like this. There was only one last exit on the hell's express and the big fellow was pushing him there. He motioned Ruth to the footstool in the big tin can that was his office and closed the door. *"Basta,"* he said to the big fellow. "That means enough. You know your Italian,

George? I've taken as much of your shit as I intend to. You're out of the lineup."

Ruth folded his hands, looked at the floor, gave him that contrite look which, when mixed in with the curses and the humping motions, was supposed to drag everybody back across the line, make you say, *Well, he's just a big kid,* and back off. It had worked every time, up to a point, but now it would not. "You're drinking yourself to fucking death, you're humping everything that doesn't run from you, and you're dropping balls you should get to. I'm not a goddamned preacher," Tosca said. "You want to throw your life away, get yourself a dose of clap that will put you under the infield, blow out your liver, that's up to you—but you're not ready to play anymore. Look at you," he said. "You stink. You stink of cheap wine, your batting average is .275, and you haven't hit a home run in three weeks. You can't even draw a walk." He felt the Italian expletives rising within him, choked them back. "I don't know that Guinea talk," the Babe would say. "Don't give me that Eye-talian shit." Worse yet, Ruppert had said the same thing to him only a few days ago when he had tried to discuss the situation with old Jake. "You hear me?" he said to the big fellow. "I'm not going to put up with this shit. You're on the bench. You got it? I'm sitting you down until you're ready to play. You don't run this club; *I* do."

The Babe shrugged. His cheeks flushed a little, but he took it very nice, very calm. That was the thing, you couldn't really get through to him unless you really did and if that happened, then he could reach out and kill you. A couple of years back, two rookies on the Browns rode him about his dark color and made a few suggestions about racial background and Ruth had taken out after them and caught them under the stands and had almost killed them. Ruppert had had to pull all the weight he had with Landis to get that one dismissed in 1925 and get the big fellow reinstated. But in so doing, Ruppert had said, he had used up all of his clout and the next time would be straight to jail, the owner had said. Of course, this was different. Ruth wasn't threatening to kill Tosca or anyone. He just wasn't playing, was humping and pissing and eating and boozing his way through every road trip and home stand, and taking down the rest of them with him.

"You're sitting," Tosca said. "You got that clear? You're on the pine until you shape up. Get the hell out of here, Babe. Just go and think about it."

"You can't do this to me," Ruth said. "I'll go to the Colonel. He knows all about you. I'll talk to Barrow. You think Barrow will make me take this shit? You think that?" Ruth screamed and reached out a furious hand toward Tosca, who slapped it away and screamed at him in Italian. *"Larghamente!"*

"I don't have to take that from some piss-ant Guinea son of a bitch," Ruth screamed and came at him again. Tosca turned and picked up the first thing he could get his hands on—the hot water bottle that he took into the dugout—and threw it at the big fellow, hitting him on the forehead. Ruth reeled back, shocked. "Get out!" Tosca said. "Get out of here or I'll fucking call the police, you understand?" Ruth bellowed something and came at him and Tosca dodged back against the wall, thinking: *this guy could kill me as fast as he could fuck a cow.* He prepared to go down screaming and defiant, but the door of the room was yanked open and Gehrig and Koenig were standing there, Koenig looking grim, and just behind them Lazzeri, who, of course, had made sense of the Italian.

"Problems, Chief?" Gehrig asked.

Ruth stopped, backed off, shook his head, and stared at Gehrig. "Lou?" the Babe said, "Lou, he's *benching* me, I can't take that crap." He began to mumble something and Gehrig put an arm around the big fellow's shoulders and guided him from the room.

"Come on, Babe," he said quietly, soothingly, and Ruth quivered against him. "Come on, come on," and Gehrig took him away, looking back over his shoulder, shaking his head at Tosca.

*I'm in over my head,* Tosca thought. *I could have been killed there if Larruping Lou hadn't saved my ass. But what could I do? He's putting us all the way down with his shit. If he goes on this way, we'll be invisible by August. And these '27 Yankees could be the greatest club I'll ever manage.*

Now and then, when he could, Tosca would take in a concert, Damrosch and the New York Symphony, or he would go to the Metropolitan Opera House and sit in the Family Circle incognito and listen to Verdi or Wagner, his favorites. Nobody knew the manager of the Yankees at either place. Tosca had always liked music, it meant a lot to him. There was no formal training, of course, after the few cello lessons his parents had scraped together when he was a little boy in Genoa, and through all the years struggling in the ports and then in the minors he had almost forgotten about it, but he guessed that the music had always been there. He still liked it a lot, sometimes would hear it in his head, odd rhythms against the sound of the bats and the crowd, and, of course, Verdi was a man who knew something about what it was like to manage a bunch like this. *Va penserio,* fly thought, that was the right thing, certainly. Fly thought far from all these ramparts; if you thought, you got into trouble. It was a strange thing, a funny thing how a little cello-playing Guinea from Genoa would wind up manager of the Yankees in New York in the '20s, hearing all the sounds of the city and taking shit from the Babe and trying to deal with a bunch of men who, with exceptions like Gehrig or Meisel, were more childish than all the urchins of his home town, but that was America for you. It was a strange and wondrous land, as the Colonel, Jake Ruppert, had pointed out to him in so many of their conversations. Jake Ruppert, a bartender and now a bootlegger, could be the greatest sporting owner in the country, little Arturo Toscanini from Genoa could become Art Tosca and take over the helm of the club which had been called unmanageable. It was a peculiar business, all right.

Tosca thought of things like this all the time, the strange and convoluted nature of his odyssey and the way in which, how peculiarly, it had come to this cir-

cumstance. First he had played ball because it was a
way to get off the docks and it was something which
interested him, the patterns, the rhythm in the hit-and-
run, and then there was the opportunity to play in the
new Pacific Coast League for a hundred dollars a
month and then, when the Seals manager had gone to
Tijuana over a Labor Day weekend and never come
back, he had found himself suddenly managing and
showing, they told him, an aptitude for it. A career
utility second baseman had turned out at the age of 50
to have some real talent for managing, or at least for
staying out of people's way, and then there had been
the sudden late-night visit with Ruppert and Barrow
who had passed through town, they said, especially to
see him, and then it was 1922 and he was managing
the New York Yankees, the champion New York Yankees just a year after they had won their first pennant
and McGraw had dropped them in the Series. McGraw
dropped them again, too, and it wasn't until 1925 that
they had won the World Championship for the first
time, but after that the '26 pennant had come easy and
for the first time in his sixty years, coming into that
'27 season, Art Tosca had felt set, had felt that there
was some permanence in his position, some real control. And then Ruth, forty pounds overweight, fat and
stupid from his triumphs in two World Series and the
47-home-run year in '26, had gone haywire over the
winter and had reported in '27 crazy and arrogant and
convinced that he was running the club, not Ruppert or
Tosca or Barrow, not Gehrig or Meisel or Landis but
only he, the Babe himself, and the season had fallen
apart on him, unraveled from April to August until
now they lay ten games back of an old Senators team,
just barely over .500 and not able to get anything going
while Babe Ruth lurched and belched all over the field
and carried bats around the dugout and fell off to .263
before anyone even grasped the seriousness of the situation. Well, it had been building for a long, long time,
all right. The confrontation was overdue, maybe things
would change now. Either way he would be out: carry
this through the season and Barrow's views would pre-

vail and he would be thrown out. Ruppert might be his
friend, but Barrow held the money and was the one
without the accent and made the contact deals with the
politicians. Everyone knew that. *I had to deal with it,*
Tosca thought. *Either way, I was lost.*

Outside of the ballpark, there was not much for
Tosca. He had married young, lost his wife and infant
daughter in a flu epidemic in the 1890s, thought about
marrying again but never got around to it, not with all
the business of baseball, the short winters, the long
summers, the travel. Like the Babe, he had planted it
here and there in his time, had calculated some moves
of his own, but when he turned fifty-five and took over
the Yankee job, most of that had seemed to pass away
from him; he simply had not been that interested anymore. He could look at the men carrying on, or hang
out at the bars on the road and see what was going on
and what it did to them, but it was something like
watching infield practice. It was fascinating and envi-
able and something which he understood but was not
himself able to carry on. It was like the music for him,
something which had happened a long time ago but
represented something which he was maybe—he hated
to think this way but it was possibly the truth—well
out of.

Ruth took the benching badly but without further
threats, and sulked his way through the doubleheader
in Philadelphia during which Grove shut them out in
the first game and they got only three hits in the second and fell to eleven games out, the Senators splitting
with the Red Sox that day, and Ruth had said nothing
at all but later, when the team was running off the
field, Meisel and Joe Dugan sprinting by him, Ruth
stopped at the end of the bench where Tosca was
slowly packing it in and said, "You put me in tomorrow, you son of a bitch, or I'll kill you. You hear me?
I mean that," Ruth said and turned away, and Tosca
could not believe that he was hearing this except, of
course, that it was exactly the kind of thing which he
should have expected to hear.

Ruth was walking away from him, just strolling through the dugout and toward the hole leading to the locker room and Tosca ran after him and said to him, "You talk to me that way, you son of a bitch? *Basta*, I say to you, I call upon you curses!" And without thinking anything more about it, he drew back a fist and hit the big fellow under the eye. Ruth staggered back and roared with surprise, and then roared again and came toward him. Tosca stood his ground as Ruth grabbed him by the NY on his uniform front and began shaking. Shaking and shaking, and Tosca, feeling the pure, high arc of rage within him, spat in Ruth's face and said, "You bastard, I'll get you suspended for life!" and Ruth hit him on the forehead, Tosca spinning away from him and back into the damned splinters and it was then that Gehrig and the rest of them, hearing this, came from the locker room and pulled Ruth away, Ruth screaming, the men shaking, Tosca shaking—and Tosca picked up a 36-ounce bat from the rack and came toward Ruth with every intention of killing the man and Gehrig, his highly trained reflexes saving him while at risk, leapt and caught him and grabbed the bat and sat him down hard.

After that much of it passed in a blur. Ruth was screaming over and over that he would kill Tosca, and Tosca was begging them to let him go so that he could try—but he wasn't very clear on this, maybe Ruth had shaken him up more than he had thought, and hours seemed to go by until the two of them were in Ruppert's office, Ruth on the couch, soaking his hand in a pot of water, and Tosca leaning back against the couch, supported by Gehrig, who looked at the two of them silently and seriously while Ruppert leaned forward and said, "I can't have this, do you understand? I cannot have this on my club. If Landis gets hold of this, you'll both be thrown out of baseball for life, do you know that? I have got to control my ball club."

"You tell him to let me play," Ruth said. "I'm here to play, and no helpless Guinea bastard who never played a day in the majors is going to sit me. If I don't play, I don't live, you hear me?"

"This is *my* ball club," Tosca said. "I was given this club to manage. Until the Colonel fires me, it's mine. You are fucking up my ball club," he said to Ruth. "I will not tolerate this."

Ruth screamed something and impossibly stood and seemed about to come at him again, and Ruppert said something terrible in German and took a gun from his desk and held it on Ruth. The big fellow saw it and slowly unraveled, falling back loosely, then heavily in the chair.

"You son of a bitch," Ruth said. "You pulled a gun on me! You pulled a gun on Babe Ruth! Are you crazy? Are you crazy enough to shoot me?"

"I'm crazy enough to shoot anyone if they're crazy enough to kill themselves," Ruppert said. "Listen here," he said to Tosca. "I hired you and I told you to make the orders, but I didn't hire you to kill this guy or to have me kill him. So I'm the owner and I'm going to make an edict, you hear me? He plays. The Babe plays. But I get one more report of fucking or boozing or carrying on in the cathouse, and you're going to be put on the suspended list and I'll have Landis make it stick. You hear me?" Ruppert said. Ruth said nothing. "I said, do you hear me?" Ruppert said.

Ruth shrugged, looked at the wall. "I guess," he said. "I guess I hear you."

"And you, Tosca," Ruppert said. "You're crazy altogether. You're sixty years old, you want to get a heart attack? You want this big stupe to kill you? You get off this case, you leave it to me. You sit on the bench and you manage, you leave the heavy problems here or to the Commissioner. I'm not going to take this anymore," Ruppert said, "I got a goddamned brewery here and a real set of problems. The Yankees were supposed to be for fun. Some fun," Rupert said. "Now shake hands and get the hell out of here."

"I won't shake the bastard's hand," Ruth said, his eyes tight and incurious behind the fat folds of his cheeks, that strange alertness which Tosca had noticed from the first now consuming him. "The son of a bitch is killing me."

"You let him kill you," Ruppert said. "But you shake his hand and you end this or it's the suspended list right now."

That was when Gehrig stood up and hauled the Babe to his feet and dragged him over. "Now," he said, "the two of you make up for the boss. I'm the captain and that's an order."

Ruth shook his head and reached out a hand. Tosca touched it, feeling the burning, feeling the force coming through the man. *If he had been a kettledrum,* Tosca thought, *I would kick him.*

They drove through August, 12 and 2 the rest of the way, and cut five games off the fading Senators and then in September the big fellow went crazy, going for the fences on every pitch and connecting often enough. He hit 17 home runs in September, getting up to 35 for the year and they went 27 and 3, winning the last 25 in a row and putting the rest of the league out of the way. Tosca stayed on one side of the dugout and Ruth on the other, the rest of them sitting in the center, and nothing touched them, nothing at all, not even the Waner boys in the Series which they won four games to none. On the last day, coming into the ninth inning with a safe lead, Ruth came over to Tosca and stuck out his hand and said, "Let's bury it, do you hear me? Let's bury it," and Tosca, too stunned to find any kind of an attitude, put out his own hand and that seemed to be the end of it, at least for then. They were World Champions and they were champions again the next year, over the Cardinals, and then it all seemed to fall apart very quickly. Ruppert got sick, the big fellow began to lose his timing, and the whole nature of the league had changed. Tosca was out of there at the end of '31, after the third Athletic pennant, kicking around San Francisco for one season of coaching before deciding to give it up and get all the way out of baseball; he got so far out of it, working as a road man when Prohibition had entered, that he was barely aware of Ruth's being dumped by the Yankees, the three home runs early in the season at Boston, and then the pitiful end. Tosca had time in the evenings for music lessons and some on the weekends, too, and learned to play the piano, although of course it was too late to be any good at all. In '41 they invited him back for the Gehrig farewell, but the letter never even caught up to Tosca; in '48 he did get the message about Ruth's farewell but decided to skip that, and also ducked seeing the cancer-ridden big fellow in the hospital at the end.

Tosca was 81 then, and it had all seeped into him. He lived in a furnished room not far from the docks he had worked fifty years ago and waited for the end. If being manager of a four-time World Champion ball club meant anything to anyone, they managed to conceal it pretty well, even though baseball after the Second World War was bigger than it ever had been. Tosca managed to keep out of the nursing home until close to the very end but when it all finished for him in January of 1957, just before his 90th birthday, he guessed that he had ended as pitifully as the big fellow, the Colonel, or anyone else. You couldn't hold it off, that was something he had known long ago, although Ruth with his boozing and mad fucking and pissing away had probably come closer than anyone to making a run at it. Tosca died in full lucidity, feeling miserably deprived, feeling as if he had wasted all of his life or at least close to all of it, but he was smart enough to know that he probably would have felt that way in any other condition and for whatever reason. Drifting in and out of coma he dreamed of throwing one bat after the next at Ruth, hurling bats, bats filling the air like musical notes, the thunder of the bats crashing and crashing against the walls, the lockers, the bony forehead of the crazed big fellow, and Tosca wondered if there was any different or better way he might have handled it. There being no satisfactory answer to this, he died to the sound of a great and empty descending cadence which—had he had more training he might have recognized this, and in fact perhaps he did anyway—composed the opening notes over string tremolo of Beethoven's Ninth Symphony. Oh, Beethoven, what a man! Was there ever such a man as Ruth?

# FOUR ATTEMPTS
## AT A LETTER

### by Michelle Sagara

*Campbell nominee Michelle Sagara is one of the up-and-coming
stars of fantastic literature. In this unique story displaying four
drafts of the same letter Golda Meir might have written,
Michelle displays the compassion and creativity that readers
have come to associate with her work.*

May 30, 1948
Dear Clara:

Please forgive me for not writing sooner. You have
been reading the news, no doubt, and you know of my
situation. Indeed, I shouldn't be writing now. It's late;
there is no power in Tel Aviv, and the candles should
be spared.

I do not know how quickly word travels, or how accurate that word is, but the situation in Israel is not
good. While we managed to smuggle in arms and am-
munition during the last days of the British Mandate,
most of these were confiscated, and our single factory
cannot turn out the quantities that a war against five
nations require. I have heard that you have continued
to be active in our cause; we need your help—and the
donations of the American Jews—now, more than ever.
In the past two weeks, weapons and disassembled
planes have arrived, and these we have put to the best
use possible. They are not enough.

Once before I traveled in America, and the American Jews responded to our cause. I am not sorry, given
the circumstances, that I declined to accept the invitation of Henry Montor's United Jewish Appeal; I am

needed here. But so is the aid of the United States. You understand as well as I the need for their aid, Clara. Tell them to hurry. Tell them it is already almost too late. Do not try to be fancy; do not try to sound erudite or philosophical. Speak only from the heart, and they will listen with the heart.

I said I would be brief; the candles have burnt low, and there is still no power.

But I can't sleep, and the darkness is unbearable to me at the moment. The candle is flickering and my hand shakes as I write. I have too much to tell you, all of it bad news. I don't know where to begin.

David Ben-Gurion died last night.

He was the founding father of Israel—but you know that. Even writing, I babble. Is it any wonder that I can't sleep? We held services for him, and Sharett, and Allon, in the early hours of morning. I could not bring myself to look at their bodies; to see his death would have been too great a defeat. I want, in part, to believe that he is still alive—that he still guides this nation that he built. But I also want to remember him as he was: formidable, always decisive, always active. What could the sight of his corpse do but take these fragile things away?

Allon is a loss that will hurt us just as badly in the short term. His was our military genius. His was the mind that preserved Israel, to this day, against the Arab invaders. But he was not Ben-Gurion, and my heart is too deadened to mourn him properly, although he was still young.

We placed a hastily scribed copy of the Declaration of Independence upon Ben-Gurion's grave, while the Egyptians prepared for another air raid. The country— *our* country!—is silent. Everywhere I walk, people are wide-eyed and pale. I tried to offer comfort or guidance to them, Clara—I honestly tried. But I, too, had little to give and too much to mourn.

The *Histadrut* is in disarray. The *haganah* and the *palmach* have been badly hurt; I do not know how long they will hold what little they have managed to retain. The Syrian and Lebanese armies have passed through and taken our settlements in the North. We've had word from Dayan; he's been forced to retreat. Thank God we haven't lost him, too.

But we have so little. The British continue to send military aid and weapons to the Arabs. Truman will not come to our aid—nor will any of the European countries; we have asked, but expect little else. In the end, the Allies allowed for the murder of six million of our kind—what difference will another ten percent make in their eyes?

I hate them, little sister. I hope they choke and die on their oil and their politics. Just as we will.

Excuse me, Clara. I cannot write at the moment. My hands are shaking too much, and I can't see the page anymore.


May 30, 1948
Dear Clara:

Forgive me for not writing to you with the news that I know you must want. But it is dark outside, and for the moment quiet. The *haganah* holds Tel Aviv; the Egyptians have not managed to bring their brigades this far. I want peace, and not war, for just a few hours, maybe even a few minutes. I will take what I can get.

How are things in America? How is your husband? How are your children?

Let me assume they are well.

Morris and I have not spoken in two weeks; I don't think he will ever speak to me again. Clara, I should never have brought him to Palestine. I should never have taken him from America. We should never have had children. The children.

You know, of course, that Sheyna and Mother have criticized me constantly about the children. Sheyna can be understanding, sometimes, in her severe way. But Mother? Never. I love her dearly, Clara, please understand that. But even living in Palestine as it became Israel—our nation, our homeland—she has never, and will never, understand the choices that I was forced to make. She thinks about Father, and about her friends, and about her children—you, Sheyna, me. Only you, she doesn't worry about, and that's because you're safe. I'm grateful that you're safe, because I, too, need one living relative that I don't have to worry about.

Even now, Mother says that I should have been a better wife to Morris, should have made our marriage work. She said I just gave up on it—as if Morris had no say at all. She's right, of course. But had I been a better wife to Morris, how much of me would have been left for Israel? Does she think a nation comes from nowhere, from nothing?

It doesn't, Clara. It comes from sweat and dedication and sacrifice. I have done all these things, even if they weren't enough, and I will do more.

Yes, I know that the Arabs of Palestine have some claim to these lands—although I say it here, for you alone. I can't say it again, ever, anywhere else. But we're family. Let us put aside the claim of land and ownership; let us ignore the fact that we, the Jews who immigrated to Palestine, bought the lands that we farm from Arabs who wanted our money. Let us forget that throughout my life here, Jews have been killed by anti-Zionist Arab factions, commanded by the Mufti of Jerusalem.

I will not argue moral imperative here; I said at the beginning of this letter that I wished to set aside war for a while. But let me say this clearly: If I have not been a good mother to my own children, I have been a mother in almost fact to those Jews that no one else wanted. They had no home but this one; no place to go, but those awful camps. They couldn't mourn their dead in peace; they were almost dead themselves. Six *million* of *my* people perished because no one, outside of the Jews, could conceive of just how hated a people they were. And hundreds of thousands of those Jews could have been saved, Clara. On the day that I signed the Declaration of Independence, I could not forget them, and embarrassed myself with public tears; I will never be able to rest wondering whether or not there was more I could have done to bring even a single child more, to Israel.

You ask me, as a mother of the Jewish people, whether I will kill my children in certainty, or cast another's child loose to fend for itself? What other answer can there be? Every mother has the right to defend her own children; to feed them and clothe them and house them.

I would never have hurt an innocent Arab. I would never have countenanced—I never did—the acts of terrorism that revolve around the deaths of the weak and the unarmed. I was willing—we were almost all willing—to live in peaceful coexistence with the Arabs. But Ben-Gurion was right, in the end. I was only willing to let them live in a house that was mine, where I could watch over the safety of all of my children in surety. And tomorrow, I will go out to the armies and I will once again reaffirm that position. Even if I know that the innocent will die at the hands of the soldiers I send into battle. Better that they kill than be killed.

But tonight, Clara, I wish that you were here. I want to call on Morris, but I know that he won't come. He was a better father than I was a mother. When Sarah came to us both, and told us of her plans to go to Revivim and live a life of hardship in the Negev, he said no. I said yes. Because I didn't want to stunt her growth. Because if I had my choice, I would be back on the kibbutz myself.

Clara, this is too hard. Thirteen days ago, my baby was killed by the Egyptians. They razed Revivim. They raped and killed every living person there. If any survived or escaped, we haven't heard about it.

We couldn't get the bodies out. I couldn't cry at the memorial service, although Morris and Mother did. Mother will be fine; she has her anger to sustain her, as I have mine. But Morris is a shadow now. Not even Ben-Gurion's death disturbed him.

Two weeks it's been, and already I miss Morris. But I miss Sarah more. The house is quiet, and she'll never cross the threshold again. How many other mothers feel what I feel tonight? How many other mothers had to stand at the memorial with a stiff face and no tears, because they had to present a strong face to Israel?

If I could issue the orders tonight, I would tell my soldiers to kill every living Arab in our territory. I would scream it, Clara—I would shout it in a voice that would be heard across the Middle East. I would carry a gun, though I have little training; I would learn how to throw grenades. And I would ride with the army through each and every Arab village to see the carnage with my own eyes.

Because tonight, even if I was a bad mother, I am only *Sarah's* mother. Tomorrow, I will be mother to the Jewish people again. God, Clara—I can't believe it. I can't write anymore. I can't believe how weak I'm being, when Israel needs my strength. But I am crying now, and these will be the last of my tears.


May 30, 1948
Dear Clara:

My time is short and this is perhaps the last news you will have of your family in Israel. I will try to be brief. Ben-Gurion, and most of his advisers, died in Tel Aviv last night, in an air raid that we were not prepared for.

Because we are in a state of emergency, I have taken some of the responsibility of running what remains of our infrastructure here. We have the advantage of organization, but the Arabs have the advantage of numbers and their weaponry is far superior to ours. Ben-Gurion was the Commander-in-Chief of our armed forces, but he relied on Allon and Dayan. Dayan has been called to the capital, and he will speak with our advisory board as soon as he arrives. If he arrives.

I used to find the night a private, comfortable time. This once, I hate it. I hate the darkness; it seems that it will go on and on without relief. I have now run through three candles; there is wax on the table, and I have a handful of cigarettes left. No coffee. I've tried twice to sleep, but I can't abide what the darkness holds.

Someone once said—I forget who, but it isn't important—that humanity has darkness because in darkness the brightest dreams are born. I nodded when I heard it; I was younger then. I am even guilty of repeating it on several occasions. But I have my answer to that now. If dreams are born in darkness, so are nightmares.

It's the nightmares I can't face now. The six million dead, and the several hundred thousand that will surely fall if we fail. Did I mention that Sarah died fighting in the Negev? I might have forgotten to tell you, because Israel has suffered so many losses in the last two weeks. Well, she comes back to me now, among the dead. So I sit here, my hands swollen with the humidity, the smell of burning wax in my hair.

I have always been certain of everything, Clara. Of Zionism. Of Socialism. Of equality and justice. I have always believed that if I put everything, my heart, my mind, my energy, into a cause, I could make things happen. Even ten years ago, if you had asked me, I would have said that this was true. But don't ask me tonight. I didn't even have the strength to face Ben-Gurion's death.

Tell me instead that in America everything is fine. That your children grow well; that they are happy, and Jewish, and safe. Tell me that your daughter is wearing hideous clothing that these young people think is fashion, that she is obstinate and willful and argues with you. Tell me that your neighbors invite you to dinner, even if they are not Jewish, and that you have a pleasant conversation, a nice evening. Tell me that the war in Israel will not destroy my country.

Because Israel is the only thing that is left in my heart that has not yet been broken. And Clara, I do not know if anything at all that I can do will save it.

Wait. I hear a humming. Let me go to the window and look.

Clara—the power has been restored; I can see the windows with their dim lights suddenly flicker on in the quiet city. They'll be shut off at once, of course. But still.

May 30, 1948

Dear Clara:

Do not believe everything you read. Israel is hurt, but it is not yet dead, and it will *never* die. By the time you read this, you will have heard of Ben-Gurion. He was Israel's greatest hero, and his death will spur us all to greater actions in his memory. We can do no less than he did, or rather, we can attempt to do no less.

I will call Montor if the phones hold. Starkly put: Israel needs money if it is to survive. Do what you can to help him; he is a good man.

The sky has turned dawn pink. I am smoking my last cigarette—yes, I know they are hard on the throat, but I'm old enough to cling to my few vices, so don't mention it—and writing to you as hurriedly as possible. Mother, Sheyna, and Morris are well. Menachem and Sarah do us proud in their service with the army.

We have suffered as a people, and we have finally brought about our own nation, our own sovereignty. Do you think that we will ever surrender it? *Never!* We have a right to be in Israel, as recognized by the United Nations. We have the right to self-rule. We will take every displaced Jew on the face of the earth, and give them a land of their own in which to live without fear. We believe this with more strength and ferocity than ever. That has never failed us, Clara—and it will not fail us now.

I see the car below; I must go. I will mail this after our meeting, if at all possible. Give my love to the children.

Golda

*Mailed on the 31st of May, 1948, from the office of Golda Meir acting Prime Minister of the State of Israel, acting Commander-in-Chief of the Armed Forces of Israel.*

# THE FIFTEEN-MINUTE FALCON

## by George Alec Effinger

*Almost half a century ago, mystery writer Craig Rice ghosted a detective novel for Gypsy Rose Lee entitled* The G-String Murders.

*I suggested to Hugo-and-Nebula-winning George Alec Effinger, author of* When Gravity Fails *and* The Exile Kiss, *that it might well be time to bring Gypsy back as a detective—and here she is, in a demonstration that Sam Spade might have envied.*

Gypsy Rose Lee's jaw was round and comely, her chin a lovely U under the luscious U of her mouth. Her nostrils curved back to make another, smaller U. Her coffee-brown eyes were horizontal. The U motif was picked up again by plucked eyebrows rising outward from twin creases above a bowed nose, and her dark brown hair fell in twin curves that framed her face. She looked rather pleasantly like a raven-tressed temptress.

She said to her sister, Baby June: "Yes, sweetheart?"

"There's a guy wants to see you, Louise. His name's Wonderly."

"A customer?"

"I guess so. You should take a look at him. He's got it in spades."

"I just hope he's got it in money," said Gypsy. "Let him in."

Baby June nodded and ushered in a tall, very handsome young man. He had dark brown hair and dark brown eyes, with just the faintest crinkling wrinkles in the corners. His face was so handsome you could eat off it, and the strong white teeth of his smile were bright enough to light a small bedroom. As he approached Gypsy's desk, he carried his expensive fedora in his hand and his camelhair coat draped over one arm. He took the seat she indicated, saying "Thank you," in a low and thrilling voice.

"So tell me what we can do for you, Mr. Wonderly," said Gypsy.

He glanced up quickly at Baby June and hesitated.

"That's all right," said Gypsy. "This is June, my partner and sister. We work as a team, and we don't keep secrets around here."

Wonderly nodded. His expression grew grave and worried. "I was hoping that you could help me with a problem. A family problem." Gypsy leaned forward better to hear the man's soft words. Baby June moved a chair from her desk a little nearer.

"It's my brother," Wonderly continued. "He's going to get himself in trouble. He's always been wild and he has a . . . a problem with fires. Do you know what I mean?"

Gypsy nodded, although she really didn't understand yet.

"My brother, Charles—he's at Jennings Prep now— has a fascination with fires. He sets them, you see. He's never really caused much damage in the past, but there's always the chance that one of his little blazes may get out of control."

Gypsy cleared her throat. "I don't quite see how we can help you, Mr. Wonderly. It seems to me that your brother has a psychological problem. We can't deal with that in our line of work."

Wonderly waved a hand. "I understand, of course. The trouble started when Charles was caught lighting a fire in a warehouse on Castillo Street. He told me later that he thought the building was abandoned."

"It wasn't?" said Baby June.

Wonderly turned to her. "No. It was owned by a Mr. Anthony Di Spumonto."

Gypsy raised her eyebrows. "Oh, now it's clear. I take it Mr. Di Spumonto—or one of his associates— has paid a visit on Charles?"

Wonderly inclined his head in agreement. His expression became almost fearful. "Charles wasn't home that evening, thank God. I was, however, and the large man Mr. Di Spumonto sent hinted that he'd find Charles sooner or later, and when he did, he'd persuade him. 'Persuade him.' Those were his exact words. I knew what he meant, all right."

Baby June said: "What can you tell us about Di Spumonto's errand boy?"

Wonderly shrugged. "Only that he's big and powerfully built, dark, mean-looking. And his name is Thursby. Floyd Thursby."

"And you want us to protect your brother?" asked Gypsy.

"Just for a little while. Our family has money, you know, a great deal of money. I'm sure I can come to a satisfactory arrangement with Mr. Di Spumonto. Until I do, however, I feel that Charles' life is in danger."

Gypsy chewed her lip in thought, staring at Baby June. Her sister returned her questioning look with a slight shrug.

"Just leave it to us, Mr. Wonderly," said Baby June. "We'll shadow your brother and if Di Spumonto's goon tries anything, well, we'll know how to handle that."

Wonderly didn't look very reassured. "If he sees you with Charles, mightn't he do something . . . something violent?"

Gypsy nodded. "He might, but you can trust us to take care of it."

"Now," said Baby June, "how do we find this brother of yours?"

"He'll be at my apartment tonight at eight o'clock." He glanced from Baby June to Gypsy. "I don't live at my parents' house on High Street. I keep a separate suite at the St. Didier Hotel. Here's the address, and my telephone number as well." He took out a black calfskin wallet and laid a business card on Gypsy's desk. He put five hundred-dollar bills beside it. "Is that sufficient?" he asked.

"That'll do just fine for now," said Gypsy, opening a desk drawer and putting the money away.

"In fact," said Baby June, "I'll take care of it myself. Eight o'clock, then, at your apartment?"

"Yes, thank you. Thank you very much." He turned to Gypsy, who offered her hand. Wonderly held it briefly. "And thank you, too."

After he left their office, Baby June said: "Maybe he spoke to you first, Louise, but I'm telling you, I get first crack at him!"

Gypsy hadn't believed a word Wonderly had said. She grinned wolfishly. "Your blood's too hot for your own good, June, that's your trouble. Yes, it is." She took out the office bottle and poured three fingers of White Way whiskey into two clean tumblers.

At half past nine that evening, Gypsy's bedside telephone rang. "Hello," she said into it.

A man's voice muttered a few terse words.

"Beaten?" asked Gypsy. "How badly? When? Where is she now?"

Just after ten o'clock, Gypsy bribed a hospital orderly to allow her to visit her sister. Baby June was resting in a semi-private room. The other bed was empty. "June," she said softly.

Baby June opened her blackened, swollen eyes. "Louise," she whispered. Her voice was dry and hoarse.

"Did he do this to you? Di Spumonto's strongarm, what was his name? Thursby?"

Baby June shook her head, then groaned.

"Di Spumonto's got more than one gorilla working for him," said Gypsy. "Don't worry, sweetheart, I'll get him. And I'll make him pay for what he's done to you. It's like Mama always said, remember? 'Down these mean runways a stripper must go, a stripper who is neither tarnished nor afraid.' Well, not terribly tarnished, anyhow."

The next morning, Gypsy caught a cab outside her apartment building and told the driver to take her to the St. Didier Hotel. At the hotel's front desk there was a clerk wearing a beige suit with an elaborate and colorful cravat. "Is Mr. Wonderly in?" asked Gypsy.

The clerk gave Gypsy an appraising look and decided he didn't like what he saw. "Mr. Wonderly checked out, just about two hours ago."

"Thanks."

Gypsy thought about that news while she rode in a taxi to her office. Somebody was playing games, but they didn't make any sense yet. They would soon enough, however.

At her desk, Gypsy began looking through the day's mail. She'd opened three envelopes and discarded their contents when the telephone by her elbow rang. "Hello," she said.

"Listen, Gypsy," said a man's voice she recognized as Detective Fouchet of the Homicide Division, "that guy of Di Spumonto's—Thursby, his name is—he's been found shot dead. We got a source that says you may know something about it. Anything you'd like to tell me?"

Gypsy pursed her lips. "Sorry, Detective. I've never even seen the man."

"Aw, don't play it that way, Gypsy," said Fouchet. "You know it'll just go harder for you in the long run."

"Rafe, if I find out anything, I'll call you later."

"But say, maybe Baby June could've—" Gypsy hung up the telephone.

It rang again a few moments later. "This is Wonderly," said the man's voice. "I'd like to see you. I'm at the Friesham on Travis Street, apartment 154. Tell the doorman you're there to see Mr. Leblanc."

"Leblanc?" said Gypsy, but now she was talking to a steady dial tone.

"Come in, Miss Lee." Wonderly had on a long, jade green dressing gown over gray slacks, a pale yellow Oxford shirt, and a blue necktie with clocks.

"Thank you."

"Miss Lee, I'm sorry about your sister."

Gypsy said: "She's feeling better today."

"I'm glad to hear it." Wonderly looked down at the floor. "I suppose I have a confession to make."

Gypsy laughed. She made herself comfortable in an armchair by the fireplace. "I didn't buy any of your act, Mr. Wonderly or Leblanc or whatever it is—"

"It's O'Shaughnessy, Miss Lee. Richard O'Shaughnessy."

"As you wish. Maybe if the situation were different—maybe if I were a male P.I., I'd be more credulous. Women spend their whole lives listening to lies from men. I can spot them very well by now, Mr. O'Shaughnessy. My sister, though, is still learning."

Wonderly looked up. There was pain on his face. "I can't help but feel responsible for what happened to her."

Gypsy smiled slowly. "You're good," she said. "You're very good. Anyway, you warned us that Di Spumonto's men were ready to play rough. Tell me what happened last night."

"Your sister came by the suite at the St. Didier Hotel precisely on time. She asked me where Charles was, and I had to explain that I didn't really have a brother. I just needed your sister's protection from Thursby for a few hours. We walked to a small restaurant I know on Montgolfier Road. We had dinner, we talked, and the time passed. June and I came back to the hotel and we shook hands at the door. She must have been assaulted sometime after that."

"You know, pal," said Gypsy, "I don't believe that either."

"I . . . I don't know what to say," O'Shaughnessy stammered.

"Well, you've paid me enough so I guess I'll keep working for you, although I don't have any idea what you want me to do. I'll keep the police away from you, at least for a little while, until I decide if you killed Thursby." Gypsy glowered at O'Shaughnessy. "And if you roughed up Baby June—"

"I . . . I never—"

"I'll talk to you later," said Gypsy, leaving

O'Shaughnessy standing by his chair with his mouth open.

That evening around the dinner hour, Gypsy was still in her office. She was holding the Chanel #22-soaked business card of one Alexandria Virginia. Although the card had an enticing fragrance, there was nothing the least bit enticing about the square-jawed Miss Virginia. She was all business, and business appeared to be good.

"What can I do for you, Miss Virginia?" asked Gypsy.

Miss Virginia had short, dull brown hair that had been hacked off at the shoulders, rather than cut and styled. Her eyes were pale blue and expressionless, and her blunt face held not the slightest hint that she had even an introduction to a sense of humor. She wore a navy-blue cloth overcoat and navy shoes that were so sensible, they could've begun their own careers as consultants. Beneath the overcoat, however, she had on a green-spangled T-bar and two green pasties with white tassels. "I wish you to recover a keepsake that is of some sentimental value to me," she said.

Gypsy doubted that. She knew that it wasn't only men who lied. Miss Virginia didn't look the type to have sentiments, let alone keepsakes. "Do you always go out in public dressed for the stage-door crowd, Miss Virginia?"

"Never mind that. I only have thirty minutes between shows. The item in question is a black bouquet of metallic roses in the shape of a horseshoe."

It sounded strangely funereal to Gypsy, but she only nodded.

"I am prepared to pay you the sum of five thousand dollars for the return of this Black Bouquet."

Gypsy stretched and lay back in her comfortable swivel chair. "Five thousand dollars is a lot of money to—"

Miss Virginia pointed a small .25 caliber automatic at her. "Now," she said, "if you would clasp your hands at the back of your neck?"

Gypsy laughed, but she did as she'd been told.

"I intend to search your office, Miss Lee, and I won't hesitate to shoot you if you interfere."

Gypsy raised her eyebrows. "Go ahead," she said.

"Please stand. I must determine if you are armed."

Gypsy gave her a disbelieving grin and stood. Miss Virginia came forward to search her. Gypsy slapped the woman's gun hand to the side, then connected with a clean right uppercut to Miss Virginia's square jaw. The woman with the gun fell to the floor, unconscious. Gypsy smiled, leaned down and took the pistol, then examined the contents of Miss Virginia's purse. It did not contain the promised five thousand dollars.

Miss Virginia recovered slowly. "You struck me!" she accused.

"Very good," said Gypsy, holding the automatic on her. "You're lucid, at least."

"I was quite serious about my offer, Miss Lee. Even though I do not have the five thousand dollars in my possession at this time, I can obtain it at a moment's notice from my employer, the Bouquet's rightful owner."

"How do I know your employer is the rightful owner? How do I know it wasn't—Thursby?" The last remark was a shot in the dark. Gypsy favored shots in the dark; every now and then they illuminated even the densest shadows.

"Thursby had no valid claim at all!" cried Miss Virginia.

"I see. Well, can you pay me a retainer, then?"

"Yes, indeed. I can give you five hundred dollars now. When you obtain the Black Bouquet, I will pay you the remaining four thousand five hundred."

"Fine," Gypsy said. "How do I get in touch with you?"

"Oh," said Miss Virginia, "I'll stay in touch with you. Now, will you return my gun?"

"Oh, sure. I'd forgotten about it." She handed Miss Virginia the automatic.

"Now," said the woman in the navy-blue overcoat,

"if you will please clasp your hands behind your neck?"

"I don't think so," said Gypsy, ignoring the pistol and slugging Miss Virginia again. The woman dropped to the floor for a second time.

"I understand that you sometimes employ Miss Alexandria Virginia," said Gypsy to the obese woman. Gypsy held a drink in her hand, but she'd long ago learned the hard way that it would be disastrous even to taste it. It was very probably drugged, and Gypsy would wake up hours from now with bleary eyes and a head that felt as if it were doing bumps and grinds to the music of the spheres.

The fat woman nodded. According to the faded, once-pink business card beside the door buzzer downstairs, her name was Jane Doe. Gypsy assumed that was yet another lie. The amount of truth going around in this case could be scooped up in a single pasty with room left over for all the sincerity in a Stage Door Johnny's proposition.

"You do understand, Miss Lee," said the fat woman, "in order to do business, I have to make use of—what shall I say?—the occasional social undesirable. At these times, I sacrifice a certain amount of my personal honor and compromise my ethical standards, and it certainly pains me to do so. I assure you, madame, that it does. Yet my competitors do not hesitate. They have no such honorable standards, believe me, Miss Lee. They have no compunction at all about committing the most heinous of crimes in order to secure for themselves even the smallest of advantages. When I hesitate to act, staying my hand in the belief that human values sometime outweigh monetary gain, my adversaries take advantage of my reluctance. Then they achieve a success that damages not only myself—and my position, relative to them, in our somewhat shadowy field of endeavor—but also those who depend upon me for their livelihood, security, and their very well-being. You see, madame, that my associates look upon me as more than an employer. I am a source of strength and,

I trust, moral guidance. I like to think of myself as a friend to those who have no friends. It is, in my humble opinion, my greatest and most important role."

Humble! It was all Gypsy could do to keep a straight face. "Yes, indeed," she said. What she was thinking was: "Can I please go home now?" The fat woman was evidently quite powerful, judging from the opposition lined up against her, competing for the ultimate ownership of the Black Bouquet. Still, like all the others, the fat woman believed that lies, deception, and intrigue were the proper techniques of day-to-day business. It was as if she had never even experimented with honesty or, if she had, had decided that it was as hopelessly outdated as the innovative financial concepts of Herbert Hoover.

"Are you sure you won't just toss down that drink?" asked the fat woman.

Gypsy shook her head. "We former burlesque queens are a sober lot," she said. She could lie, too, if she had to.

"Pity. Alexandria, pour it back into the special decanter, won't you? No sense wasting good . . . whiskey. Now, Miss Lee, as to your reward—"

Gypsy held up a hand. "Your tasseled accomplice mentioned something about five thousand dollars."

"That is correct," said the fat woman. "Five thousand dollars if you return the Black Bouquet to me, and no questions asked."

"No questions asked by whom?" asked Gypsy.

"We're certainly not going to ask any questions," said Alexandria Virginia, glancing at the fat woman, who nodded in agreement. "And we don't expect you to, either."

Gypsy rubbed her lovely jaw and smiled. "What good would it do? I haven't gotten a straight answer out of any of you yet. Now, if you'll excuse me, I have to get back to my office and wait for the next unlikely development."

"Then good day to you, Miss Lee," said the fat woman.

\* \* \*

The next unlikely development surprised even Gypsy Rose Lee, as jaded and worldly-wise as she was. While she sat behind her desk, working on her income tax form, a man entered carrying a bundle wrapped in newspaper and tied with a rope. Gypsy noticed that the newspapers were printed in a Cyrillic alphabet, but that didn't necessarily mean they were foreign.

"Just set that down over—"

"Wait," gasped the man. Gypsy looked at him more closely and saw that the man was bleeding from several severe wounds.

"Would you like a glass of water?" she asked, concerned.

"Listen," said the man, "I don't have long to live. I know that. I've made peace with my Maker on the way over here, but I have one last thing to do. This package—"

"I know, I know," said Gypsy. "It's the Black Bouquet. What else could it be?"

"Yes," said the dying man. "The Black Bouquet. Now, let me entertain you. What do you know about the Order of the Hospital of Saint John of Jerusalem, later known as the Knights of Rhodes and other things?"

"I know one thing," said Gypsy, puzzled. "That speech was supposed to come from the fat woman, not you. I've seen this movie."

"Please, pay close attention," said the man, "I don't have much longer. In 1539, these Crusading Knights—"

Gypsy rolled her eyes. "I'm really sorry to interrupt, but I don't have the time to hear the whole story, and I venture to say that you don't have time to tell it. Wouldn't you rather I called an ambulance? Don't you want to go to the hospital?"

The man waved a hand weakly. "All in good time. Now, the Emperor Charles the Fifth—"

Gypsy ignored him. She picked up the telephone and called the obese woman—"Jane Doe." Meanwhile, the dying man continued with his endless narration.

"Yeah," said Gypsy into the phone, "I've got your piece of bric-a-brac. You got my five thousand dollars? Good. I'll be right there. I've got to wait until this guy kicks the bucket here in my office. It shouldn't take long. And say, listen: We're going to need a fall guy. With people dropping dead around us, we're going to have to give the police somebody. Not me and not you. Anybody else is fine with me." Gypsy hung up, saw that the dying man was still only two-thirds finished with his tale, and went back to filling out her taxes. She thought about the five thousand dollars and grinned wolfishly. She was good at that.

Not quite two hours later, Gypsy sat on a couch at the obese woman's apartment. Alexandria Virginia was there and so was Richard O'Shaughnessy. One of these people had beaten Baby June, had killed Floyd Thursby and the man who'd delivered the Black Bouquet—who, by the way, had gasped his last all over Gypsy's shag carpet. Gypsy had phoned Rafe Fouchet, the homicide detective, and explained the situation. The nameless dead man had been carried downstairs on a stretcher and out of this story completely.

"A drink?" asked the fat woman.

"Sure," said Gypsy, taking the whiskey rocks and holding it in her right hand without the slightest intention of drinking it.

"You have the Black Bouquet?" asked the fat woman. She learned forward eagerly. Alexandria Virginia, still in her pasties, T-bar, and overcoat, leaned forward eagerly. Richard O'Shaughnessy, seeing everyone else leaning forward eagerly, leaned forward eagerly.

"I have it," said Gypsy, "and I can deliver it as soon as you pay me the five thousand dollars."

"Give me the Bouquet, and I'll pay you."

"Give me the money, and I'll give you the Bouquet."

Gypsy and the fat woman stared at each other, apparently at an impasse. At last, "Jane Doe" laughed mirthlessly. "You, madame, are a woman after my own heart, I must say. There's never an end to your surprises, and I do so like to see a person who knows where her best interests lie. Certainly, I will pay you half the money now and half on delivery, if that's acceptable to you?"

"No problem," said Gypsy. "Give me that twenty-five hundred, and I'll have the Bouquet in your hands in less than an hour."

The fat woman stared at Gypsy, measuring her with lowered eyelids. At last, "Jane Doe" made a small sign with one hand, and the stripper, Virginia, came forward. She took a pocketbook from her overcoat and counted out the money into Gypsy's hand.

"All right," said Gypsy. She went to the door, opened it, and picked up the Black Bouquet where she'd dropped it in the hall. "Here it is," she said.

"You just left it lying on the floor out there?" cried the fat woman. "It's worth a fantastic fortune, and you left it lying in the hallway?"

"Aw, hell," said Gypsy, "you've got it now. Give me my money."

The fat woman gestured to Alexandria Virginia. "Pay her."

The women in the tassels counted the money into Gypsy's hand. Gypsy filed it all away in her purse. "Now," she said, "who's going to be the fall guy?"

"Not me," said Alexandria Virginia.

"Not me," said Richard O'Shaughnessy.

"Of course not," said the fat woman. "You're both too valuable to me."

"All right," said Gypsy thoughtfully. "It's traditional to give them the gunsel."

"Gunsel?" said Miss Virginia.

"Gunsel?" said Mr. O'Shaughnessy.

"Gunsel?" said the fat woman.

Gypsy was astonished. "What? What are you saying? You don't have a gunsel? That's completely against the rules!"

Alexandria Virginia, Richard O'Shaughnessy, and the obese woman looked at each other. "I think . . . I think we neglected the gunsel this time around," said Jane Doe.

Gypsy couldn't believe it. "What am I dealing with here? Amateurs? It's like Candy Barr or Tempest Storm having to compete with some wet T-shirt girl. I thought you people were in the Big Time."

"We are," said Alexandria Virginia.

"We just forgot the gunsel this time around," said the fat woman.

"Well," said Gypsy, drawing her pistol, "that invalidates the whole contract. I knew the man was lying from the beginning, and so were the rest of you. What did you think, that I'd fall in love with O'Shaughnessy? That I'd trust you because you're women? I'm not that stupid. Rafe?"

The homicide detective burst through the door, maybe just a little more energetically than he needed to.

"Rafe," said Gypsy, "here are your villains. That man, Richard O'Shaughnessy, roughed up Baby June and may have killed Floyd Thursby. Alexandria Virginia killed the nameless guy at my office. This fat woman is their boss, the one who planned it all."

"Thanks, Gypsy," said the detective. "I owe you another one. But what's this thing?" Rafe Fouchet indicated the Black Bouquet.

"Oh, that?" said Gypsy. "That's nothing. Not even the stuff that dreams are made of. Let me have it as a souvenir?"

"Sure, Gypsy," said Fouchet absently, as he dialed the telephone, calling for backup.

Gypsy took the solid gold, jewel-encrusted Black Bouquet and quietly excused herself. She'd give her statement later at the station house. Everything was coming up roses.

# DANCE TRACK

## by Mercedes Lackey and Larry Dixon

*Isadora Duncan's profession was dancing ... but her passion
was fast cars. Did you ever wonder what might have happened
had she gone into auto racing for a living?*

*A fascinating question. And Mercedes Lackey, author of close
to a dozen bestsellers, and noted artist Larry Dixon, have come
up with a fascinating answer.*

Dora blew her hair out of her eyes with an impatient
snort and wiped sweat off her forehead. And simultaneously adjusted the timing on the engine, yelled a cor-
rection on tire selection to her tire man, and took a
quick look out of the corner of her eye for her driver.

He wasn't late—yet. He liked to give her these little
heart attacks by showing up literally at the last possible
moment. She would, of course, give him hell, trying to
sound like the crew chief that she was, and not like his
mother, which she was old enough to be—

—and most certainly not like an aging lover, which
half the Bugatti team and every other team assumed
she was.

The fact that they *weren't* had no bearing on the situation. Dora had been well aware from the moment she
joined Bugatti at the end of the war that her position in
this man's world would always be difficult.

That was all right; when had she ever had an easy
life?

"All right!" She pulled clear of the engine compartment, hands up and in plain sight, as she had taught all
her mechanics to do. Too many men in Grand Prix racing had missing fingers from being caught in the
wrong place when an engine started—but not on her

team. The powerful Bugatti engine roared to life; she nodded to the mechanic in Jimmy's seat, and he floored the pedal.

She cocked her head to one side, frowning a little; then grinned and gave the mech a thumbs up. He killed the engine, answering her grin, and popped out of the cockpit—just as Jimmy himself came swaggering up through the chaotic tangle of men and machines in the pits.

She knew he was there by the way the men's eyes suddenly moved to a point just behind and to one side of her. They never learned—or else, they never guessed how they gave themselves away. Probably the latter; they *were* mostly Italian, steeped in generations of presumed male superiority, and they would never even think that a woman could be more observant than they, no matter how often she proved it to them.

She pivoted before Jimmy could slap her butt, and gave him The Look. She didn't even have to say anything, it was all there in The Look.

He stopped, standing hip-shot as if he was posing for one of his famous publicity shots, his born-charmer grin countering her Look. The blue eyes that made millions of teenage girls suffer heart palpitations peered cheerfully at Dora through his unruly blond hair. He'd grown a thatch over his eyes for his last movie, and hadn't cut it yet. He probably wouldn't, Dora reflected. His image as a rebel wasn't just an image, it was the real Jimmy.

She pulled her eyes away from his, and The Look turned to a real frown as she took in the dark ankle-length trenchcoat and the flamboyant, long silk scarf he wore.

"Out!" she ordered, and watched his grin fade in surprise. "You heard me," she said when he hesitated. "You know the pit rules. *Nothing* that can get caught in machinery! God help us, that scarf could get your neck broken! I told you once, and I meant it; I don't care how many movies you've made, in here you're the Bugatti rookie, and you toe the line and act like a professional. And if you think you're going to make me break my promise not to compete again by getting yourself strangled, you can think again! Now get out of here and come back when you're dressed like a driver and not some Hollywood gigolo."

She turned her back on him, and back to the crew changing the tires, but she did not miss his surprised—and suddenly respectful—"Yes *ma'am!*"

She also didn't miss the surprised and respectful looks on the faces of her mechanics and pit crew. *So, they didn't expect me to chew him out in public. . . .* She couldn't help but see the little nods, and the satisfaction on the men's faces. And she hid a grin of her own, as she realized what that meant. The last rumors of her protégé being her lover had just gone up in smoke. No aging female would lay into her young lover that way in public. And no young stud would put up with that kind of treatment from a woman, young or old, unless the only position she held in his life was as respected mentor.

She raised her chin aggressively, and raked her crew with her stern gaze. "Come on, come on, pick it up," she said, echoing every other crew chief here in the pits. "We're running a race here, not an ice cream social! *Move it!*"

"Ready, Miz Duncan," said a sober voice at her shoulder. She turned to see Jimmy was back already, having ditched the coat and scarf for the racing suit of her own design. His helmet tucked under one arm, he waited while she looked him over critically.

"Nothing binding?" she asked, inspecting every visible seam and wrinkle. It was as fireproof as modern technology could make it, asbestos fabric over cotton, covering the driver from neck to ankle. Thick asbestos boots covered his feet, which would be under the engine compartment. It would be hotter than all the fires of hell in there, but Jimmy would be cooler than most of the other drivers, who shunned her innovations in favor of jerseys and heavy canvas pants.

And he would be safer than she had been, who'd won the French Gran Prix in '48 in a leotard and tights.

And if she could have put an air conditioner in there, she would have. Temperatures in the cockpit ran over 120 Fahrenheit while the car was moving—worse when it idled. In the summer, and at those temperatures, strange things started to happen to a driver's brain. Heat exhaustion and the dangerous state leading up to it had probably caused more crashes than anyone wanted to admit.

She finished her inspection and gave him the nod; he clapped his helmet on—a full head helmet, not just an elaborate leather cap, but one with a face-plate—and strolled over to his car, beginning his own inspection.

Just as she had taught him.

While the mechanics briefed him on the Bugatti's latest quirks—and Gran Prix racers always developed new quirks, at least a dozen for each race, not counting intended modifications—she took a moment to survey the nearest crews. To her right, Ferrari and Lola; to her left, Porsche and Mercedes.

Nothing to show that this was Wisconsin and not Italy or Monte Carlo. Nothing here at the track, that is. She had to admit that it was a relief being back in the U.S.; not even the passing of a decade had erased all the scars the War had put on the face of Europe. And there were those who thought that reviving the Gran Prix circuit in '46 had been both frivolous and ill-considered in light of all that Europe had suffered.

Well, those people didn't have to invest their money, their time, or their expertise in racing. The announcement that the Indianapolis 500 would be held in 1946 had given those behind the project the incentive they needed to get the plans off the drawing board and into action. The Prince in Monaco had helped immeasurably by offering to host the first race. Monte Carlo had not suffered as much damage as some of the other capitals, and it was a neutral enough spot to lure even the Germans there.

She shook herself mentally. Woolgathering again; it was a good thing she was out of the cockpit and on the sidelines, if she was going to let her thoughts drift like that.

Jimmy nodded understanding as the steering-specialist made little wiggling motions with his hand. Dora cast another glance up and down pit row, then looked down at the hands of her watch.

Time.

She signaled to the crew, who began to push the car into its appointed slot in line. This would be a true Gran Prix start; drivers sprinting to their cars on foot and bullying through the pack, jockeying for position right from the beginning. In a way, she would miss it if they went to an Indy-type start; with so little momentum, crashes at the beginning of the race were seldom serious—but when they were, they were devastating. And there were plenty of promising contenders taken out right there in the first four or five hundred yards.

She trotted alongside Jimmy as they made their way to the starting line. "All right, now listen to me: save the engine, save the tires. You have a long race ahead of you. We've got a double whammy on us," she warned. "Remember, a lot of drivers have it in for Bugatti because of me—and the Europeans aren't really thrilled with the Bugatti preference for Yankee drivers. The other thing; this is Ford country; Ford is fielding six cars in the factory team alone. None of the other chiefs I've talked to know any of the drivers personally, which tells me they're in Ford's back pocket."

"Which means they might drive as a team instead of solo?" Jimmy hazarded shrewdly. "Huh. That could be trouble. Three cars could run a rolling roadblock."

"We've worked on the engine since the trials, and there's another twenty horse there," she added. "It's just the way you like it; light, fast, and all the power you need. If I were you, I'd use that moxie early, get yourself placed up in the pack, then lay off and see what the rest do."

She slowed as they neared driver-only territory; he waved acknowledgment that he had heard her, and trotted on alone. She went back to the pits; the beginning of the race really mattered only in that he made it through the crush at the beginning, and got in a little ahead of the pack. That was one reason why she had given over the cockpit to a younger driver; she was getting too old for those sprints and leaps. Places where she'd hurt herself as a dancer were starting to remind her that she was forty-five years old now. Let Jimmy race to the car and fling himself into it, *he* was only twenty-five.

The view from her end of pit row wasn't very good, but she *could* see the start if she stood on the concrete fire wall. One of the men steadied her; Tonio, who had been with her since *she* was the driver. She handed her clipboard down to him, then noticed a stranger in their pit, wearing the appropriate pass around his neck. She was going to say something, but just then the drivers on the line crouched in preparation for the starting gun, and her attention went back to them.

The gun went off; Jimmy leapt for his car like an Olympic racer, vaulting into it in a way that made her simultaneously sigh with envy and wince. The Bugatti kicked over like a champ; Jimmy used every horse under that hood to bully his way through the exhaust-choked air to the front of the pack, taking an outside position. Just like she'd taught him.

The cars pulled out of sight, and she jumped down off the wall. The stranger was still there—and the pits were quiet for the first time today. They would not be that way for long, as damaged or empty cars staggered into the hands of their keepers, but they were for the moment, and the silence impacted the ears as the silence between incoming artillery barrages had—

She headed for the stranger, but he was heading for her. "Miss Duncan?" he said quickly. "Jim got me this pit pass. He came over to see us do *Death of a Salesman* last night and when he came back stage and found out I race too, he got me the pass and told me to check in with you."

"What kind of racing?" she asked cautiously. It would be just like Jimmy to pal around with some kid just because he was an up-and-coming actor and saddle her with someone who didn't know when to get the hell out of the way.

"Dirt-track, mostly," he said modestly, then quoted her credentials that made her raise her eyebrow. "I'll stay out of the way."

The kid had an open, handsome face, and another set of killer blue eyes—and the hand that shook hers was firm and confident. She decided in his favor.

"Do that," she told him. "Unless there's a fire. Tell you what, you think you can put up with hauling one of those around for the rest of the race?" She pointed at the rack of heavy fire bottles behind the fire wall, and he nodded. "All right; get yourself one of those and watch our pit, Porsche, and Ferrari. That's the cost of you being in here. If there's a fire in any of 'em, deal with it." Since the crews had other things on their minds, and couldn't afford to hang extinguishers around their necks, this kid might be the first one on the spot.

"Think you can handle that—what is your name, anyway?"

"Paul," he said, diffidently. "Yeah, I can handle that. Thanks, Miss Duncan."

"Dora," she replied automatically, as she caught the whine of approaching engines. She lost all interest in the kid for a moment as she strained to see who was in front.

It was Lola, but the car was already in trouble. She heard a telltale rattle deep in, and winced as the leaders roared by.

Jimmy was in the first ten; that was all that mattered, that, and his first-lap time. She glanced at Fillipe, who had the stopwatch; he gave her a thumbs-up and bent to his clipboard to make notes, as he would for almost every lap. She let out her breath in a sigh.

"Miss Duncan, how did you get into racing?"

She had forgotten the kid, but he was still there—as he had promised, out of the way, but still within talking distance.

She shook her head, a rueful smile on her lips. "Glory. How fleeting fame. Retire, and no one's ever heard of you—"

"Oh, I know all about the Gran Prix wins," the kid

said hastily. "I just wanted to know why you stopped dancing. Jimmy told me you were kind of a—big thing in Europe. It doesn't seem like a natural approach to racing. I mean, Josephine Baker didn't go into racing."

She chuckled at being compared to the infamous cabaret dancer, but no one had ever asked her the question in quite that way. "A couple of reasons," she replied thoughtfully. "The biggest one is that my dingbat brother was a better dancer than I ever was. I figured that the world only needed one crazy dancing Duncan preaching Greek revival and naturalism. And really, Ruth St. Denis and Agnes de Mille were doing what I would have been doing. Agnes was doing more; she was putting decent dancing into motion pictures, where millions of little children would see it. When I think about it, I don't think Isadora Duncan would have made any earthshaking contributions to dancing." Then she gave him her famous impish smile, the one that peeled twenty years off of her. "On the other hand, every Gran Prix driver out there does the 'Duncan dive' to hit the cockpit. And they are starting to wear the driving suits I've been working on. So I've done that much for racing."

The kid nodded; he started to ask something else, but the scream of approaching engines made him shake his head before she held up her hand.

Jimmy was still there, still within striking distance of the leaders. But there was trouble developing—because the Ford drivers were doing just what Dora had feared they would do. They were driving as a team—in two formations of three cars each. Quite enough to block. Illegal as hell, but only if the race officials caught on and they could get someone on the Ford team to spill the beans. Obvious as it might be, the worst the drivers would get would be fines, unless someone fessed up that it was premeditated—then the whole team could be disqualified.

Illegal as hell, and more than illegal—dangerous. Dora bit her lip, wondering if they really knew just how dangerous.

* * *

Halfway through the race, and already the kid had more than earned his pit pass. Porsche was out, bullied into the wall by the Ford flying wedge, in a crash that sent the driver to the hospital. Ferrari was out, too, victim of the same crash; both their LMCs had taken shrapnel that had nicked fuel lines. Thank God, Paul'd been close to the pits when the leaking fuel caught fire. He'd come in trailing a tail of fire and smoke and the kid was right in there, the first one on the scene with his fire bottle, foaming the driver down first, then going under the car with the nozzle. He'd probably prevented a worse fire.

And now the alliances in the pits had undergone an abrupt shift. It was now the Europeans and the independents against the Ford monolith. Porsche and Ferrari had just come to her—her, who Porsche had never been willing to give the time of day!—offering whatever they had left. "Somehow" the race officials were being incredibly blind to the illegal moves Ford was pulling.

Then again . . . how close was Detroit to Wisconsin?

It had happened before, and would happen again, for as long as businessmen made money on sport. All the post-race sanctions in the world weren't going to help that driver in the hospital, and no fines would change the outcome of the inevitable crashes.

The sad, charred hulk of the Ferrari had been towed, its once-proud red paint blistered and cracked; the pit crew was dejectedly cleaning up the oil and foam.

On the track, Jimmy still held his position, despite two attempts by one of the Ford wedges to shove him out of the way. That was the advantage of a vehicle like the Bugatti, as she and the engineers had designed it for him. The handling left something to be desired, at least as far as she was concerned, but it was Jimmy's kind of car. Like the 550 Porsche he drove for pleasure now, that he used to drive in races, she'd built it for speed. "Point and squirt," was how she often put it, dryly. Point it in the direction you wanted to go, and let the horses do the work.

The same thing seemed to be passing through Paul's

mind, as he watched Jimmy scream by, accelerating out of another attempt by Ford to pin him behind their wedge. He shook his head, and Dora elbowed him.

"You don't approve?" she asked.

"It's not that," he said, as if carefully choosing his words. "It's just not my kind of driving. I like handling; I like to slip through the pack like—like I was a fish and they were the water. Or I was dancing on the track—"

She had to smile. "Are you quoting that, or did you not know that was how they described my French and Monte Carlo Gran Prix wins?"

His eyes widened. "I didn't know," he stammered, blushing. "Honest! I—"

She patted his shoulder maternally. "That's fine, Paul. It's a natural analogy. Although I bet you don't know where I got my training."

He grinned. "Bet I do! Dodging bombs! I read you were an ambulance driver in Italy during the war. Is that when you met Ettore Bugatti?"

She nodded, absently, her attention on the cars roaring by. Was there a faint sound of strain in her engine? For a moment her nerves chilled.

But no, it was just another acceleration; a little one, just enough to blow Jimmy around the curve ahead of the Mercedes.

Her immediate reaction was annoyance; he shouldn't have had to power his way out of that, he should have been able to *drive* his way out. He was putting more stress on the engine than she was happy with.

Then she mentally slapped her own hand. *She* wasn't the driver, he was.

But now she knew how Ettore Bugatti felt when she took the wheel in that first Monte Carlo Gran Prix.

"You know, Bugatti was one of my passengers," she said, thinking aloud, without looking to see if Paul was listening. "He was with the Resistance in the Italian Alps. You had to be as much a mechanic as a driver, those ambulances were falling apart half the time, and he saw me doing both before I got him to the field hospital."

Sometimes, she woke up in the middle of the night, hearing the bombs falling, the screams of the attack fighters strafing the road—

Seeing the road disintegrate in a flash of fire and smoke behind her, in front of her; hearing the moans of the wounded in her battered converted bread-truck.

All too well, she remembered those frantic moments when getting the ambulance moving meant getting herself and her wounded passengers out of there before the fighter planes came back.

And for a moment, she heard those planes—

No, it was the cars returning. She shook her head to free it of unwanted memories. She had never lost a passenger, or a truck, although it had been a near thing more times than she cared to count. Whenever the memories came between her and a quiet sleep, she told herself that—and reminded herself why she had volunteered in the first place.

Because her brother, the darling of the Metaphysical set, was hiding from the draft at home by remaining in England among the blue-haired old ladies and balletomanes he charmed. Because, since they would not accept her as a combatant, she enlisted as a noncombatant.

*Some noncombatant.* She had seen more fire than most who were on the front lines.

Bugatti had been sufficiently impressed by her pluck and skill to make her an offer.

*"When this is over, if you want a job, come to me."*

Perhaps he had meant a secretarial job. She had shown up at the decimated Bugatti works, with its "EB" sign in front cracked down the middle, and offered herself as a mechanic. And Bugatti, faced with a dearth of men who were able-bodied, never mind experienced, had taken her on out of desperation.

"It was kind of a fluke, getting to be Bugatti's driver," she continued, noting absently that Paul was listening intently. "The driver for that first Gran Prix had broken an ankle, right at starting lineup, and I was the only one on the team that could make the sprint for the car!"

Paul chuckled, and it had been funny. Everyone else was either too old, or had war injuries that would slow them down. So she had grabbed the racing helmet before anyone could think to object and had taken the man's place. In her anonymous coverall, it was entirely possible none of the officials had even noticed her sex.

She had made the first of her famous "Duncan dives" into the cockpit; a modified *grand jete* that landed her on the seat, with a twist and bounce down into the cockpit itself.

"I can still hear that fellow on the bullhorn—there was no announcer's booth, no loudspeaker system—" She chuckled again. *"And coming in third—Isadora Duncan?"*

The next race, there had been no doubt at all of her sex. She had nearly died of heat stroke behind that powerful engine, and she had been shocked at what that had done to her judgment and reflexes. So this time, she had worn one of her old dancing costumes, a thick cotton leotard and tights—worn inside-out, so that the seams would not rub or abrade her.

The other drivers had been so astounded that she had gotten nearly a two-second lead on the rest of them in the sprint—and two seconds in a race meant a quarter mile.

For her third race, she had been forbidden to wear the leotard, but by then she had come up with an alternative; almost as form-fitting, and enough to cause a stir. And that had been in France, of course, and the French had been amused by her audacity. "La Belle Isadora" had her own impromptu fan club, who showed up at the race with noisemakers and banners.

Perhaps that had been the incentive she needed, for that had been her first win. She had routinely placed in the first three, and had taken home to Bugatti a fair share of first-place trophies. The other drivers might have been displeased, but they could not argue with success.

Bugatti had been overjoyed, and he had continuously modified his racing vehicles to Isadora's specifications; lighter, a little smaller than the norm, with superb handling. And as a result of Isadora's win, the Bugatti reputation had made for many, many sales of sportscars in the speed-hungry, currency-rich American market. And it did not hurt that his prize driver was an attractive, *American* lady.

But in 1953 she had known that she would have to retire, and soon. She was slowing down—and more important, so were her reflexes. That was when she had begun searching for a protégé, someone she could groom to take her place when she took over the retiring crew chief's position.

She had found it in an unlikely place; Hollywood. And in an unlikely person, a teenage heartthrob, a young, hard-living actor. But she had not seen him first on the silver screen; she had seen him racing, behind the wheel of his treasured silver Porsche.

He had been torn by indecision, although he made time for her coaching and logged a fair amount of time in Bugatti racing machines. She and the retiring crew chief worked on design changes to suit his style of driving to help lure him. But it was Hollywood itself that forced his choice.

When a near-fatality on a lonely California highway left his Porsche a wreck, his studio issued an ultimatum. *Quit driving, or tear up your contract. We don't cast corpses.*

He tore up his contract, took the exec's pipe from his mouth, stuffed the scraps in the pipe, slammed it down on the desk and said "Smoke it." He bought a ticket for Italy the same day.

"Miss Duncan?" Paul broke into her thoughts. "We have company."

She turned, to see the crew chiefs of Ferrari, Mercedes, Lola, and a dozen more approaching. Her first thought was—*What have we done now?*

But it was not what she had done, nor her crew, nor even Jimmy.

It was what Ford had done.

"Isadora," said Paul LeMond, the Ferrari crew chief, who had evidently been appointed spokesman, "We need your help."

Ten years of fighting her way through this man's world, with no support from anyone except Bugatti and a few of her crew had left her unprepared for such a statement.

She simply stared at them, while they laid out their idea.

This would be the last pit stop before the finish, and Dora was frankly not certain how Jimmy was going to take this. But she leaned down into the cockpit where she would not be overheard and shouted the unthinkable into his ear over the roar of his engine. How the crews of every other team still on the track were fed up with the performance of the Ford drivers—and well they should be, with ten multi-car wrecks leaving behind ruined vehicles and drivers in hospital. The fact that one of those wrecks had included one of the Ford three-car flying wedges had not been good enough.

"So if Ford is going to play footsie with the rules, so are we," she shouted. "They think you're the best driver on the track, Jimmy. The only one good enough to beat cheaters. So every other driver on the track's been given orders to block for you, or let you pass."

She couldn't see Jimmy's expression behind the face-plate, but she did see the muscles in his jaw tense. "So they're going to just give me the win?" he shouted back.

That was not how Jimmy wanted his first Gran Prix to end—and she didn't blame him.

"Jimmy—*they* decided you're the best out there! Not only your peers, but *mine!* Are you going to throw that kind of vote away?" It was the only way she would win this argument, she sensed it. And she sensed as his mood turned to grudging agreement.

"All right," he said finally. "But you tell them this—"

She rapped him on the top of the helmet. "No, you listen. They said to tell *you* that if you get by Ford early enough, they're going to do the same for Giorgio with the old Ferrari and Peter for Citroën. And as many more as they can squeeze by."

She sensed his mood lighten again, although he didn't answer. But by then the crew was done, and she stood back as he roared back out onto the track.

When he took the track, there were ten laps to go—but five went by without anyone being able to force a break for Jimmy, not even when the Ford wedge lapped slower cars. She had to admit that she had seldom seem smoother driving, but it was making her blood boil to watch Jimmy coming up behind them, and being forced to hold his place.

Three laps to go, and there were two more cars wrecked, one of them from Citroën.

Two laps.

One.

Flag lap.

Suddenly, on the back stretch, an opening, as one of the Ford drivers tired and backed off a little. And Jimmy went straight for it.

Dora was on the top of the fire wall, without realizing she had jumped up there, screaming at the top of her lungs, with half the crew beside her. Ford tried to close up the wedge, but it was too late.

Now it was just Jimmy and the lead Ford, neck and neck—down the backstretch, through the chicane, then on the home run for the finish line.

Dora heard his engine howling; heard strain that hadn't been there before. Surely if she heard it, so would he. He should have saved the engine early on—if he pushed it, he'd blow the engine, he had to know that—

He pushed it. She heard him drop a gear, heard the engine scream in protest—

And watched the narrow-bodied, lithe, steel Bugatti surge across the finish line a bare nose ahead of the Ford, engine afire and trailing a stream of flame and smoke that looked for all the world like a victory banner.

Dora was the first to reach him, before he'd even gotten out of the car. While firefighters doused the vehicle with impartial generosity, she reached down and yanked off his helmet.

She seized both his ears and gave him the kind of kiss only the notorious Isadora Duncan, toast of two continents, could have delivered—a kiss with every year of her considerable amatory experience behind it.

"That's for the win," she said, as he sat there, breathless, mouth agape and for once completely without any kind of response.

Then she grasped his shoulders and shook him until his teeth rattled.

"And *that's* for blowing up my engine, you idiot!" she screamed into his face.

By then, the crowd was on him, hauling him bodily out of the car and hoisting him up on their shoulders to ride to the winner's circle.

Dora saw to it that young Paul was part of that privileged party, as a reward for his fire-fighting and his listening. And when the trophy had been presented and the pictures were all taken, she made sure he got up to the front.

Jimmy recognized him, as Jimmy would, being the kind of man he was. "Hey!" he said, as the Race Queen hung on his arm and people thrust champagne bottles at him, "You made it!"

Paul grinned, shyly. Dora felt pleased for him, as he shoved the pass and a pen at Jimmy. "Listen, I know it's awful being asked—"

"Awful? Hell, no!" Jimmy grabbed the pen and pass. "Have you made up your mind about what you want to do yet?"

Paul shook his head, and Dora noticed then what she should have noticed earlier—that his bright blue eyes and Jimmy's were very similar. *And if he isn't a heartbreaker yet,* she thought wryly, *he will be.*

"I still don't know," he said.

"Tell you what," Jimmy said, pausing a moment to kiss another beauty queen for the camera. "You make a pile of money in the movies, *then* go into racing. Get a good mentor like Dora."

And then he finished the autograph with a flourish—
and handed it back to the young man.

*To Paul Newman, who can be my driver when I take
over from Dora, best of luck.*

And the familiar autograph, *James Dean.*

# WOULD HE DO WOODY?

## Nicholas A. DiChario

*As everyone knows, Charlie Chaplin was the greatest silent film star in history, a genius whose films are as funny today as they were 75 years ago.*

*Charlie was forced to be a silent star by necessity; sound pictures hadn't been invented back then. But what, asks Nicholas DiChario, one of the hottest up-and-coming stars in the science fiction galaxy, if Chaplin had been silent by choice?*

*Here's his intriguing answer.*

Charlie said nothing at the Palais des Festivals in Cannes. Not one word. Not even when he received the Palm d'Or. The journalists were hoping he would say something during the press conference at the Salon du Presse, but he didn't.

When Charlie's flight from Nice landed at La Guardia he was met by Mr. Duc's personal secretary, a beautiful Japanese woman who spoke with a lovely accent. "I represent Mr. Yhat-sow Duc."

She spirited Charlie away to a gray stretch limousine. His knees felt weak from the long flight. A light rain fell from the afternoon clouds. Charlie crouched inside the limo and slid across the seat. Mr. Duc's secretary crawled in beside him.

"My name is Yin," she said, unlatching a liquor cabinet stocked with top-shelf scotch, whiskey, bourbon, and brandy. On the seat next to Charlie, a copy of the latest *Screen International* lay folded open to page forty-eight, where Charlie's picture stared back at him. Under the picture someone had written CONGRATULATIONS in thick red marking pen. In the photo Charlie stood on the Boulevard Croisette, dressed in the baggy slacks, button-up shoes, small tight waistcoat, and bowler hat that he wore during the filming of *The Life and Times of Eddie Chaplin*. He'd worn the mustache at the festival, too, and twirled the cane, and outside the Hôtel du Cap—where the Nazi High Command had enjoyed furloughs during the World War II Occupation—Charlie performed a perfect *pas de bouree*. He was a big hit with both the French and the Americans. Not an easy trick.

Yin pushed a button on the intercom and instructed the driver to proceed directly to Mr. Duc's penthouse. She poured Charlie a Crown Royal. "Mr. Duc very interested in Chawlie Chaplin," she said, brushing back her long black hair, resting her hand on his thigh. She had bright white teeth, prune-colored eyes, and a bent nose.

Charlie knew that Mr. Yhat-sow "Daffy" Duc handled only the hottest actors and producers and directors in New York and Hollywood. He had never met the man. Charlie silently toasted Grandpa Eddie. What do you think of me now, Gramps? He picked up *Screen International:*

*. . . The finest film to come out of Cannes this year is Charlie Chaplin's silent movie,* The Life and Times of Eddie Chaplin—*a touching and tragic portrait of one man's struggle for stardom and integrity in the early years of American filmmaking.*

*Charlie plays his own grandfather, Eddie Chaplin, a vaudevillian theater actor born in 1889 in Walworth, London. The film opens with Eddie landing the opportunity of a lifetime for a young teenaged boy in the midst of an impoverished Victorian London: a chance to play America with a roving repertory company. The manager of the company employs—along with a cast of dogs and lions and chimps who provide much of the film's slapstick comedy—several bright, promising child-actors.*

*Young Eddie Chaplin soon establishes himself as an adept clog dancer, acrobat, pantomime, and natural comic. His gift to make people laugh with his facial expressions and body movements make him an instant*

*stage star in the United States. When the opportunity
to join Keystone Comedy Film Company arises (in the
form of a talent scout with contract-in-hand) Eddie
jumps at the chance to act in silent pictures along with
his companions, the strikingly beautiful Mary Pickford,
played by Isabella Rossellini, and a much less talented
lad named Arthur Stanley Jefferson, later to be known
in the "talkies" as Stan Laurel, played by Henry
Winkler.*

*Shortly after his introduction into the world of silent
movies, Eddie Chaplin suffers a bizarre (and hereat
unexplained) departure from society by taking a vow of
silence. . . .*

"Don't you feel like talking?" Yin said. "How long
since you not say any words? I understand they show
your film on opening night at Cannes. Quite an honor."
Charlie listened to the patter of soft rain against the car
windows.

Yin slid her hand between his legs.

Charlie decided to kiss her. He thought she needed
to be kissed by silence. He put down the magazine and
touched her hair. She had soft hair, soft as silk. Her
breath smelled like cherry blossoms. He pecked her
lightly on the lips and she came forward, expecting
more, but Charlie withdrew. He removed her hand
from between his legs, raised an eyebrow, and tipped
his glass to her.

"A man of integrity," she said. "I respect that. You
don't see much of that in this business." Her voice
sounded like she knew exactly what she was talking
about.

Charlie had once lost a job writing comedy sketches
for *Saturday Night Live* because the producer, Lorne
Michaels, told him his dialogue stunk. As Charlie remembered it, Lorne sounded a bit like Yin, like he
knew exactly what he was talking about. "You have
too many pauses," Lorne had told him. "How do you
expect comedy to work with so many damn pauses?
You've got to hit!-hit!-hit!"

Lorne didn't understand. Pauses were important. Es-
sential. During the best performances you could *feel*

the moments of silence. The silence, Charlie had discovered, was a natural part of him. He'd inherited it from Grandpa Eddie. So he wrote *The Life and Times of Eddie Chaplin*—an entire film with one big wonderful pause.

Yin clicked on the television set. Charlie turned off the sound. Yin leaned against him and Charlie curled his arm around her shoulders. They watched a colorized Edward G. Robinson movie until Charlie dozed off from the jet lag.

In the corner of Mr. Duc's office a dwarf bonsai and a rainbow assortment of Japanese irises occupied a large round planter. Charlie detected the faint odor of stale coffee and cigarette smoke from Daffy's furniture. A hint of blue-lotus incense lingered in the air.

"Sit, Charlie, sit," Daffy said from behind his glass desk. Charlie sat in a tall-backed chair, in front of the huge picture-windows that showed him Manhattan Island. Daffy leaned forward on his elbows. "This bit where you don't talk—a vow of silence—great gimmick. The press loves it. But you can cut the crap here with me because we need to talk hardball. I can put you on top, Charlie Chaplin. On *top!*"

Charlie grinned. Cannes would put him on top. In a fortnight, Cannes could make or break anybody in the film business, and usually did.

"When I saw that you won at Cannes," Daffy said, "I knew I had to make my move. I've been watching you for a long time. I said to myself, 'This guy is on the hot seat and he's going to need a man to feed the fire.' That's me. I feed the biggest fires in the business." He lit a cigarette and puffed several times without inhaling. "I also took the liberty of firing your former agent. I'm your agent now."

Charlie felt his stomach tighten at the thought of losing Hetty; but Hetty had been wanting to lose him for a long time. She would not be nearly as disappointed as he.

"Do you know who called me yesterday afternoon? Do you have any idea who called to talk to *me* about *you?*—Woody called me. That's right. Woody 'the Kon Man' Konigsberg. He wants you in his next production." Daffy sat back in his chair, ran his fingers through his woolly brown hair, and studied Charlie's expression. Charlie was sure Daffy wore a hairpiece or a wig or perhaps had gotten a hair transplant, like the ones he'd seen advertised on late-night television, 1-800-HAIRYME.

Daffy pursed his lips, furrowed his brow, breathed heavily through his nose. "I've studied your career, Charlie. You've been a small-timer for a lot of years. Bit parts in B movies. Commercials—Christ, you played the Dole pineapple back in '88, '89. You've never taken a speaking role. I don't want to hurt your feelings. I'm not hurting your feelings, am I?"

Charlie shook his head.

"Eddie Chaplin was a loser—hell, you know that— you wrote the damn script. Eddie passed up his shot at the big time. He turned down the talkies to stick with silent films. Where did it get him? Where, I ask you? Nowhere, that's where. He never even starred in his own picture. Stan Laurel becomes a sensation and he doesn't have a tenth of Eddie's talent. If it weren't for your film, nobody would know Eddie Chaplin's name. But you know that, right, Charlie? All I'm saying is, you played the part of Eddie and you did a damn fine job and it got you noticed. But it was just a *part*, Charlie. Move past it. Don't live your grandfather's life. It was a crappy life. He missed his shot, he lost his girl, and he died penniless and alone. You shouldn't romanticize the man. Don't make the same mistakes."

Mistakes? Charlie had taken a vow of silence, like Grandpa Eddie. He'd found his personal strength in it. How could this be a mistake?

"I've arranged for you to meet the Kon Man tomorrow afternoon at the Tokyo Tea Room. Yin will pick you up in the limo at three o'clock sharp. Be ready. When you get there, *talk* to the man. Say *YES* to whatever he offers. You get me?"

Daffy stood up, stubbed out his cigarette, and extended his hand. "How do you like Yin? She's all yours, Charlie. Comes with the package."

Charlie decided Daffy needed to be kissed by silence. He leaned forward and pecked him on the cheek.

Daffy smiled stupidly. "Charlie 'the C Man' Chaplin has arrived. This is what you've been working for. What have you got to say to that?"

Charlie thought about it. If he was inclined to say anything, he would have said, 'Isn't it amazing how much hardball we were able to discuss without me saying a word?'

Charlie nearly tripped over Hetty's suitcases when he stepped into their tiny brownstone apartment. He heard the toilet flush. Hetty Kelly came out of the bathroom and saw him standing just inside the threshold. "Shit," she said. "I was hoping to be gone before you got back. Well, it hardly matters, it's not like you'd say anything to stop me." Hetty was drunk. She listed sideways when she went for her purse.

"I got a call to do a Sani-Flush spot in L.A. I'm taking the job. It's not much of an acting opportunity, but it gets my face on camera."

Charlie nodded. Hetty hadn't gotten her big break yet.

"I talked to Daffy Duc yesterday. Congratulations on your Palm d'Or. Don't worry. I stepped down gracefully. I am no longer officially capacit—responsible—I have no more official capacity." She took a deep breath. "Duc can give you Woody. I couldn't give you Woody in a million years. Hell, we were only playing together anyway, you and me, right? I don't need you. I only hung around because you needed me. Now you've got Daffy. It's not like I should feel guilty about leaving." She picked up her purse and sat down on the couch.

Charlie glanced out the window and saw a yellow taxi cab pull up to the curb in front of their building. He sat down in the chair opposite Hetty and smiled sadly, raising his eyebrows. He loved Hetty. She knew that. But should Hetty stay with him just because he loved her? She always struggled with this, as if her inability to love him was a character flaw. Charlie's love frightened her. She would run, either to the bottle or to another man. She would always come back afterward, and Charlie would take care of her for a while. It was a regular thing.

"Are you going to do Woody?" she asked. "You'd be brain dead not to."

Charlie twitched his upper lip and shrugged.

"What do you mean you don't know? Just do what the man tells you, for God's sake. Don't be an idiot. Woody can make you somebody important. Do I have to take care of you forever? No, I don't, I'm leaving." She stood up, lost her balance, and sat back down. The cabby honked his horn.

Charlie went over to the tape deck and popped in a cassette: the soundtrack to *Eddie Chaplin*. He advanced the tape to his favorite piano concerto, the music he'd used in the big farewell dance scene, where Eddie danced with Mary Pickford under the light of a full moon on the night she left him for a clumsy, second-rate actor named Stan Laurel, a man who'd promised to give her a role in his next talkie. In the movie, Eddie and Mary gazed into each other's eyes, and they danced.

The music began to play. Charlie helped Hetty to her feet, hugged her, rocked her gently to the low keys of the piano, then led her slowly around the coffee table.

In his film, when the music came to an end, Eddie and Mary continued to dance. They danced and they wept and then Mary walked away.

The music stopped as Charlie turned Hetty toward the door. Hetty picked up her two bags and walked out. Charlie closed the door behind her and sat on the couch.

The tape clicked off and Charlie listened to the emptiness of the cloudy afternoon, of the dark blue night, of the falling moon, of the rising dawn.

*Stark;*
*terrifying;*
*lonely and lovely*
*emptiness.*

\* \* \*

"Chawlie," Yin said, climbing after him over the back seat of the limo. "I have look forward to seeing you. I could not even sleep last night thinking about you." She pushed the button on the intercom for the chauffeur. "Tokyo Tea Room. Drive slow." She clicked on the television set and turned off the sound. The New York Itsu had just tipped off against the Chicago Ima in Sony-Madison Square Garden. Yin leaned against Charlie. "Is it all right if we just sit like this, Chawlie, like we did yesterday, in the quiet?"

Charlie stroked her silky hair.

"This vow of silence shtick, Chuck—brilliant, I'm telling you—ingenious!" Woody 'the Kon Man' Konigsberg took a sip of his green tea and spat it back into his cup. "Waiter!" A lanky young man wearing a white *yukata,* a casual kimono, came up to their *kotatsu,* the knee-high tables usually found in Japanese homes. The Tokyo Tea Room was filled with these little tables, separated by rows of plastic imperial gardens. The smell of steamed vegetables and seafood wafted through the ceiling fans. Charlie and Woody sat cross-legged on cushions. "Waiter, how can you call this mouthwash tea? It's runny. I can't drink runny tea. Get me some espresso." Woody turned to Charlie. "You come to a Japanese tea room, you expect good tea. Is that too much to ask?"

The waiter picked up the tea and went into the kitchen. Woody scratched at a rash on his neck, flipped the edges of his long reddish hair off his shoulders, and nudged his thick-frammed glasses up the bridge of his nose. He had a pinched little forehead and intense eyes, as if he'd been born with a migraine headache and had spent a lifetime trying to push it out through his ears. His slight body trembled like shrubbery.

Charlie lifted the menu and browsed the house specialties:

1. 御飯 *rice*  2. 麺類 *noodles*  3. お茶 *tea*

He wasn't very hungry. He held up three fingers to the waiter and the young man brought him a cup of green tea. He thought about Hetty. He hoped she would be all right on her own. He hoped she would someday discover her silence. The world could be a very noisy place.

"You know what I saw on the news today, Chuck? A silent protest. There are a thousand or so pro-lifers and a thousand pro-choicers standing across from each other in front of some abortion clinic in Buffalo, New York, and they're all just standing there in total silence. Weird as hell. Like some kind of perverse war. Who could stay shut up longer? Somewhere in Atlanta, this guy wins the mayoral election and he stands up to deliver his acceptance speech and you know what he says? Go on, Chuck, take a guess."

Charlie didn't say anything.

"Right! The guy says nothing. Very hip. Very chic. Just stands there like a mannequin. You've started something, Chuck, a real movement. And it's only going to get bigger, and I'm going to help."

The waiter returned with a demitasse of espresso for Woody. "I want the jellied peaches," said Woody, "with whipped cream, six layers of whipped cream, you got that? If there are five layers, I'll send them back. If there are seven layers, I'll send them back. You got that?"

The waiter looked at Charlie and nodded. Charlie felt conspiratorial. Silence was not a movement. Silence, for those who understood, was a revolution, and like any good revolution no one in the elite was going to aid it, at least not knowingly.

"Let me tell you this, Chuck, before I pitch my project. I want you to know how much I respect the work you did on *Eddie Chaplin*. The music, the camera work, the lighting. Great stuff. Very artistic. Not too many people know this, but I used to be in *film noir* myself. Before I did *Jaws* and *Jaws 2* through *6*. Even before I did Bruce Lee in *Kong, Le Rex du Paris*. I did this film, *What's New, Pussycat?*—very dark, subtle, moody piece. Nobody saw it. Nobody cared. Same thing with my off-Broadway play, *Don't Drink the Water.* Depressing piece of work. Total flop. Art is deadly serious. I mean deadly. After a while it wears you down and kills you. And there's no money in it. What I'm trying to tell you is, look how far I've come."

Woody scratched at the bright red rash on his neck. "My psychiatrist blames this damn rash on stress. Soon Yi thinks it's razor burn. Who would you listen to? Your anal-retentive Ph.D. charging you thirty thousand yen per visit, or the girl who's giving you head?"

The waiter brought Charlie a bowl of rice, even though he didn't ask for it.

"I've done Cannes, of course. The *nouvelle cuisine.* The topless poolside-femmes. All-nighters over *cafe au lait* with self-important critics. Cannes can really give you the wrong impression of the film industry." Woody circled his fig-shaped nose over the steaming espresso. "But let me tell you about my project. Picture this. A major studio production silent movie. Big budget. Huge budget! I call it, *Silent Movie.*"

Charlie sipped his tea.

"High concept: Big Hollywood producer wants to shoot a silent film. Big producer needs to sign Big names to get the film off the ground. What we give the audience is a parade of stars—Kevin Costner, Julia Roberts, Al Pacino, Oprah Winfrey, Cassandra Peterson, Mel Brooks—walk-through cameos—no speaking roles. Big producer goes to all of them and makes an idiot out of himself begging and pleading them to do his film, but nobody wants to do it because it's silent. Get it? Think of the slapstick possibilities. It's wide open! Actually, I'm thinking about playing the lead role myself. Could be fun."

Charlie listened to the clinking of silverware and china. Samurai music played softly over the Tea Room's sound system. On the avenue outside, car horns honked, trucks rumbled, buses hissed. But all around him conversations had dwindled to near-nothing. This sort of sudden human silence seemed to follow Charlie wherever he went.

"Okay, get this. At the end of the film, big producer goes to the master of the *au courant* silent form, Charlie Chaplin, to be in his movie. That's you, Chuck, that's where you come in—winner at Cannes, vow of silence, the works. You turn to the camera, and in the only speaking role in the entire film, you say, 'No!' Audience erupts in laughter. Critics go wild, Christ, they go blind they're laughing so fucking godawful hard, and we're talking about opening night box-office numbers that will leave you speechless! I've already contracted cable and home-video rights and we haven't even started shooting yet. We're going to set up a 900 number that just plays a recording of you saying 'NO!' Millions and millions of yen! All because people want to hear Charlie Chaplin talk."

The waiter returned to their *kotatsu* with Woody's jellied peaches, and set down the dish. He looked at Charlie and winked, as if to say, Think of the slapstick possibilities. Charlie did, and smiled.

"Great," Woody said. "You like the idea. I knew you would." He yanked a contract out of his briefcase and slapped it down in front of Charlie, bouncing a set of chopsticks off the table. He took a pen out of his pocket and slapped that down on top of the contract.

Charlie stared at the paper and pen. Why was it so difficult for some people to understand that Charlie's grandfather had chosen silence? Many critics considered Charlie's film a tragedy—a film about a man driven to despair because his pride would not allow him the freedom to move forward, to give up the silent movies for any amount of money, or fame, or for the woman of his dreams. For stubbornness, they believed, Eddie Chaplin had sacrificed happiness. So he had died alone, watching those less talented reach for the stars.

But to die alone was not the same thing as to die lonely.

*Search for soundlessness;*
*discover it;*
*breathe it in as if it were the air,*
*or joy,*
*or God.*

*Forsake all other gods for they are false gods
filled with empty promises.*

Charlie recalled the penultimate scene in *The Life
and Times of Eddie Chaplin.* Stan Laurel had met
Eddie in a New York City restaurant. Stan had told him
he needed a partner, a sidekick in the talkies to play
straight-man to his wit. Stan had offered him fame and
fortune. There had been a whipped-cream dessert in
that scene, too.

Charlie stood. Woody glanced up at him. "Just sign
the contract, Chuck. Daffy has already approved the
draft."

Charlie decided that a kiss of silence would probably not do Woody 'the Kon Man' Konigsberg any
good. He picked up the dish of jellied peaches and
smushed six layers of whipped cream in Woody's face,
smearing it across his nose and cheeks and glasses.

A woman at the next *kotatsu* began to snicker. She
picked up her half-eaten *sukiyaki* and plopped it on top
of her boyfriend's head. An old man across the room
tossed his noodles *soba* at the hostess.

Charlie walked quietly to the exit, where Yin stood
waiting for him just inside the door. "Chawlie, the
chauffeur is on our side. I have an American Express
Gold Card with Daffy Duc's name on it. Unlimited
cwedit. We can go anywhere in the world."

Charlie glanced back at the Tea Room in time to see
a group of Japanese tourists launching marinated
shrimp from their plates of *kushiyaki* at their tour
guide.

The silent revolution had begun.

# THE WAGES OF SIN

## by Jack Nimersheim

*Everyone knows that bank robbers Bonnie and Clyde were gunned down by J. Edgar Hoover's G-men.*

*Well, as bored French philosophers are prone to say, "Everything changes and everything remains the same."*

*Jack Nimersheim, author of more than 20 nonfiction books and almost that many science fiction stories, gives you a totally different Barrow gang with oddly familiar overtones.*

> This road was so dimly lighted
> There were no highway signs to guide,
> But they made up their minds
> If the roads were all blind
> They wouldn't give up till they died.
>
> They don't think they are too tough or desperate,
> They know the law always wins,
> They have been shot at before
> But they do not ignore
> That death is the wages of sin.

The Story of Suicide Sal
Bonnie Parker, 1933–

"Do you have to light up another one of those damn things? It already smells like a goddamned crapper in here."

"I'll thank you not to complain about my smoking habits, honey." The young woman with the bright red hair took a deep drag off the freshly lit cigar and exhaled it languidly. As she did so, Bonnie Parker glared at her companion through the slowly rising smoke. "Not unless you can come up with something better to satisfy my oral fixations, that is."

Damn! He hated it when she did that. What the hell did Bonnie hope to accomplish with her constant taunts and snide comments? Did she think he enjoyed not being able to satisfy her, or what?

"Give it up, Bonnie. You oughtta know by now that it can't happen. And even if it could, I doubt that it would. Roy's my friend. How do you think he'd feel, if we started messin' around with one another and he ever found out?"

"It would serve the bastard right. Besides, what could he say? He's the one who went and got himself tossed in jail for twenty years, leaving me with nothing but his goddamned name and two hearts engraved on my thigh to remember him by. Stupidest fucking thing I ever did, letting my dear husband talk me into getting that tattoo. Now he's gone and it's still there. And I get to go through life like some prize filly, branded forever as belonging to Roy Thornton's herd."

Bonnie took another drag off the cigar. This time, the smoke exploded from between her lips. Propelled by anger and frustration, it drifted all the way across the hotel room to where Clyde Barrow lay, half-reclining on the bed, his head propped up by a pair of feather pillows. Clyde waved a hand in front of his face in a vain attempt to brush away the offensive haze.

"Ah, c'mon, Bonnie. Things ain't that bad. Hell, we've raked in a pretty good profit on this latest scam. And bilking a bunch of country bumpkins out of their money sure beats the hell out of robbing banks for a living. The way I figure it, that's about the only other thing the two of us could've done to get by, if we hadn't stumbled onto this scheme.

"Speaking of which, we got a show to do in the morning. Don't you think you better come to bed?"

"Gee, you're right, Clyde," she muttered sardonically. "It's a great life we got here. I don't know what the hell I've got to complain about." Bonnie extinguished the half-smoked cigar amidst the ashes and mutilated butts already piled up in a glass ashtray sitting on the table before her. She stood up, stretched and walked slowly across the room. "I'll come to bed, give you a platonic peck on the cheek, and then roll over and go to sleep in a cheap hotel in some backwater burg nobody ever heard of, just like I do every night. What more could a woman ask for?"

Looking out across the room, Clyde estimated the attendance at somewhere around fifty people. Not a bad turnout for a hick town like Arcadia, especially in these lean times. At five dollars a couple, he figured they'd pull down a cool hundred and twenty-five bucks this morning, minimum.

He and Bonnie had to share this with Buck and Blanche—and W.D., of course. But that was okay. The split was hardly equal. W.D. asked only a pittance. Hell, Clyde half believed W.D. would have stayed around for nothing, just to hang out with the rest of them. And he recognized the importance of having someone he could trust collecting the money at the door.

Buck and Blanche took a slightly larger cut, but not much. Again, Clyde didn't mind. This expense, also, was necessary. It amazed Clyde how reluctant folks still were to talk about sex openly. Hell, these were the 30s, weren't they?

Oh, sure, people were fascinated with sex. Had been ever since Adam first discovered that Eve possessed forbidden fruits much more appealing than a mere apple. It was easy getting them to come out and listen to someone else discuss sex. The size of the crowds he and Bonnie pulled in, regardless of where they set up shop, proved that. Convincing these same people to actually participate in the discussion, however, required a bit more coaxing. Clyde figured out a long time ago that having his brother and sister-in-law sit in the audience, ready to throw out a few well rehearsed questions if necessary, made things much more interesting than depending on the locals to keep the ball rolling.

Not that audience participation was mandatory. Curiosity alone guaranteed a good gate, whenever "The Great B&C Sex Debate" rolled into a city. But Clyde understood that their performance would have to live up to its own advanced billing, if they hoped to enjoy similar success on a return visit to a particular area.

This is where Bonnie's uncanny ability to arouse and then manipulate a crowd proved invaluable. As usual, she'd already stirred up a hornet's nest among the good folks of Arcadia.

"You're nothin' but a harlot, Miss Parker! Spreading your filthy ideas and suggestions among God-fearin' people the way you do. It's a scandal. Someone ought to run you out of town. No. Out of town's not far enough. You should be deported. Kicked right out of the country!"

"Pardon me, Miss ... um ... what's your name, please, ma'am?"

"Elizabeth Caldwell."

"And are you married, Miss Caldwell?"

"Sure am, Miss Parker. Me an' my husband, Leonard, tied the knot almost fifteen years ago. That's him, sittin' next to me." A thin man in his mid- to late-thirties—obviously a banker or some other kind of community leader, judging from his dress and demeanor—smiled and waved timidly at Bonnie. "We got three healthy, beautiful children. A son and two daughters. And we started all of them the natural way, lookin' each other straight in the eye, just like the Good Lord intended us to do."

This last comment drew a chuckle from the crowd. Good, thought Clyde. A little laughter thrown into the fray never hurt.

"And how old is your youngest child?"

"Bobby, that's our son, just turned six."

"Six, hmmm? Six years. Would that also happen to be how long it's been since you and your husband last made love?"

There are times when silence speaks volumes. This was one of them. Elizabeth Caldwell's silence, complemented by the crimson flush that suddenly colored her face, provided a more eloquent answer to Bonnie's question that mere words ever could have. Once again, the crowd chuckled—this time, a little louder.

"Don't any of you dare laugh at this woman!" Bonnie shouted. The room fell silent. She looked directly at the humiliated Mrs. Caldwell and flashed her sweetest smile—which was sweet, indeed—before continuing. "I apologize, ma'am. I didn't meant to embarrass you. I was merely trying to make a point.

"I don't doubt for a moment that you and your husband—Leonard, was it?—love one another." The woman nodded. It wasn't obvious which point she was clarifying. "But there's no reason your demonstration of that love can't include some, shall we say, creative physical encounters, as well.

"I'm familiar with the word of God, also, Mrs. Caldwell. Quite familiar with it, in fact. I've read the Bible several times, from Genesis to Revelations. Aside from condemning a few specific acts that I'm sure all of us agree are loathsome and unnatural in the extreme, nothing in the Good Book specifically prohibits the free expression of love between a husband and wife.

"It isn't my place to pass judgment on you, my dear lady. All I'm suggesting is that, with a little imagination, you and others like you can reignite the spark that initially stoked the fires of your relationship—and bring a twinkle to the eye of your husband in the process, if you know what I mean." Bonnie winked to emphasize her point.

Most of the men in the crowd (and quite a few women, as well) snickered at this last observation. Even the previously upset Mrs. Caldwell smiled sheepishly, although her face blushed a bright crimson as she did so.

Damn, Clyde thought, Bonnie sure was on a roll today. She had the audience eating out of her hand even more than usual. And that was saying something! He'd have to piss her off the night before every show, if this was how she responded.

"Mr. Barrow, what do you think of Miss Parker's libertarian views?" It was Blanche, right on cue.

Blanche and Buck had instructions to keep controversy raging, once it arose. Should sentiment sway too far in favor of Bonnie, it fell to one or the other of them to direct the discussion back to Clyde. He, of course, responded with an opinion directly opposed to the well-rehearsed convictions Bonnie professed.

Clyde recognized the irony in this strategy. It was, after all, nothing more than a new twist on an old and highly effective form of manipulation he'd fallen prey to, back in his younger days. How many times had various Texas law-enforcement agencies pulled the "good cop/bad cop" routine on him? More than Clyde cared to admit, to be sure. Their first few attempts even succeeded. Then, he wised up. Clyde's 1930 arrest for car theft was the result of solid criminal investigation—not intimidation and self-incrimination, as were most of his earlier incarcerations.

Clyde wised up in other ways, as well, during the almost two years he spent behind bars following his 1930 conviction. That's when he concluded that bending the law made a lot more sense than breaking it. That's also when Clyde decided there was probably more profit to be found in lechery than larceny.

It was bitterly cold, that February morning in 1932 when Clyde walked out of prison for what he swore would be the final time. He had only three things to his name: $20, a cheap suit, and a dream. He immediately spent the $20 to replace the suit with one of a more dapper design. His final possession he held onto only slightly longer, until August of the same year. That's when Clyde Barrow finally teamed up with Bonnie Parker. Only then did the seed planted by his dream blossom into a profitable reality.

"So, lover, what's the final take?" Bonnie was curled up in a chair by the window. Her arms were wrapped around both legs. Her chin rested on her knees. As usual, a cigar dangled from the corner of her mouth.

"$132.50. That means we had, um, fifty-three people. Hmmmm. An uneven number. I thought I made it clear, W.D. I want to limit the audience to couples only. What happened?"

"Uh, well, boss, um, it's like this. This one guy showed up all by himself. Said his wife was planning on comin', but then she took ill last night and couldn't make it. If you ask me, though, his wife, if he even had one, just didn't want to be seen with him in public. This guy was ugly, had a face like a bulldog. But his money was as green as everybody else's. So, I figured, what the hell, and let him in anyway."

"Ah saw him," Blanche chimed in. She was sitting in a sofa on the opposite side of the room from Bonnie. Blanche and Bonnie, who didn't get along very well, kept their distance from one another. That's not quite right. Blanche kept her distance from Bonnie. Bonnie did what she wanted, when she wanted, where she wanted. Although she held no love for Clyde's sister-in-law, Bonnie wasn't about to inconvenience herself for anyone. It was Blanche, therefore, who always waited to see where Bonnie settled in and then found her own spot—usually as far away from the other woman as circumstances permitted.

"He was sittin' about three rows in front of me and Buck," Blanche continued."A short, ugly guy, just like W.D. said. He didn't say a word to anybody. In fact, he hardly moved. Just sat there, starin' at you and Bonnie, the whole mornin'. He was kinda spooky, if you ask me."

"We didn't, dearie."

"Ah, c'mon, Bonnie. Lighten up on Blanche." Clyde's brother Buck tried to maintain an uneasy truce between the two women. He failed miserably in these attempts, but his heart was in the right place.

"Why should I? And what the hell's she trying to scare us with this 'spooky' stuff for? He paid his two bucks and change and, in return, he got to hear a pretty girl talk about sex for a couple hours. Probably just some lonely guy lookin' for a cheap thrill.

"It wasn't nothing more than that. Spooky. Geez! Who ever heard of such crap? That's some imagination you got there, Blanche."

"All right, everybody, settle down. We got a pile of cold cash here just waitin' to be divvied up. So, what do y'all say we get down to business and start divvyin' it."

The bickering stopped immediately. Where Buck could only try to maintain peace, Clyde succeeded. Always. Even Bonnie bowed to his will—in front of the others, at least.

"Why do you egg Blanche on like that, Bonnie? She ain't so bad. Besides, Buck loves her. Things would go a whole lot easier if you just backed off a little bit."

They were alone in the room. The others had departed right after getting their share of the take. Buck and Blanche were probably eating dinner together at a local restaurant, as they did almost every evening. W.D. never talked about what he did in his spare time. Clyde never asked.

"Ah, c'mon, Clyde. That's garbage, and you know it. Blanche is a pain in the ass, plain and simple. She always has been, and she always will be. I swear, I don't know what Buck sees in her. Unless, of course . . .

Clyde couldn't remember the last time he'd heard Bonnie laugh. It had been a while, he knew that. But she laughed now. Bonnie laughed so hard it shook the bed. Hell, it rattled the whole room. She didn't regain her composure for several minutes.

"What the hell was that all about?"

"I just had a weird thought. You don't suppose Blanche actually buys into all that crap we shovel out to the crowds, do you? God knows she's naive enough. I mean, can you imagine her and your brother doing some of the things we talk about? I just had a vision of Buck and little miss priss-butt going at it with one another like a couple of pigs in heat. It ain't a pretty sight."

Recounting the image started Bonnie to laughing all over again. This time, Clyde couldn't help but join in. Sure, he loved his brother. But the idea of Buck and Blanche caught up in the throes of passion, fucking each other's brains out in any way other than the good old missionary position, *was* funny. Funny, hell. It was downright hilarious.

\* \* \*

"Y'all ain't gonna do nothin' that'll hurt Clyde, are you?"

"Of course not, W.D. It's my duty to protect Americans."

"Then why do you and me have to keep meetin' in secret like this? Wouldn't it be better if you just sat down and talked with Clyde and explained to him what you're worried about?"

"I don't believe that's a good idea. For one thing, I'm not sure he'd listen to me."

"I don't understand. Why not?"

"Tell me something, W.D. Does Clyde ever listen to you?"

"Well, no. I can't say that he does."

"To be honest, that's one of Mr. Barrow's biggest problems. He thinks he knows everything, that he has all the answers. Because of that attitude, he doesn't feel the need to listen to what anyone else has to say."

"That's not right. He listens to Bonnie."

"Are you sure about that? Or does he just pay lip service to Ms. Parker, and then go ahead and do whatever he wants to?"

W.D. winked before responding. "Oh, he gives Bonnie plenty of lip service, sir. You can bet your last dollar on that. My guess is he's probably givin' it to her right now, if you catch my drift."

The man in the dark, double-breasted suit tried to conceal his disgust at W.D.'s all-too-obvious "drift." He wasn't completely successful in his efforts. Not that W.D. noticed. He was still giggling at his own joke.

"That could be true, W.D. Nevertheless, you know Mr. Barrow would never listen to me. You also know he'd be extremely upset, if he found out that you and I have been talking with one another these past few evenings. That's why our meetings must remain clandestine in nature, at least for the time being. If only to protect Mr. Barrow from his own pride."

"I understand. But it still don't feel quite right, sir, goin' around behind Clyde's back like this. Heck, I even lied to him earlier today. I had to make up some silly story to explain why I let you into the show alone—y'know, like you asked me to. I've never lied to Clyde before. An' I didn't like doin' now. No, sir. Not one bit."

"I'm sure you didn't, W.D. But did he believe you?"

"Seemed to, especially after Bonnie told everyone you probably just came to get your rocks off listenin' to her talk."

Once again, a look of contempt chiseled even deeper lines in the man's already craggy features. Once again, W.D. Jones didn't notice.

"*Hurrumph!* Well. Be that as it may, W.D., I need your help, if we're to help Mr. Barrow. You're not thinking about backing out on me now, are you, son?"

"Oh, no. No, sir. I mean, I wanna help Clyde, too. No matter how bad he treats me sometimes, he's the closest thing to a brother I ever had. So, you just tell me what you want me to do next, sir, and I'll do it. You bet I will."

"That's good, W.D. I'm glad to hear it. And don't worry. The next favor I'm going to ask of you won't require dishonesty of any kind. All I need to know is what city you're scheduled to visit next and the route you plan on using to get there."

"Well, I'm think we're goin' to Shreveport next. Yeah. I'm sure that's what Clyde said this afternoon. Said we were headin' for the big time, finally. As for how we're gonna get there, I guess that's pretty much up to me. Clyde said he wanted me to drive the next leg of our trip."

"Good, W.D. Tell me, are you familiar with parish road 262?"

"Nope. Can't say that I am."

"It runs west from Arcadia to Gibsland. That's the road I want you to take tomorrow. If you do, I can have my men make sure you get to Shreveport safely."

"Safely. What d'ya mean, safely?"

"We can't be too careful, W.D. Look, you know Mr. Barrow and Miss Parker don't mean any harm with all the talk about sexual liberation that they're spreading around. I know that, too. We both also know that this is just a scam, nothing more than Clyde's latest get-rich-quick scheme. And as such schemes go, at least it's legal—which is more than I can say about anything Clyde's done in the past. That's why I can't just step in and force him to stop, even if it is for his own good."

"His own good? That's the part I don't get. If Clyde's not doin' nothin' wrong, what does he have to worry about?"

"That's an interesting question. Keep in mind that I said Clyde hadn't done anything illegal. I didn't say that what he's doing isn't wrong."

"Is it?"

"Well, now, W.D., that depends."

"On what?"

"On who you ask. You see, whether a particular action is legal or illegal is a pretty easy question to answer. If the law doesn't forbid a specific activity, it's legal. If the law says you're not allowed to do something, it's illegal. A straight and narrow line divides one from the other.

"But right or wrong? Well, W.D., I'm afraid those concepts are a little more difficult to define."

"Why?"

"Because everyone draws the line between right and wrong in a slightly different location. Some folks hear what your friends are saying and think they have some pretty good ideas. If you ask them, there's nothing wrong with pushing back our sexual boundaries a little bit. But there are other people in this country who disagree vehemently with that philosophy. In their opinion, to even suggest such behavior is not only wrong, it's totally reprehensible.

"There's another, even more important difference between what's illegal and what's wrong, W.D. Do you know what that is?"

"No, sir. I'm afraid I don't."

"It's how people react to each. Most folks, if they see someone doing something illegal, well, their first instinct is to call a cop. Stopping a crime, they figure, is someone else's job. But righting a wrong? For some reason, people consider that to be a personal, almost sacred duty. It's a responsibility they can't resist carrying on their own shoulders. Believe me, W.D., some people will go to any length to put an end to something they think is wrong. These are the kinds of people I'm trying to protect Clyde from—with your help, of course.

"You better get going now, W.D. You've got a long drive ahead of you tomorrow. Besides, I still have some things to arrange before then. Just remember, I'm expecting you to take parish road 262 to Gibsland.

"And don't worry, W.D., everything's going to work out just fine. I promise."

It was hot and muggy, a typical May afternoon in the deep South. The tempers of the five people crowded into the black car, always simmering, had already reached the boiling point at least a dozen times. Even with the windows wide open, the sun beating down on the roof made it feel like they were riding in an oven.

Someone had been bickering, complaining, or outright arguing constantly. Almost from the moment they pulled out of Arcadia. Buck was the one yelling now.

"Damn, W.D.! Of all the stupid things you've ever done, this has got to be the stupidest. Why the hell you insisted on taking this godforsaken road, I have no idea. If you'd a' listened to me and cut straight across Route 80, we'd've been in Shreveport an hour ago."

"Calm down, Buck," Clyde said. "W.D. just figured it'd be nice to get off the main highways for a change. He had no idea how bad a shape these parish roads were in. Besides, it's not like we're in a hurry or anything. Our next show's not until tomorrow afternoon. We got plenty a' time. So why don't you just sit back, shut up, and enjoy the scenery."

They all were sweating. But no one more than W.D.

Something didn't feel right. W.D. wished he could figure out what it was, but he couldn't. Clyde probably could've. Clyde was smart like that. He had a knack for putting together the pieces of a puzzle and coming up with the whole picture.

But W.D. couldn't tell Clyde anything. Not without

telling him everything. And that was the last thing he
wanted to do. He knew that would upset Clyde. So
W.D. just kept driving. His eyes looking straight ahead.
Then darting left and right. Looking for even the
slightest sign of trouble.

Blanche was the first one to see the truck blocking
the road in front of them.

"Now ain't that strange? I wonder what it's doin'
there."

The truck wasn't just broken down on the side of the
highway—a common sight in these times, in these
parts. Instead, it was turned sideways, blocking both
lanes of the narrow parish road.

"Shit! There ain't no way we got enough room to go
around that thing. So what do you think about W.D.'s
bright idea now, little brother?"

"How the hell could he have known this was going
to happen? We'll just wait a little bit. I'm sure whoever
it belongs to is around here somewhere. He'll be back.
Hell. If nothin' else, we can help him move it.

"Just relax, Buck. Pass me one of those peanut butter sandwiches Bonnie's eating. Like I said, we're in
no hurry. We got all the time in the world."

W.D. saw the man with the bulldog face walk out
from behind the other side of the truck a split second
before the woods on either side of the road exploded.
So did Blanche. She didn't get the chance to tell Bonnie a second time that she thought he was spooky.

A thin, gray haze hung suspended in the hot, humid
air. The acrid smell of cordite permeated the area. Almost two hundred bullet holes perforated the black se-
dan. Inside, five bodies lay twisted, intertwined with
one another in impossible poses.

The man with the bulldog face plucked a cigar from
between Bonnie Parker's lifeless lips and threw it on
the ground. Walking around to the driver's side of the
car, he looked down disdainfully at the bloody corpse
of W.D. Jones.

"Sorry, kid. But it's like I tried to explain to you.

Sometimes you have to do whatever it takes, to get rid of something that's wrong.

"All right, men. Get rid of this mess. And bury those goddamn perverts back in the woods somewhere, where nobody'll ever find them. Can't have anyone making martyrs out of them. C'mon. Hurry it up. I've already spent too much time in this godforsaken state. I got a whole damn country to clean up."

"Sure thing, Mr. Hoover, sir. We'll get right on it."

# FRANZ KAFKA, SUPERHERO!

## by David Gerrold

*The strange, warped, paranoid viewpoint of Franz Kafka's writ-*
*ing is so famous that it actually gave birth to a descriptive ad-*
*jective that can be found in most dictionaries: Kafkaesque.*
*   So it is only fitting that the strangest story in this anthology*
*should be about Franz Kafka, Superhero, and his battle against*
*the nefarious PsycheMan.*
*   The referee—excuse me; the author—is David Gerrold, who*
*has such books as* When H.A.R.L.I.E. Was One *and the*
*bestselling* War Against the Chtorr *series to his credit.*

The rattle of the red roach phone—a noise like an angry cicada—brought him to instant wakefulness. He
rolled out of bed in a single movement, scooped up the
handset and held it to his ear. He didn't speak.

The familiar voice. The words crisp and mellifluous.
"One-thirty-three. How soon can you leave?"

He bent to the nightstand and switched on the lamp
with a loud click. He opened the World Atlas that lay
directly under the lamp glow to page 133. A map of
Vienna. He glanced at the clock. The minute hand had
long since fallen off, but he'd become proficient at telling the time by the position of the hour hand alone.
"I'll be on the ten-thirty train."

"Good," said the voice. The line clicked and went
silent.

He undid the laces tying up the throat of his nightshirt, letting the wide neck of the garment fall open
and away. He began shrugging it down off his shoulders, pulling it down to his waist, shedding it like an
insect pushing its way out of its cocoon, all the while

darting his eyes about the room in quick, nervous little glances. It fell forgotten to the floor. He stepped out of it, pink, naked, and alert. A whole new being. His eyes glistened with anticipation and excitement.

He dressed quick, efficiently. He put on a shiny black suit. He selected a matching black tie. He buttoned his dark red vest meticulously. He wound his watch and tucked it into his vest. He opened the top drawer and selected his two best handkerchiefs; then, after a moment's consideration, he selected a third one as well—his *silk* handkerchief, the one he used only for special occasions.

He pulled on his heavy wool overcoat. He grabbed his carpet bag from the closet, already packed. He was ready to go.

As he walked, he considered. Fifteen minutes to the train station. Five minutes to buy a ticket. Twenty minutes to spare before the train arrived. Yes. He could purchase a newspaper and have a coffee and a croissant in the cafe while he waited. Good.

He could feel the power in his step. He was ready for battle. His mind was clear. This time, he would confront the arch-fiend PsycheMan in his lair. Yes! The enemy would know the taste of ashes and despair before *this* day was through.

In his ordinary life, he pretended to be just another faceless dark slug—sweaty, confused, trapped by circumstance. He moved through the maze of twisty gray streets, almost unnoticed. If by chance he did attract the attention of another being, they would see him only as one more squat shape, brooding and uncommunicative.

In his ordinary life, he pretended to be a writer of grotesque fantasies, a mordant storyteller of obscure, deranged, and unpublishable dreads. His visions were tumbled and stifling—almost repulsive in their queerness. People avoided the possibility of close contact, which was exactly what he wanted and needed—

—Because in his *extra*ordinary life, he was Bug-Man! *The human insect!*

Transformed by a bizarre experiment in Marie Curie's laboratory—accidentally exposed to the life-altering rays of the mysterious element *radium*—he had become *a whole new kind of being*. A strange burst of power had expanded throughout his entire body, shredding the very cells of his flesh.

For a single bright instant, he comprised the entire universe, he knew *everything,* understood *everything*. His skin glowed white as the very essence of life itself infused his whole being. For just that single instant, he became a creature of *pure energy!* And then the transforming bath of radioactive power had ebbed and the entire cosmos collapsed again, down into a single dark node at the bottom of his soul. When his vision cleared, he realized that the insect specimen he had been holding had vanished completely, its essence subsumed throughout his flesh.

That night, under the intoxicating rays of the full moon, he discovered a new plasticity to his flesh. His bones had become malleable. His muscles could be used to pull his body into a shape that was at first painful and frightening, then curious, and finally invigorating and powerful. His skin toughened like armor. He turned and saw himself in the mirror as something strange and beautiful. A shining black carapace. Glistening faceted eyes. Trembling antennae. He could hear symphonies in the air that he had never known were possible before. He could see colors previously undreamt. The strength in his limbs was alarming! Thrilling! He had become a *master of metamorphosis*. Franz Kafka, superhero!

In the days that followed, he learned to control his new powers, leaping from buildings, tunneling, biting, scrabbling through the earth in the dead of night. He became a force to be reckoned with, seeking out those who preyed on the weak, snapping them in two and feeding on their flesh; the cost of his ability to metamorphosize was a ferocious hunger. He satisfied it by preying on the predators of society. Soon, the dark underworld elements of Austria learned the fury of his appetites. The word spread. *The night belonged to Bug-Man.*

Soon he became an ally to the great governments of Europe, battling arch-fiends all over the continent. His exploits became world-famous. His twilight battles were the stuff of legend. Where evil spread its nefarious claws, the cry would soon go up: "This is a job for Bug-Man!"

Now, he hurried to Vienna, eager for the final confrontation with the greatest monster of them all: the terrible master of confusion, Sigmund Freud—more commonly known to the League Of United Superheroes Everywhere as *PsycheMan!*

The evil doctor Freud terrorized his victims by summoning up the monsters of the id. He used their own fears against them, plundering their treasures, and leaving them feeble and empty. Freud's victims babbled in languages of their own, meaningless chatter. They capered like monkeys, simpered like idiots, grinning and drooling; he filled the asylums with his victims. Franz Kafka could not wait to catch this monster on his own overstuffed couch. He dabbed at his chin with his handkerchief, lest someone observe him drooling in anticipation.

The train lurched and rattled and crawled across the Austrian countryside. By the time it finally clattered into the Vienna station, it was nearly four in the afternoon. Dusk would be falling soon, and with it would come his terrible hunger. No matter, tonight he intended to feed well. He would soon suck the marrow from the bones of Dr. Freud. He could hardly wait to sink his gleaming pincers into the soft white flesh of the little Viennese Jew, injecting him with his venom, then tasting the liquefied flesh, inhaling its aroma, taking it hungrily into his metamorphosed self, refreshing himself, invigorating his energies. He would turn the monster's very flesh into fuel for his own divine crusade against evil!

Wiping his mouth again, covering his excitement with his now-sodden handkerchief, Kafka hurried to the post office window and asked if a letter had been left there for him. The squint-eyed clerk handed it across without comment. Kafka shoved it into his coat pocket without looking at it and scuttled away out of the glare of the bright lights overhead. At last he flattened himself into a dark corner and opened the envelope quickly. Inside was a small square of paper with an address neatly typed on it. Kafka repeated the address to himself three times, memorizing it, then wadded up the paper and shoved it into his mouth, chewing frantically. It was several moments before he was able to swallow the wad, and during the entire time his little dark eyes flicked back and forth, watching for suspicious strangers. But no, nobody had noticed the dark little creature in the corner.

Kafka swallowed the last of the paper and left the station, relieved to be away from the screech of the trains and the crush of so many people. He headed north, walking briskly, but not so fast as to call attention to himself. He headed directly for the address on the paper. He had to see the house before the sun set. The narrow cobbled streets of Vienna echoed with his footsteps.

All the buildings clustered like newborn wedding cakes, close and ornate. The streets and alleys between them were already sunk in romantic gloom, and the first smells of the evening meal were already filling the streets. He passed open shop doors and restaurants. His heightened senses told him of the spices in the sausages, the honey in the pastries, the butterfat in the cream. A horse-drawn wagon clattered by, dragging with it the animal scent of manure and sweat. Smoke from the chimneys climbed up into the oppressive sky. The heavy flavor of coal pervaded everything.

Kafka found the street he was looking for and turned left into it as if he was a long-familiar resident. He slowed his pace and studied the houses on the opposite side of the avenue, one at a time, examining each as if none of them held any specific interest for him. They were tall, narrow structures, each hiding behind a wrought-iron fence. The high peaked roofs offered multiple opportunities to hide and possible easy access through the gabled windows; but Kafka ignored them. He let his attention wander to the cobbled street itself, the sewers and the drains. If he was satisfied with what he saw, he gave no sign. He continued on down the street toward the end.

At the end of the block, he turned right, crossed the street and headed up toward the next block. He turned right and headed up the row of houses looking thoughtfully at each one. As luck would have it, the building directly behind Dr. Freud's suspected lair was a small hotel for retired gentlemen.

He climbed up the front steps, entered, and rang the bell at the registration desk. Shortly, a wizened old clerk appeared and Kafka inquired politely if there were a quiet room available in the back of the inn. There was, and he immediately secured it for two days. He would need a private place in which to accomplish his metamorphosis, and he considered himself extremely fortunate to be so close to his quarry.

Wiping his chin, he let himself into the room, put down his carpet bag just inside the door, turned, and locked the door behind him. At last! He was so close to his archenemy, Freud, he could almost taste his blood! He crossed to the window and parted the curtains. Across a narrow garden, he could see the shuttered rear windows of Dr. Freud's house. He wondered what nefarious deeds were going on behind those walls.

He'd know soon enough; the moon was already visible above the rooftops. He pulled the curtains aside and opened the window, the better to admit the healing rays of the moonlight. He began pulling off his clothes, almost clawing his way out of them, exposing his pallid flesh to the intoxicating luminance.

He opened the carpet bag and began laying out the equipment that he would need. A large rubber sheet—he spread it across the floor. A large block of wood—battered, chipped and scarred; he placed that carefully on the sheet.

The transformation began slowly. He felt the first twinges in his shoulders and in his knees. He began to twitch. The long hours cooped up in the train had left him stiff and uncomfortable; this metamorphosis would be a painful one. Good! A flurry of little shudders shook his body; he grabbed hold of a chair for support until the seizure eased. He knew he had to be careful, he knew he didn't dare risk losing consciousness; he had to stay awake and deliberately shape himself for the battle ahead.

His head. Most important. His mandibles—

His teeth began to lengthen in his mouth, pushing his jaw painfully out of its sockets. He shoved his fingers into his mouth and started pulling his teeth painfully forward, shaping them into the digging and grinding tools that he would shortly need.

Next, his skull. He put his right hand under his chin and his left hand on top of his head and pressed them toward each other as hard as he could. The bones of his skull creaked and gave. His head began to flatten. His chin spread, his eyes bulged sideways, his jaw widened out, his teeth splayed forward, his eyebrows sprang out like antennae—blood began to pour from his nose. He pressed harder and harder, until the pain became unbearable, but still he pressed until he no longer had the strength in his arms or the leverage with which to press.

Already his spine was softening, could no longer support his weight. He dropped to the floor, grunting as the air was forced from his lungs. His arms flopped wildly. He pulled his knees up and grabbed hold of his feet as hard as he could. As he straightened his legs again, his arms began to lengthen. His elbows popped, the bones pulling out of their sockets—he screamed with pain; rolled over and grabbed the block of wood in his mouth, bit it as hard as he could. He did this again and again, stretching his arms into long, black, hairy appendages.

Yes, the hair! It was sprouting all over his arms and legs. His legs were softening now. He pulled his knees up to his chest, and now, grabbing them again with his hardening arms, he pulled at his knees until the sockets popped and now his legs could lengthen naturally. He clutched his feet, working them into clawlike shapes, stretching his toes, pulling at them mercilessly, grunting with the pain, and still continuing to pull. And yes, now the side appendages were large enough to grab, to pull, to stretch. He worked his muscles savagely, massaging them into shape, strengthening them. Yes, this was going to be one of the best! The more pain he experienced, the better the transformation!

He rolled around on the floor, rubbing his back and sides against the rubber sheet, hardening his carapace. He wiped at his multifaceted eyes with his front legs, cleaning them of bloody residue. His antennae twitched. He was almost done. Almost there—and yes, in a final spasm of completion, he *ejaculated*! Spurt after spurt after spurt of sickly yellow-looking ichor. The shaft of his metallic-looking penis retreated again inside his chitiny shell, and Bug-Man raised himself aloft on his six exquisite legs, chittering with satisfaction and joy!

Bug-Man was a simple being. He had no knowledge of anything but the blood of his enemy. He cared nothing for Franz Kafka or the League Of United Superheroes Everywhere. He knew little of trains and croissants and newspapers. Bug-Man was a creature of hunger and rage. He knew only the ferocious desire for vengeance. He lived for the hot red fulfillment of delicious gluttony. His mandibles clattered in soft anticipation. He drooled with excitement. He wanted one thing only—the flesh of *PsycheMan*! He could not rest until he'd crunched the skull of Sigmund Freud between his diamond-hard teeth!

He leapt to the window, flinging it open, pulling himself out onto the balustrade, poising himself, stretching himself up into the darkness and the holy glow of the full moon above. Across the way, he heard a gasp, and then the sound of a window slamming. A light vanished. He heard the sounds of running footsteps. He ignored them all. He leapt.

He landed lightly on the soft black earth of the garden below. Instantly, he began digging, down and down into the deep delicious soil, his six legs working frantically, flinging the dirt, backward and upward, scattering it in every direction. His mandibles chewed and cut. In moments, he was gone, sliding into the cool dark space beneath the lawn, tunneling his way toward the house of Sigmund Freud, the monster.

The night fell silent. The moon rose higher and higher until it was directly overhead, casting its lambent radiance down across the gabled old houses of sleeping Vienna. And then a noise . . .

The sound of something creaking, cracking, crackling as it broke—

The ancient floorboards came away in ragged chunks. The hole widened. Something was chewing up through the ground, widening the hole in quick, malicious bites. And then it was climbing up and into the cellar of the house. Bug-Man was here! Inside the house of his archenemy! He scrabbled purposefully across the floor, sniffing the air with his antennae. He slid up the stairs, not bothering to open the door at the top, breaking through it instead like a flimsy construction of cardboard.

He was in the pantry! The overwhelming pantry, reeking with conflicting flavors and aromas—all the spices and ingredients of a thousand different meals, coffee-chocolate-butter-garlic-sausage-cheese-pepper-bread—they all repulsed him now. He moved swiftly to the kitchen, to the dining room, to the stairway in the hall, and up the stairs, breaking away the banister as he climbed to give himself room.

There was no dark at the top of the stairs. The light came on abruptly. Someone was moving up there. Bug-Man's glistening multifaceted eyes caught the image in a shattered reality. There—silhouetted against the glare of the electric lamp beyond—stood the terrible demonic form of Sigmund Freud, the *PsycheMan!*

He stood alone, wearing only a nightshirt, a robe, and fuzzy blue slippers. He rested one hand on the top of the broken banister to support himself. He looked incredibly frail, but his eyes gleamed with turquoise power! His high forehead bulged abnormally, the fringe of white hair around it was not enough to conceal its freakish expanded shape. His predatory chin was concealed by the long white beard. His bony knees stuck out from beneath the hem of his garment like awkward chicken legs.

The transformed Kafka lifted himself up, as if about to leap. He uttered a low sound, a moan of anticipatory lust, a growl of warning, a challenge, a chittering of danger.

"Ach!" said Freud. "It's only you. Well, come in, come in. I've been expecting you. You're late again." He waggled his finger warningly. "You superheroes, you think you can come calling any time, day or night, without an appointment—"

He started to turn away, then suddenly, turned back toward Bug-Man, his eyes blazing with red fire! *"Well, I won't have it!"* He knocked the ash off his cigar into his hand and carefully pocketed the residue. Then lifted the cigar like a baton, holding it outstretched toward the man-bug. With his other hand he stroked the cigar, once, twice, a third time—suddenly the cigar emitted a crackling bolt of blue-white lightning. Bug-Man ducked his head just in time. The blast of fire splattered off his back singeing the walls, scorching the wallpaper, striking little fires among the chips and sawdust of the broken banister all the way down and leaving the air stinking of ozone.

Kafka was stunned. For a moment, he almost forgot that he was Bug-Man. Freud was much stronger than he thought. He must have been gaining converts faster than they had realized, far more than they had estimated. He must have been draining the life force of hundreds, perhaps thousands of hapless souls, distilling their very being down into his own evil essence.

Bug-Man recovered himself then. He stopped thinking, stopped considering, stopped caring—he remembered his purpose. *To feed on the flesh of Sigmund Freud!* He charged up the stairs after the monstrous little man. But Freud's frail demeanor was only another deceit. The old man scampered away like an animated elf, disappearing into the darkness at the far end of the hall.

Bug-Man followed relentlessly, his six long hairy legs scrabbling loudly on the hardwood floor. His claws left nasty scratches in the polished surface. He plunged into the darkness—

And found himself in a maze of twisty little passages, all alike. A maze. The maze. Twisty little passages. A twisty little maze. All alike.

His eyes swiveled backward and forward—and he hesitated. For a moment, he had to be Kafka again. Had to rely on his innate human intelligence instead of his insect instinct. Reminded himself. *Freud has no power of his own. He borrows the power of others. He summons monsters from the id. You will destroy yourself fighting your own fears. Ignore the illusions. Concentrate on what's real!*

Bug-Man's hesitation stretched out forever. His chitiny shell began to soften. His mandibles clattered in confusion. *But—but how do I know what's real?* he wondered. *Everything that a being can know is ultimately experiential. I have no way to stand apart from the experiential nature of existence! So how can I access what is real and distinguish it from illusion?*

It seemed as if all time was standing still. Kafka's mind raced, his thought processes accelerated. *Be who you are!* he shouted to the Bug-Man! *Don't let him define you! You are the Bug-Man! You are the greatest superhero ever! Ignore the lies! Anything that contradicts the Bug-Man is a lie! Remember that!*

The Bug-Man snarled. Unconfused. He knew himself again, submerged himself once more in crimson fury and fire; the hunger and rage suffused his body like a bath of acid. He clicked his mandibles, reached out with his pincers and started pulling down the ugly twisty little walls and their dripping vines and wires, started pulling down the twisty little maze of darkness and fury, sending creatures of indeterminate shape scuttling out into the fringes, started pulling down the twisty little passages all alike, pulling and chewing and breaking through—

He was in a tunnel. Blackness behind him. Blackness ahead.

The tunnel slanted downward into the bottomless dark. The walls were straight; they were set wide apart, but the ceiling was low. Everything was cut from dark wet stone. The water dripped from the walls and slid downward into the gloom ahead. His eyes refocused. What little light there was seeped into the air from no apparent source.

Far in the distance below, something moved. He could smell it. His antennae quivered in anticipation. He lifted his pincers. He readied his stinger, arching his tail high over his head. His venom dripped.

The thing below was coming closer. In the blackness ahead, a formless form was growing. It opened its eyes. Two bright red embers, glowing ferociously! The eyes were screaming toward him now!

*Stinger?!*

Bug-Man remembered just in time. *Ignore the lies!*

The red eyes went hurling past him, vanishing into darkness. The screams of rage faded into distant echoes that hung in the air like dreadful memories—

*I could have stung myself, right behind the brain case*—he realized. And then, realizing again how narrowly he had escaped the trap of the Freudian paradigm, he repeated anew his warning to himself. *You are the Bug-Man! Don't let him define you or your reality! Monsters from the id aren't real!*

The Bug-Man headed down the tunnel. Its angle of descent increased abruptly, getting steeper and steeper, until he was slipping, sliding, skidding, tumbling—

—onto the hard-baked surface of a place with no sun, no moon, no sky, and no horizon. Tall black cylinders surrounded them, leaping up into the gloom and disappearing overhead. They looked like the bars of a cage.

Freud stood beside one of the bars, surveying him thoughtfully. "You are resisting the treatment," he said. "I can't help you if you don't want to be helped." He waggled his finger meaningfully. *"You have to really want to change!"*

Bug-Man roared in fury. It consumed him like volcanic fire. He became a core of molten energy. The blast of emotion overwhelmed him. Enraged, he charged.

Bug-Man galloped across the space between them, tearing up the floor with his six mighty claws. He thundered like a bull, hot smoke streaming from the vents of his nostrils. The black leviathan leapt—

—and abruptly, Freud was gone!

Bug-Man smashed against the bars of the cage like a locomotive hitting a wall, his legs flailing, his body deforming, the air screaming out from his lungs like a steam whistle. He shrieked in rage and frustration and pain. He fell back, legs working wildly, righted himself, whirled around, eyes flicking this way and that—focusing on Freud again. The *PsycheMan* waited for him on the opposite side of the cage. The Bug-Man didn't hesitate! He charged again—

—and again, he came slamming up against the bars. Helpless for an instant, he lay there gasping and wondering what he was doing wrong. Transformed Kafka shuddered in his shell. But he pushed the thought aside, levered himself back to his feet, focused again on his target, readied his charge, sighted his prey—

This time, he would watch to see which way the *PsycheMan* leapt. He would snatch him from the air. He held his pincers high and wide. Instead of charging, he advanced steadily, inexorably, closing on his elusive prey like some ghastly mechanical device of the Industrial Revolution gone mad. His mandibles clicked and clashed. His eyes shone with unholy fury. A terrible guttural sound came moaning up out of his throat—

—came slamming hard against the bars of the cage as if he'd been fired into them by a cannon. The discontinuity left him rolling across the floor in pain, clutching at his aching genitals and crying in little soft gasps. He pulled himself back to his knees, his feet, trying to solidify his form again. He stood there, wavering, almost whimpering.

"What's wrong?" he asked himself. "What am I doing wrong?"

Kafka looked across the cage. Freud stood there grinning nastily. The old man laughed. "You battle yourself!" he said thickly. "The rigidity of your constructed identity cannot deal with events occurring outside of its world view. You become confused and you attack shadows and phantoms!"

Kafka took a deep breath. Then another, and another. "I am Franz Kafka, superhero!" he said to himself. "I am here to destroy the evil paradigm of Dr. Freud! I will not be defeated."

*No!*—he realized abruptly. *That way doesn't work! I am the master of metamorphosis. I must metamorphose into something that the doctor cannot defeat!* At first he thought of giant squids and vampire bats, cobras and Bengal tigers, raging elephants, bears, dragons, manticores, goblins, trolls—Jungian archetypes! *But, no*—he realized. *That would be just more of the same! Just another monster to fight a monster. I must change into something ELSE*—

He stood there motionless, staring across the cage at his fiendish opponent, considering. His mind worked like a precision machine, a clockwork device ticking away at superfast speed. His thoughts raced, exploring strange new possibilities he had never conceived before.

*Ego cogito sum*—he considered. *I have been reacting to his manipulations. Reactive behavior allows him to control the circumstance. Proactive behavior puts me in control. I should attack him, but attacking him is still reaction. Yet, if I don't attack him, I cannot defeat him. How can I be proactive without being reactive?*

Bug-Man wavered. His confusion manifested itself as a softening of his shell, a spreading pale discoloration of his metallic carapace. His mandibles began to shrink. His arms and legs began to plump out, seeking their previous shape. *No!* he shrieked to himself. *No! Not yet! I haven't killed him yet*—

Bug-Man felt himself weakening, growing ever more helpless in the face of his enemy. He felt shamed and embarrassed. He wanted to scuttle off and hide in the woodwork. His bowels let loose, his bladder emptied. His skin became soft and pallid again. He stood naked before Freud. Franz Kafka, superhero. But the Bug-Man was defeated, discredited—

*No!* said Kafka. *No! I won't have it. I am Franz Kafka, superhero! I don't need to be a giant cockroach to destroy the malevolence of Freud! I can stop him with my bare hands.*

And then he knew!

"Your paradigm is invalid," Kafka said. "It's powerful, yes, but ultimately, it has no power over those who refuse to give it power; therefore, it is not an accurate map of the objective reality, only another word-game played out in language." Freud's eyes widened in surprise. Kafka took two steps toward him. "You're just a middle-aged Viennese Jew, who smokes too much, talks too much, and suffers from—your word—*agoraphobia.* You can't even cross the street without help!" Freud held up a hand in protest, but Kafka kept advancing, continued his unflinching verbal assault. "You're a dirty old man. You can't stop talking about sex, you want to kill your father and copulate with your mother—and you believe that everybody else feels the same thing, too! You're despicable, Sigmund Freud!"

Freud's chin trembled. "You—you don't understand. You're functioning as a paranoid schizophrenic with psychotic delusions. You've constructed a world view in which explanations are impossible—"

"That won't work, Siggie. It's just so much language. It's just a load of psyche-babble. The distinctions you've drawn are arbitrary constructions that only have the meaning that we as humans invest them with. Well, I withdraw my investment. Your words are meaningless. I will not be psychologized. You are just a disgusting little man who likes to talk about penises!"

The old man made one last attempt to withstand the withering assault of Kafka's logic. "But if you withdraw all meaning from the paradigm—" he protested, "—what meaning can you replace it with?"

"That's just it!" exulted Kafka, delivering the death blow. *"Life is empty and meaningless!"*

Horrified, Freud collapsed to the floor of his living room, clutching at his chest.

Kafka stood over him, triumphant. *"It's meaningless, you old fart!"*

Freud moaned—

*"It doesn't mean anything! And it doesn't even mean anything that it doesn't mean anything! So we're free to make it up any way we choose!"*

"Please, no. Please, stop—"

But Kafka wasn't finished. "Your way is just a possible way of being, Sigmund—but it isn't the only way! The difference between you and me is that because I know the bindings of my language, I also know my freedom within those bindings! You have been focusing on the bindings, you old asshole, *not the freedom.*"

Freud was shuddering now, impaled on Kafka's impeccable truths. He lay in Kafka's arms, trembling and sick. "Forgive me, please. I didn't know what I was doing."

Kafka knelt to the floor, gathered Freud up in his arms, held him gently, cradling him like a child. He placed one soft hand on the old man's forehead. "It's all right now, Siggie," he soothed. "It's all over. You can stop. You can rest."

Freud looked up into Kafka's gentle expression, questioning, hoping. He saw only kindness in the superhero's eyes. Reassured, he let himself relax; he allowed the peace to flood throughout his body. All stiffness fled. Sigmund Freud rested securely in Franz Kafka's arms. "Thank you," he whispered. "Thank you."

"No," said Kafka. "On the contrary. It is *I* who should thank *you*." And with that he plunged his needle-sharp teeth into Sigmund Freud's pale exposed neck, ripping it open. He bent his head and fed ferociously. The hot rush of blood slaked his incredible thirst, and he moaned in delirious ecstasy.

Triumph was delicious.

# IF HORSES WERE WISHES

## by Ginjer Buchanan

*Do you remember Ruffian, the gallant filly trained by Frank
Whitely, who was unbeaten and unextended until her tragic
match race with Foolish Pleasure in 1975? She was winning the
race when she shattered her ankle in front of 60,000 fans and 20
million television viewers and had to be destroyed.*

*Ginjer Buchanan, science fiction editor of Ace Books, remem-
bers. She also remembers Flame, the fictional hero of Walter
Farley's* The Island Stallion—*and here she shows you just what
a science fiction writer can do when she sets her mind to it.*

Many years ago, in a verdant land of rolling hills and
peaceful streams, a girl child was born into a noble
family. Her mother was the daughter of a great warrior
and her father the son of a king and the grandson of a
proud ruler who had been known for his fierceness in
battle. He himself had had a season or two of success
in the field until injury had sent him early to hearth
and home.

The child had black hair, with a wild white streak
over her forehead, and when her naming time came,
they wrote "Ruffia" in the book where the names of
the generations were kept.

Like her sisters and brothers and cousins, the Lady
Ruffia spent her early years in careless play. But the
ways of her kind were warrior ways, and even if there
was no enemy to fight, sooner rather than later, the
children of the palace were taken away and turned over
to the Weapons Master.

In the years when Lady Ruffia was being educated,
the Master's name was Whitely. At first he despaired

of her. Her blood was the best, but she was tall, ungainly, soft, and too fleshy. Still, it was his job to train the young nobles, so he would make the best of it.

Then Ruffia picked up a sword and shield and became another creature. A thing of quicksilver and wind, a dancer on the edge of death. She thrust and parried; she lunged and retreated; she was inexhaustable and terrible and, to Master Whitely, wonderful.

Word of her prowess spread slowly in the kingdom. Many thought that Master Whitely was perhaps exaggerating to please Lady Ruffia's father. Still, at her maiden tourney, she caused quite a stir. In her armor, bearing her shield with the red and white crest of her illustrious family, she stood taller than any other girl on the field. And she carried herself, as all could see, with a dignity and sense of purpose beyond her years.

She won handily, and stood alone on the field at the end of the afternoon accepting the accolades due the victor. She removed her helm, shaking loose her long black hair with the wild white streak, and bowed gravely to the crowd. She found that she liked to win, and that she liked the cheers.

Around the training yard and in the maiden's quarters, she was known to have a temper. Her greatgrandfather's blood, they said. Yet she was never mean or a bully. Focused, however, and determined. The Weapons Master knew he was training a true warrior.

After her first win, envoys came from a neighboring kingdom proposing that their foremost maiden champion, the Lady Coepernica, be permitted to participate in the next tourney. The Lady Coepernica was wellknown. The child of foreign royalty, she had been born half-blind. But such was her blood and her determination that she had overcome this handicap and prevailed over all in her own first fight.

The invitation was extended and on a sunny day in June, battle was joined. Lady Coepernica fought gamely, but in the end, Lady Ruffia triumphed once more.

And so it went, all that year. Ruffia defeated the best

maiden warriors of her age group with style, grace and uncanny speed. She was the darling of the people, but behind her back, in the dining hall and along garden paths, the whispers and the quiet laughter never quite stopped. Such a *big* girl! What a *hearty* appetite! Did you hear, she once *slapped* her squire!

Ruffia kept to herself and continued to do what she did better and better from day to day. Only once did an opponent truly test her, causing her to falter and stumble. She found that she did not like to be nearly bested. And she found that the stumble was a costly one. Shortly thereafter, she awoke with a dull pain in her right ankle. She could not practice, she could not fight. She brooded, took to her bed, and began skipping meals.

Master Whitely was alarmed. Though she was noble and he but a servant, albeit a very important one, he spoke sternly to her, reminding her that she had many years of tourneys to come before she returned to her father's house to be betrothed. It would not do for her as a warrior to make herself more ill than she was.

So Ruffia bided her time and healed. She stayed in the maiden's quarters, read books on strategies of the sword, exercised lightly, and watched as many of the girls of her age, having done their duty, returned to their houses to be bid and bargained for. She could have, too. A year of competition fulfilled honor. But of course, she did not.

When spring came, the Lady Ruffia was older, wiser in the ways of the sword, and even stronger for her enforced rest. What had been fleshiness was now muscle. What had been the ungainliness of youth was now leggy poise. She was still a big girl, but to any but the most jealous eyes, she was also a beautiful one.

As though she were still tilting at the straw targets in the practice yard, she easily won all three of the major tourneys of the season. Her feats were unprecedented. She had already become the subject of verse and ballads. Folk who had previously paid scant attention to what was thought of as the games of the nobles, and who thought even less of these games when they were played by maidens, now stood for hours to see her fight. She was awarded the accolade of Champion of Champions by the King himself. At the season's end, everyone expected her to resign from the lists, and return in triumph to her father's house, where, it was said, a list of suitors was already vying for her hand.

Master Whitely knew better. The Lady Ruffia was a girl—no, a woman now—who was a warrior to the bone, to the center of her heart. And a warrior must match herself against the best. At the beginning of the summer he spoke with her and shared his daring idea. Her eyes glowed. The challenge was issued.

His name was Lord Plasir. He was the Champion of Champions among the young men. In his first year of competition, he had been undefeated five out of five times (as had Lady Ruffia). And in his second year, he had proven himself against the best of his age in the Grand Spring Tourney. He had his own pride—and his own curiosity. So, though it caused great scandal in the land, when the challenge was made, Lord Plasir accepted.

The crowd that gathered that hot day in July was enormous, buzzing with excitement and anticipation. In contrast, Lady Ruffia and Lord Plasir were calm, concentrating on the fight to come.

The two champions strode to the middle of the field, swords and shields to hand. Though it should have been no surprise, many in the crowd gasped to see them together. The Lady Ruffia stood taller and broader than Lord Plasir, who was by no means a small man. Yet there was about her still a delicacy, so that even in armor all could tell which was man and which was maiden.

Trumpets were blown and the fight was joined. Plasir struck first, but Ruffia's good shield protected her. She parried, he defended. At each blow, the crowd shouted with one voice. They were evenly matched these two, it was obvious. It might well be that they would fight until exhaustion overcame them both.

Then Ruffia's own strength nearly proved her undoing. She struck such a mighty blow that the force of it as Plasir blocked it with his shield shattered her wrist with a crack that could almost be heard above the crowd. In years to come, Master Whitely would claim that he did hear it, but that day in truth all he knew at once was that Ruffia was in dire straits.

Her sword fell from her senseless fingers and she stumbled. Because of who he was and what he had been trained to do, Plasir fought on. And because of who she was and what she was, Ruffia did not go down. Dodging Plasir's sword, she switched her shield to her damaged arm, and scrambled for her sword with her good hand. In a space of heartbeats, she was standing tall again, toe to toe with Plasir. Inside her helm, sweat runneled her cheeks and her lips were thin with pain.

But she was a warrior. And she fought on. Step by step she pushed forward, and step by step Plasir gave ground. Finally, one clever backhanded blow disarmed him, and brought him to his knees. Slowly, he raised his helm, regarding with a mixture of awe and fear the woman who had bested him. In a clear voice, which spoke of his own blood and breeding, he yielded to her.

Ruffia nodded in acceptance, lowered her sword, and turned to salute the crowd. Her right arm hung useless, the broken wrist further shattered by the weight of the shield. She stood silent a moment, and then pain overcame her. She fell at the feet of the man she had defeated.

The wrist was ruined. Only the stubborn insistence of Master Whitely as Ruffia lay feverish and dazed prevented the physicians from taking her hand. It was saved and she was saved. But there is no place in the lists for a one-armed warrior, champion or not.

So the Lady Ruffia returned to her father's house. As she had known it would, her victory had drawn even more suitors. Tall and broad she might be. Crippled she might be. But what sons and daughters might well come from such a magnificent woman! Her great-grandfather's blood ran strong in her, there could be no doubt of that.

It had come to that, as it nearly always did. Ruffia brooded as she roamed her father's fields or sat in her room gazing at her arms which hung now over her bed. To bear children, that thought did not displease her. But to live—*only* to bear young, given to some small man for his pleasure because he offered a higher dower price or because his bloodlines were the most desirable—was this a life for a warrior?

Time went by, and no betrothal took place, however. Ruffia did what she could toward that end. On days when suitors appeared, her arm often pained her greatly, causing her to take to her bed. On days when she was forced to parade around in her finery before some emissary from this prince or that prince, she was unpleasant as she could possibly be. After all, everyone know she had a temper. Nearly a year passed so. In secret she practiced her left-handed sword skills, but it was mere shadow play without a worthy opponent.

Finally, though, the deed was done. Articles of betrothal were exchanged between Ruffia's father and the King of a far-distant land. (The very King who had fathered the Lady Coepernica.) He was of the noblest blood, he was immensely wealthy, and she would be the youngest and most treasured (his emmisary assured her father) of his many wives.

As her ship set sail on the journey that would take her to the King's bed, Lady Ruffia did not weep. She was a warrior, after all. She gave Master Whitely, whom she had not seen in a year, a nod and a smile. He had come to bid farewell to the best pupil he would ever have, and he took pride in her for one last time as she turned from the rail and withdrew to her cabin.

There, from amid the laces and silks in her travel chest, she removed her sword and sat running her good hand over the blade.

Ruffia did not take to sea travel. Few of her blood did. She was restless, nervous. She ate and slept poorly, stayed in her cabin and allowed the servants who had been sent with her only minimal access to her person. She brooded as she had not since the injury that had cut short her first tourney season.

On the fourth night out, vicious clouds began scudding across the full moon. The wind rose, and then rose higher. Alone in her cabin, Ruffia was startled awake by the rolling of the ship and the crashing of—thunder? The waves? She could not tell. She huddled below, clutching her sword as though it were a magical amulet, as the crew battled storm and sea, and the moon crossed the turbulent sky above.

Dawn approached, and Ruffia judged from the shouts and screams that the sea was winning. She gathered a warm cloak, some bits of bread and cheese left from her dinner and her sword, and made her way onto the deck. No one, least of all her servants, noticed her. As the ship listed farther and farther into the wet darkness, she cast about for something that might give hope of survival. Master Whitley had not covered shipwrecks, but Ruffia was resourceful. She found an empty barrel on the slippery deck, and with some effort, climbed into it. Scant moments later, the deck fell away beneath her, and though she was soaked through, the barrel did not follow the ship into the deep.

Sunrise and then sunset and then sunrise again. Ruffia ate her bread and cheese. She grew hungry and very thirsty. She thought a while about the ease of drowning. Perhaps tied to her sword? Not, she decided, a thought worthy of a warrior. Finally, she slept.

When she awoke and raised herself carefully, she saw that it was dawn again. And she saw in the near distance, a dark bulk against the sky. Gradually, the current of the water drew her barrel closer, closer still, until it began to scrape and bump on the bottom of sea.

Using her good hand and her sword, Ruffia scrambled out, and stumbled on legs half-numb from cramping onto the sand. She was a child of pleasant green places, and the land beneath and around her was strange and uncomfortable. But it was solid. Dragging her sword, she moved farther away from the sea, and slept again.

In the days that followed, she explored the speck of rock and sand at length. It was oval, a pile of stone surrounded by scrubby plants, coarse sand, and endless ocean. A trickle of a stream descended from the rocky cliffs. She shared the water with several kinds of birds, none of which she could have named.

As she had in times past studied her opponents in the practice yard and on the field, so she took note of the strange birds, their habits, their comings and goings. She also grew increasingly familiar with the sea creatures, both finned and shelled, that swam and crawled in the shallows. She became as great a hunter as she had been a fighter, and the sword that had bested the best did duty as fish killer and crab cracker. Not perhaps the noblest of endeavors, and not one that would send the blood singing in her heart. Still, something that had to be done, a task to be mastered, like any other.

Ruffia survived. Flesh that had grown soft during her year in her father's house hardened again into muscle. She became brown from the sun. She braided her long black hair, to tame it, though the wild white streak often escaped the braid. Her left arm grew stronger, and when she fought with shadows, she imagined a field alive with color and sound, and the crowd cheering the One-armed Warrior, who was a champion still.

She was in the midst of just such a dream one morning, lying stretched out at the foot of the cliff, in the small shade of the rocks. In her dream, her opponent began throwing dirt in her face, to cloud her sight. She brushed at her eyes with her good hand, and brought herself awake, as more debris struck her on the face and chest. In an instant, she was on her feet, sword at the ready. A rock the size of a man's head narrowly missed her foot. She looked up, just as a cascade of such rocks began pelting down. Above them, a goodly sized boulder teetered on the brink of a ledge, then broke free and fell toward her, gathering momentum with astonishing speed.

Master Whitely had long ago taught her to fall and roll to dodge a blow from above. The boulder bounced by her, and rolled across the sand, splashing into the shallows. She looked up again, and caught a flash of yellow, a white face peering over the ledge. In a voice grown hoarse from lack of use, she shouted a challenge, but the face disappeared.

Reason said that a one-armed woman, even one who was a warrior, could not climb a cliff face, sheer or not. But reason had also said that no girl warrior, no matter how skilled, could defeat a male champion. It took some hours, and Ruffia's sword saw duty as staff and handhold gouger, but she kept her focus on that flash of yellow until she at last reached the ledge.

Behind the ledge, a deep cave opened out, its depths cloaked in shadow. Ruffia had no torch, no source of illumination save that which penetrated from the outside. To go on challenged reason even more. But, she realized, to go *down* might not be possible, unless she chose the way of the boulder.

Ruffia rested a while, brushed the effects of the climb from her clothing, tied down her hair more securely, and ignored the pain in her right hand and arm. She cleaned her sword and sat looking out at the boulder far below as the endless sea eddied around it. She was bone-weary, yet strangely exhilarated. Weariness won out, and she fell into a deep slumber.

The rising sun woke her. And, she was pleased to see, shone directly into the cave, revealing that it opened into a wide tunnel, a tunnel that beyond doubt must lead to the figure in yellow.

The tunnel narrowed in places, but nowhere did she have even to stoop. Ruffia did not think of her growing thirst and hunger. When the light dimmed, she used her sword as she remembered those without sight using strong sticks, to tap her way cautiously along.

For a time, darkness was complete. Then gradually, the darkness lightened, until Ruffia could see a point of light ahead. She moved forward steadily, and so came little by little, out of the tunnel, onto a hillside overlooking a valley as verdant as the land of her birth.

Below her, she could see a small village, and the movements of folk going here and there, about the business of daily life.

To shout aloud at this sight would not be the way of a warrior. But it was not unseemly to descend the slope on a well-worn path with some speed. Sword in hand, of course.

She approached the village boldly, as befitted her, but she was ever alert for any signs of hostility, or of a figure clad in yellow. The villagers regarded her with lively curiosity, gathering around her, abuzz with questions. Ruffia held herself aloof, nearly overwhelmed after so long a time alone.

As a Lady, as a warrior and a Champion, she demanded to know who among them had assaulted her from the cliff. She had been imperiled, and she sought satisfaction.

No one was forthcoming, though an uneasiness went through them at her tone and manner. One woman stepped forward then. She wore a sword belted at her waist, and she stood as tall as Ruffia, though she was finer boned, and fair. She named herself as Chloe, and extended the hospitality of her hearth.

Ruffia succumbed to the twin pressures of hunger and thirst. She must be at her best when she found her foe, it was a warrior's duty to tend to her body as she did her weapon.

Chloe led her, not as she had thought, to the maiden's quarters, but to a simple dwelling. As they drew near, a pair of children bolted out the door, and attached themselves to Chloe, hanging one on each arm, chattering away. Inside, a man waited. He embraced Chloe and gave his name as Kelvan.

Ruffia stayed with them for some days. She met Chloe's sister, Elane, and the man with whom she lived. Neither of them bore weapons of any kind, and they teased Chloe gently as she and Ruffia spent time in mock fighting in the yard of the small house.

Ruffia met the folk of the village. She met the healers and the hunters and those that tilled the fields. She met the weapons masters, and the warriors, both men and women. She kept some of herself private, since she did not trust that these folk would believe that one who was handicapped could have ever been Champion of Champions. And she looked and asked repeatedly about the yellow-clad figure on the cliff.

Until one afternoon, she chanced to encounter outside the alehouse a young man who grew pale and nervous when he looked upon her face. At once she knew. She drew her sword, and challenged him there and then. He stammered, and did not deny his deed, but claimed that he had meant only to irritate, not to threaten. He begged for pardon. She pressed him with her sword, and once more issued a challenge. Her heart beat faster, and color flowed into her cheeks. He backed away. Fear had begun to pull at the corners of his mouth. Her warrior blood was singing. He was young, yes, but she was one-handed, so the fight would not be beneath her honor.

From behind, a voice full of the tone of command called on her to halt. She turned to face a man taller than her by a handsbreadth, flame-haired, boldly built. By the sword at his belt, the way he held her eye, and the pride of him, she recognized a true warrior.

She drew herself up and questioned his authority. He named himself as Azul, and added that the land that she now stood on was his, by virtue of blood and sword. And he called her challenge of the young man unseemly, for he did not go armed, and was not a warrior born or trained.

Ruffia frowned. She threw her braid with a toss of her head, and said that she, the Lady Ruffia, Champion of Champions, nonetheless *demanded* satisfaction for the attack that had been made upon her.

Azul smiled and claimed kinship with the young man, and the right to fight as his champion, if she so insisted. Ruffia accepted, and the two withdrew to the training grounds at the edge of the village. Nearly everyone followed them, and the noise of the crowd was music to Ruffia.

They faced each other then. Azul tied back his flame-colored hair, and drew his sword with a flourish. He made no mention of the fact that Ruffia fought one-handed, and it was not until much later that she recalled that he had done likewise. At the time, she was back in her dream, Master Whitely's warrior, the best of the best, facing at last a worthy foe.

They circled and thrust and parried. Azul was skilled, though not as skilled as Lord Plasir had been. But he was more experienced, and he had a greater reach because of his size. Ruffia felt alive in a way that only a warrior could understand. This was true combat! No armor, no shields, sword to sword, heart to heart. The sun, the dust, and the crowd receded. Except for the cheers. The cheering drove her on, as it always had.

A touch of her sword point drew blood on Azul's arm. He swept his sword at her legs, and she leapt to avoid it. She pressed him back, and he came at her with a high blow, which she rolled away from, as she had from the boulder. Back and forth they went, and Ruffia was challenged as never before.

He would not yield. She would not yield. On it went, until Ruffia felt as though she could not raise her arm for even one more blow. He sensed this and went on the attack. She feigned a falter, and with the same backhand move that had brought her to victory before, she took him by surprise, sending his sword flying into the crowd, where it narrowly missed impaling the young man who had been the cause of the fight.

The Lady Ruffia stood once more triumphant. Azul bowed his head, and yielded to her. She nodded in acceptance and turned to the villagers, who cheered her as though she were their own.

Azul took his sword from the young man, who at a stern look from him, again expressed to Ruffia his sorrow at the threat that he had been. This time she graciously acknowledged his words.

The villagers, warrior men, warrior women, mothers and fathers, one and all, gathered around Ruffia, full of good-natured praise. There were no accolades, but there was a sense of being at home that she had never felt in her father's house. In the excitement, Azul withdrew. Ruffia, when she noticed this, felt regret.

Three days later, he sent to the village, to the house of Kelvan and Chloe, to ask the Lady Ruffia to dine with him. He suggested that she bring her sword, that she might demonstrate to him some of the skills she had used against him. It was an invitation from one warrior to another. Something stirred in Ruffia's blood. She went that evening to the house of Azul, who was not a lord but was noble nonetheless.

And she stayed.

# ARS LONGA

## by Nancy Kress

*What would you do if you were an art instructor and your favorite student insisted on wasting his time drawing little sketches of anthropomorphic mice and ducks? As multiple Nebula-winner Nancy Kress demonstrates, it's not all that simple a question when the student is a kid named Disney.*

The first time I saw Walt, I knew he would be a great man. Oh, I know everybody and his brother says that about the famous, or those about to become famous. But in my case it's absolutely true. I saw that earnest little boy dressed in his hand-me-down knickers and torn shirt, and I just *knew.* I wouldn't say that if it wasn't true. The town of Marceline entrusted me with their precious children for fifty-two years, until my retirement. I'm a member in good standing of the First Congregational Church. You may ask anyone in Marceline about Annie Peeler's veracity.

I've never been interviewed for a newspaper before. Would you like more tea, Mr. Snelling?

Yes, of course, about Walt. Of course I understand your time is limited and this will only be a small article, although I do think the papers might pay more attention to the fine arts instead of all these cheap movies and so-called pop songs with their suggestive lyrics and . . . Art is the thing that unites us, lifts us out of baser and more jaded selves. Art is what justifies our being.

Yes, I *did* tell Walt that. I told all my pupils that, right from the first day of school. It's a great mistake to think third-graders can't understand. Children hunger for greatness, and in a place like Marceline they see so little of it around them. That's why I've always hung fine art prints all around my classroom, even in the early years when they cost me most of my salary. I used to travel to Kansas City on the Atchison, Topeka, and Santa Fe to buy them. Renoir and Rosetti and Monet and Whistler and of course Burne-Jones. Children will open like blossoms in the presence of great art, with proper guidance. I've always believed that. Why, when I graduated from Normal in 1894—

Yes. Walt.

As I say, I knew right away he was special. He sat at his desk in those patched hand-me-downs—his father, you know, was as mean with money as with everything else—drawing his little pictures in the margins of schoolbooks so old they had pages missing. I think they'd been his older brothers' books, and Walt's father just didn't give a hoot if all of Milton and most of long division had just been wantonly ripped out.

His mother? *What* mother?

Oh, don't write that down, I'm sorry I said it. It wasn't a very Christian thing to say, was it? I'm sure she did the best she could, poor thing, married to Elias Disney. Never any money, of course, and what was worse, no education or refinement, no chance to pass on a sense of the finer things in life. Just the same, to let him go around in those torn knickers, scrounging pencil stubs out of wastebaskets, sketching his little things in the margins of schoolbooks because no one recognized and nurtured his talent at home . . . If ever a boy needed mothering, it was young Walt.

I bought him his first sketchbook, you know, and a box of decent pencils. His little face just lit up. He was a grateful child, always, and quick to see an opportunity. Right away he started copying Edward Hicks' "The Peaceable Kingdom." He liked animal pictures, although of course later on I tried to steer him toward people. I always impressed on the children that the human form is the noblest expression of the painter's art.

Young Walt's first copy wasn't very good, of course—he completely missed the painting's spiritual dimension—but he kept at it all year, and gradually his drawing improved. I remembered he copied Burne-Jones' "The Mill" very credibly, and also Gauguin's "The Yellow Christ." Oh, yes, we had Gauguin, even though some of the parents didn't like it. Too strange and—I don't want you to get the wrong impression here, these are all lovely people in Marceline, good solid Christian people, but they do have provincial tastes. There's no getting around it. But I kept Gauguin up on my walls even when a delegation of parents went to the principal to object. I've always had a little rebellious streak of my own. And more important, of course, is that education must never bow to the trivial or the provincial. Education of the young must always embrace the highest of ideals and attainments.

Which is why I was glad when Walt's family moved to Kansas City at the end of the school year. Oh, of course I was torn up inside; some days I truly didn't think I could bear losing him. But I thought that in KC he could have proper art lessons, go to museums ... Ha! Just shows you how much I knew about Elias Disney!

He bought a newspaper route, you know, for the *Kansas City Star.* Little Walt and his big brother Roy had to get up at 3:30 in the morning to meet the delivery truck and deliver hundreds of papers before school, struggling through the snow and rain in the dark. It almost broke my heart when Walt told me that in the winter he would lie down and doze in the corridors of apartment buildings, because they were warm, and in the summer he'd play with toys left overnight on the porches of children whose fathers weren't the skinflint, lucre-minded louts that Elias—

What? How did he tell me that? Oh, I went to KC every few months to visit him. By then I knew I was that poor, talented little boy's only hope. I met him during the noon recess of his school, a dreadful place full of coarse children and underbred teachers. It disgraced the name of education. I took Walt to a decent tearoom for lunch, and I brought him art supplies, and most of all I encouraged him. Never give up, I told him

over and over. Look at Van Gogh. Look at Paul
Cezanne, with his own dreadful father. There is more
in life than daily drudgery to bring ephemeral journalism to uncaring philistines.

More tea?

Yes, Walt did continue to draw during those years. I
remember a lovely still life, a fruit piece, a little bit in
the style of Cezanne. Very promising. Of course,
nearly all his time was taken up by the newspaper
route, and finally I saw that something would have to
be done. So when Walt was fourteen I went to see
Elias Disney.

"You have to send that boy for Saturday lessons at
the Art Institute," I said.

He squinted at me with his mean little eyes and
didn't say anything. Walt had told me his father used
to beat him. He'd stopped *that* by now, but he looked
as if he wanted to beat me. But I stood my ground.
And all the while his timid, ineffectual mother cower-
ing in the background. I'm sorry, Mr. Snelling, but I
really cannot respect a member of the fair sex who will
not fight for her young. Had I ever been privileged to
bear a child like Walt . . . But that's hardly germane to
our interview, is it?

"I am prepared to pay for the lessons myself," I told
Elias Disney. "All you must do is excuse Walt from
work on Saturday. His obligation to his own talent is a
higher one than to commerce."

Elias looked at me and spat his tobacco on the
ground—a filthy habit, that, and one I was glad to see
disappear. He said, "I always heard you was an inter-
fering old maid."

Well, you can imagine the effect that had on me. I
am directly descended from Ebenezer Zane, the fron-
tier hero who saved the Ohio Valley from the savages.
On my mother's side. I just drew myself up to my full
height and said calmly, "Mr. Disney, I don't care how
you insult me, that boy must have his chance. Art has
called him, and your feelings and mine are irrelevant.
If you will not allow me to give him the opportunity he

deserves, then I will see that he wrenches it from you by moral force."

Well, Elias looked a little confused, and to tell the truth, so did Walt. He was still very young. But Elias' older three sons had already all run away from home, so maybe that's what made Elias back down. Or maybe Art can even touch a man like him, in his secret soul— would you be so rash as to deny the possibility, Mr. Snelling? I think not. At any rate, he spat again and said, "Ain't my lookout how you spend your money."

Immediately I pressed my advantage. "Then Walt may have Saturdays off? And carfare to the Art Institute?"

Elias nodded. I hid my triumph—it wouldn't have been Christian to gloat—and the very next week I took Walt to register at the Institute.

He didn't? Not anything about the Institute? Well, I'm afraid there's a reason for that. Let me just find the words to put this diplomatically.

There, I'm ready now. Are you writing this down?

The Art Institute is a good and worthy institution. But Kansas City, after all, is not New York. Had the young Walt Disney enrolled in an art school in New York, the greater sophistication and perspicacity of the teachers would have immediately led them to recognize his unusual talent. But in Kansas City, provincialism meant that his teachers were not as impressed with Walt as they should have been. That explains the mediocre response he received there. As I'm sure you know, the same negative reception initially greeted the Impressionists and the Pre-Raphaelites—why even Rosetti and Burne-Jones were initially scorned!

Not, of course, that I can approve of Rosetti's manner of living. But his art—

Please don't keep looking at your watch, Mr. Snelling. I assure you I'm telling this as fast as I can without leaving anything out.

Walt actually made good progress at the Art Institute. At the proper time, I bought him oils, brushes, and an easel. As much of my salary as was necessary went to support his art. That's what the profession of educator once meant to some of us. It was a calling, no less sacred than that of physician or minister, not merely a job to be unionized like any common workmen, as we see happening today. Put *that* in your paper.

The next thing that happened was that Elias Disney moved his family to Chicago. The newspaper route scheme had failed, of course, and now Elias was ready to try something else. A jelly factory, I believe. Walt went, too. I was devastated. Chicago was too far to visit regularly. But the Lord helps us to bear what we must, Mr. Snelling, and Art anoints her servants. Walt found a place on the McKinley High School paper, doing drawings and photography both.

Here I must trust you, Mr. Snelling. I want to tell the whole truth—you remember that I told you at the beginning of the interview that I revere truth—and yet not give you the wrong impression. Walt and I were as close as ever. We wrote each other every week. He was studying at the Chicago Academy of Fine Arts, and every month he sent me his work to critique. He relied utterly on my guidance, my greater education, my superior taste. But at this point in his life—he was seventeen, remember—young men are apt to be rebellious. That's only natural.

So sometimes—only sometimes—he sent me crude little line drawings, sketches of cute animals or smiling flowers. They were amusing, I suppose, but they represented a regression. He was so much better than that. His still lifes and rural landscapes were beginning to have real power. I remember especially a pastoral, somewhat in the style of Turner, that was remarkable for a boy his age. And then to spend his talent on debased line drawings!

Do you know the Biblical story of Onan, Mr. Snelling?

There, I've shocked you. Well, I did warn you that a life dedicated to Art can brook no evasions. And that was what young Walt, in his inexperience, was doing. Evading service to the highest ideals of Art and turning to the vulgar because it was easier.

I wrote him so, in the strongest possible terms. He replied by sending me drawings illustrating a children's fairy tale. It seems that he had gone to the motion pictures with a friend and seen Marguerite Clark in "Snow White and the Seven Dwarfs." It had sparked something in his fertile mind, and he had translated that crude film into line drawings that, he thought, might illustrate a children's book.

How can I tell you what I felt? What would any mentor feel who sees real talent turning, in its youth and inexperience, to the lures of commerce that will corrupt it utterly?

I caught the next train to Chicago. I found him after school hours outside his father's factory, a pitiful concern already on the brink of failure. When Walt saw me, he turned as white as your shirt, Mr. Snelling.

"You are betraying yourself," I said quietly. I wanted him to be shocked by my lack of social preamble. I wanted him to realize how important this was.

We went to a tearoom and talked for hours. He had grown; he was good-looking, manly in figure but still unformed in soul. Oh, can you blame me that I fought so hard for that soul to belong to Art? If only more of our young people had someone to care about their futures!

And I reached him. At least, I think I did. He was sullen, which is certainly natural at seventeen, but he did promise me he would not stop painting what was best and true in the world. However, he *didn't* promise not to continue with his vulgar little line drawings.

And I didn't ask him to. I hadn't taught children for twenty-three years for nothing. One can only push so far, and then one must rely on righteous guilt.

I remember clearly one thing Walt said that day. I didn't hold the comment against him. I still don't. He was so young. He said, "There's no money in real art."

I said gently, "But there's soul in it."

And, of course, he had no answer to that.

The next month America entered the war. Walt wrote me that he'd joined the Navy. But all during his time at the Naval base in Connecticut, and all during

his time in France driving supply trucks, he wrote me
that he kept studying and learning, copying fine paint-
ings. He wrote that he had a copy of Whistler's "The
Little White Girl" in his kit bag, and wrinkled and
stained though it became, he looked at it every night,
drinking in the lines and composition.

It was only later that I learned about the cowboys he
drew on the supply trucks, and the fake Croix de
Guerre he painted on soldiers' leather jackets for ten
francs each.

Well, I'm sure you can see where this is going, Mr.
Snelling. I notice that you're not looking at your watch
*now.* Isn't it amazing how all the epic human battles
can be fought on such humble grounds? Altruism versus selfishness in every hospital. Civilization versus
barbarism in every classroom. And the highest ideals
of Art versus base commerce in letters carried by the
humble Postal Service.

We had it out when Walt come home. He came to
see me in Marceline, the first time he'd been back
since he was nine. He used a portion of his Navy pay.
That alone was proof to me that the values I had tried
to give him had not been dulled by the roughness of
war. He came to see me even before he visited his
mother.

I waited for him in the parlor of my boardinghouse.
I can still see that room, with its plush green sofa and
red figured rug and Tiffany glass lamp above the round
table. I remember it seemed incredible to me that the
other boarders going in and out, good respectable souls
that they were, had no idea of the importance of the
meeting to come. And how Walt had changed! He was
a man, still in uniform, with a man's power. But I
knew that my power, that of Art, was at least equal to
his. In fact, there is no power greater, save that of the
Creator Himself.

"Hello, Miss Peeler," Walt said. He seemed nervous,
and a little defiant. But so glad to see me!

"You've returned," I said, and then—I don't blush to
admit this, Mr. Snelling—I cried a little. No one knew

the fears I'd had for Walt's safety during the war. I made it my business that no one should know.

His defiance left him immediately. He sat beside me on the sofa and took my hands, and for nearly an hour he entertained me with stories of his gallant comrades in arms. People went past, watching us curiously, but I introduced him to no one. For that hour, doubly precious because of the battle to come, he was mine.

Let me say something here, Mr. Snelling. I count it as not the weakest proof of Walt's talent that he came to me in his hour of questioning. He was always attached to me, but this was more than mere attachment. Only the most idealistic and noblest of souls recognize that they can profit from the guidance of those that have trod the same way before. I am not, and never was, an artist. I was not entrusted with that gift myself. But I was a teacher, devoting my life to nurturing that which is highest in my students, and Walt at his crossroads recognized that.

He pulled a sketchpad from his traveling case.

"Now, I want you to look at this with an open mind. Promise me!" I had never seen his face so serious.

"I will," I said, and it was a solemn promise between us.

He opened the pad. Page after page of drawings of a mouse with a human face, dressed in red velvet pants with two huge pearl buttons, grinning merrily. "Mortimer," it said on some pages. Later in the sketchpad Mortimer Mouse was joined by a lady mouse. Both were shown boarding a plane powered by a dachshund wound up tight like a rubber band. The plane almost hits sketched-in mountains and trees. At the end both mice parachute to safety, the girl with a great display of patched bloomers.

The drawing was unbelievably crude. "Mortimer's" head was no more than a circle, with an oblong circle for a snout. His so-called legs were mere lines. The whole was merry, mocking, vulgar, nauseatingly cute, without taste or real emotions or any meaning beyond the desire to provoke the most simple-minded laugh.

"It's preliminary sketches for an animated motion

picture," Walt said. "Roy's already talked to some fellows at an outfit called The Kansas City Film Ad Company. They do advertising, mostly, little one-minute animated shorts for local theaters. But they might be interested in trying for something bigger. This could be my opportunity!"

I remember that I closed my eyes. It was a prayer for eloquence.

"Walt," I finally said, "this is a turning point for the rest of your life. If you give your talent to . . . to *this,* it will be exactly like using a fine horsehair brush to paint a barn door. In a short time the brush is worn and damaged, unfit for anything else. But unlike a brush, dear Walt, your talent is not replaceable—once dulled, *you can never obtain another.* Your talent is given you only once, and to waste its freshness, its fine edges, on *cartoons . . .*"

For a moment I thought I couldn't go on. But then words found me. Art itself came to my rescue, giving my words wings. I spoke of Gauguin, turning his back on his comfortable stockbroker life to paint from his heart in the South Seas. I spoke of Delacroix, staying faithful to the patrician and the sublime despite the scorn heaped on him. I spoke of Art's scared mission to capture the essence of man's soul, and of—oh!—the emptiness of the lives of those who accept tawdry, secondhand substitutes for that soul. I scarcely know what I said. I would have said anything to keep him faithful to the best that was in him, the highest of which he was capable.

He listened, but I wasn't reaching him. I could see that. He was only eighteen, and he was on fire with the vulgar hustle the war had brought to the cities. The post-war era—the first war, I mean—was a sad time for true culture, Mr. Snelling. Not that the present day is any better.

A cookie with your tea?

Oh, of course the story's not over! It's just that I never quite know how to tell people the next part. It always sounds . . . mystical. And in 1950, who has the spirituality to credit mystical intervention? Especially

in what Art has become now? When I think of the
soulless so-called Cubists, elevating technical exercises
above the—

Yes. Of course. What actually happened on the green
sofa.

I could see Walt was not persuaded. I had failed.
The greatest talent it was ever my happiness to nurture
was voluntarily turning himself over to Mammon. I
was distraught. I begged, pleaded, argued. Finally,
Walt left me, striding away with that sullen expression
I knew so well from two and a half decades in the
classroom. But you must remember—he was so young!

I followed him out to the street. He started to cross.
I grabbed his sleeve. He shook himself free and ran
into the street. And at that moment—the neighborhood
where I boarded wasn't at all what it had once been,
remember that please—at that moment a rat darted out
from behind a trashcan in the adjacent alley. It ran
straight toward me, and I screamed. Walt stopped in
the middle of the street, and half-turned, and immediately was struck by one of Mr. Ford's mass-produced
model Ts.

Just give me a moment, please.

There.

Walt said that? I am glad of it. You see, he recog-
nizes as well as I do that the accident was his true moment of decision. If it *was* an accident. Walt has
always denied the mystical intervention of Art herself.
Still, you men persist in thinking of yourselves as so
much more rational than we women, do you not?

At any rate, Walt is certainly right when he says that
dreadful time in the hospital changed his life. I visited
him every day. We talked for hours. I took a formal
leave from my classroom to be with him, and have
never regretted it. Teaching goes on in many ways, Mr.
Snelling, and education is never confined by four
walls.

It was a year before Walt recovered from his injuries, which I'm sure he told you were extensive. There
was damage to the lungs, ribs, and hips, followed by
infection. Now, of course, we would have these won-

---

derful new antibiotics to aid his recovery, but not then. All Walt had was the sustaining belief in the highest ideals of Art, which I strengthened and girded every day. He came out of the hospital a chastened man.

The rest I'm sure he's told you. He's worked thirty-two years now on the *Kansas City Star*, in the illustration department to be sure, but only to support himself. His real effort, his real soul, has gone into his painting. He has endured many hardships and disappointments—not unlike the masters before him. It's a disgrace to the world, of course, that he should only have his first show at forty-nine, but then the world has always been slow to acknowledge genuine merit. And of course Walt paints the true soul of his subjects, not like these cold travesties who think painting is about the paint, Mondrian and Rothko and this Pollock person. . . . When Walt's show opens next week, you'll see what I mean. His work bears comparison with the best of past masters. Why, there's one picture that might almost have been painted by Burne-Jones himself.

Dear me, I had no idea it was so late. Do you really have to go?

Well, let me leave you with just one summary quote for your paper. Let me see, I want to choose my words carefully. How about this: "Miss Annie Peeler has had faith in Mr. Walt Disney's talent from his childhood. His show at the Kansas City Public Library is long overdue, and this humble beginning will undoubtedly be the harbinger of acknowledgment by the art world. Miss Peeler will say of her own contribution to Mr. Disney's career only that she did no more than any proud member of our educational system *should* do, striving always to keep our pupils' eyes fixed on the highest of which humanity is capable. If we do this, our children's success is inevitable."

There, how's that?

One last cup of tea?

# A DREAM CAN MAKE A DIFFERENCE

## by Beth Meacham

*We have had three celebrities who remain as popular today as when they were alive: Elvis Presley, James Dean, and Marilyn Monroe. Probably the most intriguing is Marilyn, who not only made a name for herself in Hollywood, but was also romantically linked to both John and Robert Kennedy. To this day speculation continues about her life, her death, her love life—and now Beth Meacham, executive editor of Tor Books and a truly fine writer as well, speculates about Marilyn's career had Fate taken a slightly different turn.*

"And so, on this tragic thirtieth day of March, 1981, we look back at the life and death of a President of the United States, gunned down in the streets of Washington DC. To recap for those of you just joining us: This morning as the President was leaving a breakfast meeting, a man named John Hinkley, Jr., rushed out of the crowd, and fired three shots. One of those bullets struck home in the lovely curves of—"

"Cut! Cut, damn it! Dan, you can't talk about the President of the United States' tits. Especially when she's dead."

The anchorman stumbled to a halt. He wasn't used to doing standups outside the White House anymore, and the rain had rattled him. He glared at me, and I glared right back, waiting for him to realize that I was right. He did, too. I've worked with worse.

"Sorry. I just can't quite believe she's gone." Like nearly every man in the country, Dan was in love with President Monroe. She always did have that effect on men.

"Take a break." I turned to the rest of the crew. "Hey, ten minutes. Jim, go see if you can get some coffee. We've got half an hour to air, and I bet we get it in the can next time around."

I walked around our truck, through the maze of cables, and over to NBC's crew. They had Brinkley out in the rain, but he was hitting his marks just fine. He's an old pro, all right. I remembered watching him do the same thing right after the Kennedy assassination.

"Come to check out the competition, Linda?" That was Jane Mason, one of the best producers I know, except for me, of course. I just shook my head at her—we're old friends.

"Nope. Just getting away from the boys. I'm getting damn tired of fighting about the film clips; I don't know how many times this afternoon some jerk has had the bright idea to run that skirts-flying-in-the-wind shot against a sunset. Makes me want to puke."

Jane was sympathetic. She'd heard that one, too. But, "Linda, you can't get too upset about that. She always did use sex appeal to distract them from what she was really doing."

"It's true. Man, I can't believe she's gone. It's like JFK all over again."

"Do you remember during the '76 primaries, when Buchannan came crawling in with that poll?"

"You mean when the Republicans had decided to accuse her of being JFK's mistress, and then Ford's people found out that if they did, she'd win for sure?"

"Yeah. Scandal from the past. They thought they had her. I wish I'd been there when those bastards realized that they were about to give the election to the Democrats." Jane seemed even more upset than I was. More angry.

Someday, maybe someday soon, I was going to have to write my memoirs of the Monroe years. I'd start when I stopped wanting to cry about it. Meanwhile, Danny-boy had had a long enough break. It was time to get this standup in the can. I wished to God that the White House would put out a new statement, so we wouldn't have to keep saying the same thing over and over. But Vice President Carter—no, President Carter—was still en route back from Central America, so there wasn't much to say. Hinkley was still being booked at the local precinct jail.

I first became aware of Monroe when I was in high school, because the boy I had a crush on only had eyes for her. It's funny. I don't remember his name, but I remember stuffing Kleenex in my bra and sneaking red lipstick to try to look more like her. That was in 1964, I guess, when she was making her comeback after the divorces, the suicide attempts, the Kennedy assassination. She had a lot of guts, I realize now. Back then, I hated her. And I wanted to be just like her.

Three years later I was a freshman at UC Berkeley, and she was running for governor of California. Everybody laughed about it—Hollywood was casting real-life politics, with the sex goddess of the century in the leading role, and Ronald Reagan co-starring as her opponent. We all said that script-logic called for the two of them to run off and get married after the election, just like a second-rate Tracy-Hepburn film. But Reagan was fronting for the right-wing loonies who wanted to keep us in Vietnam, and Monroe was the Democrat's secret weapon candidate. And they were old enemies. I found out later that Marilyn blamed Reagan for Arthur Miller being called up in front of the McCarthy hearings, and had hated him since way back when. She told me once, in an off-the-record conversation, that the thing that finally made her agree to run was the thought of shoving it to Reagan. Of course, the fact that Bobby Kennedy himself had come to beg her to do it didn't hurt either. Oh, that woman had finally learned to make men jump through hoops.

That campaign was the dirtiest anyone's ever seen, before or since. Reagan's handlers dredged up all the stories about Monroe's affairs, and abortions, and drug addiction. They began to realize that they were making a mistake when the nude pictures turned up all over the country on people's walls. They knew they'd made a big mistake when Monroe went on TV and talked about how the studio doctors had forced her into the drug addiction to keep her skinny and passive, just like they did Garland and Taylor. I don't think I'll ever forget her performance that day, sitting there talking to Billy Graham, tears streaming down her face, about how in the dark of one August night she hit rock bottom and found God there waiting for her.

I guess nobody knows what really happened that night, but it was the last time Marilyn Monroe was ever known to have taken drugs. She left the U.S. and went into a sanitarium in Europe—the studio was furious that she wouldn't come back and finish *Something's Got To Give*, even though they'd fired her from it two weeks before. I heard rumors years later that the Kennedys had something to do with it, but by then her political links to Bobby and Teddy were so strong that nobody paid any attention.

She won the election. I had been working on her campaign, and was at the Monroe headquarters election night as a reporter from the Free Press. She walked right past me to get up to the stage to give her acceptance speech, and I saw her turn on the men who were escorting her. They'd been holding her arms on each side as if they were taking a prisoner to execution. She stopped in front of me, and jerked her arms away from them. She suddenly looked like she was ten feet tall, and she stared at all of them, one by one, and said, "I'm the Governor of California, not some doped-up party girl. Keep your hands off me from now on." She was whispering, like she always did, but it wasn't sexy.

Then she went up there and made a hell of a speech, all about how California was the richest state in the country, rich in money, but also rich in resources and people. She was going to make sure that those resources were invested for the future, by investing in people, all the people.

We got the White House standup done, and about half an hour later the rain finally let up. I had to get back to the newsroom; the network was starting to get pissed about my decision to tape the show on location—my job these days is producer of the Evening News. It isn't glamorous on the surface—hell, I'm not glamorous on the surface—but a lot of people depend on me to be there in the studio in case anything goes wrong. Nobody could understand why I assigned myself to this. I didn't understand it myself just then. I just knew I had to be there. Jane Mason understood. She was far too senior to be out in the rain producing standups. In fact, as I checked out who was on location at the White House this afternoon, I noticed a lot of senior women who shouldn't have been there— newswomen I first met on the Monroe campaign trails.

I got a call, then, that that bastard Hinkley was going to be transferred from the local precinct jail to the Federal Courts Building. I told Dan to stay at the White House in case there was any word from the vice-president. Then I called a backup crew and said I'd meet them at the Courts.

I saw her again a year later, in '68, at the Democratic National convention in Chicago. Martin Luther King and Bobby Kennedy had been assassinated, and the convention was in turmoil. She was there as head of the California delegation, of course, and she was tight with the civil rights people. I was out in the streets with the demonstrators against the war, real close to the hotel she was staying in. She walked out of the hotel into the middle of a riot, with a lot of TV cameras. There were always cameras following Governor Monroe. Some of the cops tried to make her go back inside, and some of the other cops tried to smash the TV cameras. They didn't want film of them beating up the demonstrators. But Monroe just walked out into the middle of the crowd and stood there in front of the cameras. A cop in riot gear came at her, and she batted her eyes at him and said that the last time anyone had swung a club at her it had been in Selma, Alabama. Everything calmed down real fast. Then she went to the convention hall, marched onto the stage and grabbed the microphone away from Daley. "Do you know that out there in the streets the Chicago police are beating up children?" she asked, breathy and trembling and aghast. Daley tried to shut her up, but couldn't bring himself to attack her physically for the mike. She talked for a long time about how the people outside were the children of the people inside, and how the convention should listen to them instead of punishing them for speaking out. She was electrifying.

Of course, the election went to Nixon in the end, but Monroe had become a national political figure. People started talking about 1972.

By '71 I was working for a San Francisco TV station, and I was assigned to cover the Governor. That was a pretty strange time. All the top political correspondents were men in those days, believe it or not. But after Monroe had read Friedan's book, she made a rule that she'd only do a press conference when there were at least ten women reporters in the room. And she kept giving exclusives to women, because she liked to talk in the ladies room during official functions. So all the papers and TV stations were scrounging around for females to send to Sacramento. We didn't get much air time; when Monroe was talking to the men she'd turn on the high-voltage charm, and that was what the bosses wanted to show. But when it came to reporting the real news, they had to get it from us.

One night she found me sitting and crying in the ladies' lounge of the Beverly Hills Hotel. I was covering a speech she was making to the ACLU, or at least I had thought I was. The bastard of a news director had just told me on the phone that he was pulling me off the assignment because I had refused his advances two days ago. I wasn't cooperative, he said, and he only worked with *cooperative* women. Well, it got to me. Sometimes it seemed it didn't matter how good you were—the men in charge could only think about sex when a woman stood in front of them. So I was hiding out and wondering if I was going to say yes the next time some man made sex the price of a job, and hating myself for even thinking about doing it.

She came up behind me and said, "What's the matter, Linda?" in a real gentle voice, and I started talking before I turned around and realized who it was. I was embarrassed, I hadn't even realized that she knew my name. But I couldn't stay embarrassed for long, because she started imitating all the men who'd ever made her put out to get a job. God, she was a good actress. It was horrible, but in five minutes I was laughing so hard I'd forgotten that I'd been crying. Then she stopped, and said that she'd walked around for years just terrified of what she might be forced to do, until she realized that they *wanted* her to be afraid all the time. Because if they could terrorize her, they wouldn't have to admit she was as good as they were. "Honey, that man wants you to be in here crying, so you aren't out there competing with him. It stinks."

Then she pulled me to my feet, made my face up for me to hide the puffiness, and made me go out with her to the speaker's table. That was the first night she gave her famous sexual harassment speech. That was also the night I decided that she had to be President. See, she made that speech completely ad lib. She may have been planning to talk about women's rights, but she made all her points by linking them to the story I'd just told her, two minutes before.

I got to the Federal Building about 45 seconds before the other network crews did. A lot of people had gotten phone calls, it seemed. There was a message for me from Sauter saying that I'd better know what I was doing, because I'd missed the night assignments meeting. I knew that. We set up, and I grabbed a shirt and blazer from the wardrobe closet. I was going to have to go in front of the cameras for this one, and I wanted to look nice.

The Secret Service guys at the door said they didn't know a thing about moving Hinkley. Well, that's their job. But one of them had been with Monroe for years, since 1975, and he pulled me aside.

"Shut off that mike, Linda."

"Tim, I have to know where they're bringing him in—I need to see him. My viewers need to see him."

"Linda, shut it off," he repeated.

It was already off, of course. I showed him the switch.

He told me that the car was going to come in at the loading dock—I didn't even know the building had a loading dock. The only access was one alley, already blocked by blue-and-whites, so we couldn't get the truck in. I went and talked to the crew, and we decided I'd go with a transmitter and a camerawoman. As I strapped on the battery pack, I saw Jane talking with Tim. That man couldn't keep a secret, it seemed. Of course, Jane had been with us for years, too.

Monroe had a lot of support for the 1972 nomination, but not enough. I don't think she could have beaten Nixon, anyway; I don't think anyone could have. But after Watergate the country was disgusted with politics-as-usual. It was time for a change.

I had to make a tough choice at the end of 1975. I had two job offers—CBS News offered me a job as producer of their morning show. And Marilyn Monroe offered me a job as her media spokeswoman. I finally opted for the job with CBS, but it was hard. Monroe said she understood—I guess she did, too. During the campaign all that long year, she'd call me up in the middle of the night to talk about how things were going. She never once asked me to do her any favors, and I never once told my boss that she was doing it.

I did let her know what the press was thinking about, sometimes. Early on, during the primaries, people started wondering about men in her life. She was single, and had been for years. It hadn't bothered anyone in California, but they said that in Peoria people worried about single women. When I told her about that during one of our late night chats, she was pissed, but the campaign took steps to defuse the issue. I also warned her that stories about her and the Kennedys were starting to circulate again. She was actually happy about that one. She called it the Camelot Effect, and said it would win the election for her. She was right, too.

Whatever anybody might say now, in early 1976 nobody really believed that a woman could be elected President. The media followed her campaign for the nomination very closely, but that was mostly because she was so damned photogenic. The press attention kept her in the public eye, though. And people came to hear her speeches; after all, she was Marilyn Monroe and everyone knew her. They came to stare at her, but they couldn't help but listen to what she said. And what she said made a lot of sense. She talked a lot about the Constitution, and about civil rights, and about how we had a republic instead of a monarchy because individual people counted. She talked about her own past—there was a real Abe Lincoln-log cabin story—and explained why that meant she would be everybody's President, not just the bosses' President. People ate it up. They voted for her.

So she came into the 1976 convention with the nomination sewed up. The only question was who her running mate would be. I happened to be there, setting up for an interview, when she first met the Carters. The governor of Georgia had run a small campaign for the nomination, but he'd bowed out early when Monroe's strength became clear. He came to see her on the first day of the convention, and brought along Rosalyn and his mother, Miss Lillian. I expected fireworks—everybody knew that Lillian Carter was a rock-rib Southern Baptist. They talked for a while, and then Jimmy said straight out that he'd be honored if she'd consider him for her running mate. I think you could have knocked Monroe over with a whistle, she was so surprised.

"Jimmy," she said finally, "if you really mean it, we'd win for sure. But they're gonna drag my morals all over the press. Can you handle that?"

Miss Lillian snorted. "Of course he can handle it. I've been watching you, Marilyn, and you're a good woman now, whatever you might have been once." Her sweet Southern drawl fell into a preacher's singsong. "I've told Jimmy, and I'll tell everyone else who asks, that if Jesus Christ could forgive Mary Magdalene, then Jimmy Carter can sure forgive Marilyn Monroe."

Marilyn looked angry at that. "I don't need your forgiveness for doing what I had to do to survive."

Miss Lillian nodded. "You bet you don't. But those good ole boys out there think you do. And if you get forgiven by the Southern Baptists, there's nobody going to dare bring up the subject again."

That old woman was sharp, and her son was a canny politician. And the combination of the Kennedys and the Southern Democrats was more than the Republicans could stand against.

I got into the Federal Courts building through the front door, then followed the crowd down into the basement. There were cops and Secret Service, and FBI, and about a dozen reporters and cameramen. Jane Mason was there, of course, but also Sue Leonard, and Barbara Short, and Sue Hardy, and a couple other women I recognized but didn't know. The five of us had spent a lot of time together covering Governor, and then President, Monroe. I wondered if they got late night phone calls, too. I wandered over to them.

"Hi. Guess we all had the same idea," I said.

"Guess so." That was Sue Hardy. There was a world of bitterness in her voice.

"Do you suppose we can get him to talk?" Jane asked.

That was what we were there for, obviously. If the Secret Service didn't want him to talk, we'd never have gotten this far. Tim was pretty transparent sometimes.

"Heads up!" someone shouted from down the corridor.

We turned like a pack of hounds and almost ran to the door. I slipped through the crowd toward the front, then turned and gave Janet, my camerawoman, a high sign and a sound check. She nodded. Jane bumped up beside me.

The doors swung back with a bang, and the corridor erupted in sound, cops shouting "Get back, get back!" and reporters shouting "Mr. Hinkley, Mr. Hinkley!" and "Commissioner!"

I took a breath, and stepped out right in front of Hinkley, so he had to stop. A hand in a blue sleeve reached for me, then was pulled back by another in a gray suit. I shoved the mike at his petulant mouth, and said, "Do you want to say anything to the American public?" Figuring, of course, that he must. They all did.

He blinked at me. Then he put on his TV face— everybody these days has a TV face—and said, "Yes, I do."

All the noise stopped, just like that. The Secret Service guys grinned. The cops looked sick.

"Can I say hi to my mom and dad?" he asked.

"Sure you can. Mr. Hinkley, why did you shoot the President?" I figured I might as well get to the point before somebody came to their senses and threw me out.

His face twisted. "She didn't love me," he said. I went cold inside. "She made me want her, and then she didn't love me." His voice rose. "She was a whore! She deserved to be punished, beaten. I could have made her listen, made her see that she shouldn't show herself like that, stand up in public like that. Women should take care of men and have babies, not spurn their love and make a public spectacle." He narrowed his eyes at me. "You're another one, aren't you. Another one of those half-women who like to make men small, like to see them crawl. Yes, I know who you are, you make men do everything for you, then you laugh at them and turn away—"

He went on like that. He was sweating, and the smell was nauseating. I wanted to throw up. The crowd was pulling back from him, but the cameras kept rolling, getting it all on tape. I felt a jab in my ribs, and turned toward Jane.

She had a gun in her left hand, the one by my side. She'd elbowed me, pulling it out of her pocket. I looked away quickly, and saw that Sue Hardy had one, too. I was still holding the mike in Hinkley's face, so I jerked it a little to distract everyone's attention. That brought the cops back to themselves, and they grabbed tighter hold of him and got ready to move again.

That's when they shot him.

I remember lying awake late one night, thinking about all kinds of things. I'd just gotten off the phone with the President, who still called her old friends when she couldn't sleep at night. We'd talked about how well the Camp David meetings had gone, and what a good job Carter had done in making Sadat and Begin listen to reason. We'd talked about the new Job Corps program that she was going to propose, based on the California model that had been so successful. The economy was really taking off. I remember thinking how different everything would be if she hadn't run for governor, how close this country came to disaster during the Nixon years, when politicians really began to believe that the government was the master, and not the servant of the people.

Monroe brought compassion back to politics. She took that power she had, the power to make men want to please her, and turned their hearts toward kindness, made them want to heal the sick, and house the homeless, and teach the children, and not think of any reward but the knowledge of doing good.

She had told me about a dream she had once, that she was able to travel back in time to visit herself when she was fifteen. She'd open the door of her room, where she was lying on the bed crying and shaking. She'd walk in there, and take the pill bottle away, and tell the girl that if she'd just hold on she'd make a difference in the world some day. Then Marilyn said that in her dream she was flying from room to room, girl to girl, all over the country, and telling all of them to just hold on, they could all make a difference in the world, and then the world would be a better place.

\* \* \*

Most of the men were satisfied with a smile from her. Most of them, but not that man who lay dead on the concrete at my feet. He thought that he could own her, like a dog or a slave. And he thought that he had the right to kill her if he chose, like a dog or a slave.

It was like the world had freeze-framed, or everything was in slow motion. I grabbed the gun out of Jane's hand, then someone grabbed it from me. The cops had dropped to the floor when they heard the shots, so they didn't see. The Secret Service guys deliberately turned their heads away. Both guns ended up on the floor at the back of the crowd, and when the FBI tried to pull prints, all they found was a blur of a hundred different ones.

I'm told that when the sequence was run on the news, Hinkley spewing hate and then the gunshots and his head exploding, people cheered. The thing I regret the most is that I wasn't able to cover her funeral. And without me there to stop it, Sauter ran the damn skirt shot.

They arrested us all, of course. They had to. After five days of questioning they let everyone but Jane and Sue and me go. But none of the video showed who had fired; and they couldn't tie the guns to any of us, because of the messed-up prints, and the fact that there weren't any serial numbers. The powder traces were on everyone who was close to Hinkley. And Tim was never called to testify. So the Grand Jury couldn't indict us, and we walked. Lost our jobs, of course. But we've formed a new media consulting company, Some Like It Hot, and we're doing better than ever.

I hope that Jimmy Carter can keep her dream alive into the 1980s. I think he's a better man than Lyndon Johnson was. I hope so.

# UNDER A SKY MORE FIERCELY BLUE

## by Laura Resnick

*Laura Resnick, award-winning romance writer and Campbell nominee in the science fiction field, spent a couple of years living in Sicily, where gangster Lucky Luciano, the most celebrated Mafia chief in New York's history, was deported half a century ago. Here she gives you a hint of how he might have fared under slightly different circumstances.*

In July of 1943, the Allies invaded Sicily, and the Fascist government toppled five weeks later. Despite two decades of decline under fascism, the Sicilian Mafia quickly stepped into the power breach—with notable help from the Americans.

Charles "Lucky" Luciano, who was serving a thirty-year prison sentence in America, was paroled in 1946 due to his "extensive and valuable aid to the Navy during the war." The most powerful figure in organized crime, he was immediately deported to Italy, where he lived in reluctant exile until his death in 1962.

Luciano is officially recorded as having used his influence on the New York waterfront as part of a counter-intelligence effort to prevent anticipated sabotage by the Nazis. It is rumored, however, that he did far more than that. Although Luciano denied it until his death, legend has it that he was personally smuggled into Sicily in early 1943 to convince Don Vizzini and the Sicilian Mafia to assist the Allied invasion, in exchange for which they would be given the run of the island after the war.

* * *

The almond trees were in bloom the day he fell out of the sky. Their blossoms were puffs of pale pink, their appearance strangely similar to the round, sun-burned faces of the German soldiers. My mother always said that the almond tree, the first of all trees to flower each year, was a symbol of hope. But in February of 1943, Sicily was a place where hope had been eaten alive by foreign invaders. And not just the Germans; the Nazis merely stole whatever the Fascists neglected to take.

We ate what little was left over, rations which were not fit to feed a rat—and which were barely plentiful enough to sustain one, anyhow. All that winter, oranges were our main sustenance. And so at thirteen, I was a small, skinny boy with sunken eyes and sallow skin. How pathetic and sickly I must have looked to him, a man who had lived like a king in the gold-paved streets of America.

At first, I ignored the airplane as it soared above the ancient hills of Western Sicily. But when the parachute blossomed against a sky more fiercely blue than any other, my heart burned like the heart of a fire, and I hid behind some rocks to watch its slow descent. I knew that a solitary man falling out of the sky and landing secretly in this rocky, barren landscape could only mean one thing: the Allies had finally sent someone to Sicily.

Of course, one man was not an army, and I quickly began to suspect that *this* man was not even a soldier. He fell to earth with a harsh crash and cursed fluidly in Sicilian dialect as he rolled downhill, getting tangled up in his parachute. I watched as he finally fought his way out from beneath its folds, rose stiffly to his feet, and gathered the billowing heap of silk into a careless bundle which he then hid beneath a prickly pear tree. That made me grin, for I knew no Germans would want to look for it there; I had seen them howl like children after trying to pick the sweet fruit of the *fico d'India*.

Having hidden the parachute, he retrieved the small knapsack he had dropped upon landing and looked around, as if trying to guess where he was. Who knows how different the shape of my life might have been, had I stayed hidden and let him go his way? But I realized that he was Sicilian, despite his foreign clothes, for such things are clear to the ear and the eye. I was a more curious boy than my mother had taught me to be, and, hoping the stranger had food with him, I cautiously came out of hiding.

He was as alert as a wild animal, for he fell to the ground, rolled away, and drew a pistol out of nowhere in one smooth, swift movement. I crossed myself and tried, with a dry, sluggish tongue, to confess my sins before God.

"Holy shit," he said in English, and I frowned at the strange sound of the words. "A kid."

He rose slowly from the ground and looked around again, more carefully this time.

"Are you alone?" he asked. His Italian was guttural, like my mother's. I nodded. "Where's your father?" he demanded, as if he supposed I was lying.

I found my voice. "Dead."

"Ah. Then where are your brothers?"

I was silent until he cocked the hammer of the gun. "Marco and Rosario are dead. Tommaso has been in Africa since 1938." I looked at the ground and admitted, "He might be dead, too."

There was a long silence between us, and it grew so heavy that I finally looked up. Our gazes locked, and I couldn't have looked away if my life had depended upon it. In that moment, his eyes were as cold and flat as a snake's, utterly indifferent to my youth and my fear. I did not tremble or beg for mercy, for I had been raised to be a man; but I know that I could throw myself into the fires of Mount Etna more easily than I could face a look like that again. If I live another century, I will never forget the expression in his eyes as he decided whether or not to kill me.

Finally, perhaps seeing how harmless I was, he lowered the pistol. "What's your name?"

"Toto."

"Short for Salvatore?" When I nodded, he smiled beguilingly and said, "That used to be my name, too."

"Used to be?"

He nodded. "Salvatore Lucania. But I changed it." He stuck the pistol into the waistband of his trousers, at the small of his back where it was hidden by his dull brown jacket. "Where are we, Toto?" he asked.

I stared at him without responding, for nothing is given away lightly in Sicily, least of all knowledge.

"Jesus," he muttered at last. "Welcome home, Charlie."

He sat down on a rock, pulled out a packet of cigarettes, and lit one.

I crept closer and looked at the packet.

"Want one?" he asked.

I shook my head but said with interest, "American cigarettes."

His eyes went cold again, and I looked down rather than be caught in his web. A moment later he laughed softly, startling me. "Yeah, I know. Not too smart, if I get caught with these on me. But fuck it. Nobody is pushing me out of a goddamned airplane and dropping me into fucking Villalba without a pack of cigarettes."

"This isn't Villalba."

"Well, they weren't just going to drop me into the main piazza for all the Germans to watch, kid." He inhaled deeply on his cigarette, then asked, "How far away are we?"

I shrugged.

"Fucking typical." He looked disgusted. "Look, I'll make it simple for you. If you started walking right now, how long would it take you to get to Villalba?"

I shrugged.

"Guess!" he snapped.

"A long time, I suppose. I heard once that Villalba is almost thirty kilometers from Caltanissetta, which is already a long walk from here."

*"What?"* He looked at me strangely. "What is the name of your village?"

I looked away again, for I knew better than to answer anyone's questions, particularly the questions of a stranger. But then, he was not just any stranger. He had fallen out of the sky to land at my feet, and he had chosen not to kill me.

"My village is Serradifalco," I said at last.

*"Porca miseria!"* He threw his cigarette to the ground and put his head in his hands. "Can't those assholes get anything right?"

"They were supposed to drop you near Villalba?" I guessed.

He nodded. "Goddammit! And people wonder why it took those bastards twenty years to catch me! Hell, they didn't even catch me—the motherfuckers set me up." He sighed and lit another cigarette. A fresh one, not the good one he had thrown to the ground. Such waste amazed me.

"You were sent by the Americans," I said. "But you are not American."

He didn't agree, and I saw then that, unlike my neighbor Signor Cataldo, this was a Sicilian who had never intended to come back home. He closed his eyes and admitted, "I was born here. In Lercara Friddi."

"Then they should have sent you to Lercara Friddi, so your family could help you."

That made him grin. "You could say I've got family in Villalba, too."

"Oh." I thought it over. "If you're going to Villalba, you'll have to be very careful. The soldiers are very strict."

"I'll need help."

"You're a stranger here. Who will help you?"

His smile was more subtle this time, as if I had said something very naive. "You don't know who I am, do you?"

He said it formally, in good Italian—*Lei non sa chi io sono*. His tone almost made a joke of it, because he was confident that if my eyes had not been so dazzled by the spectacle of his parachute, I would have seen immediately, as anyone could see, that he was a man of respect. A friend of the friends—*un amico degli amici*. My face flushed with shame at my foolishness.

"You are of the Society," I whispered, afraid to say it aloud. Then I frowned. "You live in America?"

"Well, that remains to be seen." His voice was rueful.

"Born in Lercara Friddi ..." It was as if the Madonna whispered his name in my ear then, for I knew instantly who he was. My throat filled with awe as I cried, "Luciano!" Then, horrified that I had thrown his name so carelessly to the wind, I clapped a hand over my mouth and backed away.

"Hey, it's okay, kid, calm down. If there's any spot in Italy more godforsaken and lonely than this, I'd be surprised. No one heard you."

I let my hand drop and continued to stare in wonder. *"Luciano,"* I breathed. *"Il capo di tutti capi."*

"Cut that shit out." He shook his head and grinned again. "Ain't you heard, Toto? I modernized things in America. We don't do things the old way anymore. There's no boss of all bosses. I'm more like a chairman of the board."

I bit my lip, embarrassed at my indiscretion. No matter how they did things in America, there were many things which we never even said out loud in Sicily. This was my first encounter with such a powerful man, and, wishing to make a good impression, I searched for something to say. "Signor Cataldo returned to our village the year before the war started," I told Luciano. "He was in America for twenty years and came home a wealthy man. He owns a *car."*

"Uh-huh."

He was clearly unimpressed. I decided not to mention the *signore's* other fabulous possessions, and said only, "He has told us many tales about you."

"Oh?" Luciano didn't bother to look at me, but I could tell he was interested now. What great man does not enjoy hearing his own legend repeated and embellished?

"Signor Cataldo says that by the time you were eighteen, you were already a man of respect. He has told us stories of the Night of the Sicilian Vespers and other great victories. And once, your enemies attempted to kill you, but by a miracle of God, you survived; the knife left a scar on your face, and you bear a new name in honor of it. It's . . . an American word."

"Lucky. Charlie Lucky Luciano."

"Yes. Signor Cataldo says that while still a young man, you organized all the . . . the friends in America, and you became the most powerful man in the whole country."

He grinned. "Not quite, kid. Just the most powerful man among my friends."

"Oh." I frowned. "But why did the Americans drop you out of the sky? Don't they want you anymore?"

He actually laughed, and the expression on his face made me remember the tales Signor Cataldo had told of Luciano's legendary charm. Finally, still looking amused, he said, "They sent me to do a job for them, a job nobody else can do."

"You're going to kill the Nazi *capo!*"

"Hell, no. That kind of thing is for soldiers—jerks who run around happily killing each other for a dollar a day."

"But if anyone could kill him, *you* could," I insisted, forgetting my manners, relishing the thought. How I hated the Germans!

He shook his head. "We don't need to kill no Germans, kid. The Allied soldiers are coming here to do it for us. Soon, too."

I sat down on a rock, not sure what to think. The old men in my village had argued ferociously about this for months. Some longed for the invasion we all believed the Allies were planning, for Sicilians had suffered under the Fascists and Nazis for so very long. But, officially, we were Italians, part of the Axis, so the Allies were our enemies. Moreover, the Nazis and Fascists would not give up Sicily without a fight, and many of us might well be killed in the battle the great powers would wage for control of our country. Given a choice between the invaders who ruled us and the invaders we awaited, who could say which was the greater evil? We all knew that Roosevelt and Churchill, like Mussolini and Hitler, made their plans without concern for us, our families, or our empty bellies.

I asked the only important question. "Will this end the war?"

"The invasion?" Luciano shrugged. "They expect it to, but not right away. This is still a long way from Rome, kid. Not to mention Berlin."

"My mother says that Rome is on the other side of the moon."

He squinted against the harsh sunlight and looked around. "She's right." His voice was bleak.

"So if you're not a soldier, why are you here?" I had by now asked him more questions in a few minutes than I had asked anyone else in a year.

"The Allies want to save their strength for the mainland battles they'll have to fight. They want a warm welcome here, so they won't lose too many soldiers at such an early stage. The Americans sent me because they want help from my friends."

"But such friends are . . ." I tried to think of a phrase that would not insult him. It wasn't easy, for power is everything to such men, and theirs had been stripped away like flimsy garments. "Many such friends have been jailed, and others, though they are respected, have little, um . . . The Fascists changed many things here," I concluded awkwardly. "Your friends may not be as influential as they once were."

"So I've heard. But nothing ever changes *that* much. Especially not here."

"So you are going to Villalba to see Don Vizzini?"

He looked at me thoughtfully. "You know him?"

I shook my head. "But everyone knows *of* him. A man like you would have no other reason to go to Villalba."

"Toto, do you know someone reliable? Someone who can take me to Vizzini?"

Suddenly excited, imagining myself in a heroic scene, I said, "I can take you!"

"Forget it. You're a kid. Anyhow, you've never been to Villalba."

"You'd have trouble finding anyone in Serradifalco

who's older than me and younger than my grandfather. Trouble, too, finding anyone in my village who *has* been to Villalba."

"What will your mother think when you don't come home?"

I had thought he would ask, since no man, not even a man like Luciano, ignores his mother's wishes. "When I come home, she will be proud if I can tell her I helped you."

"But think of how she'll suffer until then."

"She has suffered before," I said with the callousness of youth.

"Since she lives here, I don't doubt it." He rose to his feet. "Are you sure you can take me to Villalba without getting caught?"

"For three years I have stolen fuel and meat from the soldiers without getting caught. I've smuggled cheese and grain through these mountains to my family, and I've traded on the black market." Pleased that he seemed to take my accomplishments seriously, I concluded, "I can get you to Villalba safely."

He agreed to let me guide him, and we set off toward Villalba. As the hours passed, I discovered that he enjoyed conversation, though he preferred to ask questions rather than answer them. I explained that, when he appeared, I had been on my way to the estate of a *latifondista*—a landowner—to steal a sheep.

"Of course, many *latifondisti* are not as wealthy as they once were," I said as we followed a dry riverbed through the hills, heading north. "First the Fascists, then the war . . . Still, they are richer than we are, and I think this one can certainly spare one sheep for my family."

"There's just you, your mother, and your grandfather now?"

"Yes. And my grandfather is very ill, so it's my duty to make sure we have something to eat."

I could see that he was no longer a young man, and he obviously wasn't used to hiking through rough terrain, but he didn't complain or ask to rest. Nevertheless, out of respect, I slowed my pace when I saw he was tiring. We stayed far from the roads, of which there were very few anyhow, and encountered no soldiers. When the sky began to darken, we decided to find shelter. Whenever I traveled by myself, I slept outside and ate what my mother had packed for me, since no one would want to shelter or feed a strange boy from another village. But sheltering a man like Luciano would obviously be another matter.

"We will stay the night with *contadini*," I said. "They will give us something to eat."

"Peasants? Do you think they'll *have* anything to eat?"

"For you, they will find something," I said with confidence.

Just as night descended, we stopped at a stone dwelling perched atop a parched and stony hill. As we approached it, the door opened and a man greeted us with a *lupara*. My blood ran cold as I looked down its barrel and thought about how a simple movement of his finger could rip open my flesh. But the man, whose name was Piersanto, put aside the *lupara* when Luciano spoke. The words revealed nothing, except that we needed food and shelter and could pay for it. But the tone, the proud stance, the aura of command . . . Well, even in the dark, this miserable *contadino* could see what kind of man Luciano was. He welcomed us into his home then, silent, unsmiling, respectful, a little afraid.

Piersanto, his pregnant wife, their three surviving children, the donkey, a goat, and four scrawny chickens all lived together in one dark room with a dirt floor.

"Jesus," Luciano muttered. "Jesus, I'd forgotten." I looked at him questioningly, but he only repeated, "I'd forgotten."

The bread was brown, coarse, and dry, and the *minestrone* was thin and strangely bitter. And the oranges, which I had grown to hate anyhow, were bitter, too, as if no sweetness could enter Piersanto's home. Still hungry, I curled up in a smelly corner, with Luciano's jacket thrown over me, and fell asleep on the floor as he enjoyed a cigarette with our host. When we departed before dawn, Luciano left behind a yellow silk kerchief with a black "L" on it as a mark of his favor. Who knew what respect, what advantage, Piersanto or his sons might someday gain through ownership of this souvenir?

We encountered two priests that day, and many people saw us enter Villalba that night and approach Vizzini's home, but it didn't worry either of us. Although we didn't wish to flaunt our presence or be seen by soldiers, we had no fear of betrayal. Even those who hated Vizzini would cut out their own tongues before they would reveal Sicilian matters to outsiders, strangers, foreigners.

We were spotted by Vizzini's men long before we reached the gate of his house, and the first man to recognize Luciano couldn't have looked more surprised if he'd seen the Blessed Virgin standing there in the chilly night air. Upon being told who wished to pay him a visit, Vizzini himself came outside and greeted Luciano as a father would greet a son. As a sign of trust, Luciano was permitted to enter the don's home without being searched for a weapon, though they must surely know he had not come without one.

Vizzini's house was the grandest place I had ever seen, though I suppose it looked humble to Luciano. Vizzini himself was already quite old, a fat, wrinkled man with thick features.

"And who is this?" he asked Luciano, upon noticing me.

I returned his gaze boldly, feeling my own importance. *I* had guided Lucky Luciano through the mountains!

Luciano introduced me and added respectfully, "Toto's father and brothers were killed in the war. He's the man in his family, now."

I looked up at Luciano and started to say that my father and brothers hadn't been killed in the *war*, but Vizzini was speaking again, his voice too loud and rumbling for my own thin one to be heard. Then the don guided us into the kitchen and offered us food, and

I forgot about everything except the gnawing pain in my belly.

Luciano grinned as I fell upon the bread and pasta like a ravening wolf, swallowing before I had chewed, taking huge bites before I had swallowed.

"Careful, kid, or it'll come right back up."

I didn't care. The taste of last night's bitter meal had fouled my mouth all day, and the sauce I was eating now was spicy and delicious—almost as good as the sauces my mother could prepare if the ingredients were available.

"Only at Easter, once a year, do we eat like this," I sighed, shoving more pasta into my mouth.

A woman—Vizzini's wife, I supposed—fussed over me then, putting more food within my reach, taking off my cap and ruffling my dirty hair, remarking on how thin I was. I tried to smile politely and thank her for this feast, but my hands could not seem to stop reaching for more. Fresh green salad, olive oil, cheese, thin slices of *prosciutto*! It was a banquet of ecstasy.

I was finally full when Vizzini sent the woman out of the room, but I continued to slowly savor the sweets she had given me, sitting quietly in the shadows as the two men talked.

"Do you like the *cannoli,* Toto?" Vizzini asked jovially. I nodded, and he grinned, "All boys have a sweet tooth, eh?"

I nodded again, my mouth too full to respond, but I remembered suddenly another boy with a sweet tooth. The previous year, my family had traveled all the way to Agrigento, the farthest from home I had ever been, to celebrate Easter with my mother's sister. I remembered walking past the bakery and seeing a boy, perhaps eight or nine years old, being thrown out of the shop by the baker for having attempted to steal some sweets. The boy stood crying in the street as a man came out of the bakery carrying a box of *cannoli*. He was fat and well-dressed; a man such as Vizzini, a man of respect. The boy threw himself at the man's feet and begged for something to eat. Even at Easter, his family had no money for sweets, and he pleaded for one, just *one* of the man's precious *cannoli*. The man hit him and walked away, never looking back to see the boy's tears, or the blood which gushed from his nose.

I suddenly wondered, as I sat in Don Vizzini's kitchen amidst the remnants of that meal, why did *they* always seem to have enough to eat, while the rest of us went hungry? Why was Vizzini's wife plump and nicely dressed, while my own mother wore rags and grew thinner every day? Why did *they* have hot and cold running water in their houses, while the rest of us had to carry water home from public fountains which often ran dry?

I continued to chew, but the creamy ricotta cheese and crisp pastry lost their sweetness and grew bitter on my tongue.

"I thought you were in jail," Don Vizzini said to Luciano, now that his wife had left them alone. "Did you escape?"

"No."

"You can't mean to say the Americans simply let you out? They sentenced you to thirty years!"

"The war has a way of changing the best laid plans. Hadn't you noticed? The Americans called a sit-down and came up with a deal. If I help them out with their war, they'll let me go free."

I listened in surprise, for Signor Cataldo had neglected to mention that the great Lucky Luciano had been *imprisoned* in America. I was astonished that the Americans, whom everyone knew were very strict about such things, had actually released him. I wondered why they had sent him here alone, without a guard. Didn't they know he could disappear forever in Sicily? Not even his enemies would betray him to foreigners.

"They said they'd free you? Let you go back to your business?" Vizzini stared at Luciano, clearly torn between amusement and disgust. "And you believe that? Have you grown stupid over the years?"

"You don't know the Americans. I do. They keep their word, even to guys like me."

"And how do they expect you to help them with the war?"

Luciano removed his pistol from the waistband of his trousers, laid it on the table between us, and leaned back in his chair, looking relaxed and confident. "I started off by using my influence on the New York waterfront to prevent Nazi sabotage. That got me a reduced sentence." He swallowed some more wine. We had not had wine in our house since my oldest brother's wake. "Then they came to me with another deal."

The proposition was simple, and it was clear why they had chosen Luciano. What other man in America had his connections? What other man from that country could wield such influence here?

"You help them out, you make sure the population of Sicily offers them no resistance," he said to Vizzini, "and they will return the favor."

Vizzini listened as Luciano outlined the promises of the Americans, who were offering to hand over the country—our country, *my* country—to Vizzini and others of his kind, the very men who had controlled Sicily before the Fascists had taken over. Special privileges, control of the black market, official government positions—whatever these friends of Luciano's required, the Americans would give to them, provided they used their influence to ensure civilian cooperation during the invasion.

I knew without being told that Luciano's friends would willingly assist the Allies, if for no other reason than that they were all passionately antifascist, many of them having spent years in Mussolini's jails. The promises which Luciano was making on behalf of the Americans were merely added inducements.

The *cannoli* seemed to turn to paste in my stomach as I stared at Luciano. He wasn't a great man in America, I realized. He was just a criminal, not a warrior or a hero. And the Americans had thought it appropriate to send a criminal here to speak on their behalf, as if there were no Sicilians worthy of negotiating with a real American hero.

And, as Luciano spoke with Vizzini, I realized that,

worse than being a criminal, he was also a fool. He truly believed that the people who had dropped him into German-occupied Sicily were going to take him back to America after the battle was over and let him return to his former life as "chairman of the board." Vizzini knew it would never happen, but he made only one attempt to tell Luciano, for, in the end, a man believes what he chooses to believe.

I realized then how clever the Americans were. Of course they could send Luciano here alone—they knew he had no desire to remain in Sicily. His longing to return to America was so evident in his face, it almost made him look like a child. And, if he failed to fulfill his bargain with the Americans, they could simply betray him to the Nazis, who would hunt him down like an animal; it would simultaneously waste German resources and make Luciano's life a misery. Yes, the Americans had left Luciano very little choice when they made their agreement with him.

Having listened to Luciano, Vizzini finally said, "I feel certain I can accept on behalf of all our friends. Do you have some way of notifying the Americans?"

Luciano nodded. "They'll be waiting for my signal. Two days from now."

"And then you'll leave?"

"God, how I would love to! I can't stand this shithole, and I should daily bless my father for having emigrated. But, unfortunately, it's a lot easier to drop someone off in hostile territory than to pick him up again. I'm stuck here until the American forces arrive."

My eyes clouded as he spoke, and my heart grew heavy. He was not the only fool, I realized. I had seen yesterday that he had no love for this devastated land, but I had thought nothing of it. After all, which of us had not cursed the merciless sun, the dry river beds, the rocky hills? Which of us had never longed to leave the certain poverty of life here for the riches which awaited a man in America? But, like my father and grandfather before me, I had, deep in my heart, continued to love Sicily throughout every moment that I hated her for draining away my life before it had even begun.

And here was a man who didn't love her, who had clearly never loved her, and he spoke on behalf of men who had never even seen her, but who were now deciding her future.

"I'll have to get to the coast," Luciano told Vizzini.

"Will you need a guide?" Vizzini asked.

Luciano smiled at me. "No, I don't think so. I have a feeling this kid can get me just about anywhere, and he's a lot less conspicuous than any of your men. You think we could pass for father and son?"

Only that morning I would have been honored to pose as Luciano's son, but now I found the idea distasteful. "No," I said rudely. "Anyone can see you're an outsider."

He looked at me in surprise for a moment, then turned his attention back to Vizzini. My father and brothers would have been ashamed of me for speaking to Luciano like that. But then, they were dead, and I couldn't afford to worry about what they would have wanted me to do.

Luciano and Vizzini continued to make plans, deciding whom they should contact, which men should be placed in which positions, and which commodities they most wanted to control.

"It'll be like the old days," Vizzini said with relish.

"It can be better, if you plan ahead. Think big. You don't have to just milk the *latifondisti* and squash the peasants," Luciano said contemptuously. "Think like a businessman, like a politician. Once the Allies hand over a little to you, you can *take* the rest. Who's going to stop you? Not the Italians; they'll be busy losing the war. Not the Americans; they won't give a damn what happens here once they've begun their invasion of the mainland." He leaned forward, resting his elbows on the table and said, "Listen to me. You can own this whole damn island if you use your heads."

And when would *we* own it, I wondered angrily. If the Americans kept their promises to the friends of the friends—and, as Luciano had pointed out, they had no reason not to—nothing would change for people like my family. When the war ended, there would be a little more food, but no more than there had been before the war had started. As much as I hated the Fascists and the Germans, I suddenly hated the Americans more. The old men who said that none of the great powers cared what would happen to us during a battle for Sicily didn't know the half of it. We were worth less than dust to them.

I wished hotly that the Americans would never come, even if it meant living under German occupation forever. But then, a thought occurred to me. What if the Americans came and found that Luciano had failed? What if they couldn't find Vizzini, the *capo di tutti capi,* and didn't know who else to contact? Without organized cooperation from the *amici,* the battle for Sicily would be longer and bloodier, but perhaps the Americans would drive out the Fascists and Germans and leave Sicily to the Sicilians—for the first time ever.

I felt the hand of God on my shoulder, the whisper of His breath in my ear. This was my destiny. This was why Luciano had fallen out of the sky to land at my feet, why he hadn't killed me when he'd had the chance, why he had taken me with him to Vizzini.

Vizzini went to a cupboard and pulled out a map of Sicily. Luciano rose from his chair and rounded the table so he and the don could study the map together. As terrified as I was, I knew this was another sign. He was making it so easy for me, I knew that I had to do it. I stared at the two men, willing my hands to move, feeling my dinner churning in my stomach as I pictured the act in my mind.

Luciano glanced up, as if he felt the intensity of my gaze. He studied me speculatively, his expression slightly puzzled.

Vizzini finally looked up, too, and smiled lazily. "You're listening with interest, aren't you, Toto? You're a smart boy, and brave. Some day, you will be one of us. Would you like that?"

I shook my head slowly. "I don't think so. My father was one of you, and that's why he's dead."

Luciano straightened, holding my gaze. "Your father was of the Society?"

I nodded. "And my brothers, Marco and Rosario. Not important men. Not rich men, like you. We were always poor. But they were men of honor. Of loyalty."

I think Vizzini guessed the truth before Luciano—maybe because they did things differently in America. Vizzini said, "They didn't die in the war, did they?"

"No."

"Did the Fascists kill them?" Luciano asked very quietly.

I shook my head again. *"Vendetta."*

Luciano's eyes grew cold and wary. "Why are *you* still alive?"

"I killed their killers." To my shame, my voice broke as I remembered the explosion of the *lupara,* the men's abrupt screams, the splattering of shattered bone and mangled flesh, the stench of blood and death. "They were the last ones. There's no one left in my village except women and children and old men. Now it's over. We would leave, but my brother Tommaso might be alive. He might come home from the war someday, and I don't know how he would find us if we left."

Luciano's eyes flashed uneasily to the pistol which lay on the table, so near to me, so far from him.

"I can't leave," I said.

"Toto . . ." Luciano said slowly. "We could—"

"No! It's over." I picked up the pistol before he could move. "No more." My hand shook as I cocked the hammer. "You want to make us all live that way, your way, my father's way." I shook my head and whispered, "No."

"Toto." Luciano's voice was commanding, threatening. He took two steps toward me.

"Stop!" I shouted.

I smelled their blood even before I shot them. I think they both died from the first two shots I fired, for I had a good aim and they were only a few feet away, but I kept pulling the trigger until the chamber was empty. Then I dropped the gun and was instantly, violently sick.

It's a miracle that I escaped the house alive, but I was a small, pathetic-looking boy, and I doubt if Vizzini's men realized that I, and not an intruder, had killed both men until long after I had slipped out of the window and melted into the darkness.

I disappeared into the hills, stole a sheep two days later, and returned home to my mother, who clutched me so fiercely I could scarcely breathe, then beat me for being gone so long with no explanation.

The Allies invaded in July of that year, and there was such confusion and chaos that the battle for Sicily took over three months. Palermo and Messina, as well as many villages, were devastated by Allied bombing, and we were left to clean up the mess by ourselves; since the invasion of Sicily had taken twice as long as expected, the Allies were practically running after the retreating Nazis in order to make up for lost time and adhere to the plan for the Allied offensive on the Italian mainland.

Tommaso did survive the war, and he eventually came home. He had been a prisoner of war in Kenya since 1939. Although the experience had taught him to hate the British bitterly, he had fallen in love with Africa. He stayed in Sicily only long enough to marry his childhood sweetheart, then he took her back to Kenya where he started farming.

After my grandfather died, I took my mother to live in Palermo, leaving behind Serradifalco and its bitter memories—as well as Signor Cataldo and his enduring stories about the great Lucky Luciano and the gold-paved streets of America. I returned to school and eventually became the first man in my family to ever attend the university. After receiving my diploma, I worked for the government as a civil engineer, developing modern methods of distributing water throughout Sicily, so that no ordinary man would ever again have to carry water home from a public fountain because the water supply was controlled by certain "friends."

I was still a young man when the Americans, for reason known only to themselves, decided to seek out and prosecute Charles Luciano. They didn't have much luck, despite their repeated requests to the government in Rome to assist in Luciano's extradition from Sicily, where he had "escaped to" during the war.

Naturally, no one ever bothered to tell the officials from Washington or Rome that Luciano had been dead since 1943. They were, after all, outsiders.

# SINNER-SAINTS

## by Kristine Kathryn Rusch

*One of the more famous and ill-fated romances between people
in the arts was that between playwright Lillian Hellman and al-
coholic detective writer Dashiell Hammett, creator of* The Mal-
tese Falcon *and* The Thin Man.

*Here Kristine Kathryn Rusch—Hugo-and-Nebula-nominated
author, and the editor of* The Magazine of Fantasy and Science
Fiction—*examines that romance as it might have existed under
other circumstances.*

*From the unfinished autobiography of former Senator
Lillian Hellman:*

He was the most interesting man I've ever met. Even
now, decades later, I think about him at the oddest
times, when someone mixes a martini or when twilight
sun streams in my living-room window. Some people
thought I have not spoken about Dashiell Hammett because I am still keeping secrets too potent to reveal. If
I possess secrets, I do not know it. I have not spoken
of Hammett because I have too much to say.

We met when I was twenty-four years old and he
was thirty-six. I was a rebel who worked as a secretary
and had a husband who didn't understand how my re-
belliousness leaned toward politics. Hammett was the
hottest thing in Hollywood and New York.

It is not unusual to be the hottest thing in either
city—the hottest kid changes for each winter season—
but in his case it was of extra interest to those who collect people that the ex-detective who had bad cuts on
his legs and an indentation in his head from being
scrappy with criminals was gentle in manner, well educated, elegant to look at, born of early settlers, was
eccentric, witty, and spent so much money on women

that they would have liked him even if he had been none of those good things. When I met him, he was at the end of a five-day drunk and his wonderful face looked rumpled and his tall thin figure was sagged and tired. He spent no money on me. Instead, we wandered out of the restaurant in Hollywood and sat in his car all night, smoking cigarettes and talking of things I can no longer remember.

Sometimes I imagine that night we first spoke of my political career, young as it was, and he told me what he would tell me for years. "There will come a day, Lil, when they will ask you to sell out your friends." The first time he said it, I got angry and swore I would never sell out my friends, and he looked at me with a sadness I only saw in those last days in '61, in the hospital room before he died.

Those words started to haunt me in the spring of 1947 when Truman threw us back into war. J. Edgar Hoover started talking about the Communists as a fifth column, and Truman ordered his Attorney General to draw up a list. The list contained organizations with four ties—Communist, Fascist, totalitarian or subversive views—and membership in one of them would indicate that an applicant for a government job would suffer an investigation. The list was published later in the year, and opened the door for all the civil rights violations that would follow.

But in the early thirties, those far-off days were an unspeakable imagining. Most of the country lived in the deepest Depression the nation had ever seen, and only in a few isolated places—Hollywood being one of them—did people have the money to laugh and drink all night as if the twenties had never ended. I left my husband and moved in with Hammett, and for a few wild and heady years, we acted as if the Depression did not exist. Then poverty crept back into my life in the form of ragged children on roadsides, beaten men standing on corners, asking for jobs but unwilling to take a nickel from strangers, faded and aging young women begging outside grocery stores for someone to buy their babies milk.

Hammett tossed them money, but I thought about other solutions. I had studied in Bonn a few years earlier and the rise of National Socialism out of the economic ruins of Germany frightened me. For the first time I had realized I was a Jew. I went home and saw afresh how my Southern family had made its fortune on the borrowings of poor Negroes, and the roots of my rebellion dug deep. Those roots called to me on bright California afternoons as I passed defeated people hunching together in little tent villages.

Hoover made proclamations and did nothing. FDR, then a bright speck on the political horizon, quoted vague ideas that seemed to come from a wealthy man's view of the unfortunate masses. The Republicans had crashed with the market, and the Democrats were glorying in their new position instead of looking for answers. We watched the Spanish Civil War with fascination and dread—perhaps something like that would happen here. Some of Hollywood joined the Communist party. Others spoke of the virtues of Marxism. I remember all night discussions about the need for a third party, one with no ties to any other system.

During one of those all night discussions, a man by the name of Hubert Wallens asked me if I knew how such a party would start. Wallens was a dapper little man whose eyes shifted around the room as I spoke to him. I remember thinking, through the cigarette and alcohol haze, that he was merely biding time with me until someone more important came into his view. Later I learned he did this because he didn't want to miss anything happening around him. In fact, he had absorbed all of our conversation and could repeat it almost to the last word.

He told me he was raising money for a third party presidential bid, and I told him he was wasting his dollars. He would never find the right candidate, the perfect hero for which the country was looking, and the larger parties would shatter his choice into little pieces. He reminded me that his method had worked in the nineteenth century, and I reminded him that we lived in the twentieth.

Our voices must have carried over the general din of conversation because the room gradually grew quiet. I told him that third parties had to begin with the people and sweep the country, ward by ward, district by district. His money would be better spent financing small heroes who could convince small areas that the new party was better. He would have to choose heroes who would deliver, whose personal force would gather people around them. He laughed then, and said maybe I had a vision in me after all.

The conversation ended, and others began. I found Hammett at my side, looking serious. He didn't trust politicians. I knew that. Later he would say, when he refused to compromise his principles in a trial that would lead him to jail, "I better tell you that if it were more than jail, if it were my life, I would give it for what I think democracy is, and I don't let cops or judges or politicians tell me what I think democracy is."

He was drunk. His eyes had that red-rimmed look and his mouth grew tight. "You walk down this path, Lil, and you can never turn back."

He was right. I never did.

Now when I think of him, standing beside me, wearing white without a stain on him despite the long-night drunk, I wonder what he was really saying. He was a proud man who asked for nothing, but sometimes in the echoes of his words, I hear the request of a man who never made them. The night before he died, when I visited his hospital room, he reached for me as if he would never let go, and I knew then what I had been too blind to see before, that we were two of a kind and always belonged together. He had known it, and I had not.

I started to spend a lot of time with Wallens in dark rooms and dirty restaurants, plotting, planning. This much money in this ward would bring that result. Hammett disappeared into his book. He wrote the last of his five novels that year, and it wasn't until his final interview, published by the *New York Times* just after his death, that I learned he had modeled Nora Charles on me. It is nice to be Nora, married to Nick Charles, maybe one of the few marriages in modern literature where the man and woman like each other and have a fine time together. Surely the only successful marriage I ever made.

Somehow those discussions in dark rooms turned to running me as a candidate. Wallens thought me perfect. I was outspoken, mannish in my attitudes, but feminine enough to attract the male vote without alienating the female. I hesitated. I had never considered myself a political person. I was more of a rebel.

The final conversation took place at an afternoon party held at a starlet's estate. I had taken my drink beside the pool, preferring to sit in the sun while Hammett and the others argued art in the living room. The chlorine-scented water shone blue in the bright light. I closed my eyes, tired of conversation and endless parties that went nowhere, when I felt someone sit on the edge of my chair.

"See, Lil," said a voice. It was Wallens. "This life isn't for you. It bores you."

"I'm tired, Hubert," I said.

"You're tempted," he said, and I opened my eyes. With the sun at his back and the light framing him, he looked like an angel. A dark angel, I corrected myself and smiled at the reference. He thought that meant I agreed with him. "Lil—"

I raised a hand to silence him. "If I disagree with someone, I'll tell him, Hubert. If I dislike someone, chances are I'll tell him, too. If I think someone's policies stink, I say that, in public most likely and at the wrong time."

"Good," he said. "It's time for honesty in politics."

"Honesty and politics don't mix," I said. "I would hate to be the proving ground of an old cliche."

"You're as excited about this as I am," he said. "Why not run with it?"

I closed my eyes and leaned back, unable to respond. He knew me better than I thought. I was excited and tempted and scared. Fear was a great motivator. I was also young. "I'll damage the party."

"You'll help it."

"I'm better behind the scenes."

"We need someone like you out front."

The arguments were no different than they were before. But perhaps discussing them in the light, beside a rich woman's pool, gave them more credence than they had had in dark rooms. I agreed, and felt a little thrill of delight run to my stomach.

Hammett caught my arm after Wallens left and I went inside to replenish my drink. He scanned my face without asking a question. I knew from his expression that he had seen Wallens beside me. "I'm going to do it," I said. "I'm going to run."

He said nothing. I refilled my drink, a little uneasy about his lack of response. The chair beside the pool lost its allure and I wandered through the grounds, alone, thinking about what I had done. I could think of no arguments to change my mind.

Later that evening, Hammett and I had a fight in front of the remaining guests. He said it started because I objected to the way he kissed the starlet. I had seen him kiss other women before and it had never bothered me. I do remember screaming about the starlet, but I think I was angry about his silence. In everything else, Hammett had given me total support. In this, he withdrew.

He didn't come home that night, nor the next, nor the next. Sometimes, he and his friends would go on several day drunks, so that was not unusual. But he hadn't touched anything heavier than beer since he began the novel, and he had not stayed away at night in nearly a year. By the time he came home, I couldn't decide if I was hysterical with fear or with anger.

He looked as rumpled as he had the day I met him. The twilight sun streaming in from the windows caught him. His white hair, white pants and white shirt made a straight, flat surface. I thought: maybe that's the handsomest sight I ever saw, that line of a man, the knife for a nose, and I yelled at him, "So you're a Dostoevsky sinner-saint. So you are."

He said he didn't know what that meant, and it

didn't matter anyway. I could keep the apartment, he said, but he would be moving on.

Moving on, as if I were his starlet, or the women he had talked about when he began to write in the twenties. Maybe he had said that to his wife and two daughters when he left them. Or maybe he had only said it to me.

He took his books and his clothes and a few items of furniture. Not much, perhaps because he thought I had no money, or perhaps because he didn't want it. I said nothing as he left and nothing years afterward. I sank myself into my campaign with a single-minded zeal I had not realized I was capable of.

And in all those years, in all those campaigns, through all those interviews, no one said a word about Dash.

He contributed to all of my campaigns even, I later learned, when he had no money to spare. Over the years, he finished the novel, wrote screenplays, and then stopped writing at all. The party grew—especially in California—and I moved from the House to the Senate with a small group of like-minded people following me up the ranks. I was as outspoken as I had warned Wallens I would be, and usually he tolerated it, although he didn't like it as much as he thought he would. Still, I had a constituency, and the press liked me, and there was even talk, in those early days, as running me to be the first female President.

In 1941, the war came, as I had been fearing since I saw the National Socialist banners in Bonn. I supported a strike against the Nazi evil and my vehemence startled my friends, but I remembered how it felt to walk the streets of a city and be conscious that I was a Jew. I heard the stories, unsubstantiated, of camps and prisons and Krystalnachts, and I decided that Fascism had to stop, even if I wasn't certain of the methods.

I had returned to California for town meetings when an old friend told me Hammett was being shipped out in a few days. I was shocked and assumed that a bureaucratic mistake had caused a forty-eight-year-old man to fight in a war designed for the young. He was still living in the old neighborhood. Going to see him was like stepping back in time. I almost pulled the shabby door open, and stepped inside, removing my gloves and shoes and settling into a chair before lighting a cigarette.

But I did not. I rapped on the door firmly, the sound muted by my gloves, adjusted my hat like a school girl and wished for the old familiarity. I didn't like the nerves that tickled at my throat. I blamed them on thirst. When the door opened, Hammett stood before me, still thin, still handsome, eyes twinkling as if I had been the one on the two-day drunk.

"The clothes suit you, Lil," he said as he pulled open the door.

I stepped inside and removed my hat before I thought about it. The room was cluttered with books and old magazines. Gadgets of all sizes and in all states of repair leaned against the undecorated walls. Hammett lived alone. The possessions told me that. I had never expected it of him.

We had not spoken since the day he left. The old hurt was there, throbbing like a reopened wound. I longed to shout at him and have him shout back—to know that all was right in the world again.

He pulled books off a metal kitchen chair, and I sat on it, feeling prim. We stared at each other for a few minutes, unwilling to say the clichés of old lovers. Then he took a chair himself.

"So what exactly did you mean," he asked, "Dostoevsky sinner-saint?"

I told him I didn't know, and maybe at that point, I didn't. I did later, when I realized the sinning had passed—whatever sinning was—and he became the Hammett of his final years. I tried then to explain it to him, but he said it was all too religious for him.

His question wiped away the barriers and made me want to ask my own question, the one that had haunted me since he told me he was going to move on. A little plaintive whine played in my head, begging to know why he had left, what had caused him to close the door behind us. I said nothing. Hammett knew that I wanted to know. He would tell me when he was ready.

"I heard you're shipping out soon," I said, pulling off my gloves. The gesture was that of a genteel Southern Lady, a pose I adopted when I was nervous. "You know you don't have to go, Dash. I can fix whatever bureaucratic error caused the problem."

Color suffused his face, then faded, followed by an all-too-familiar smile. "No error, Lil," he said. "I enlisted."

"What?" The genteel Southern Lady was gone. In her place, the brash and brassy woman with whom Hammett had fallen in love. "You're too old, Dash. Let the children fight this war. We need you at home."

At first I thought my outburst didn't disturb him. Then he stood up and his hands were shaking. "Need me for what, Lil? To write war propoganda for the moving pictures? To show the young enlistees what kind of future they can hope for?"

"What about the scars on your lungs?" Scars he had gotten in the First World War, battling tuberculosis.

He shrugged and smiled and poured me a drink. I didn't take it. "That fire serves you well on the Hill."

"Dash, I can't let you."

The laughter stopped. He set the bottle down, looked at me with a look I hope no one ever uses on me again, and said, "I never expected you to say that."

I had been prepared to pull every string I had to keep him stateside, to keep him out of the shooting and the fighting even before I knew where he was going to go. His look made me feel like a wayward child who had disappointed an indulgent parent.

"I enlisted, the army accepted me, and I'm going to go. You can't stop me, Lil. You have no right."

I pulled my gloves back on and grabbed for my hat. My response had startled me. I spent my entire career defending the rights of people who had none and I was about to take away the rights of a forty-eight-year-old man all because I loved him. Still. "I have to go."

"Like hell," he said.

"I have meetings."

"Meetings be damned if they lead you to think you can screw with someone else's life."

He was right and I didn't know how to tell him. I could only think of getting out of the room. "I made a mistake."

"That's right," he said. "And you're going to stay here until we make sure you're not going to make that mistake again."

It took Wallens two days and half a dozen missed meetings to find me. The old gang was gone, but the all night discussions were the same. Hammett had a touch of tenderness I had forgotten, or perhaps it had appeared in the years we were apart. When Wallens called, Hammett let me go with a wave and smile, and no discussion about whether I would ever be back.

Soon after that, the first reporters asked questions. Wallens smelled a scandal—"How could you have lived with him without marrying him, Lillian?" "I was already married at the time, Hubert."—but it got buried under the weight of the war. Hammett was a war hero, even though he never fought on any front, just the idea that a man like him would enlist was enough. And I had other battles to fight in the Senate, battles that were more important than a decade-old relationship and the mistakes of a young girl.

He sent me letters from the Aleutian Islands. I have many letters describing their beauty and for years he talked about going back to see them again. He conducted a training program there for a while and edited a good army newspaper: the copy was clean, the news was accurate, and the jokes were funny. I never knew what attracted a man like him to the army. Maybe it gave him, a man who never sought out other people, a place. Maybe he felt a sense of pride that a man of forty-eight could keep pace with boys half his age. Or maybe he liked his country and felt this was a just war and had to be fought.

I never asked Hammett about his politics. It seems odd, I suppose, considering how much happened because of them. But in the early years, we discussed my political changes and in the later years, I no longer felt the need to ask. What had happened had changed us; we could not go back. I do not know if Hammett was a Communist Party member. I do think he was a Marxist. But he was a very critical Marxist, often critical of the Soviet Union in the same hick sense that many Americans are critical of foreigners. I know that, whatever he believed in, whatever he arrived at, came from reading and thinking. He took time to find out what he thought, and he had an open mind and a tolerant nature.

When we won the war, I believed that we had vanquished evil and the world was a rosy place. Perhaps that was a product of the times. I had enough knowledge of human nature to know that each of us carries our own contradictions, our own good and evil views, Dostoevsky sinner-saints on the small view, and I was fooling myself that ticker-tape parades and dead dictators could make up for willful American ignorance about death camps and Asian cities destroyed by a single bomb dropped from a great height. I rode in those parades and made speeches about the glories of our country and saw Hammett once after he returned.

He had a wildness I had never seen before, and a way of looking through me that I didn't like, and we fought about my speeches and his enlistment and we both went away sour. The memories of the days before the war were overshadowed by the new fight and the drinking.

Those weren't the only shadows. The Attorney General's list and Alger Hiss rose like specters on the collective horizon. I spoke out against them, but no longer had my fingers on the pulse. The letters from my constituents grew angry and frustrated. They wanted our party to disavow any ties with other third parties, including the Communist Party from which many of our early members had come. I refused. I found myself repeating many times during those days that I could not and would not cut my conscience to fit this year's fashions.

The test of that statement came when Hammett went

to prison in 1951. He and two other trustees of the bail bond fund of the Civil Rights Congress refused to reveal the names of the contributors to that fund. He was prosecuted for withholding information, but the truth was that Hammett had never been to the Congress' offices, and didn't know the name of a single contributor. It was his particular honor that led him to jail, and his particular honor that opened the door to all that was to follow.

Even though Hammett had written little in the last decade, the memory of his days as the hottest thing in New York and Hollywood had not faded. Reporters questioned him and his trial was big news in all the major papers. And then someone remembered the rumors about me.

The information wasn't hard to find. Hammett and I did live together twenty years before. Sometimes we acted like a married couple and sometimes we acted like roommates. In those days, when everyone would testify to anything to avoid being destroyed by a congressional committee, no one had to lie about the fact that Dashiell Hammett and I had once had a strong and passionate relationship.

But now the press wanted to know if Hammett was a Communist and if I had ever "harbored" him. The rumors were thick and damaging. Wallens called for a meeting. His offices, as the head of the party, were also in Washington, up a long windy stairway in one of the older buildings just down from the embassies. I hated going up there and would often complain that I felt as if I were going to see a Mafia don. Wallens smiled at the comparison, and toward the end, I always felt as if I wanted him to deny it.

That afternoon, he poured me a drink before talking with me. His office had no window and was dominated by a huge leather chair that a patron had given him years before. The chair even dwarfed his desk. He had a liquor cabinet off to the side, built with mahogony, just like his bookcases, and the crystal glasses were more for show than for sharing. So when he reached for them, I knew the discussion would be serious.

"Tell me about Hammett, Lil," he said as he handed me my glass.

I continued standing. The pictures decorating the office caught my eye. Wallens and I at a party fundraiser. Wallens sitting before a congressional committee. Wallens with FDR. Wallens with Truman. Wallens shaking the hand of Churchill. We had come a long way, Wallens and I. "Dash is in jail."

"I know," he said. He perched on the edge of his expensive desk. Funny how I had never questioned his money or the party's backing before. "I mean, what can you tell me about your relationship with Hammett?"

"You know about my relationship with Dash. I was living with him when you and I met."

"Yes, and we've managed to keep that quiet until now."

I remember thinking that I didn't want the surprise I felt to show on my face. I didn't know this man. I had worked with him for two decades, started a political movement with him, but I didn't know him. "I haven't kept anything quiet," I said.

"Who have you told?" His face held a kind of alarm.

"Until recently, no one has asked. The information is private, so I haven't said anything. But I don't keep things quiet, Hubert. You know that."

He knew that but had forgotten it, or had chosen to forget it. He downed his drink so fast I thought he was going to choke. "I think we need to keep it quiet now, Lil," he said. "Or it will kill us. You, me, the party, everything we've worked for."

"If I lie to protect everything we've worked for, then it's all gone anyway," I said. "We started this to be different, and I warned you that I was outspoken. The party is based on honesty. What makes you think I can lie?"

"It will make no difference to Hammett," Wallens said, and his voice had a whine I had never heard before. This was what powerful men sounded like when they begged. "He's already in jail."

"And what happens when he gets out? When someone with photographs or proof shows him that I have denied a relationship that once meant something to both of us. It cheapens me, Hubert. It cheapens the party. And it cheapens what Hammett and I had."

"What did you have, Lil?" Wallens asked, face studying the drops remaining in his tumbler. "He left when you decided to become your own woman."

"He did, didn't he." I felt around my heart the old wound I had had those days with Hammett before the war, when I let myself believe that our separation hadn't mattered, that time, patience and a bit of healing would reconcile us again. In that moment, I understood the fear and bitterness that made people sell out their friends, sell out their beliefs, to protect themselves. "But that changes nothing, Hubert. It happened. And I will not lie and say it didn't."

"Think about it," he said. "Talk to me in the morning."

"In the morning," I said. "I will not have changed my mind."

I left my drink untouched on his desk and walked down those long gloomy stairs. My feet tapped a rhythm on the wood and with each beat, I heard his demands over and over. What had caused us to go from that jubilation I had felt at the end of the war to this paranoia? What had caused Wallens to cave in to it? And what was causing me to listen to him?

By the time I reached the street I knew that I would need some other solution. The questions about Hammett would surface again and again, and I needed an answer or at least an attitude.

I thought about writing to Hammett, for he was the wisest man I knew. But he was in prison and his mail was censored, and all I needed was for some prison warden with dreams of fame to publish our mail. Still, I was angry at Hammett for his stubbornness. If he had told the truth about the bail bondsmen he wouldn't be in jail and I wouldn't be struggling with this dilemma on my own. But if he had told the truth about the bail bondsmen, he wouldn't have been Hammett.

Funny how I felt I needed him then, even though I

had struggled through other difficult questions on my own. Perhaps it was because I had been defending him or perhaps because his words were haunting me, his words on my post-war speeches, on the inevitability of the road I walked, on betrayal: *There will come a day, Lil, when they will ask you to sell out your friends.*

The day had come, a day I had been too naive to believe in.

I didn't sleep the night I saw Wallens. Instead, I wandered around my Georgetown apartment, staring at the city lights and letting my thoughts drift. In addition to Hammett's statements about loyalty, I heard my own voice claiming boldly that I did not cut my conscience to fit this year's fashions. And Hammett again, just before he went to jail, telling me that no cop or judge or politician would tell him what democracy was. No one would tell me either.

I knew that my decision would destroy the party. And I knew it would destroy my political career. But since I had discussed it with no one and since I had no backing but my own conscience, I never realized the difficulties buried in such a decision. I had always considered myself a smart and honest woman who would do what she must in difficult times. I dedicated myself to truth and sense in all things. I helped what people I could, gave back what things I could, and made policy based on my beliefs. Hammett once called me a Jeffersonian politician—one who believed not so much in the leadership of the people, but in the people's ability to choose someone with the moral courage to represent their interests. Few such Jeffersonians were left. And even fewer stood up on the Hill.

The next morning, I called a press conference. We held it in the press room on the Hill and every reporter in town appeared on very short notice. I read a prepared statement that not even my staff had seen. It was short and I had memorized it, so that I could see the faces around me as I spoke.

"In the last week, you have asked me many questions about my past. I have not answered, because in these times, an answer is often taken as a confession to a crime no one understands. I have never lied about my life. Indeed, I am proud of most of it. The way I lived before I went into public life created the politician I now am. That is, I think, a good thing."

Wallens slipped in the back of the room. His face was white, but he nodded as I spoke and I assumed I was on the right track. The reporters were scribbling furiously and beneath the podium, tape recorders whirred. A few flashbulbs went off in my face.

"Many of you have asked about my relationship with Dashiell Hammett. I cannot describe it to you because I cannot describe it to myself. We shared a home in the early thirties after I had left my husband and we had a friendship that remains, to me, special. Beyond that, I will not discuss him because you want to know about his political views and the only political views I understand are my own."

Wallens no longer looked pale, he looked sick. He leaned against the wall for support. The reporters continued scribbling. I felt as if I were lecturing a class.

I stepped back from the podium and instantly a dozen voices shouted "Senator! Senator!" For a moment, I thought of ignoring the questions, but decided that was cowardly. I had set my ground rules. I would stick to them.

The questions flew like spitballs. I could not see who fired them.

"Was Dashiell Hammett your lover?"

"Aren't you still married, Senator?"

"Are you advocating living in sin?"

"Did you know he was a Communist when you met him?"

"When will you purge your party of its 683 Communist members?"

I had stood silent before the podium, letting the questions pelt me. I did not duck, but I had no response to most of them. Finally, I heard a question I could answer.

"Are you a Communist, Senator?"

The questioner was a new, young reporter for the *New York Times*. He later became the head of his own

paper and pretended he had been a liberal his entire
life. I would remind him of his anti-Communist lean-
ings in the fifties, and he would leave me alone. Now
he stood in front of me, young and brash and full of his
position as a cub at the *Times*. His black hair tumbled
into his eyes and his sleeves were rolled above the elbow. He leaned forward with an eagerness of a dog at
the hunt.

I ignored the other questions and stared at him. "I
am not a Communist," I said. "Nor have I ever been
one. There is no Communist menace in this country
and you know it. You have made cowards into liars, an
ugly business, and the things our country stands for
and fought for in a war not ten years gone have disintegrated into the petty squabblings of frightened children. The search for a Communist under each rock and
bushel will destroy us as quickly as an atomic bomb
dropped overhead. And you who report these stories
with the glee of slavering dogs are as guilty of that de-
struction as my colleagues in Congress who do not
know that the business of running a government in-
cludes the concepts of justice, honesty and fairness no
matter what a person's political stripe."

In the silence that followed, Wallens disappeared out
the back door. The reporters stared at me, reprimanded
only momentarily. Then hands went up and the cries of
Senator! Senator! began again. I stepped away from
the podium, for good this time, and walked off the
stage.

What I remember of the next four hours has blurred
with time and pressure. People I never expected—
silent Congressmen and Senators—patted me on the
back and thanked me for speaking out. Richard Nixon
pointedly avoided me in the halls.

The headlines were grand—HELLMAN SPEAKS
OUT FOR FREEDOM. SENATOR FIGHTS BACK.
COMMUNISTS NOT A MENACE, SENATOR
SAYS—but they lasted a mere heartbeat before the
fight began again. Old pictures of me with Hammett
graced the front page of the *Times* with my young
friend's byline on the stories, claiming that I had ac-

companied Hammett to Communist Party meetings. More and more of my friends appeared before the House Un-American Activities Committee and more and more of them lied when pressed—yes, I saw Lillian Hellman at a Communist Party rally. Yes, I saw Lilly flash her Communist Party card. I did not know I had liked so many cowards. Wallens publically denounced me, and in the fall elections, the voters denounced me, too.

The days were empty. I did not retire, an elder statesman, as I had once thought my due. No one spoke to me about Washington or the Communist menace. I bought a farm in New England and retired there, away from the crowds.

Hammett sent me a letter. Two confusing sentences that I stared at for days before I finally set it aside. *I'm sorry, Lil. I should have trusted your strength.*

I did not see him again until the week before his death, although we corresponded through the remaining years. That week he was too tired for meaningful conversation and, I think, we saw no need for it. A mutual friend had told me he was alone in the hospital, his daughters refusing to come although they were paying the bill, and I went not knowing what I could find.

Disease had blunted the knife-edged handsomeness and his eyes were dulled by pain. His grip on mine was stronger than I expected. We spoke little and what we did say was of old times, of good times, when we were young. The stories had the feeling of code, the kind an old married couple uses when the tales have been remade into comforting legend. We pretended that we had had more of a life together than apart.

He died, his grip still tight upon my hand.

His daughters let me go through his papers. I found among them a scrap I thought an excised part of a story. I later realized it was part of a journal he kept on random slips of papers, scattered throughout his manuscripts. The date on it marked from the night he left me.

*Maybe the way she was looking when I walked
out the door made me reconsider. That little lost
stare on a face that had never looked lost before.
I almost went back inside. But I knew if I did
that, everything she wanted would disappear or I
would kill it, just by my presence. She wouldn't
have to betray me. We would betray ourselves.*

He had moved on because he thought our relationship would kill my dreams. Or maybe he was less noble than that. Maybe by not trusting my strength, he
failed to believe that I would defend him—defend us—
when the time came. Maybe he was afraid that my life
as a politician would offend his sense of democracy.

I sat in his office, which smelled of sickness and
pipe smoke and Hammett and clutched that piece of
paper so hard my thumb pierced it through. Our
silences—the perfect understandings of Nick and Nora
Charles—transformed into unspoken needs and wants
and led to a misunderstanding that resulted in three decades apart instead of three decades together.

When I think of Hammett, I think not of the fights
nor the silences but of the longing I felt sitting across
the table in his sloppy kitchen, my gloves and hat beside me, a glass of Scotch in my hand. I wanted to
breach the distance between us, but instead we danced
and played and argued about things that mattered only
on the periphery and not inside.

The paper sits beside me now, my rip an angry scar
along its bottom. His letter beside it, another silent request from a man who never made them, a request I
did not understand. I want to shake him for taking care
of me, yell at him for not asking what I wanted, hold
him as tightly as, in the end, he held me.

The distance remains, and the longing remains, and
the silence remains. Forever.

*Author's Note:* Some descriptions of Dashiell Hammett
were taken from Lillian Hellman's excellent autobiog-
raphies *An Unfinished Woman* and *Scoundrel Time.*

# OUT OF SIGHT

## by Janni Lee Simner

*Helen Keller is probably the most famous handicapped person
in our history. The award-winning play,* The Miracle Worker,
*showed spellbound audiences exactly how she overcame these
handicaps and was able to function in the world.*

*Now Janni Simner has created an alternate time-track in
which Helen must still deal with handicaps—but not her own.*

Susan was fastening the back of Helen's dress when
the baby started to cry. Helen lifted it from the bed,
where it lay wrapped in a soft woolen blanket. "Always crying," she muttered, positioning the infant
awkwardly in the crook of her arm. She jiggled it up
and down, as she'd seen other mothers do, but it continued to weep, hard choking sounds that shook its
small body.

"Not like that, Miss Keller. Like this." Helen
watched while Susan took the baby and drew it to her
shoulder, humming softly as she rocked it back and
forth. The baby quieted, snuggling against her cotton
blouse. It clutched the blanket with one hand. "Such a
pretty girl," Susan said, stroking its downy head. "Like
her mother." She kissed the infant lightly on the cheek,
then set it back down on the bed.

Susan started on Helen's hair, brushing the tangles
out of her long, blond curls. "Mr. Flannery came by today," she said, drawing the curls together. "He wanted
to know when he could see you."

Helen looked down at her pale, slender hands. "Rehearsals won't begin until tomorrow. Peter knows
that."

Susan laughed, twisting Helen's hair into a bun with

one quick motion. "Oh, Miss Keller, that's not what he meant. He wants to see *you*." She lowered her voice to a whisper. "You and the baby."

"I'm sure he does," Helen said. "My hat, please."

"You know what he told me?" Susan asked. Her voice rose, and she laughed again. "He told me he wants to marry you. Isn't that grand?"

"I know he does," Helen said. Her voice was flat. "I've already refused him once."

"You've already what?"

Helen looked at herself in the mirror, brushing a stray curl from her face. She grimaced. Susan had let out the tight waist of her dress, and it hung awkwardly about her hips. She'd need to lose weight by the end of the month. "My hat, Susan. And my cloak."

"Yes. Yes of course." Susan gave them to her. "You really said no?" she asked. Her eyes were wide.

Helen drew the fur-trimmed cloak around her shoulders. "Yes, Susan. I really said no. Have you sent for a cab?"

"Not yet, Miss Keller. I'll go do that now. What address shall I give?"

"I'll handle the address," Helen said. Her voice was sharp, but Susan just nodded. She looked at the baby, sleeping contentedly on the bed, then back to Helen. "Mr. Flannery's missed you, you know."

"Yes, Susan, I know. I've missed him, too. Now if you'll call that cab . . ."

"Yes, Miss Keller. Right away." Susan looked as if she were going to say something more, but then she pursed her lips together and left the room, lifting her long skirt as she walked out the door.

Helen picked up the baby once more, holding it carefully beneath her cloak. The infant stirred, but didn't wake. It felt awkward in her arms. Helen sighed. She didn't know much about babies. At the sanitarium they'd tried to teach her, but she hadn't stayed long enough to learn. She'd spent the pregnancy there, telling the public she needed to settle her nerves. Then her agent had cabled with a role for her, a lead in a new Clyde Fitch comedy opening at the end of the month.

Helen would have been a fool to turn it down. She'd returned to New York as soon as she could.

Helen shifted the baby onto her shoulder. When had she even held an infant before? There was her sister, but—Helen took a deep breath. She didn't want to think about Mildred. Trembling, she sat down on the bed and shut her eyes. But sitting there, the baby's weight on her shoulder, she couldn't help it. The memory came, so strong that it almost seemed real.

She was five years old. Outside, rain fell in steady sheets. It ran in small rivers between the trees, and even inside, Helen could smell the wet dirt. No one would let her play outside, and the light that filtered in was so dim that she couldn't bear staying in, either.

She paced the house for a while, dragging her rag doll Nancy along behind her. She discovered that when she pulled Nancy down the stairs, her bead eyes banged against the wood, making a pleasant clomping sound that echoed through the stairwell. Helen climbed up the stairs to try this again, but the nurse came out and told her to stop, that the noise was disturbing her mother. Helen didn't want to stop, so she stuck out her tongue. The nurse grabbed Helen's arm and pulled back a hand to slap her, but then Helen's father appeared behind them, and the nurse drew her hand away. Helen's father carried her back downstairs.

Helen wriggled out of his arms, onto the soft blue couch. Her father picked her up again, setting her down on his knee. His gray beard scratched Helen's face, but she never minded that. He bounced her gently up and down, and Helen, settling back against him, asked, "Papa, what will the baby look like?"

Her father brushed a yellow curl from her face. "A lot like you, I suppose. Only smaller. Unless it's a boy, of course."

Helen thought about that. From all the warnings she'd received about how she'd better behave once the baby was born, how she shouldn't disturb the baby or her mother, she'd figured she'd find a monster when she entered her mother's room. She tried to picture a tiny girl instead, so small it fit in the palm of her hand. The thought was so funny she laughed aloud, and her father laughed with her, his deep voice filling the room. Helen snuggled contentedly against him.

Later, when one of the servants finally led Helen to her mother, what she saw wasn't a monster, and it wasn't a little girl who could fit in the palm of her hand. Wrapped in its blankets, the small red thing looked more like a doll than anything else.

Helen picked it up. The baby felt warm and heavy against her shoulder. She liked it better than Nancy. Helen's mother, looking pale and thin against the pillows, told her the baby's name was Mildred.

Helen cast her doll aside to play with her new sister. She spent hours, sitting beneath the magnolias outside the house, running a brush through Mildred's fine brown hair. She fed her with a small silver spoon. She even rocked Mildred to sleep in Nancy's cradle, which fit Mildred so well that Helen's parents stopped using the larger one they'd brought in from the shed.

"What a good girl she's become," Helen's mother said, watching Helen play. "Not at all the wild thing I feared she was turning into." The servants, when her mother talked like this, always nodded. They began to smile at Helen, too, when before they'd mostly scolded. All this, of course, made Helen love Mildred all the more. She played with her whenever she could.

Then Mildred got sick. She was sick for a long time. And when she got better, everything changed.

"Miss Keller? Miss Keller, your cab is here."

Helen blinked, focusing once more on the bedroom, on the polished wooden dresser and the mirror that hung beside it. Looking out the windows, she could see the bare treetops of Central Park in the distance. The gray sky promised snow, but for now only a stiff wind blew, shaking the bare branches. The buildings outside were much like Helen's own, low brick structures with two or three apartments to a floor. Thin metal trolley tracks ran along the paved streets between them.

"I'm coming," Helen said. She followed Susan downstairs.

Susan opened the outside door, and the wind hit Helen at once. Helen struggled to pull the cloak tighter around her. It was awkward, with one hand holding the baby on her shoulder. The infant whimpered at the cold, and Helen made certain the cloak covered it completely.

The cab was waiting; the brown horse hitched to it breathed clouds of frosty air. The driver, a middle-aged man with a thick brown mustache, climbed down when he saw them. He took his hat from his head and bowed slightly. "Miss Keller?" he asked.

"Yes," Helen said. She nodded at Susan, who silently reentered the building.

"This way," the driver said, and Helen followed him to the carriage. He looked at her a moment, then asked, "You're not really Helen Keller, are you? The Broadway actress?"

"Yes, that's me," Helen said, more sharply than she'd intended. She hoped he couldn't make out the bundle beneath her cloak. She didn't want word to get around, not with a play opening so soon.

"My wife's talked about you," the driver said, his voice rising. He gestured eagerly. "I'm not into the theater much myself, but she saw you in that Shaw play, *Mrs. Warren's Profession*, before the police shut it down. That was about a year ago, wasn't it?"

Helen nodded. She shivered, and the baby stirred at her sudden movement. Helen prayed it wouldn't cry.

The driver rambled on. "I never did understand all that fuss. Anyway, my wife says you were very dynamic, lots of energy. Dynamic—that's the sort of word theater people use, isn't it?"

"Yes," Helen said. "Yes it is." Her teeth chattered as she spoke.

"Oh, I'm sorry, Miss Keller. Here I am talking on and on, leaving you out in the cold. Here, I'll help you up." He opened the cab door, reaching out a hand for Helen. "If you give me the address," he said, "we'll be on our way."

Helen handed him a folded slip of paper she'd tucked behind her belt. His eyes widened as he read it, but he only said, "I'm going to tell my wife I met you. She won't believe me, but I'm going to tell her anyway." He stepped back, swinging the door shut behind him. Helen blinked, adjusting to the dim light. The cab jolted forward as they started moving; Helen could hear the horse's hooves clopping against the pavement.

She sighed and leaned back. She certainly wasn't feeling very dynamic. All she'd wanted to do, since returning to New York, was sleep. Well, rehearsals began tomorrow. Maybe that would wake her up.

Helen closed her eyes. Faint white sparkles danced in front of them, reminding her of—

She sat bolt upright, eyes wide open again, fighting the memory. But in the darkened cab, she couldn't stop it. Faintly, she heard her father's voice.

"The baby can't see," her father said. "The baby can't hear."

They were sitting outside on the steps. The air was warm, but the leaves were beginning to drop from the branches, letting the pale blue sky show through where they fell. Helen leaned back against her father, squirming uncomfortably. The doctor had just left, and in the house, her mother was crying.

"You mean Mildred can't open her eyes?" Helen asked, trying to understand. She shut her own eyes, so tightly that bright white sparks danced in front of them. She could still hear, though—the birds chittering back and forth, the clipping of the gardener's shears as he walked among the trees. She couldn't imagine not seeing and hearing both.

Helen opened her eyes. In the bright sunlight, she had to blink several times before she could see again.

"It will be hard," her father said. "There'll be a lot of things Mildred won't understand. Since she can't talk now, she'll probably never learn. You're her big sister, Helen. Will you help us take care of her?"

Helen nodded. She wondered what it would be like to close her eyes and never open them again.

"All right," her father said. "Let's go in to your mother, then." He stood, and Helen, reaching for his hand, followed him into the house.

In the months that followed, Helen helped out as well as she could. At first, nothing seemed very different. Helen still brushed Mildred's hair, still rocked her to sleep. Mildred no longer looked up when Helen entered the room, not unless Helen's footsteps were hard enough to shake the floor, but as soon as Helen picked her up, Mildred knew who she was and gurgled happily. Or tried to gurgle; as she grew older, she made noises less and less often, until all that remained was her laugh, a high wheezing giggle that Helen never forgot.

Then Mildred started walking, and wouldn't let Helen hold her anymore. She began bumping into things, or reaching for objects that were hot or had sharp edges. She knocked things off shelves, too, glass and china that shattered onto the floor.

Helen felt bad for her. When she had been younger, she'd knocked things down a lot, too, even though she could see. She still did sometimes, when she ran too fast across a room. Her mother always yelled at her, and told her to act like a lady.

No one yelled at Mildred. Helen understood that; Mildred couldn't hear them. What Helen didn't understand was why she got yelled at instead.

Like on her tenth birthday. Helen's mother had made a cake, chocolate with white icing, and after dinner her father sliced it. Mildred sat beside Helen, sucking on a ribbon she'd pulled off her dress. She didn't stop when the cake was set in front of her, not until her mother walked up and put a fork in her hand.

As usual, Mildred threw the fork to the floor and reached for the cake with her hands. Helen's mother sighed, but sat back down and didn't try to stop her. Mildred shoved a handful of cake into her mouth, smearing it on her face and collar. Bits of white icing stuck to her hair. Mildred giggled, and reached for more cake.

Helen looked away, focusing on her own cake instead. She held her fork as her mother had taught her, cutting off a neat slice of cake and eating it slowly. One neat piece, then another. Before she could take a third, Mildred reached in and grabbed some of Helen's cake for herself. Helen cried out, but Mildred, not hearing, reached for another handful.

Helen jumped to her feet, taking her plate with her. Mildred, reaching out again and feeling only the linen tablecloth, struck out with her arms, spilling Helen's glass. As the maid rushed over to wipe up the lemonade, Mildred threw her own plate to the floor. It shattered beside her chair. She started pounding on the heavy oak table, so hard that it shook. Tears ran down her cheeks, leaving red splotchy marks. Her mouth was open, and she breathed deep, heaving breaths.

Helen's mother darted up, grabbing Mildred by the shoulders and whispering, "Hush, baby. Don't cry." She was the only one who still talked to Mildred; Helen couldn't understand why.

Mildred continued to thrash, kicking as well as punching now, and her mother stroked her hair. "Helen, come here," she said. "Share your cake with your sister."

Helen had no problem with sharing, but grabbing was another matter. "It's my cake," she said fiercely, shoving a forkful into her mouth. "Mine!"

Her mother let go of Mildred and wrenched the plate out of Helen's hands. Helen's fork clattered to the floor. "You'll listen when I talk to you. If I say to share with your sister, you'll share."

"That's not sharing," Helen said, staring at the empty space in front of her. "That's taking."

Her mother set Helen's plate in Mildred's lap, but Mildred threw it across the room. It knocked over the flower vase, and water trickled across the tablecloth.

"I want more cake," Helen said.

Helen's mother ignored her, picking Mildred up and setting her down on the floor. "Don't cry," she said. "It's all right. Mama's here." She reached down to stroke Mildred's face, but Mildred pushed her away. "All right," Helen's mother said, sounding suddenly tired. "Go cry yourself out, if that's what you're going to do." She turned and looked over to Helen.

"How many candles were on that cake?" she demanded.

"Ten," Helen said, wondering what candles had to do with anything.

"Ten years," her mother said. "You're ten years old today. A young lady. You're not a baby, a baby who can't even see or hear. Mildred can't help herself. I expect more from you."

"More than what?" Helen asked, wondering if this meant she wouldn't get any more cake. It wasn't fair. It was her birthday, not Mildred's.

Helen's mother sighed, pushing her hair back from her face. "You may leave the table," she said. "You can come back when you understand."

Helen opened her mouth to protest, but her father called, "Come here, Helen. Come sit with me a while."

Helen followed him from the room, through an open archway. He sat on the couch, and Helen sat beside him. She wouldn't look at him, though, not even when he set her in his lap.

She stared back into the dining room. Mildred had stopped crying, and her mother sat beside her on the floor. She wrapped her arms around Mildred, rocking her back and forth. Mildred leaned back against her mother, falling into a fitful sleep.

Helen's father ran his fingers through Helen's hair. He began whispering in her ear, telling her how she should try to understand, how it wasn't Mildred's fault. Helen didn't listen. She watched her mother, holding Mildred to her chest, humming softly.

I understand, Helen thought, the taste of chocolate bitter in her mouth. I understand perfectly.

"Miss? Miss Keller?"

The voice jarred Helen awake. She blinked and looked up. The driver stood by the open carriage door, his thick brows wrinkled together. Behind him, tall brick buildings stretched into the gray sky, their windows cracked, their shutters swinging loose on the hinges. Light snow had started to fall, coating the street with a layer of white. A few men pushed carts along the uneven stones, bending their heads against the cold. A wind gusted into the cab, carrying with it the smell of sweat and bad whisky.

"You sure this is the place?" the driver asked.

"Yes," Helen said. She stepped down into the street. The movement woke the baby, and it began to whine.

The driver started at the sound. He stared at Helen, making no move to depart.

"You can go now," Helen said. "You were paid before we left."

The driver frowned. "I assumed you wanted me to wait. It's a bad neighborhood for—"

"No," Helen said. "There's no need." She didn't want anyone waiting around. She didn't want anyone to know where she was going.

The driver continued, as if he hadn't heard, "This isn't the place for a lady like you—"

"You can go," Helen said, her voice taking on more of an edge. The baby was still crying.

The driver shoved his hands into his pockets. He shifted awkwardly. "All right, Miss Keller. But you take care, okay?"

He climbed back onto the cab, watching her. He hesitated a moment, then flicked the reins. The cab moved slowly off.

Helen stood there a moment, looking down the street, repeating to herself the directions that she'd memorized. Then she started walking. The baby squirmed, and Helen had to hold it with both arms to keep it from wriggling away. Her cloak flapped up behind her, and the wind cut through her dress.

She turned off the main street and into an alley, where trash overflowed battered cans, spilling onto the unpaved dirt. Five and six story buildings rose up on either side, clotheslines strung across their rusting fire escapes. A child leaned against one of the buildings, her feet bare on the snow-dusted ground, her dress barely covering her knees. Two men sat a little farther

on, hunched over a small fire. The air smelled of
smoke and rotting meat. Helen shivered, and pulled the
baby closer. It drooled on her shoulder. The moisture
soaked through her blouse, feeling cold and clammy
against her skin.

The place Helen wanted was a block farther on, near
the corner where the alley opened back onto the street.
It was only two stories high, a squat little building
squeezed between higher neighbors. The sign nailed to
the bricks was completely faded, the wood worn
smooth by the storms of many winters. Paint was peeling off the door. Helen raised her hand to knock on it.

And hesitated. She looked down at the baby. It had
stopped crying, and was sucking on a ribbon that hung
from Helen's blouse. Saliva dribbled out one corner of
its mouth. Helen should have been disgusted, but she
wasn't. She stared at the infant's small fingers, clutching the woolen blanket, at the brown fuzz that covered
its head. Susan had been right; it was a beautiful baby.
Helen wiped its mouth, ran one finger along its smooth
cheek. She could feel it breathing softly against her
chest. She almost turned around.

But even as Helen considered it, she knew she had
to knock. There was nothing else she could do. Not after Mildred. Not after what Helen had done.

Another teacher was leaving. Helen knew by the
suitcases in the hall, by the way the bed in the guest
room had been stripped bare, though the servants nor-
mally didn't go upstairs until after lunch. Besides,
Mildred had locked her teacher in the guest room for
the third time in a week, and unable to find the key, her
father had had to carry Miss Sullivan out the window.

Mildred had developed a fascination with keys.
She'd locked her mother in the pantry less than a
month ago. Her mother had pounded furiously on the
door, while Mildred sat outside, giggling. She didn't
understand, Helen's father had later said, that being
locked in the closet caused her mother any distress.
She only knew that she liked the vibrations the pounding caused, when the door and the wooden floor shook.

Helen thought about her own teacher, a tutor who visited three times a week. She was a severe woman, with gray hair tied on top of her head and thin lips pursed close together. Helen didn't like her. Yet she'd been Helen's teacher for four years, since she was twelve. Mildred's teachers never lasted more than a few months.

Helen had liked Mildred's teacher this time. She was young, with dark hair and thick glasses. She'd successfully taught a blind and deaf student in Boston, Helen's mother had said, a young girl who had died of tuberculosis two winters ago.

The new teacher had tapped words into Mildred's hand, like many of the others, but unlike the others she wouldn't stop when Mildred cried. She had punished Mildred, too, when she ate from other people's plates, or pulled Helen's hair, or knocked things off the shelves. Helen's parents had complained, but they hadn't interfered.

It didn't matter. Day after day the teacher had spelled into Mildred's hand, and day after day Mildred hadn't understood. Her tantrums had grown worse than ever. Helen, her mother, and Miss Sullivan all had the bruises to prove it.

In the living room, Helen heard voices. Miss Sullivan and her parents, settling on a final payment. Helen sighed, and started up the stairs.

The door to her bedroom was locked. Helen knocked, then pounded. From the other side of the door, she heard giggling. There was a crash, and silence for a while, and then Mildred started laughing again.

Helen flew down the stairs two at a time. Her boots banged loudly against the wood. "Do be quiet!" her mother called from the other room. "Act like a lady."

Helen didn't care how much noise she made. Mildred was in her room, throwing her things about, and she couldn't get in to stop her. Helen ran outside, slamming the door behind her. The sky was gray, with dark clouds moving in from the west. The trees were thick with green leaves, and the air smelled of dirt and summer thunderstorms.

The ladder was still outside the guest room, and Helen dragged it to her own window. She climbed up slowly, the soles of her boots sliding on the wooden rungs. At the top, she pushed her window open and looked inside.

Mildred sat in the middle of Helen's room, facing the door. Broken pottery lay scattered about, the remnants of a china doll, of a piggy bank Helen's father had given her, into which she'd put the first penny she'd ever owned.

Helen pulled herself through the window, tumbling to the floor. Mildred must have felt something, for she stood and turned around. She was tall now, and her brown hair fell past her waist. She'd shot up the past year. Like a beanstalk, Helen's father said.

Mildred had something in her arms. A pile of rags—it was Nancy, Helen's old doll. A tight feeling settled in Helen's stomach. It took her a moment to recognize the feeling as anger. Why should she be angry because Mildred held a doll that Helen herself hadn't touched in years?

Helen stared at her sister. Outside, there was a low rumble of thunder, and rain began to fall, gusting in the open window. Mildred returned to the floor, setting the doll in her lap. She pulled on one of the legs, harder and harder, until the leg came free with the sound of tearing cloth. The sound made Helen's stomach tighter, twisting the anger into something so hard it hurt. Mildred giggled and threw the leg across the floor. She began pulling on Nancy's head.

"No!" Helen flew across the room, wrenching the doll from Mildred's hands. Mildred screamed, a strange guttural sound, and lunged at Helen. She knocked her sister to the floor, so hard that for a moment she couldn't breathe. Helen almost yelled for her parents, but she knew what her mother would say. "You're not a little girl. Mildred doesn't know any better. Leave your sister alone."

Something about the words made the knot in Helen's

stomach burst, turned it into a white hot rage. She threw Mildred down, pinning her shoulders to the floor. Mildred tried to twist away, but Helen held her tightly, so tightly her fingers dug into Mildred's flesh. A roaring sound raced through Helen's ears, drowning out the gurgling noises Mildred made. Helen shook her sister, shook her hard, and for once, no one tried to stop her. Mildred's head hit the floor once, twice, three times, but Helen kept going, even when Mildred stopped fighting and hung limp in Helen's hands, like a doll.

Helen heard someone pounding on the door, but the sound seemed distant, not real. Then the door crashed open and Helen's mother was there, wrenching Mildred from Helen's arms. She slapped Helen, and Helen fell backward, rubbing the spot where the blow stung her face.

Helen watched as her mother took Mildred into her lap. Her mother looked down at Mildred, an awful, fierce look on her face. She brushed Mildred's damp hair back from her forehead, kissed her softly on one cheek. Her mother was crying, Helen realized, tears streaming down her face.

Mildred, in her mother's lap, never stirred.

Helen's father stood in the doorway. He silently entered the room, kneeling by her mother's side. Her mother buried her face in his shoulder, breaking into loud, choking sobs. Helen's father held her tightly, rocking her back and forth. He wouldn't look at Helen.

Helen watched them with growing horror. Mildred's still body, her mother's face red from weeping, even her father crying. Helen backed away, realizing what she'd done. The awful tightness returned, twisting her stomach into painful knots.

She couldn't bear it. She flew past her parents, down the stairs, threw the door open and ran outside. The rain soaked through her dress, but she didn't care. She ran as fast as she could, through the muddy fields. She kept seeing Mildred's small body, limp in her mother's lap. She wished she could run faster.

She ran for a long time, until well after dark, when

the rain stopped and the air was still. Even then, Helen couldn't face her parents again. So she climbed the ladder to her room one more time, packing some clothes in an old carpetbag. She crept downstairs, into her father's office. Though she felt sick all the while, she took some money from his middle desk drawer, the one he used when paying the bills.

She boarded a train at the nearest station, not really caring where it went.

She'd stolen more money than she'd realized. Three days later she was in New York.

Helen stared at the worn wooden door, one hand still poised to knock, the other holding the baby. It was sleeping again, its face warm and soft against her neck. Helen was shaking, as if she had only just stopped running, as if it hadn't really been ten years ago. The years in between seemed a numb blur, not as real as the awful thing that had sent her running in the first place. Once in New York, she'd taken whatever work she could find—mending clothes, waiting tables, singing in an underground saloon—and one thing had led to another. She'd had talent, but she'd also been lucky. That happened in theater sometimes.

Helen took a deep breath, steadied her hand, and knocked on the door.

She heard footsteps. The door flew open, letting out a smell of sweat and decay. Like the odor in the alley, only stronger, more human. A man stood in the doorway. His shoulders were stooped, his face drawn and tired. "Yes?" he said. His voice was thin, irritable. Somewhere in the dim rooms behind him a woman screamed and was silent.

Helen's mouth felt dry. She swallowed. "The baby," she said. "I want you to take it."

The man studied Helen intently. "Is it deranged?" he asked.

"No," Helen said. "No, it isn't."

The man's face hardened. "This is an asylum, Miss, not a nursery. If you're unwilling to care for this child, it is not our affair."

"But I can't—" Helen's throat tightened. She continued, her words hoarse sobs. "Its eyes. Look at its eyes. It can't see."

She couldn't raise a blind child. Not on her own, not with Peter, though he was honorable enough that he would marry her. She couldn't—not after Mildred. The baby would be better off here.

The infant stirred. Helen brushed the cloak aside and took it in both arms. The man stretched out a finger to the child. It didn't grasp it, not until he touched the small palm. He passed his hand in front of the baby's face, once, twice, three times. The child did not respond. He snapped his fingers. The baby started at the sound, but did not blink.

"Very well," the man said at last. "We'll take the child. If you're certain you wish to leave it with us."

"Yes," Helen said. "Yes, I'm certain."

But her arms ached as she handed him the child. He held it in the crook of his arm, jiggling it up and down. The baby started to cry. The man turned away from Helen without speaking. He stepped back inside, slamming the door shut behind him. Through it, Helen thought she could hear hard, choking sobs.

"Not like that," Helen whispered, staring at the door. "Like this." She moved one hand to her shoulder. It felt damp and warm. She pulled her arms tightly around herself.

The snow continued to fall, dusting her shoulders with white. Helen shivered. She turned, pulled her cloak tighter about her, and started for home.

# MOTHER, MAE I?

## by Lawrence Schimel

*Imagine the least likely place to find the most notorious blonde bombshell, the immortal Mae West. Which is precisely what Lawrence Schimel did.*

"Oh how the women
grip and stretch
fainting on the horn."

—Anne Sexton, "The Little Peasant"

## I. Matins—The Start of the Hunt

It was barely detectable under her black nun's habit as she walked across the Cuxa Cloister, novice in tow, but Mae West still had a whisper of that "wiggle" which had brought her fame. She blinked as they entered the tapestry room, letting her eyes adjust to the dim interior, then turned to the novice. "You're sure this is what ya saw?"

"Yes, Mother."

Mae looked back at the tapestry in front of them, her mind racing. "Ridden by a pregnant gal?"

"Yes, Mother."

"Don't you know that's impossible?"

"Yes, Mother."

"Then how can you say you saw it?"

"How can we say that rain falls from the sky, or the sun rises every day? I am sure of what I saw: a unicorn—like that one—with a pregnant woman on his back."

Mae sat down under the window and thought. The stained glass cast colored shadows across her habit and the wooden bench. The novice waited expectantly for an answer, an explanation of her vision. Mae thought for a long time. Hard. At last she looked up at the novice and said, "It had to have been the Madonna."

"The Virgin?"

"Exactly. It's the only way this makes any sense. Only a virgin can ride a unicorn, and Mary's the only gal to stay one even after she was pregnant. The poor thing."

"But why did I see her?"

"I'm still working on that one."

## II. Prime—The Unicorn at the Fountain

"Mother Mae! Mother Mae!" Angela came running into the Bonnefont Cloister where Mae sat in contemplation of the definition of sin. "It happened again. But only the unicorn. Oh, what am I going to do? Am I going crazy? It's one thing to have visions of the Virgin, but to see unicorns?"

"If ya can believe in a virgin birth, why's it so hard to also believe in unicorns?"

"Then it's real? Oh, Mother Mae, why has it come for me? Have I done something wrong? If I have, it was done in ignorance! I swear it!" Angela clapped her hand to her mouth, suddenly realizing that swearing was a sin.

"Siddown child," Mae ordered, getting up to allow the novice to sit in her place. "I wanna explain three things to ya. First, I wanchya to relax. Ya can't think straight if you're all nerves like this, and I need ya to tell me everythin' you can 'bout what ya saw." Mae held up two fingers. "Second, always remember: it's better to be looked over than overlooked. An' lastly: just 'cause you saw it doesn't mean it's come for ya."

Angela relaxed visibly at the last. "Then it might have come for someone else?"

"Exactly."

"But who?" Mae didn't say anything. Could it be

her? the novice thought. "But—but considering your past . . ."

"Women with 'pasts' interest men because men hope that history will repeat itself."

"But this is a unicorn we're dealing with—not a man."

The look Mae gave her said: You have so much left to learn. What Mae actually said was, "What we're dealing with is Christ."

### III. Terce—The Unicorn Leaps the Stream

They were back in the tapestry room. "Let's start with the basics," Mae began to lecture. "The unicorn is Christ, represented by the whiteness and purity. I used to be Snow White—but I drifted. An' now I've drifted back.

"Anyway, we've got seven tapestries that show a unicorn being hunted. He's killed in the sixth tapestry, an' yet, he appears again, alive, in the seventh. A metaphor for Christ's resurrection. You'll notice the obvious wounds on the unicorn in this last tapestry, representing His stigmata, although some secularists suggest that they're the drippings of the pomegranates under which he's sitting.

"Here in the second tapestry the unicorn is removing the serpent's venom from the water, just as Christ redeemed mankind from the Fall caused by that first serpent in Eden. Here in this fragment—sadly all that remains of the fifth tapestry—there's an apple tree in the center of the garden where the unicorn is captured at last. An' here, as the dead unicorn is brought to the castle, he's got a crown of thorns round his neck."

"Why does she do it? She must have been especially pure and good to have attracted a unicorn. How could she let them kill him like that?"

"Goodness had nothing to do with it—she just had to make him believe she was virgin."

"You can almost see the betrayal in her eyes. Why did he go to her?"

Mae laughed. "When women go wrong, men go right after them. But that's not the virgin who's catching the unicorn. She's not shown in these fragments, though you can see her hand around the unicorn's neck as she strokes his mane. That woman you see is the one who's on top of things. She was likely the virgin's lady-in-waiting, but in this she's in charge. She's the worldly one. She has the power. Look how she gives the signal that the unicorn can be taken."

Angela shivered. "And the unicorn is supposed to be Christ still? Betrayed by a woman."

"Notice the A and backwards E sewn into the background in the left fragment. It appears in every tapestry, often many times. It even appears as the insignia on the dog's collar, here. It's another symbol for Christ, who said 'I am the Alpha and the Omega.' The beginning—"

"And the end," a voice said behind them. "If it isn't my little chickadee instructing a friend o' hers. How do, ladies?"

Angela spun around at the voice, having thought they were alone. She imagined her jaw gaped, although was not sure. "Ar—aren't you W.C. Fields?" she stammered at last.

"Why, yes, so I am. And you are, love?"

"Mother Angela." She blushed. "Or I will be soon."

"Mother Angela. Lovely name, and quite appropriate for a nun."

Angela gestured to his own outfit. "I never knew you'd been ordained."

"I joined for the Holy Water, m'dear." He lifted a flask to her in a toast, took a swallow, and left the courtyard.

## IV. Sext—The Unicorn Defends Himself

"And you, Mother Mae? Why did you become a nun? If I may ask you that," Angela added hastily.

"That's what I'm here for, ain't it? To give you an education." Mae gave a thoughtful look toward the archway Fields had disappeared through, as she eased into another lecture. "It happened just after the war. Y'see my husband was one of the first men to get killed overseas, and it really got to me. Now, most people never knew I had a husband an' that's the way I wanted it. Marriage would've ruined my career, an' I wasn't about to let it. I needed to keep my public happy, make 'em believe I belonged strictly to them.

"I never liked the man much, didn't wanna marry him in the first place, but I was young an' out on the vaudeville circuit. There was talk, naturally, since I was gettin' the attention of every man everywhere I went. An', well, one day it just happened. Marriage can do that to ya sometimes.

"Allow me to tell ya a little story. My father was a street fighter. He fought in the ring since he was eleven years old an' he was always ready to do physical violence when the urge came upon 'im. He was known as Battlin' Jack West, Champion of Brooklyn. But he gave it up when he married my mother. He became a businessman. Had a livery stable business: carriages, surreys, an' coaches for hire, an' in winter horse-drawn sleighs with jingle bells. How's that for a fightin' man? Marriage saps the life out of 'em, makes men respectable. Notice the unicorn in the final tapestry's got a collar round his neck. He's not just enclosed, but chained to a tree. There's no way he can break free.

"These tapestries were a marriage gift. The F and the R at the top of the third tapestry are the initials of the couple, an' all over there're symbols of fertility an' love. There're dogs in almost every tapestry, for the loyalty they show their master. Here at the fountain there's a lion with his mate, again symbolizin' fidelity in love. This little rabbit over here is renowned for his fertility, as are these goldfinches, or the pomegranates with their luscious red fruits an' abundance of seeds. Ya might say there's marriage in the air, in these tapestries.

"An' while marriage wasn't right for me when it happened, soon as it was gone I felt somethin' was missing. I wasn't satisfied with my life in Hollywood.

The reality of a star's life isn't all glamour. I lived a quiet life. I didn't go out much. Yes, I had my men, but a star's life is very lonely. Everyone's in love with who you are on the screen, no one wants who you really are. An' I'd been missing New York like crazy, even though it brought back memories of my mother. So, I came 'home' an' joined our Order, resolved that this time I would honor my vows." Mae sighed. "I'd even lied about my age for the marriage certificate.

"But the real reason," she said, winking, "was I'd heard so much about Christ's Passion, I wanted to sample some for myself."

## V. Nones—The Unicorn is Captured by the Maiden

"I still don't understand why I have these visions," Angela complained as they walked back out to the Bonnefort Cloister.

"What puzzles me is the double Christ. Not that I'm complainin'. I'm used to having more than one man in my life, an' since I'm married to Him, the more the merrier, I say."

"How are there two of them?"

"In your first vision, the unicorn was one, an' the unborn child the other. The only things I can think of it standin' for are the Resurrection or the extra Messiah from the Second Comin'. Unless Mary got herself knocked up by God again." She looked thoughtful a moment. "Which, I guess, would be *her* second comin'." It was a variation on an *old* joke, but Mae guessed that Angela had never heard any of them. And she was there to provide the girl with an education, wasn't she?"

Angela did not notice, asking, "What does this mean? Why has He chosen me that I am receiving visions of the Second Coming?"

"*He* hasn't chosen you for anythin'. *I* have."

"I don't understand—"

Mae pointed over Angela's shoulder. "Look."

Angela turned around. The unicorn had entered the

garden and was approaching them. He looked exactly like the one in the tapestries, tall and white and regal. Angela turned back to Mae to ask what she had meant, but forgot as she watched Mae pull a lasso from under her habit.

"Ya don't make so many Westerns without picking up a few tricks," Mae said, lifting the rope over her head.

Angela figured out on her own what Mae had chosen her for. She was the bait. The virgin lure. And now . . .

"No! How can you—"

But it was too late. Mae had already let fly the rope, which landed perfectly around the unicorn's neck.

"You should see me twirl a six-shooter."

## VI. Lauds—The Unicorn is Killed and Brought to the Castle

"So, is that a horn in your pocket, or are ya just glad to see me?" Mae began slowly coiling the rope, pulling the unicorn to her from across the garden.

"What are you going to do with him?" Angela asked angrily.

"What comes naturally. Ya never saw my play *Catherine Was Great,* didja? Fascinatin' woman. She rules thirty million people and had over three thousand lovers. I did the best I could in two hours."

The unicorn now stood between the two of them, and he looked from one to the other as if he were deciding between them. He stretched his neck out to sniff at Angela's habit. Mae put her hand out to stroke his neck, reminding him of her presence with a simple yet calculated caress. The unicorn took a step toward her and nuzzled her hair.

"Glad to see me, then," Mae said, gloating just a little bit at her victory. "I like that in a man. Or a horse."

The unicorn tossed his head. "Careful there, fella." Mae turned to the novice. "It's been swell, kid, but the two of us 're gonna make tracks now. Take care of

y'rself. Too many girls follow the line of least
resistance—but a good line is hard to resist." Mae
turned to leave the cloister. Over her shoulder she said,
"Don't be a stranger. If you've got nothin' to do, an
plenty of time to do it in, come up 'n' see me sometime. We'll compare notes on Christ or somethin'."
The unicorn bumped Mother Mae with his neck, as if
he were trying to keep her in the cloister. Mae smiled
at Angela over his shoulder. "Give a man a free hand
and he'll try and put it all over you."

Angela didn't know what she could do. She wondered if the maiden in the tapestries had felt so frustrated when she found out she'd been used. Had she
cried out when they led the unicorn off to be killed?
Was there anything she could do to stop this? Mae had
picked up the rope again to lead the unicorn away. She
also plucked a rose, and held it before him as an en-
ticement.

But the unicorn didn't want to go. Did he know what
Mother Mae planned? Angela wondered. She felt like
she had to do something. But what?

Before she could do anything, however, the unicorn
reared back, and then pierced Mae through the chest
with his horn. Angela gasped. What she'd tried to stop
had happened anyway. The unicorn killing Mother
Mae was just as bad as Mother Mae killing the unicorn. How could she know what Mother Mae's plans
had been? Maybe they were completely innocent.
Angela wrung her hands in frustration. What could she
do, but stand there and watch in horror?

Mae looked down at the horn extruding from her
chest, rather shocked. But then she smiled. "I do," she
cried out, tossing the rose up into the air. "Oh, how I
do!"

It was terribly small for a bouquet, but Angela
caught it anyway. After all, the unicorn might have
worked up an appetite by the time he was done.

Watching the pair of them, Angela felt a tingle of
Christ's Passion as well. Was it envy? No, Angela
thought, as she looked down at her hand and smiled.
One of the rose's thorns had pierced her finger. "I

never knew a rose by any other fame could feel so sweet," she whispered.

## VII. Vespers—The Unicorn in Captivity

Angela looked up at the sound of hoofbeats in the St. Guilhem Cloister. A shadow passed the doorway to the Fuentidueña Chapel where she was praying. She smiled as she watched Mother Mae riding off into the sunset on the unicorn's back. "She's still so Hollywood sometimes." Angela wondered where they would go for the honeymoon. The Garden of Eden to rediscover original sin, if Mae had anything to say about it.

Angela sighed and returned to the evening prayers, remembering that it had been a fortunate fall. She couldn't have married Christ herself, otherwise.

However, Temptation whispered in her ear, if Sloth had been the original sin she could be in Eden right now.

# THE *DEFIANT* DISASTER

## by Kate Daniel

*Amelia Earhart, whose life ended in a mysterious plane crash, was the most famous female pilot of the first half of the twentieth century. Author Kate Daniel brings her back in this alternate timeline to see if she truly possessed The Right Stuff.*

### Courage

Courage is the price that Life exacts for granting peace.
The soul that knows it not, knows no release
From little things.
Knows not the livid loneliness of fear
Nor mountain heights where bitter joy can hear
The sound of wings.

How can Life grant us boon of living, compensate
For dull gray ugliness and pregnant hate
Unless we dare
The soul's dominion? Each time we make a choice, we pay
With courage to behold resistless day
And count it fair.

—Amelia Earhart, 1927
appeared in *Survey* magazine
July 1, 1928, p. 60

"Sixty-five miles altitude and you're looking good, *Defiant*."

"Roger, Ground Base." The static didn't disguise the southern drawl. "This is one hot airplane."

"Not much air left at that altitude, *Defiant*. Seventy miles."

The director of NSEA stood near the back of the

crowded control room that was Ground Base. Her fingernails dug holes in her palms. She had nothing to do at this point, except wish she were flying the rocket plane herself.

"Seventy-five miles." The atmosphere had no clear boundary. Their goal for this mission was an even one hundred miles altitude. At that point, the question would be academic. They would be in space.

There was an unusually loud burst of static from the loudspeaker. The single word, "control," cut through the noise, then the speaker settled to a steady hiss. Simultaneously, the radar man raised his voice. "We've lost the trace."

"Engine temperature trace spiked, then zeroed out."

"Fuel pressure's gone crazy, there's no reading."

"Still no radar trace."

"We've lost him."

The director pushed her way outside and looked up, straining her eyes for something she knew she'd never be able to see. The harsh blue Mojave sky was empty. Inside, tightly controlled voices confirmed one after another that all trace of the *Defiant* had been lost. A loudspeaker on the outside of the small building echoed the hissing static that was all the radio was receiving now. She listened to the empty radio until someone inside the building shut it off. Her eyes searched the sky again, knowing someplace, miles above, a brief star had blossomed.

But its light was lost in the brilliance of the desert sky.


"I would remind the witness that the United States Congress is not on trial here!" The senator glared at the slim woman seated across from him.

"This is a Congressional inquiry, not a court; no one is on trial. Neither the Congress nor the witness." The committee chairman spoke sharply, and the Senator leaned back in his chair. "Please answer the question, Miss Earhart, and without the lectures, if you don't mind. I think we've had enough of those for one day. This isn't the time to play politics."

As though the junior senator from Wisconsin ever had anything else on his mind. Amelia Earhart gave McCarthy another of the level looks newsreels had made famous and said, "To repeat what I have said many times before, then, no, Senator, I do not consider the risks excessive. Nor . . ." For a moment, she hesitated, then continued. "Nor did Colonel Yeager. And he would still agree with that assessment, even if another had piloted the *Defiant*."

Eyes turned to the black-clad figure of Glennis Yeager sitting near the head of the National Space Exploration Administration. The senator cleared his throat; he had no desire for the papers to show him mocking America's first space hero in front of his widow.

"Colonel Yeager was a brave American, of course," he said. His tone was properly respectful, shifting to a sharper edge as he continued, "But that's hardly the point, is it, Miss Earhart? You have yet to prove to the satisfaction of this committee"—which meant to his satisfaction—"that the benefits are worth the risk to these brave young American men." He flushed slightly. "And women."

That sticks in his craw, she thought with grim satisfaction. A.E. had been head of NSEA since its formation during the last administration. The new agency had taken over many of the functions and much of the personnel of the older National Advisory Committee for Aeronautics, but with the advent of Amelia Earhart as boss, the closed fraternity of male test pilots had been opened to a few women. There had been fights over that, the first major ones of her administration, and she'd won.

"Senator McCarthy, the dream of space is more than numbers on a chart . . ." The carefully scripted speech was delivered with the ease of a polished speaker. The words sounded impromptu, but they were anything but spontaneous, and the intended audience wasn't here in the Senate Hearing Room. She lifted her chin slightly, looking steadily into the television camera and making sure her voice was clear enough to be understood over the air.

The hearing adjourned shortly after that, and she made her way through the cyclone of reporters thrusting microphones at her. "No ... no comment ... NSEA will be releasing a position statement shortly ..." The journalistic wall parted abruptly and Glennis Yeager joined her, wrapped in a bubble of silence. The widow's face was under rigid control, but it looked as though she'd make it out the door without breaking. The two women walked out of the Capitol building together. As they passed, microphones withdrew and voices and questions died away. Once they were outside, they parted with only a few words.

"Take me back to the agency, Janice," Amelia directed her driver. This particular perk of bureaucratic Washington made sense. As much as she loved driving, traffic got worse in this city every year, and she had too much on her mind to navigate the streets safely.

She had opposed the war for as long as she could, right up until Pearl Harbor. But aviation had jumped forward during the war, its progress fueled by blood. German rockets and British jets convinced her that rocket planes soon would be able to fly faster and higher than she had dreamed of back at Kinner Field. Amelia had spent her life promoting commercial air travel; rocket planes were just another step. She had pushed the idea in Washington while working as a consultant for the government, and her words had gone higher than she'd realized. When Truman asked her to head the new agency after the war, she'd been surprised. But she was a natural, and it reinforced the civilian nature of the agency. Truman was no pacifist, but she pointed out the damage done by German rockets falling on London and the incredible power of the atom bomb. Any American agency joining those awesome forces needed to be nonmilitary, for the world's peace of mind. Korea had brought demands that the Air Force be put in charge, but interservice rivalry had left NSEA intact with Amelia still at the helm.

*"You know what Chuck would have said."* That was

all Glennis had said, and it echoed in Amelia's mind. Chuck would have been madder than hell at those vultures. The program wasn't dead yet. But losing Chuck, having him blow up right on the edge of true space flight—it wasn't just the blow to the agency. He was a flier, a good one. She had the fatalism of all pilots and had had her share of close calls, but this one hurt.

Once she got back to her office, she plunged into a whirlwind of papers. The number had doubled since *Defiant* had exploded on the threshold of space four days earlier. There were reports to sign, projections of new budgets, press releases, press releases, and more press releases. She delegated as much as she could, but it was too much, always too much. Why has she let President Truman talk her into flying this desk in the first place? She took her time over one folder: *Preliminary Analysis of Defiant Flight 17*. Seventeen wasn't supposed to be an unlucky number.

Figuring out what had happened was going to be rough; when a rocket plane explodes 78 miles up, not many pieces make it to the ground intact. From the instrument charts, it looked as though there'd been a sudden spike in the temperature of the main engine. Their best guess was that the lining had burned through, throwing the FH-1 out of control and flashing back to the main tanks in an explosion. The agency's engineers were working overtime with the people from Bell, trying to pinpoint what could have caused it, but the sequence of events had taken less than a minute. At least Chuck hadn't had more than a few seconds to realize something was wrong. And it hadn't been pilot error. He would have been glad of that. The equipment might have failed, but he hadn't.

She had just laid the folder back on her desk when the door opened and Jack Ridley, head of Flight Test Operations, strode in. He dropped into the chair across from Amelia.

"Jack, do you know what happened yet?" she asked.

He ignored the question. "A.E., what are them sumbiches planning on doing?"

"Grounding us."

He started swearing and she cut him off. "Jack, we all feel that way, but we haven't got time for it now. Have you got anything I can throw at McCarthy tomorrow to convince him the ship isn't a flying bomb?"

"Hell, no, A.E., it *is* one, you know that. A controlled one. This time it didn't stay under control." His face twisted.

Hers was impassive. "Then we'd better think of something to do, or there won't *be* an American space program."

". . . your known opposition to the military." McCarthy's voice was taking on a familiar rhythm. Any moment now, he'd reach in his pocket and pull out a list with her name on it, A.E. thought. She shifted in her seat.

"I am a pacifist, if that's what you mean," she said. "That has nothing whatsoever to do with the safety of Far Horizons." She glanced over at the chairman, but he said nothing. Up for reelection this fall, she recalled, and running scared of McCarthy like everyone else in Washington.

"Safety. That . . . that *bomb* you call a rocket plane has cost the life of a fine young American." Senator McCarthy leaned forward, his eyebrows lowering dramatically. "We expect our men in uniform to take risks. But he wasn't in uniform, was he, Miss Earhart? He had to leave the Air Force to fly for NSEA."

"NSEA was established by Congress as a civilian agency," she said. He knew that, of course; she was speaking for the cameras again. That was the heart of his opposition: a civilian agency headed by a pacifist had to be suspect. He'd fought against the bill establishing the agency. It had been a close vote, and McCarthy had lost it. He didn't like losing. "I'd like to ask Mr. Jack Ridley, who is in charge of our Flight Test Operations, to give a brief summary of the reasons for this, and the history of the Far Horizons project."

Jack cleared his throat as the cameras turned his way. His delivery wasn't as polished as A.E.'s, but it gave her a chance to watch the rest of the committee and judge how they were reacting. It didn't look good. They were politicians, looking ahead no farther than the next election. Her thoughts drifted as Jack spoke, gaining confidence as he went.

They weren't talking about shutting down NSEA. Not even the Far Horizons flight test program. But grounding the planes while they waited for perfect engineering would be the beginning of the end. Jack was pointing out the risks inherent in any new advance now, reviewing the old NACA X-1 program. It was a shrewd example; Colonel Yeager had broken the sound barrier in that plane, the direct ancestor of the FH-1, before joining NSEA. And Jack's point was obvious: if you worry too much about crashing, you never take off. But the committee wasn't buying it.

"... pending a complete investigation of the cause of this disaster, the National Space Exploration Administration is hereby directed to suspend all testing, in particular high altitude flight, of the Far Horizons rocket plane." The chairman banged his gavel. "This hearing is adjourned."

The cruciform shadow of the plane raced ahead over the cloudtops. She banked slightly, positioning the sun directly behind the plane so the shadow was leading her toward the western horizon. The twin engine Aereo-Commander responded perfectly, unlike the committee. She shut off that line of thought, choking it before it could progress to the unending, repeated list of *If onlys*. If only McCarthy had lost to La Follette. If only Chuck had been in *Defiant's* sister ship, *American Eagle*. If only maintenance had caught the weak spot. If only, if only, if only. None of it changed what *was*. Chuck Yeager was gone, and with him Far Horizons.

The planning meeting in her office had lasted almost as long as the hearing. Wake would be a more honest term; there was nothing left to plan. There would be a prolonged investigation. A few newspapers would call for vision; more would question the need for rocket planes. Lindbergh would testify, but McCarthy would sneer at him once more for his pre-war isolationism. Some in Congress would never forgive his sin of being right about German air power, and the rest would applaud politely, look at McCarthy's following, and say nothing.

She dropped lower, closer to the clouds. The shadow still led her toward the horizon. She loved this plane; it was a distance plane, with more speed and power than the Vega which had carried her over the Atlantic twenty-two years earlier. The changes in two decades . . . If Congress grounded Far Horizons, the next two might show far less improvement in aircraft. If they could push ahead, actual space planes would be possible.

The one thing that might save the program was a public outcry, but not that many people understood or cared about aviation. Most of the excitement of the early days was gone; people no longer gawked at the sight of a plane, any more than they did at the sight of an automobile. The difference was, most of them owned a car, and almost every person in the country had ridden in one. Even counting the military, less than a quarter of the population had ever been airborne. As for flying beyond the atmosphere, most people thought of that as something out of Buck Rodgers, not the next logical step in aviation.

It was a shame G.P. wasn't around, Amelia thought. The divorce, two years after her almost fatal crash off Howland Island during her round-the-world flight, had garnered almost as many headlines as her first Atlantic crossing, but it had been amicable enough. Sometimes she thought they would have separated sooner if it hadn't been for the crash. Even after George's remarriage, they'd remained friends. He would have helped, and no one could promote like George Palmer Putnam. But G.P. had died four years earlier.

Thoughts of G.P., of her early record-setting flights, of the impending ruin of Far Horizons, all faded to a background ache in her mind as she concentrated on flying, racing the Commander's shadow as though this were the National Air Races instead of one lone

woman flying to forget. The sound of wings hypno-
tized her.

The idea, born of memories and frustration and flying, hit hard. Alone in her cockpit, Amelia grinned at
the horizon.

"Barnstorming."

She stood the wings of the Commander on edge in a
side slip and the plane quietly slid down the sky, cutting through the clouds and its own shadow.

"Barnstorming? A.E., have you gone loco?"

"I don't think so, Jack," she said. Her face was
calm, with only a slight smile and no trace of excitement. Her eyes betrayed her; they sparkled, for the first
time since the explosion. "What's wrong with the
idea?"

"What's wrong with it . . . ? Look, first of all, we've
only got one rocket plane left. And that sumbich is too
damned hot to play hop scotch round the country. And
anyways, them bastids said we can't fly her till they
finish their damned 'investigation,' And . . ."

Amelia waved the objections aside. "Barnstorming
is just an easy thing to call it. I know we can't land
*American Eagle* in a corn field. But we *can* fly it
around the bigger airports. Or at least a few of them."
She pointed to the map she'd laid out on her desk, with
half a dozen cities ringed in red. "We were ordered not
to do any more testing. They didn't say we couldn't fly
it at all. All we'll do is cut it loose from the mother
ship and have Jackie land at those airports. That's not
testing."

"Even with television, that's not going to reach
many people, A.E." Jackie Cochran raised an eyebrow,
inviting more. With Yeager gone, she was the senior
pilot. Jackie was Amelia's closest friend; she knew
there had to be more involved than a few landings.

"It will be a start. For the rest of it, we're hitting the
road. All of us, every person in this agency who can
manage to say two words in a row. The lecture circuit."

The landing of *American Eagle* two weeks later at

Idlewild Airport drew crowds of New Yorkers, fascinated by the boom when the *Eagle* broke the sound barrier. Amelia was waiting on the ground. The rolling echoes made her think of Chuck, who had made that first clap of artificial thunder just seven years before. *They won't ground us,* she promised him mentally. *We're going to keep flying higher, faster, farther.*

She used that theme in her first lecture that night. The hall was only three-quarters full, but the television cameras were there. With television, the newest town crier, Amelia would reach far more people than could crowd into a lecture hall.

"The oxcart is safer than the automobile," she said. "But I saw no oxcarts drawn up in front of the hall tonight. Every advance exacts a price, and all aviators know this. We lost Colonel Yeager. He wasn't the first, nor the last. I brushed by death more than once in the past. The Atlantic solo could have killed me, as it did so many pilots back then. Now two decades later, hundreds of passengers cross daily in safety. When a great adventure is offered to you, you don't refuse it. And our country must not refuse this one."

The next night, crowds packed the hall. Amelia Earhart was still America's "First Lady of Flying." During the day, people pushed and shoved in lines passing by the twin planes, the FH-1 *American Eagle,* its fuel exhausted in the brief flight, and the modified B-29 that served as the mother ship. After landing the *Eagle,* Jackie had taken off with her husband for Washington and more speeches. Her husband lent his clout to the effort, and as head of General Dynamics, Floyd Odlum had plenty. Politicians listened to his money; the crowds listened to her descriptions of flying a plane that could punch through the sky and reach space.

Jack Ridley kept saying he was no good at talking, but his reminiscences about Chuck and the X-1 were better than any stiff presentation of goals. *Life* did an issue on the future of aviation, interviewing Jack. The writer caught the enthusiasm of the NSEA people, and he portrayed the X-1 and the FH-1 as linked steps along the way, not a final goal. Lindbergh wrote articles, measured, rational, and filled with the poetry of flight. Each dead-stick landing of the rocket plane drew larger crowds, and more coverage from the newspapers and radio. Television cameras were everywhere. The shape of the *American Eagle* was imprinted on the national mind, along with the words "Far Horizons" and "space." America had reached the Pacific; now politicians started to talk about Manifest Destiny reaching to the sky.

And letters began to land on Congressional desks.

". . . Three . . . Two . . . One . . . Drop."

"Separated from the mother ship. Lighting first chamber in twenty seconds."

The second voice sounded calm over the loudspeaker. Amelia kept herself still with an effort. After all these years, she still had never gotten used to being the one on the ground. She wanted to be up there with Jackie. As a flyer, bad radio discipline had almost killed her off Howland. Now she was linked to the FH-1 only by the radio waves broadcast from Jackie's mike and the instruments on the rocket plane.

"Ignition." There was a cheer in the control room at Edwards as the instruments echoed the successful firing of the first rocket motor. They were flying again, the whole agency.

Flying faster, and higher, and farther. As the rocket plane climbed, so did the tension in the control room. The Bell engineers had assured NSEA that the *American Eagle* was safe, but there were still a dozen ways it could kill.

"Roger, *Eagle,* everything looks good from here." The radio operator sounded calm, as though the *Defiant* had never flown. But his posture was rigid, betraying the tension he was keeping from his voice.

Once they'd captured the imaginations and hopes of the nation, the temporary freeze on flight test had been removed by Congress. It helped that the Army had at long last managed to discredit McCarthy. The Tail-Gunner had been shot down. But support from the public was what had saved Far Horizons.

"Chase plane Able on station. She looks good from here." The Air Force had loaned the project two of their hottest fighter jets this time, along with a couple of Korean War aces. They'd follow the rocket plane as high as they could, tracking from high altitude in case anything went wrong again. But if they lost this one, the program would be dead. NSEA had no more rocket planes.

The tension in the room showed in the lack of jokes and wisecracks. The strip-charts were monitored, each quiver in a line being reported almost before the pen could make the trace. The chase planes reached their maximum altitude and started to circle, still tracking visually. But Jackie was roaring away from them, and was soon lost even to their sight.

"*Eagle,* you're halfway there." There was a suspicion of a break in the radioman's voice. "Fifty miles altitude."

As she passed the seventy-mile mark, then the seventy-five, everyone in the room fell silent, except for the steady voice of the radio operator. Jackie's voice over the loudspeaker held the professional calm of the pilot.

"Seventy-five miles altitude ... eighty miles altitude ..." There was another cheer, this one louder, but it quickly choked off. Jackie was now flying higher than any human before her, higher than Chuck had reached, but the flight wasn't over yet. The minutes crept by, until the words came, "Approaching the one-hundred-mile mark ... ninety-eight ... ninety-nine ... one hundred miles altitude. You're in space, *Eagle.*" This time the cheering didn't die down.

Amelia picked up the telephone. The connection had already been made. Strange, her hands were shaking. That had never happened before.

"Mr. President? At 10:37 Pacific time, Jacqueline Cochran achieved one hundred miles elevation in the

Far Horizons rocket plane." She took a deep breath to steady herself, then went on. This was just the beginning; they'd fly farther and faster yet. And higher.

"The *Eagle* is flying."

# SOUTH OF EDEN, SOMEWHERE NEAR SALINAS

## By Jack C. Haldeman II

*James Dean was obsessed with cars and speed, and it was that obsession that finally killed him.*

*Still, his memory lives on, and he remains as big a name today as when he was alive. One can almost imagine him in some alternate plane of existence, getting into his race car while his girlfriend, Natalie Wood, and his best buddy, Sal Mineo, watch him take the track with mixed emotions. And, if you have a little trouble imagining that scene, here's Jack Haldeman to help you.*

Natalie Wood looked up at James Dean and smiled.

Dean didn't notice. His eyes were locked on Bill Vukovich as he wrestled the Hopkins Special around the track at Indianapolis for his qualifying run. Dean didn't need a stopwatch to tell that Vucki was lapping at well over 140 mph. Yesterday it would have been good enough for the pole. But yesterday rain had cut the qualifying session short, and Vucki hadn't been able to run. Dean had managed to get his run in.

James Dean, at age 24, had the pole position for the 1955 Indianapolis 500, driving the Baker House Special around the brickyard at an average speed of 140.045 miles per hour.

"Excuse me. Mr. Dean?"

James Dean sighed, ran his hand through his sandy hair, and brought his attention back to the reporter.

"He's the man you want, Miss Wood," said Dean, waving at Vucki as he took his cool-down lap. "No

one has ever won the Indianapolis 500 three times in a
row. This could be the year."

"My name's Natalie," she said. "And it's you that I
want."

Dean laughed. "Fair enough, Natalie. And you can
call me James or Jimmy." He looked over to see
Vucki's time being posted. It was a new track record at
141.071 mph. Yesterday that would have bought him
the pole.

"Okay, James," said Natalie, taking out a notebook.
"What do you feel about dying on a race track?"

Dean fixed her with a hard stare, turning up the collar of his jeans jacket and sliding down in his seat in
the grandstand, propping his boots on the seat in front.
He reached down and picked up his cowboy hat and
set it low on his head.

"I thought you worked for a reputable publication,"
he mumbled.

*"The Saturday Evening Post,"* she snapped, *"is* a
reputable publication. Readers want to know about the
hot new driver."

"New driver? I've been racing since I was sixteen
years old. My uncle brought me here when I was eight
years old, and I knew then I was going to be a driver.
I never considered doing anything else."

"And you're clearly very good at it."

Dean looked at her and nodded. "I am."

"Then you must occasionally think about death."

Dean unfolded himself and stood up. "I think that
magazine sent the wrong person to write this article,
lady. You're chasing a story that isn't there. I drive,
and I drive fast. That's all there is to it."

"I don't believe that for a minute," Natalie said.

Someone called Dean's name from the track and he
waved.

"I've got to go," he said. "My chief mechanic needs
me."

"I'll just tag along," said Natalie. "Maybe I can
learn something. I'll stay out of the way."

"Women aren't allowed in Gasoline Alley," said

Dean. "Its tradition, like the jinx on green cars. Just not done."

"I think that's stupid, tradition or not."

Dean shrugged.

"You'll be at the reception tonight, won't you?" asked Natalie.

"I don't have any choice," said Dean. "My sponsors would have a fit if I didn't show up."

"Maybe we can continue the interview there."

"Maybe," said Dean. "Maybe not."

Natalie watched James Dean leave. The lanky race driver was going to be a tough interview, but she'd known that from the start. He had that kind of a reputation. Nice looking man, though. Very nice.

Down on the track, Dean threw his arm around Sal, his chief mechanic, and they started walking toward Gasoline Alley.

Sal Mineo was everything that James Dean wasn't, and they were best of friends. Dean was tall, and Sal was short. Dean had tousled sandy hair that was continually out of control, while Sal's heavily-greased black hair was always combed in a carefully prepared pompadour. Where Dean was ruggedly handsome, Sal had a soft, innocent, baby face that would probably make him look eighteen forever. The fact that he always had a couple of comic books stuffed in his back pocket didn't make him look any older.

But Sal, the only son of one of the best mechanics in the business, had been born with a spanner in one hand and a torque wrench in the other. He was a genius, as Dean knew well. There wasn't anyone alive who could do more with the 270 cubic inches of a Meyer-Drake engine than Sal. Before qualifying, the Baker House Special had checked out at 335 horsepower at the rear wheels, almost 5 horsepower greater than the competition.

"So what's up, Boy Wonder?" asked Dean.

"Not much," said Sal. "You looked like you needed to be rescued."

"I did."

"She's a cute one, that reporter," said Sal. "A real Lois Lane."

"I didn't notice," said Dean.

"Right," said Sal, giving Dean a light punch in the ribs. "And the Pope ain't Catholic."

They laughed together and kept on walking.

Dean hated the days between qualifying and the actual race. It was a circus of interviews, parties, and personal appearances, none of which had anything to do with racing, as far as he could see. As the pole sitter, his sponsors missed no opportunities to parade him in front of anyone with a camera or a microphone. He was expected to be polite and articulate. Sometimes, to his sponsors' surprise, he was.

But not at the reception that night. He'd shaken too many hands that day, and engaged in too many meaningless conversations with people he had absolutely nothing in common with. After he almost snapped at the Mayor of Indianapolis, he knew he had to get away before he did something that would get him into serious trouble.

Dean looked around the large hall. Sal was over at a table, trying to make some moves on Deborah Drake, a photographer from *Life*. He was playing the little boy role to the hilt. Vucki was surrounded by people. Dean found himself looking for Wilbur Shaw, who was always good to talk with. But Wilbur wouldn't be back this year, or ever. Dead in a plane crash.

Then he saw Natalie Wood, leaning against the far wall, drinking a soda. She was wearing a plaid pleated skirt and a light blue cashmere short-sleeved sweater. Penny loafers. She smiled at him, but made no move to come over. Dean liked that.

Someone grabbed him by the arm. "Jimmy, I'd like you to meet—"

"Sorry, Mr. Baker," said Dean, pulling away. "Gotta take a whizz."

He walked over to Natalie, took her by the hand.

"Let's get out of here," he said.

They slipped out a side door to a covered porch and down the stairs to the parking lot. Dean opened the passenger door to a small red two-seater convertible with the top down and Natalie got in.

"Nice car," she said.

Dean shrugged as he slipped behind the wheel. "Ford Thunderbird. Nice lines, but it's still nothing but Detroit iron. It'll move in a straight line, but can't corner worth a damn. I wouldn't have one, but they rented it for me while I'm in town." He paused and smiled at Natalie. "My sponsors like to keep up my image."

"They seem to be doing well in that respect," she said.

"It's all show business," said Dean, shaking his head, firing up the engine and pulling out of the parking lot, laying twenty feet of rubber in the process.

"Where are we going?" asked Natalie, fastening her seatbelt and grabbing the dashboard.

"The brickyard," said Dean, pressing hard on the accelerator.

The reception had been held in a hotel outside of town, and on the back way into the track, Dean pushed the Thunderbird hard, its headlights illuminating the winding, tree-lined road.

"How fast are we going?" Natalie asked, the wind whipping her dark hair.

"Not fast."

"How fast?"

"Seventy-five."

"This road is awfully narrow," said Natalie.

"I'd be pushing one hundred twenty if we were in my Porsche," said Dean. "The D-Jag I'll be driving in Le Mans could take this at one hundred forty. This is nothing."

When they reached the dark track, a security guard waved them inside. They drove across the racetrack and parked in the deserted infield.

It was quiet. Light clouds drifted across the star-studded sky. They walked out on the track and stood on the brick surface.

"This is incredible," whispered Natalie, as if they were in a shrine. "All those empty seats."

"In a few days they'll be packed," said Dean, standing with his hands in his pockets, his shoulders hunched. "It looks like a mountain of people from down here, if you have time to watch."

"You'd really like to win this, wouldn't you, James?"

"Sure," said Dean, starting to walk slowly down the track. "Who wouldn't? I finished second to Vucki the last two years, and second is nowhere in this business. If I'm going to win, he's the man I have to beat."

"He's fast," Natalie said.

Dean nodded. "Maybe."

"He holds the track record here," she said.

"Vucki is a man with an obsession," said Dean. "Indianapolis is his whole life. He doesn't do any of the other races, just Indy. He wants it so badly, he takes chances that maybe he shouldn't take. They don't call him Wild Bill for nothing. Don't get me wrong, he's a friend, and I admire the heck out of him, but if he makes a mistake, I'll beat him. Or maybe something will break. In '52 he was leading with nine laps to go when his steering went. Anything can happen here."

"You take chances, too," said Natalie.

"I drive right on the edge," said Dean. "I know exactly what the car can do, and what I can do with it. I push it to that precise point. There's a difference."

"But what if something happens? If you're going that fast, there must not be much time to react."

Dean shrugged. "Things happen. You do the best you can to minimize the damage. I've been into the wall twice here. The first was at the end of this straight during the '52 race when I hit some oil. In practice last year a tie rod let go and I went into the wall in turn four. Turns out our backup car was faster than the original, so it all worked out."

"It sounds like practice can be as dangerous as the race," Natalie said.

Dean didn't respond. Manuel Ayulo had been killed in practice this year.

As they approached the end of the grandstands, the brick surface gave way to asphalt. Dean stood there, lost in thought. He closed his eyes and visualized all

200 laps, and how the brick straight in front of the grandstands threatened to jar your teeth out and how it felt like glass when you went from the bricks to the asphalt, just in time to get set for turn one. Repeat 200 times, in heavy traffic.

"Your parents must be proud of you," Natalie said.

Dean turned to her, his face hard. He balled his right hand into a fist and pounded it into his left palm several times, then turned and walked briskly back down the track. As Natalie caught up with him, he broke into a run, left her behind, and didn't stop until he'd reached the car. A few moments later Natalie, out of breath, came up. They sat next to each other on the hood.

"I'm sorry, James," she said. "I didn't mean—"

"My parents don't understand," he said evenly in a cold, level voice. "I doubt if anyone does, but them especially. They wanted me to be a lawyer or a doctor. Anything less amounted to failure in their eyes. I couldn't do it. I couldn't do anything to please them. Are you going to write about *this*?" he asked sharply, tears in his eyes.

"No," she whispered.

"I couldn't sit still in school, though I did well enough in class when I was there. I wanted to be moving. I wanted to be moving fast. Back then I *did* take chances, before I learned better. I wanted to live fast, and I didn't much care if I died young in the process. Now I want revenge. I want to be the best damn driver in the world. There's no way in hell they can ignore that." He turned his back to her, dried his eyes.

"Jimmy," she said, touching his back. He flinched.

"I know what you mean," she said. "My mother wanted me to be a model or an actress. She thought I was wasting my time with words. To her, journalism was not a fit career for a woman. Actually, more to the point, she felt women didn't need careers; what a woman needed was a husband. I need a husband like a frog needs a bicycle."

Dean laughed.

"Looks don't last," she said, gently touching the

back of his neck. "I figured that out early on. But words will last as long as there are books and magazines. I won three awards for feature articles last year, and I'm damn proud of them. They mean nothing to my mother, but they mean everything to me. I quit living my life for her—or against her—years ago."

James Dean turned, and caressed the side of her cheek. They kissed, gently at first and then with a passion. They drew apart, looked at each other for a moment and then laughed.

"Your place or mine?" asked Dean.

"Mine," said Natalie with a smile. "Definitely mine. We'd never have a moment's peace at your place."

They stayed in bed until noon. James Dean missed two interviews and a personal appearance at the local Goodyear Tire store. Natalie Wood learned a lot about James Dean, none of which was suitable material for *The Saturday Evening Post.* He learned a lot about her, too. It was a mutually satisfactory exchange of information. Sal chased them down about one in the afternoon.

"Jimmy," said Sal. "Have you gone crazy?"

Dean was sitting shirtless in Natalie's hotel room, wearing only jeans, with his bare feet propped up against the radiator.

"Hardly," he said.

"Everyone's looking for you," Sal said, taking an offered cup of coffee from Natalie, who was wearing a terrycloth bathrobe and not much else. "What are you going to do?"

"Oh my, oh my, what *shall* I do?" said Dean dramatically, wringing his hands and giving Natalie a wink and a smile. Then he looked at Sal. "So is the car set, Boy Wonder?"

"You know it is, Jimmy." He looked a little shocked and hurt that Dean might think anything else.

"And that body panel I crunched coming into the pits. Got that fixed?"

"Lawson is the best body and paint man in the business."

"Then what I'm going to do is drive the hell out of

it on Monday. Until then, if anyone asks you where I am, tell them that as far as you know, I've gone to a mountain top to practice my bongos. They'll believe anything about me if it's strange enough."

And they did.

By the time James Dean arrived at the track Monday morning, every reporter covering the event wanted an interview with the beatnik driver who played the bongo drums. He ducked them all. But he couldn't escape Clayton Baker III, the major sponsor of the Baker House Special.

"And where the hell have you been, Jimmy?" said Clayton, grabbing Dean's arm as the crew rolled his car out to the track. "I had you scheduled for meetings all over the place, and you disappear with some cock-and-bull story about drums."

"You want a driver or a puppet, Mr. Baker?" asked Dean.

"What?"

"If you want a driver, you've got the world's best. If you want a puppet, you've got the wrong man."

"I've lost a lot of face here, Jimmy. You've cost me a ton of money."

"Wrong," said Dean. "I've made you a ton of money. There's no way in the world you could have bought this kind of publicity. Now get out of my way. I've got a race to run." He turned and walked away, leaving the car owner standing alone and flustered.

Sal caught up with Dean. "I see you're still biting the hand that feeds you," he said.

James Dean didn't reply. Sal realized he was putting his game face on again, mentally preparing for the race, and walked quietly beside him.

It was this way before every race. Dean would slip into a cold and distant place, a place where nothing existed but the car, the track. The other drivers ceased to be friends or acquaintances; they were simply obstacles between him and the checkered flag.

Everything else slipped away while he focused his concentration. The pageantry flowed around him unnoticed. The invocation, the National Anthem, Dinah

Shore singing "Back Home Again in Indiana," the traditional command by Tony Hulman of "Gentlemen, start your engines." All a blur until the engine kicked over and Sal tapped his helmet for good luck, saying "SHAZAM," as he always did.

Like a fuzzy picture suddenly made razor-sharp, Dean became acutely aware of everything within the confines of the track. He put the Baker House Special into gear and pulled away from the starting grid, following the Chevrolet convertible pace car around the track for their warmup laps.

Dean was feeling the car out as he weaved from side to side to get the tires hot. He listened to the engine, checked out the steering, accelerated and decelerated a couple of times to see what it felt like with a full load of fuel aboard. Everything was fine. They picked up speed.

The pace car pulled off into the pit road. The crowd was on its feet, roaring. Dean put his foot into it as he pulled out of turn four and was flying as he led the other thirty-two drivers past the green flag.

He dove low and hard into the first turn, barely nosing out Steve Charnes, who was fighting him for position. As Charnes tucked in behind him, Dean hit the throttle, accelerating as he exited the corner, and pulled away.

This was the kind of racing Dean lived for. He was in the lead, with nothing but clear track ahead of him. He drove the Baker House Special to its very limit, waiting for the last instant to decelerate for the corners, barely tapping the brakes, feeling the g-forces pull at the tires and the weight of the car. He was dancing right on the edge and he loved it.

He felt alive, as he did at no other times in his life.

He led the first lap, the second, the third. On the fourth, he glanced at Nick Steel, who was holding a chalk-marked sign by the wall. The sign told him he was eight seconds ahead of the second place car and twenty-three seconds ahead of Vukovich.

On the tenth lap Nick's sign showed he was ten seconds ahead of the second place car and twelve seconds ahead of Vukovich. Two laps later Vukovich was in second place and closing. Five laps later, they were side by side going down the back stretch at full speed.

Dean knew they'd both have to decelerate to make turn three. It was all a matter of who lifted his throttle foot first. It hung that way for an instant, then Dean felt the limit of his car approaching and backed off. Vucki barely ducked under him on the inside, the back end of his car sliding dangerously close to the wall.

When they hit the straight in front of the grandstand, Vucki started pulling away. Dean nodded grimly. The man had either found something extra or was driving past the limits of his car. There was nothing to do but hang in there and see what happened.

By lap 100, the midpoint of the race, Vucki had stretched his lead over Dean to seventeen seconds. A few laps later it happened.

Dean couldn't see what started it. They were working their way through lapped traffic when the cars in front started spinning. Dean slowed, his eyes searching for a pattern in the spinning cars, a way through. It seemed to last forever, but it only took a split second as Vucki headed for a clear space only to have a sliding car close it off at the last instant. Vucki's car rode up on the other car's wheel and flew into the air, spinning crazily end over end as it vaulted over the fence and crashed outside the track, exploding in a churning ball of flame.

Dean wove through the scattered cars and fell in behind the pace car as the yellow came out. As they drove past the scene of the wreck, it was still burning.

He pulled into pit road, and as they were fueling the car, he looked at Sal. Sal shook his head. The door in Dean's head slammed shut.

Dean pulled out of the pits. From the outside, he looked as if he was totally concentrating on the job. Inside it was completely different. As he followed the pace car slowly around the track, he was drifting, visiting an all-too-familiar place.

He imagined he was in a mansion, standing alone in the middle of an incredibly large room. All around him were doors to other rooms, thousands of them. People stood in many of the doorways; friends, strangers. Natalie waved to him from her doorway, Sal sat cross-legged in his, reading a comic book. Wilbur Shaw's door was closed. And now, Vucki's door was closed, too, closed forever. As long as Dean stayed in the central room he was safe, invulnerable. He was convinced he could be hurt, but not killed, in this special place, this place he had visited far too many times. It was a fugue state, almost hypnotic. It was protective.

For the duration of the yellow flag, James Dean stood alone in the middle of the room, safe, untouched. The caution period was a long one, twenty-seven minutes. When the green flag started the race up again, he immediately snapped back. Nothing existed except the track, the car.

He drove spectacularly, right on the edge, but never beyond it. James Dean won the 1955 Indy 500 by almost a full lap.

The celebration in victory lane was subdued. Dean, his face smeared with dirt and oil, accepted the traditional bottle of milk and the traditional kiss. As he posed with the trophy, he saw Natalie standing at the back of the crowd of reporters. Deborah, the *Life* photographer, had her arm around Natalie. It looked like they had both been crying.

Later, after a seemingly endless series of interviews, Dean slipped away and found Natalie.

"I'm sorry," she said as he came up to her. "I know he was your friend."

"I'm sorry, too, but things happen. It's over, and time to move on." His eyes were hard. "We need to think about Friday."

"What's special about Friday?"

"You're flying to France with me."

"I am?"

"Le Mans," he said. "Better start packing."

She did.

Natalie had never been to France before, and the strangeness of everything was a shock at first. After a few days she settled in, and was almost comfortable as they sat together at a table outside a creperie the evening before the race, sipping cider from eathenware cups.

"Are you worried, Jimmy?" she asked, breaking a long, uncomfortable silence.

"Only about Mercedes," he said.

"That's not what I meant."

"I know." He sighed, and sipped his cider, holding the cup with both hands. "But Moss is going to be hard to beat. He tore up the Mille Migle this year, and that's one tough road course. Those 300 SLs are fast, and he's one damn fine driver."

"Jimmy!" snapped Natalie. "Don't you ever think about anything but racing?"

Dean reached out and touched her cheek. "Sometimes I do."

She blushed. "Seriously," she said.

"I get offers all the time," he said. "Jaguar and Porsche both want me to run car dealerships. I've been approached to do television commercials and bit parts in movies. Sun Records wants to turn me into the next Tab Hunter, even though I can't carry a tune in a bucket. I turn them all down."

"Why?"

"All I know is racing, Natalie. I'd be lost without it. I can't stand still. After Le Mans I'm headed back to Bonneville for a shot at the land speed record. Next year Jaguar wants me to drive Formula One for them. I could be the first American to win the World Championship."

A waiter set two small cups of coffee in front of them. Dean added sugar to his before even tasting it.

"Have you ever turned down a racing assignment, Jimmy?" asked Natalie, sipping the strong coffee.

"Once," said Dean. "Lee Petty wanted me to drive a stock car, but I don't see the point. Stock cars will never get off the ground. No one wants to watch Detroit iron go around in circles. You might as well stand above an LA highway and root for all the red cars. Stupid idea."

"I don't know," said Natalie. "It doesn't sound any

more ridiculous than driving 400 miles per hour across a desert."

"We've been all through this, Natalie. No one has ever done that before, and I'm going to be the first. I can't help being what I am."

Natalie reached over and touched his hand. "Let's go back to the hotel," she said. "It's going to be a long day tomorrow."

Dean nodded, and reached for his wallet to pay the check.

It was a cool morning for June in France, but James Dean didn't notice. He was driving first shift. If all went well, his codriver, Mike Hawthorn, would relieve him in two or three hours.

The drivers lined up along the track, opposite their cars, for the traditional Le Mans start. James Dean was focused, for he knew it would be crowded and chaotic with all the cars accelerating at once. It was better if you got out first.

The signal was given. The drivers raced across the track for their cars. Dean had practiced this a hundred times. He vaulted into the open cockpit of the D-Jag, slapped the ignition, popped the clutch, and pulled out into the weaving traffic.

He was fourth into the first turn, behind another Jaguar and two Mercedes roadsters. As he tucked in behind Bob Immler and reached the apex of the turn, he got on the throttle. The Jaguar engine responded beautifully, and the car leapt out of the turn. Dean settled down to race.

He loved road courses, and this one was over eight miles of tight turns and long straights. It was a test of endurance, both for the cars and the drivers. At times he would be blasting along at over 180 miles per hour and a few moments later he would have to slow down to 20 in order to negotiate a turn. It was a challenge to run on the edge for so long, but Dean was up to it, and he knew Mike Hawthorn would be, too. The biggest threats would come from the powerful Mercedes roadsters and the legendary Juan Fangio.

Being in fourth place did not particularly bother

Dean. It was a long race. A lot could happen in twenty-four hours.

It happened just a few laps later. A Jaguar pulled sharply into the pits, causing an Austin-Healy to lock its brakes and spin. It developed very quickly. Pierre Levege never had a chance. He was going flat out at 185 miles an hour down the grandstand straight when the car skidded into his path. His Mercedes climbed the back of the Austin-Healy and was instantly airborne, clearing the fence and plowing into the crowded grandstands, cutting through the spectators like a deadly scythe.

Dean saw the tragedy unfold. A part of him locked down and as he concentrated on driving through the wreckage, he could feel the doors closing.

He expected them to bring out the red flag and stop the race, but instead they only brought out the yellow in the area of the accident. He continued driving around the course, but every time he passed the grandstands a part of him slipped back into that cold mansion and he watched the doors slam shut one at a time as he stood, invulnerable, in the middle. A few laps later he pitted, and Mike Hawthorn took over.

The sitting was the hard part; the waiting was far more difficult than the driving. He tried to rest, but couldn't. Mercedes had withdrawn all its cars. Much of the crowd had left following the accident. He and Mike were in the lead and adding to it with every lap.

It went that way through the afternoon and evening. Dean and Hawthorn rotated regularly. When he wasn't driving, Dean tried to sleep. It was impossible. Instead, he sat and stared at the lights of the cars weaving through the night like fireflies.

The next morning, Dean was driving as the clock ran down. The last lap was a madhouse. The stewards came out onto the track, waving all their flags at once in the traditional salute. At the finish he had to inch his way through the crowd, because Le Mans lets spectators on the track at the end. As expected, he and Mike went through the motions of spraying the gathering with a huge bottle of champagne. Neither of them were smiling.

As soon as he could get away, he found Natalie Wood.

"The reports are that almost a hundred people were killed," she said, anguish making her voice crack.

James Dean just nodded. He was wearing dark glasses and his face was hard and cold.

"We're catching the next plane out of here," he said.

"Sure, Jimmy," she said, slipping her arms around him. "I want to get away from this place, too."

"It's not that," said Dean, pulling away. "I've got a car waiting on the Bonneville Salt Flats."

Natalie shuddered. But she followed him.

She followed him all the way to Bonneville, where she stood under the merciless sun with Sal, watching Dean pose for the publicity pictures before his run.

"What do you think his chances are?" she asked. The car was a deep blue streamlined teardrop, flattened on top and incredibly low to the ground. It shimmered in the heat like a living creature.

"Pretty good," said Sal. "Those twin Rolls-Royce aircraft engines check out fine. There's no wind. I'd say he has a decent chance to break Cobb's 394 run."

"That's not exactly what I meant, Sal," she said.

Sal looked embarrassed. "I know," he said, shaking his head. "Bad luck to talk like that."

They walked over together as Dean got ready to get into the car. Natalie gave him a kiss, and as he put on his helmet, she hugged him tightly. He looked over her head, already mentally halfway across the desert. When he climbed inside, Sal slapped him on the head, and said "SHAZAM" as always. Then they clamped the cockpit closed.

Dean was alone. He waited patiently as the technicians finished their last-minute adjustments and the spectators got a safe distance away. When he got the signal, he fired up the engines. He sat for a minute, watching the gauges and feeling the horsepower build. Then he eased the RPMs up, put it in gear and started flying.

The acceleration was incredible, like nothing he had ever felt before. Pressed back into his seat by the g-forces, he floored the sucker, passing 100, 200, and 300 miles per hour. The car was a handful, but manageable. Unexpectedly, it tended to drift left. He corrected and pressed on, tweaking every last bit of power out of the engines. He was so busy when he flew through the timing lights he didn't see how fast he was going. As he passed the end marker, he cut back on the engines and popped the chutes. He was thrown forward violently against his harness as the chutes caught and almost blacked out. He rolled to a stop and the team at the other end swarmed over the car.

"How'd we do?" he asked.

"Four hundred and seven, plus change," said a tech. "Back it up on the return and we're set."

Dean didn't get out as they turned the car around and got it ready for the return. He thought of nothing but the back-up run necessary for the world record. He integrated all he'd learned on the first run and when they signaled everything was ready he nodded and fired the engines.

It was beautiful; couldn't have felt better. The crush of acceleration as he pulled away was like an old friend. He was convinced he was going to do it. He passed 200 mph, 300, 350.

At 375 miles per hour the car started getting loose. Like a boat skimming over waves, he was in a cycle where the nose of the car lifted and fell. When it lifted, he had no control at all, but regained it when the car touched down. He realized he had only two choices. He could shut down and lose everything they'd worked for, or he could hope that the next time the nose came down it would grab, and the application of more horsepower would keep it down. It floated up, and the next time it came down, he jammed the accelerator.

The nose of the car lifted even farther up, and as the air caught it, the car rose completely off the ground and did a slow backward flip in the air. Dean hit the chutes, but it was far too late.

There was nothing he could do now but play this

game to the end. In the instant before the car hit the ground, he closed his eyes and imagined the mansion. The room was shaking, doors were falling from their hinges. He was on his knees in the middle of the room. The ceiling was falling in pieces all around him.

Then the car hit the ground and disintegrated.

Natalie Wood wanted to close her eyes, but couldn't. The horror etched itself in her brain as she watched.

"Jimmy!" she cried and found herself running with Sal across the hardpacked surface to what remained of the twisted car in the distance. A truck stopped to pick them up.

"Stay here, Natalie," said Sal. "You don't want to see this."

"I *have* to see this," she said firmly. Sal looked at her and nodded. They rode to the smoldering wreckage and when they got there, she wished with all her soul that she hadn't come. It was terrible.

For ten days, James Dean lay in a coma. His arms and legs were shattered, his skull was fractured. He had four cracked ribs, a broken pelvis, and internal injuries. He was not expected to live. As the nurses worked around him, they often talked as if he were already dead.

He drifted for those ten days. Unconscious to the outside world, he dwelled in the mansion, being careful to stay in the middle of the room and away from the doors. On the eleventh day, he opened his eyes and saw Natalie Wood standing at the foot of his bed.

"Jimmy," she said. "Jimmy."

He smiled at her, winked, and fell asleep.

Although the long-term prognosis looked grim, James Dean's strength, determination, and drive surprised everybody. A week later, as Natalie was coming by for a visit, she met Sal outside Dean's room. He was carrying the steering wheel from a racing car.

"No!" she cried, grabbing it from Sal's hands. "No!" She pushed open the door to Dean's room.

"What's this?" she shouted.

"A steering wheel," said Dean.

"The doctors said you'd never walk again. What do you need this for?"

"I don't care about walking, but I *need* to drive," he said. "They have to rebuild my arms and hands. I'm not going to have much motion when they're finished and I want to make sure they put me back together in a way that I can grip the wheel. I asked Sal to bring it in for measurements."

"You never give up, do you, Jimmy?"

"No," he said, smiling at her. "I never do."

It should have taken years, but it actually took only a couple of months. James Dean rented them a house outside of LA and hired a physical therapist to work with him every day. While he worked out with weights and in the swimming pool, Natalie tried to finish the article for *The Saturday Evening Post*. She threw away twenty pages for every paragraph she saved. Sometimes she was too sad to write, but more often it was her anger that kept her from finishing the article. The day he took the Porsche over to the track at Riverside to run a few practice laps was the worst. They didn't speak for days following that. Then he dropped the bombshell.

"I'm taking the Porsche up to Monterey," he said casually over coffee that morning.

"Why?"

"I've entered a road race," he said. "I'm meeting Sal and the guys in Bakersfield."

"Jimmy!" She slammed her coffee cup down so hard it shattered the saucer. "You can't even walk without a cane! It's too soon."

"I have to do this," he said slowly. "Are you with me?"

She nodded, but her heart wasn't in it, and she had to fight back tears.

The Porsche Spyder that Dean was so proud of was a beautiful and powerful machine. As they headed north, Dean pushed it hard.

"Slow down, Jimmy," said Natalie. "We're going too fast."

"I know what I'm doing," he said.

"At least fasten your seat belt."

"I hate those damn things," he said. "I never wear them unless I have to. I'm safer without them. If anything happened, I'd be better off being thrown clear."

"Like at Bonneville?" she said. "At 400 miles per hour?"

Dean shrugged. "The clock said I was only doing 378 when I flipped."

He would not back off, and seemed driven by demons that Natalie could only guess at.

On the outskirts of Bakersfield, they were pulled over by a cop. He walked to the driver's side and Dean flipped him his license.

"This isn't a racetrack, Mr. Dean," the policeman said.

"Is that right?" he said. "I never would have guessed."

"You were doing 110 miles per hour in a 35 mile zone."

"So?" Dean said.

"So you could have killed someone."

"If you're going to give me a ticket, just hand it over," he said. "Spare me the lecture."

"Damn right you're getting a ticket." He wrote it out and handed it to Dean. As he walked back to the patrol car, Dean crumpled it up and shoved it under the seat. Then he drove to the restaurant where they were meeting Sal and the rest of the crew.

When he turned off the ignition in the parking lot, Natalie got out and slammed the door.

"This is where I get off, Jimmy," she said.

"What?"

"I love you, but I don't want to watch you die. I can't take it anymore."

He looked up at her as she walked around to the driver's side. "You're serious, aren't you?" he asked.

"I'm afraid so." She bent over and kissed his cheek, then patted his head and said "SHAZAM."

He watched her walk away. Sal and the rest of the crew came out of the restaurant.

"What was that?" asked Sal.

"I'll never know," said Dean. "You want to ride up to Monterey with me? The other guys can follow."

Sal got in and they drove off.

The time passed awkwardly as they sped through the back roads. Finally Sal spoke up.

"I'll miss her," he said.

"I will, too," said Dean, drifting through a bend in the road. "But she has to be who she is, and I have to be me."

"Where are we?" asked Sal.

"About eighty miles south of Salinas. Coming into some burg named Cholame."

"Watch out!" cried Sal. A car was running though a stop sign in front of them.

"The guy's got to stop," said Dean. "He'll see us."

As Dean slammed the brakes and worked the wheel he flashed for one last time into the mansion. All the doors to the living room were closed. The floor tilted sharply and he tumbled to the downward side. Wilbur Shaw was there, as was Vucki and Pierre Levegh and so many others. They welcomed him with open arms.

The next morning Natalie Wood finished her article. With tears in her eyes she wrote the following words:

"Noted racecar driver James Dean died on September 30th, 1955 in a tragic and senseless accident in Cholame, California. His chief mechanic, Sal Mineo, who was wearing a seat belt, survived with minor injuries. James Dean will be missed by all those who knew and loved him."

Loved him.

Loved him.

Loved him.

# CLEM, THE LITTLE COPPER

## by Thomas A. Easton

*When I invited Tom Easton, long-time reviewer for* Analog *magazine and author of* Greenhouse *and* Woodsman, *to submit a story for this book, he asked if he could do a variation of Red Skelton.*

*It wasn't until the story arrived in the mail that I realized just how much of a variation he had in mind. I now invite you to meet Clem Cadiddlehopper, hard-boiled cop supreme.*

Mama Teresa's tablecloths were a bold red check. The four shakers in each table's rack held salt and pepper and Parmesan and red pepper. A bowl was full of little envelopes that passed for sugar.

The chair was an inch higher than any other chair in the place. The owner provided it just for Clement.

The low-silled window was full of faces. Four of them. Three men, wrapped to their ears in too-big overcoats and ancient sweaters, uncut hair poking like hay from beneath stocking caps, rheumy eyes, runny noses. One woman, her gender apparent only because she didn't have a beard and her lips were painted a red so bright it was thirty years out of date. Behind her, a shopping cart full of old shoes was dimly visible.

All four were staring at him.

He glared at them.

They paid no attention at all.

They weren't staring at him after all, but at his plate. At lasagna and salad and house chianti.

He fished his wallet from his jacket pocket, flipped it open to show the badge, and held it over his food.

When he looked up once more, they were gone, shopping cart and all.

He grunted with satisfaction. At four foot six, he was not a very prepossessing cop, but he was a cop, thanks to an uncle with the clout to persuade the city to ignore the height minimum. He could make life miserable for them, and they knew it. Not that they always paid attention.

All that remained in the window was his reflection. Fading red hair surrounding a large bald spot. Lines and freckles, the latter dating back and back and ...

What was that? Was one of those bums back? But no. This face was dim, like a reflection, too. Sad and round, a fringe of gray hair, a battered top hat.

He turned to look behind him, but there was no one there. Certainly there was no clown like ... Yes, it was still there. No, now it wasn't. Blown away on the cold October wind he could hear outside the restaurant. Blown with the litter that scampered through the gutters.

He took another mouthful of lasagna and grinned at his reflection. He was glad he was indoors, warm and well-fed, even if the fat guy at the next table did smell faintly of sewers.

Fuck the homeless.


The beat cop was standing by the meter Clement hadn't fed, his hands behind his back, his stick swinging from its thong. "You ran outta time, Clem. Good thing I recognized the car."

"I thought you might, Carson." He had bought the high-tired Ranger so he could sit a little taller than his fellows for a change. "You coming to the party Friday?"

"Not unless you've got a new costume." Carson followed the shorter cop around the front of the car.

"Fat chance." The key snicked in the lock. "Ain't much in my size but plastic kid stuff."

"How about some new jokes, then?"

They both laughed.

Carson saluted and turned away.

Clement started his engine and the scanner with the same motion.

A few minutes later he decided not to go home quite yet.

The dispatcher was calling every available cop to the corner of Fifth and Washington. Gacy's Department Store. A bunch of bums had smashed three display windows, and now they were blocking traffic. They wanted to be arrested.

His two-room bachelor apartment wouldn't be anywhere near as much fun.

He turned left at the next light. He passed the lightless marquee of a boarded-up movie theater. Torn posters. Graffiti. Rows of display windows empty but for dust and broken boxes. A burned-out apartment building with the gleams of small fires in a few of its glassless windows. He had seen the fireplaces—sheet metal propped on bricks, old stainless steel or porcelain sinks. If someone tripped, the building's contents burned again.

Buildings full of trash. White trash. Black trash. Even yellow and red trash.

Trash fires.

There really wasn't any mystery why these bums were waiting for the cops. It was October. The weather was already cold, and soon it would turn nasty. A month from now, if he flipped his badge at bums drooling over his dinner, they would flip him the bird.

They *wanted* to get arrested. Jail was warm and dry. It had toilets and showers. And the city served meals.

There had been 73 in the tank that morning. By noon, a judge had heard their cases and set bail they couldn't make. They would stay in jail, cozy and fed, until their trial, and then for thirty days after that.

He shook his head. Turn 'em loose, and they'd do whatever it took to get back in. It would be simpler and cheaper to give 'em bus tickets to the sunny south. But that wasn't allowed anymore.

He thought of the parking lot beside the station, a square of asphalt surrounded by chain-link fence. Herd 'em in there. Feed 'em, but no roof, no warm. They'd *beg* for those bus tickets.

But that wasn't allowed either. No matter how crowded the jails got.

The intersection of Fifth and Washington was chaos. Six squad cars and three paddy wagons strobed the dark with their flashing lightbars. Traffic and street lights added to the visual din. Glass glinted wherever the sidewalk showed between the milling spectators.

Two dozen cops stood between the vehicles and a circle of what must have been a hundred ragged bums, their arms interlocked at the elbows. The circle moved clockwise, and as it moved, the bums chanted, "Don't pass GO. Go to jail. Don't pass GO. Go to jail."

The crowd on the sidewalk was laughing.

The cops were slapping riot sticks against their palms, waiting for just the right moment to arrive.

He stopped his car in the middle of the street behind Car 283. He twisted in his seat and reached into the back for his own riot stick. It was two-thirds his own height. The tip had been drilled and filled with lead shot. The grip was wrapped with black tape.

When he straightened up, the clown face was back, filling the window beside him. Its mouth was an open O, and to one side was a hand, fanned wide, chalk-white digits jutting from an ancient, fingerless glove.

He parked the squad car next to a hydrant and stared at the ancient flop across the sidewalk. It was too seedy to be called a hotel even by courtesy. The glass in its front door was patched with weathered cardboard so old even the graffiti had graffiti.

He yawned.

He wished he had stayed in bed.

But no. He had showed up at the station even though he knew the others would be in bed, sleeping off their exercise. They were on the evening shift. He was not.

He had held a cup of bitterly vile coffee in one hand and massaged his shoulder with the other. He had listened to the chatter: "You thought the tank was full yesterday? You should see it now. Two dozen more.

They brought 'em in last night. Regular riot. Injuries? Nah. A little muscle strain, maybe. Look at the Demon Midget there. The bums? Most of 'em were able to run away, but who cares? The ER sent over a couple of PAs."

A radio had muttered of slaughter in Belgrade and Dacca, thousands dead in floods and earthquakes and famines, a new record for unemployment figures, city blocks in flames set by pro-life rioters.

Not here, thank God. Not in *his* city.

And there hadn't been a hint of police brutality.

Not until he had gone to the cooler to wash the taste of the coffee out of his mouth. He had stood on tiptoe and bent over the spout. He had mashed the button with his thumb. And it had sprayed him like a firehose.

He had sworn.

Three cops had laughed.

And that damned clown had appeared in the polished steel of the cooler, a shadow-image howling with its eyes squeezed shut and its half-gloved hands holding up a *Herald-Post* as crystal-clear as television.

A *Herald-Post?* There was no such thing.

But its headline had seemed real enough: "Rioting Police Batter Homeless."

Except that no one else seemed to see a thing.

He needed more sleep.

He was seeing things. Nonexistent newspapers. An alarum that would alarm no one in his world.

The flophouse was another matter.

He got out of the car. He did not lock it. Even in this neighborhood, no one would dare to steal a cop's wheels.

He pushed the cardboarded door out of his way and found a dirty floor, stained and scuffed wainscoting, a rickety dinette table that served as a front desk, and a skinny, rabbit-toothed manager.

"Where's the body?"

"Upstairs. In back." The manager's voice was a sticky whine.

"Show me."

Once this place had been a respectable hotel. It had

had wide hallways, meeting rooms, a banquet hall, rooms with space for two double beds, a table, and a bathroom. Now most of the bathrooms had cots instead of plumbing. The larger rooms had been subdivided into cubicles no larger than the bathrooms. Half the width of each hallway was a row of still more cubicles. The building stank and murmured and droned.

As the manager led the way to the murder scene, Clement glimpsed whole families crowded into spaces too small for single adults. Children burst from their cells to follow, their parents after them, just as curious. They climbed a flight of stairs.

"Get those kids outa here," said the manager.

No one paid any attention.

"It's right in there." He was pointing at a door as flimsy as the partitions that made the building such a hive.

Clement pushed the door open.

"It" was an emaciated young woman, naked. She lay on a thin pink blanket soaked with blood beneath her torso. A rusty hunting knife lay beside her.

Her throat bore a bloody line where a locket had been ripped away while she was still alive. A finger lay on the floor; the bloodless stump on her hand said a ring had been stolen after death.

"She was a hooker," said a young voice.

Clement looked behind himself and saw a bright-eyed boy leaning eagerly forward. Adults were nodding in confirmation.

"She got AIDS?"

There were other things that stripped the meat from skull and limbs and ribs. But not many. He kept his mouth shut and glanced at the filthy mirror on one wall, almost expecting to see a mocking clown face.

A gravelly voice said, "She din't have much choice."

"No jobs."

"No more unemployment."

"No dough for dole."

This time Clement looked. The gravelly voice belonged to horn-rimmed glasses, shaggy eyebrows, and a fat cigar, unlit.

"This ain't the first," said the manager's whine.

"No one's safe," said the gravel. "You got money or rings or just a pretty ass, and it's gone."

"You don't like it," said the kid. "And you're dead. Like her." He did not sound shocked. Bum kids didn't keep their innocence long.

"Who did it?"

The manager shrugged.

Clement glared at the spectators, daring them to laugh.

But most of them didn't look like they thought anything was funny. Their faces were grim, their clenched lips pale. They could guess, their eyes said, but they didn't dare.

Only the boy spoke. "Cops never caught anybody before. You won't either."

He didn't answer the little bastard. He faced the manager. "How about a search? Or do I need to get a warrant?"

"Go ahead." *This* bastard didn't have as much nerve as the brat. "No such thing as privacy here anyway."

He turned his back on the body and pushed his way into the hall.

The room next door held a blank-eyed zombie and a sour odor. "Meds," someone said.

The room across the hall was empty, though the shit in the corner smelled fresh.

In the next, a dazed-looking man in a T-shirt slouched on the cot. A filthy hypodermic lay on the floor beside his foot. His arms were covered with needle scars. A thin gold chain was wrapped around his left wrist.

Clement hadn't expected it to be so easy.

"Whaddaya mean, no charges?"

"What's the point?" asked the Assistant DA Clement had stopped in the courthouse corridor. His blow-dried hair didn't twitch when he moved his head.

"He killed her!" Clement's voice actually squeaked.

He hated it when it did that. "The chain was broken. The links fit the marks on her neck! and I'll bet his semen matched . . ."

The Assistant DA said, "We didn't even check."

"Why the hell not?"

"She was a whore. She must have had six men's squirts inside her."

"So who cares? Right?"

"Something like that, yeah."

"Just a bunch of bums."

The Assistant DA turned away.

"So the punk walks."

"Not for long." The assistant DA looked over his shoulder. "We gave him an ounce that hadn't been cut yet."

A hand hit Clement's shoulder. Rafferty. They'd shared a beat once. "Hell, kid. Happens all the time. Good riddance, eh?"

Clement made a disgusted face.

The girl hadn't deserved to die that way. No one did.

The punk, on the other hand . . . With needle tracks like his, and a megadose of horse in his pocket, he wouldn't last the night.

The trouble was, he'd die happy.

He was easing the squad car down Twenty-eighth when he saw the kid. She was wearing shorts and a tee at least a size too small. The clothes were filthy. So was her face. She was maybe ten, just budding.

Her eyes were dead.

The man holding tight to her upper arm looked absolutely middle-class normal.

Clement pulled the car over and got out. He was in uniform, but he owned a leer he thought might serve. He put it on, and when the pair came abreast of him, he said, "Good-lookin' kid. Yours?"

The man studied him for a long moment before pulling a twenty out of his pocket and saying, "Hell, no. But you can have a piece when I'm done. Or she has a brother." He tucked the twenty in Clement's shirt pocket. Then he tossed his head. "Back there. The alley. My treat."

Clement looked, and there was the alley, half a block away. There was a woman wearing a too-large sweatshirt, leaning past the corner of the building, staring anxiously after her daughter. Staring at him, dark eyes saying she had seen the twenty.

So she hadn't lost it all, he thought. She could still worry. Still hate.

She should.

He turned back, and the man was gone. But an old hotel was just a few steps away, the paint on its door and window casements peeling, the wood cracked and gray, the glass almost opaque with dirt.

The place was a notch above that flop where the whore had died, but he wouldn't want to send his mother a postcard from it. She might catch something.

He was willing to bet that the threadbare sheets would still be warm when the man threw the kid down.

He wondered how many times the kid had been in there. And her brother. And her mother.

It wasn't any of his business, was it? He should call the vice squad.

And they'd say, "Who cares? They're just bums. Fuck 'em."

Yuck, yuck.

He was reaching for the squad car door when something made him glance toward the alley once more. The mother was still there, still leaning past the edge of the wall. Staring at him.

Was that hope in her eyes? Or just despair?

Had her husband been dancing in the street outside Gacy's the other night? Singing "Don't pass GO. Go to jail."

Fuck 'em.

Fuck the homeless.

He let go of the door handle and went to the back of the car. He opened the trunk. He stared at the shotgun in its clamps. That fired tear gas canisters, rubber bullets. Just the thing for crowd control. Overkill now.

But his number two riot stick. The same lead weight

in the end. The wood a little darker. The handle covered with pebbled rubber. Not quite the same, but good enough.

When he pushed the lobby door open, he was not surprised to see that shadowy clown face once more, nodding and winking and grinning. But he ignored the apparition. The desk clerk in front of him was just a kid, not much older than the girl, all pimples and Adam's apple.

He slammed the riot stick on the counter so hard that he left a crease in the ancient wood.

"A man and a little girl," he said. He did not show his badge.

He didn't have to.

The kid swallowed. His throat yo-yoed. He said, "Two oh three."

When Clement left, there was blood on his stick.

The Odd Fellows had donated their hall for the department's annual Halloween party. People would be trickling in already, expecting to see Clement there to greet them with a pratfall and a joke.

This year . . .

The garment bag lay open on the bed, displaying his usual costume. A shirt and jacket and pair of pants covered with colorful patches. The bottom of the bag held his oversized, floppy shoes and a baggy containing his pink rubber skinhead and makeup. There was a bindle, a kerchief tied up around a bundle of rags. There was his riot stick, to sling the bindle over his shoulder.

A bum suit.

He would lurch around the party, staggering in parody of drunkenness, laughing at hunger even as he ate, pretending to fear those cops who had come in uniform. Making fun, making mock.

While every cop and their wives and girlfriends and daughters laughed and laughed and laughed.

Behind him, opposite the foot of the bed, stood a massive oak dresser. On its top were scattered keys and coins, a wallet, a pair of nail scissors. Above it, on the wall, was a rectangular mirror. Above that was an ornate crucifix, complete with suffering Jesus.

But he was not looking in that direction. He therefore missed the face in the mirror, clearer than it ever was in windows and water coolers.

Sad-face makeup, fright wig, top hat. A coat of rags and patches.

A clown in a bum suit.

But not his bum suit.

Clement shook his head. He turned to the closet and sorted through the hangers until he found a black shirt. He put it on.

Then he went to the bureau and yanked open a drawer. He did not seem to see the clown in the mirror.

There was an unopened package of T-shirts in the drawer. He extracted the snow-white cardboard that stiffened it. He used the nail scissors to cut an inch-wide strip from the cardboard.

When he was done, he buttoned the throat of his shirt and fitted the cardboard strip under the collar. He looked at himself in the mirror and nodded. He still did not seem to see the clown.

He was ready. He stared up at the crucifix for a long, silent moment. He crossed himself.

The last thing he did before he left was to turn back to the bed and stare at his old costume with much the solemnity he had given the crucifix.

He shook his head and muttered, " 'Tain't funny, Magee."

He shook his head again. " 'Tain't funny anymore."

When he had left, the face in the mirror winked, tipped its hat, and vanished.

# A BUBBLE
# FOR A MINUTE

## by Dean Wesley Smith

*Everyone knows that Edward gave up the throne of England to marry American divorcee Wallis Simpson in one of history's most unlikely love stories. In fact, it was so unlikely that when I invited Dean Wesley Smith, publisher of* Pulphouse *and author of several fine works of fiction, to contribute to this anthology, I suggested that he write a story in which Mrs. Simpson stays in her own backyard, so to speak, and has her romance with an American head of state—Franklin Delano Roosevelt, to be precise.*

The last notes of the old song, "Paper Moon," faded into the thick antiseptic smell of the small nursing home room and the needle of the record made an impatient clicking, demanding that someone stop it.

In the wheelchair beside the bed, the old woman named Wallis Simpson nodded, almost in time to the clicking needle. She had a faint smile and distant haze in her eyes that gave her ninety-eight-year-old face a peaceful look. Seventeen-year-old Gary Sullivan studied that face for a moment, shaking his head at the incredible story she had just told him. A story of her youth and her marriages. A story identical to the stories she had told him every day for the last week. Identical, that is, right up until the story reached 1932. Right up until she stopped and asked him to put on the long-playing record of "Paper Moon."

Gary pulled back the sleeve on his sweatshirt and leaned forward in his chair over the old-fashioned phonograph. Carefully he picked up the arm and put it back on its holder. It was amazing something this old still worked and even more amazing that the old record hadn't been worn into dust since she listened to it so much.

He clicked off the machine and the small tape recorder on the nightstand beside it, then faced Mrs Simpson. "Would you mind if I came back again tomorrow?" It was the same thing he had asked for the past two weeks.

She took a moment to come back from whatever time she had been inside her own head, then smiled at him. "Of course not." Her voice was soft and almost hoarse after the workout she had given it telling him her story today. But her voice still had a tremendous power and aliveness that he had admired since the first day he had interviewed her.

"Besides," she said. A light smile slowly filled her face and smoothed out some of the wrinkles. "Who else would I have to talk to? Who else would believe in me?"

"Great," he said, with as much enthusiasm as he could muster, even though he had no idea what she meant by believing in her. It was just part of that song she loved so much.

He stood and, for the first time in the last half hour, noticed just how hot and closed-in this modern little room was. It felt like a prison and suddenly all he wanted to do was run for the door, escape, see what had changed.

What had changed seemed to be his constant question. Today, her story had ended with her marrying a businessman by the name of Harvey. With him she had two children. Gary had no idea what that would do to the world outside. But he doubted it would be enough to help his dad. So far, in two weeks of trying, none of her stories had been enough. But somehow he knew that if she just kept telling stories, in one his dad would still be with him and his mother.

Mrs. Simpson turned her wheelchair slightly to face where Gary stood. "You know," she said. "This little experiment of yours has made me the envy of the wing. No one ever comes to talk to most of these folks, except on holidays and the like."

He took a deep breath of the hot air and forced himself to smile. He didn't have the heart to tell her that his little experiment, as she called it, had started out as nothing more than a history paper for a senior high class. A simple assignment that had been done and turned in two weeks before. But he had kept coming back because at first he didn't understand why she kept changing the last part of her stories.

And then, after a few days, he needed her to keep changing the stories until she came to the right story. The exact right story that would bring his dad back home.

"Well," Gary said, "how about the same time tomorrow afternoon? You know how important reputation is to high school students."

She laughed. "Thanks for believing in me," she said again. She said that at least once every day and it was starting to give him the creeps. He just nodded and turned into the hall. The name beside her door now said Mrs. Harvey. It had been the twelfth time her name had changed, yet he still thought of her as Wallis Simpson, the name she had been the first time he asked her to tell a story.

Gary forced himself to walk slowly and carefully to the front door, smiling at the nurses at the nurse's station and taking slow, deep breaths of the thick antiseptic and death-filled air. The front door was only a few yards ahead.

He wondered what world he would find beyond it this time.

The assignment had been given by Coach Kinser, the heavyset ex-jock who taught Gary's third period. He was also Gary's football coach, which made getting a good grade even more important. "Go to a nursing home," Coach Kinser had said, "ask permission to talk to a resident, and interview that resident about his or her past."

The entire class had groaned and the coach had just

smiled. "History is an oral tradition," he had said. "You will enjoy it."

Gary, of course, had waited until a few days before it was due and then found Mrs. Simpson. "Wallis," as she said she liked to be called. Her room was the standard modern nursing home room, just like the one Gary's grandmother had died in. There was a bed with metal rails, a small desk, a small night stand, and a television across from a rocking chair. Nothing else decorated her room and the place instantly made him feel like he was being smothered. His first thought was to make the interview fast and get it over with. But Wallis Simpson was a good storyteller and, as Mr. Kinser had said, Gary enjoyed listening to her. It took over an hour the first day and filled a tape.

That first day she told him about her early years. She was from Baltimore and had been married twice. Her first marriage was to a naval officer by the name of Earl Spencer, whom she divorced in 1927. Her second marriage was to a Washington DC businessman named Ernest Simpson.

From the way she talked it was clear that she loved Ernest and everything he gave to her. She talked about how much they traveled and how she met kings and presidents while at his side. On a business trip to England she and Ernest had become fast friends with the Prince of Wales, who later became King Edward. She said she had many wonderful stories about trips with the Prince and parties at his castle.

But when her story reached the summer of 1932 and the party she and Ernest attended at the White House, everything suddenly changed.

The Prince of Wales had gotten them an invitation to the party to meet the new American President. It was at the mention of the party that she asked Gary to put the long-playing record of "Paper Moon" on her old phonograph. He did as she asked and while that record played, she told him about the party and meeting President Roosevelt and the First Lady and then about how Ernest was killed in London and how she returned to the States and never remarried. Her story ended with the record and Gary thanked her and went home, thinking he had more than enough information for his paper.

But it turned out he didn't. He actually wanted more information about the White House party and the young President Roosevelt, figuring that would make the most interesting paper for the coach, since the coach had a thing for the Roosevelts. So the next afternoon Gary stopped by the nursing home again to see Mrs. Simpson. She seemed happy to see him and again she went over the same story of her life, right up until the party at the White House.

And again, when she mentioned that White House summer party, she asked him to put on the record.

This time she told him much more about the party and about how she and Ernest had taken a limousine from the hotel. Then she went on to tell him about how she had fallen for the limousine driver. Two years after the party she went back to Washington, leaving Ernest in London, and got a divorce. She married the limousine driver, a man by the name of Barkley. He died five years ago and she was now all alone.

At first Gary had wanted to ask her about her change in her story, but then just shrugged it off to senility. And he was so startled by the change in story that he forgot to ask her more about President Roosevelt. She thanked him for believing in her and, as he left the room, he noticed the name tag on the door. It now read Mrs. Barkley, where the day before he was sure it had read Simpson.

As a lark, and with the same excuse that he needed more information about President Roosevelt, he went back the next day. In that day's story she met a businessman at the White House party and married him three years later. Not only had her name again changed on her door, but on the way home that afternoon his mom's favorite grocery store, DANNY'S, was gone, replaced by a small shopping mall. He asked his mom about the store, but she just gave him a blank look and shook her head. And there was no store by that name listed anywhere in the phone book.

The next day DANNY'S Grocery was back after

Mrs. Simpson told him a story about how she and Ernest traveled to Africa, where he died in a hunting accident. By this point Gary had figured out what seemed to be impossible: that her stories were somehow changing the world.

And he had also figured out that maybe, if he got to the right story, his dad would come back. His dad who had left him and his mother when he was five. A dad who his mother would never talk about and who he had dreamed about for as long as he could remember.

So he kept going back every day, listening to Mrs. Simpson, or whatever her name was that day, tell the same story right up to the hot summer of 1932, right up to the White House party. Then he would listen to her change the world around them.

On Gary's seventeenth visit to Mrs. Simpson he finally got his wish. His dad came back.

Her story the day before had left her with two children and today, for some reason, there was a vase of fresh flowers on her night stand. She looked happier and healthier than he had seen her and he commented about it.

She thanked him and they started into the same routine. She told him about her early life, her uncle and her grandmother, both of her marriages, and all the traveling she did. Gary had this part memorized and it never varied. And as always, when she reached the summer party at the White House, she asked him to put on the record of "Paper Moon."

"Why 'Paper Moon'?" he asked her as he placed the record on the turntable.

She smiled, her mind obviously a long way back in time, remembering. "It was the song the big band at the White House played three times. I danced and danced that night, feeling like a princess gone to the ball. I remember wanting the song and the night to last forever." She smiled at him. "So I bought the record. And besides, didn't you know that music has magic in it? With music, the world can be more than just make-believe."

Gary just nodded as the shivers ran up and down his back. With his hand shaking he carefully started the record.

"He was so handsome," she said, her eyes glazed as she looked off into the past, "standing there beside Eleanor, greeting his guests." She paused and looked at me. "You know he couldn't walk, don't you?"

"President Roosevelt?"

She nodded. "They had his braces locked in place so he could stand and greet his guests. He told me later that hurt him, which was why he didn't give many parties."

Gary had a sinking feeling that he didn't want to know where this was heading, but he just nodded and she went on.

"After dancing a few times, I got this message that the President would like to talk to me. He told me I danced beautifully and wished he could join me." She smiled, remembering an obviously joyful event.

"He was sitting in a large overstuffed chair and when he said that, he reached down and knocked on his braces through his pants. 'Not much chance of that,' he said and then laughed as if it were funny. I laughed with him."

She swayed back and forth in time with the music as she talked. "I remember I was hot from the dancing and the humid evening, so I sat on the footstool in front of him and we talked for the next hour between interruptions of other guests and business from his advisors."

She looked up at Gary as the song continued. "You know it was that hour that I think I fell in love with him. I know that seems hard to believe, but it only took an hour. After that evening Ernest and I went back to England, but Franklin and I kept in touch and I saw him three or four times a year for the next few years.

In 1936 I went back to Washington and divorced Ernest. Franklin and I saw each other much more during his second term, usually meeting in the home I owned in Maryland. Even though the people wanted him to, he decided to not run for a third term in 1940. He divorced Eleanor in 1941 and we were married the next year."

Suddenly she seemed to age and her face turned pale. "I'm sure you know he was executed right after the invasion of fifty-two. I've been alone ever since."

The last note of the song ended and faded into the dingy-looking room. Gary took a few deep breaths trying to calm the panic filling his stomach. Oh-God-oh-God-oh-God. What had he done? He picked up the arm of the record player and stopped the clicking. Invasion of '52? What was that? What had happened?

Slowly, he looked around the room. The flowers were gone and the bed had become a wooden frame with nothing more than a stained mattress and a rumpled sheet on it. This was the first time that the changes in her story had actually come into her room. He had no memory of when they had happened, even though he had been sitting here the entire time. In her other stories he had always remembered what had changed, but had never been near anything when the change took place.

Mrs. Simpson, or he would assume now, Mrs. Roosevelt, looked to be almost in a coma. Her eyes were glassy and she seemed about to collapse. Only the belt strapping her to the wheelchair held her upright.

He patted her hand and thanked her, but she paid no attention. He stood and turned for the door. His legs felt weak and his stomach twisted as if he had just been caught with his pants down in front of the entire school.

"Tomorrow?" he asked as he reached her door, not really wanting to go beyond it. But again she didn't notice his question.

Even though it was still mid-afternoon, the hall was almost dark, with only a few bare bulbs in the ceiling fixtures. The smell was of a musty attic, and the floor was stained and unwashed. Very, very different from the modern nursing home he had entered less than an hour before. This felt more like a jail for the elderly.

At the end of the hall, near the entrance hung a huge

sign in a foreign language Gary didn't recognize. All he had taken in school was French and hadn't really paid much attention to that. Behind an old wood desk where the nurses station had been when he came in was an old guard wearing a black uniform and reading a tattered paperback novel.

As Gary took a deep breath and started toward the front door, he remembered.

He remembered what life had been like before she told her story and what life was now like for him in this world. Memories like clear plastic, one over the other, flooded into his mind.

This time he remembered his dad. In this world he had a father who had not disappeared when he was five. In this world Germany had joined with Russia and won World War Two. Japan controlled the West Coast of what had been the United States and Maryland was now nothing more than a German satellite state.

And in this world his dad was a drunk who beat him and his mother. His dad never worked and blamed his mother for almost everything that was wrong in the world. He was an ugly, sadistic man who hated everything and everyone around him. Nothing like the dream father Gary had imagined him to be.

Gary staggered against the wall out of sight of the guard and forced himself to take deep breaths as the coach had taught him to do in pressure games. How did Roosevelt not running for President in 1940 cause America to lose the war? How could one woman change the world so much? It wasn't possible, yet Gary knew it was.

And how could his father hit him? Gary looked down at his arm where the angry red bruise had appeared.

He looked quickly in both directions down the hall. His memory of the clean, modern nursing home overlaid the prisonlike feel of this old building. But his memories of the world before were quickly fading. He would have to get Mrs. Simpson to switch it all back, to tell a new story. But what if her new story was worse than even this? What would happen if in the next world he hadn't even been born. Then what would happen?

He wanted to pound his fists against the wall and scream. Why hadn't he thought of that before now? How could he have been so stupid, hoping that he could find a world where he would know his dad? Well, it had worked and he had real vivid memories of his father now. Real vivid memories bruises and beatings and of wishing his father were dead, night after night, over and over again.

He eased back into Mrs. Simpson's room. She still sat beside the old phonograph, her eyes glazed.

"Mrs. Simpson, I mean Mrs. Roosevelt?" Gary said, sitting down across from her and keeping his voice low. "Would you mind telling me a story about your life?"

Nothing. She didn't move and Gary passed a hand in front of her unseeing eyes. No blink. Nothing. As far as he knew she might have been like this for years in this world. Maybe there was no going back. He took a few more deep breaths to fight off the panic, but this time it didn't seem to help. "Mrs. Roosevelt. Can you hear me? Please talk to me."

He shook her shoulders, slowly at first, and then harder, but her blank stare went right through him. He stood and paced back and forth in front of the door. He had enough memories of this new world to know that if he was caught in here, he would be in trouble. Big trouble.

Carefully he poked his head out and looked toward the guard. The old guy was still reading and except for a low moaning coming from a room down the hall, everything was the same. No movement. Nothing.

Gary went back and shook Mrs. Roosevelt one more time without luck. She was dead to this world. And now he was stuck here.

Footsteps came from down the hall and Gary quickly darted in behind the open door. The guard passed by, walked to the end of the hall, and went into a room there, letting the door bang closed behind him.

The banging echoed down the hall and Gary turned to see if Mrs. Roosevelt had noticed. She still sat there blankly staring over the old record player. And for a minute Gary stared at it, too, remembering what she had said and remembering the words of the song she loved so much. That just might do the trick.

Gary quickly stuck his head out the door to check on where the guard had gone, then went over to the old machine. It was still on and still had the record of "Paper Moon" in place. Maybe that would take her back to the party and both of them out of this nightmare.

He listened for a moment to make sure the guard had not come back out of the room, then put the needle in place and started the record. As the first few notes filled the room he wanted to stop it. It sounded so loud, far loud enough to bring the guard.

He went to the door quickly and checked the hall. The opening of the song seemed to be amplified in the stark hallway. It could be heard all over the building, he was sure.

He went back over to Mrs. Roosevelt and again shook her shoulders. "Wake up! Please? "I'm playing your song for you."

Slowly, he felt some life come back into her shoulders. He let go and sat down. After a few bars Mrs. Roosevelt's eyes flickered and she smiled faintly.

"Tell me about the party," Gary said, trying to keep his voice under control and not panic-filled. "Tell me who you met there at the White House. Please?" He glanced at the door and then back to her.

"Why," she said, her voice gaining strength and power with each word. "I met the President and the First Lady and a lot of others. It was a wonderful party and I danced and danced all night. You know, after Edward and I were married I thanked him for getting me invited to that party by taking him on a tour of Washington, DC. It was such a sweet thing for him to do, don't you think?"

"Edward?" Gary asked. "Who was Edward?"

Mrs. Roosevelt laughed, a strong, hearty laugh. "You are teasing me, aren't you? Why, he was the

Prince of Wales and then the King of England. After
his abdication we were married. I am the Duchess of
Windsor."

She reached over and patted Gary's hand. "A young
man like you should study his history more."

Gary only nodded in agreement and glanced around
at the room. The air shimmered like a heat wave had
hit it and the layers of the dark prisonlike room faded
away, replaced with a modern nursing home room.

And the old record player was also shimmering and
fading, as was Mrs. Simpson. In her place sat an elderly gentleman named Harrison and he was finishing
a story about how he fought in the Pacific and how the
kids of today just didn't understand how important history was and how smart it was for Gary's history
teacher to have them do this assignment.

Gary agreed, quickly thanked the man, and headed
for the front door.

The relief washed over Gary as he went down the
hall. He felt light, almost like dancing. He could still
remember his dad from the other world, but it was fading into the background like remembering a bad nightmare, pushed into the corners by the warm sun and the
smiles of the nurses. He doubted if he would ever
again wish for a father he didn't have.

And for one final time, faintly from down the hall,
he thought he heard Wallis Simpson say, "Thanks for
believing in me."

# SPACE CADET

## by Janet Kagan

*It has always been difficult for some people to take Dan Quayle seriously, but there's never been any question that a Vice President of the United States certainly qualifies as a celebrity. Here Janet Kagan, author of* Hellspark *and* Mirabile, *examines the same man in a slightly different reality.*

The laboratory was almost as the President had imagined it: banks of blinking lights, large and small machines humming happily to themselves, each in a slightly different tone, as if they were some great chorus singing for him. He frowned slightly—not enough to cause his face to wrinkle, of course—for now he noticed that something was missing. "Where's the, uh, thingie that makes the sparks?"

The scientist seemed not to understand English. Probably foreign from the looks of him. The President tried again, more loudly this time. "The sparker," he said. His hands described the arc. "Ziiiip!" he said. "Zaaaaap!"

"Do you mean a Jacob's ladder?" The scientist gave his assistant the ghost of a smile. "We don't need one of those, Mr. President. We're not bringing anyone back to life."

"Oh. Right. Let's see it, then." He was anxious to get on with this. The eggheads at the CIA had promised him ... well, never mind what they'd promised him. If he didn't get his money's worth, he'd see to their budget for the next four years!

"If you'll step this way, sir." He made a gracious gesture, and the lab assistant opened the glass door of the booth.

The President hesitated. The booth reminded him of something—that scene from *The Fly*. As if he were a mindreader, the scientist said, "Don't worry. We had the exterminator in this morning." The lab assistant laughed. Mistake, thought the President. Bad move to laugh at the boss' jokes when they aren't jokes. See if you get reappointed after *that*.

The scientist patted the side of the booth. "Here she is—our TATSbe. That's what we've taken to calling her: sort of an acronym for 'Things As They Should Be.' It offers us the chance to change our world for the better. Now the principle behind the machine you see here—"

The lab assistant shook his head. This time the President agreed; with a wave of his hand he cut the scientist short. "Just tell me what to do," he said. "I'm a busy man, and the sooner we get this done the better."

"Just step into the booth, close the door completely, and press the button on this."

The little box he was handed looked much like the remote control for his TV set. He grinned boyishly. "You mean this switches from one channel to another, until I get one I like."

"That's about the size of it. Though we have discovered that the worlds tend toward optimum—that's why we named it 'Things As They *Should* Be.' "

"Tend toward optimum?"

"They get better and better," said the lab assistant. "Each time you press the button. So if you don't like the one you get first, try, try again. It will only get *better*."

"Too bad I can't use this on my TV." That would sure fix all those snotty reporters who were always on his case. Well, if he understood this TATSbe thing, it *would* fix all those snotty reporters.

He gripped the remote control firmly in his hand and stepped into the booth. Things as they *should* be—he could hardly wait.

He pressed the button. . . .

\* \* \*

Harry looked totally exasperated. "Dan, pay attention now. All you have to do is stick the keys *in* the lock, open the door, come *through* the door facing the camera, and look surprised. So—could we get it right this time?"

"Sure," he said. A movie star, he thought gleefully. I'm a movie star and that's Barbra Streisand I'm being in a movie with. I can do this! This is great!

"Places, people! And roll . . . ." "Speed." *Snap!* "Scene 24a; take sixteen . . ." "Dan, do it!"

Walk to the door. Insert the keys in the lock. His hands were sweaty with excitement; the keys were slippery little buggers. Ooops. Jangling, the keys dropped to the ground. "Oh, shit," he said.

"Cut!" yelled the director. He put his head in his hands and said to no one, "Why me?"

Streisand said, "Danny, Danny. . . . Your poor mother, rest her soul, how did she raise such a klutz? Oy!"

"All right," said the director, getting a grip on himself. "Let's do it one more time."

Streisand said something he didn't catch and the director laughed. It wasn't a nice laugh.

The hell with you, thought the President. This is too much like work, and all this makeup makes me feel like a pansy. Besides, I'm not getting any more respect than I was before. Things as they should be—let's just see about that. He reached into his pocket and pushed the button. . . .

He felt a sense of motion, a rolling motion that made him feel a little nauseated until he realized he was on a boat. Not a yacht, he found, as he looked around. Why wasn't it a yacht? He turned for a better look and almost fell over his flippers. Ah! He was scuba diving . . .

The Frenchie said, "Are you ready, Dan?"

The President nodded, smiling for the video camera, and gave a thumbs up. Scuba diving with Jacques Cousteau—now *that* was something, all right. Famous diver, on TV all the time—and none of that makeup shit.

I get to swim with dolphins. Oh, boy! I always wanted to do that ... never could get near them, except in the Oceanarium, and how much fun was that?

"Okay, Dan, into the cage."

Cage? He followed their lead. He climbed into the cage. The next thing he knew he was being lowered into the icy water, cage and all. When at last he got his bearings, he swung the light around. Wonderful! He was surrounded by dolphins.

The dolphins circled closer. Odd, he thought. I thought dolphins were— Then he noticed the dorsal fins. And the teeth. And the *jaws.*

Something slammed into the cage behind him. Because he was unprepared, the slight motion rocked him against the bars. Enormous teeth aimed right for his faceplate. He paddled frantically back to the center of the cage as the shark began to gnash its teeth against the bars.

Sharks! Holy shit, sharks!

Blind with panic, he finally found the remote control. Things as they *should* be, he said, stabbing once, twice, three times at the button.

He was before TV cameras again, sweating under the lights. Ah, a televised debate—*that* he could do in his sleep. . . .

It was a presidential debate, too. He leaned back, feeling very much in his element, and turned to his opponent.

His jaw fell. "Marilyn?" he said. "Marilyn? Don't you know me?"

His wife said, "Yes, I do. I knew Jack Kennedy, too. I served with Jack Kennedy. Jack Kennedy was a friend of mine. And, J. Danforth Quayle—*you're no Jack Kennedy.*"

"Lieutenant, we've got a sniper out there!"

He was sweating still—this time from the heat and the humidity of the jungle. The whole pack stank like fireworks and chemicals. What didn't stink of fireworks and chemicals stank of *green.*

Thank God for that phone call that had gotten him his commission. That meant he could kill gooks the right way, not the namby-pamby way Nixon was going about it.

"All right, men! Get that sniper! Charge!"

For once, they actually obeyed him. He followed after, keeping low, his back aching with the amount of equipment he carried. The weight of his gun was appalling. The heat was worse . . .

The men seemed to veer off as they reached the rotting tree that lay across the path. Fuck it. He'd take the short cut over it. He'd take that sniper out himself . . .

There was an ear-splitting sound and the world went tumbling. He knew he was screaming in pain, but he couldn't hear himself over the ringing in his ears.

Two of the men came and stood over him. One of them knelt. "Looks like the lieutenant's a goner," he said, as if it didn't much matter.

"Looks like," said the other.

"Think next time we'll get a looey that cares whether we live or die?"

The second shrugged. "Don't matter. I got another VC trip mine stashed away, just in case." He gave a toothy grin that reminded the President of the sharks.

A clear crisp fall day . . . He was part of a long line stretched out across the field. He breathed a sigh of relief. Hunting, that was something familiar to him, something pleasant.

"Okay, fellows. The President's ready—"

The President straightened. That was more like it. But he *wasn't* ready. All he had was a damn stick . . . what kind of hunt was this?

"—Let's see he gets his money's worth." The rest of the line started to thrash its way through the field.

The President felt a stiff jab to the shoulder.

"Danny, fer chrysake, quit daydreaming. Beat the godfersaken bushes, will ya? That's what you're getting paid for!"

A shove sent the President stumbling forward. A

covey of birds shot from the bushes and into the air. Shots rang out . . .

The President felt a searing pain in his right arm. Blood! More blood! He screamed again.

"Fer chrysake, Danny, it's only a flesh wound." The guy in the Coors cap clamped a hand on his arm to stop the bleeding. The President sat abruptly.

George and a bunch of Secret Service men rushed to the President's side. The man in the cap said, "Don't worry, Mr. President. It's only a flesh wound. Coulda happened to anybody." He was talking to George. *George was president!* Unbelievable.

"Sorry, son," George said to him. "Hope you don't take it personally. It's not my, uh, thing to go around shooting people—only meant to bag a few quail."

The man in the Coors cap laughed himself red in the face.

"Something funny, mister?" one of the Secret Service men said in a surly tone of voice.

"Sure is. You got yourself a quail, Mr. President. This here's Danny Quayle in person—and you sure brought him down!"

Even George got the joke, this time. He gave that irritating halfhearted laugh of his and the Secret Service men all laughed with him dutifully.

The President reached left-handed for the remote control. "Take that, George," he said, as he pushed the button.

The lander came to rest amid the rocks and red dust with a gentle thump. The President glanced at the monitor and remembered to notify NASA. For some reason, it would be a long time before they acknowledged—but the sooner he talked the sooner they would.

Still—Mars! He was on Mars!

The cameras showed him not far from one of the canals. Even better.

Exultant—he'd gotten the hang of the TATSbe at last—he eyed the monitor. He'd been in charge of the Space Program for a long time: this was the payoff.

Presidents might be forgotten—he knew he couldn't remember but a handful—but the first man to set foot on Mars . . . Now, *that* was making history!

For once, he'd get the respect he deserved.

And he was damned if he'd wait for those jerks at NASA to tell him which foot to move when. Laying aside the remote control, he opened the hatch and stuck his head out to take a good deep breath of the Martian air . . .

Back on Earth, Chief Justice of the Supreme Court Barbara Jordan had just finished swearing in the new President of the United States, Pat Schroeder. The TATSbe had done its job and had winked out of existence . . .

Things were as they should be.

# HITLER AT NUREMBERG

## by Barry N. Malzberg

*It's almost impossible to think of Adolf Hitler as a celebrity, or, indeed, as anything but a genocidal maniac. But it is the job of the science fiction writer to attempt the impossible, and here Barry Malzberg, author of* Hervoit's World *and* The Sodom and Gomorrah Business, *does just that—for a live, imprisoned Hitler, awaiting trial at Nuremberg, would certainly have been the most celebrated prisoner of this millennium.*

The humiliation.

Not the incarceration. That I accept. I would have done the same to any of them: Eisenhower, Churchill, that traitor Joe Stalin in the dock, manacles removed only when in full court. One must intern the enemy. The enemy is not there to be humored.

But to be assembled with these lying subordinates, to be enmeshed with them. Himmler, Goering, Streicher, that dog. To take the air, eat the meals, meet the lawyers chained to these fools. A head of state is entitled to be managed with respect, and that I do not forgive them. Also these foul, stinking quarters, the piss-cans, the scraps of uneaten food in the corners, unclean, unclean! *tref* the kikes say, and the sound of the dogs in the courtyard. These are not quarters I would have given them. I would have placed interned enemies in better places, isolated, given Stalin or Truman the respect due a leader. This foul air grips, it clings, I can feel the indelicate heave of the stomach and the need to vomit but no, I am disciplined. I will not give them the satisfaction. I will not show weakness.

My generals, he thinks, my aides, my partners and collaborators in the great adventure of the Reich. Who would have known? he thinks. I had no idea what they were doing in my name. No head of state can be responsible for everything. If there is no delegation of duties, there is only fragmentation and disorder. I permitted them autonomy, I treated them as I would have been. Who was to know? Who could have possibly known what was going on there? The camps, the exterminations, the trains, the mad accountings, the accumulation in the refineries, the crematoria working frantically in the beginning of '45 just before it all fell . . . I knew nothing of this. The Russians obsessed me, the failures of the Luftwaffe, the betrayals and incompetence of the generals. The poverty of Dunetz's face when he looked at me and said, "It is all over; I think we should sue for peace." These are the issues which concerned me, great matters of state, of defeat, of the fall of empires, of the final, frozen, perilous march to the abyss. Not the Jews and their Final Solution. I had no position on that at all.

I was sick of Jews, he says in open court. Sick of them, do you hear me! Usurers, thieves, international bankers, Communists and spies, yes, but I could not be concerned with them anymore; if in half a millennium the Inquisition had not been able to bring peace to the continent and disperse them, then my own feeble efforts would be unavailing. I did not want anything more to do with the Jews. Let Eichmann take care of it, I said to Himmler. *Poof!* I clean my hands of this, let Eichmann arrange for their deportation. *Arbeit machen frei.* Keep them at their tasks.

He needs the microphones more as his testimony continues. At the beginning he had entered the dock straight and angry, dark with pride and the consistency of his purpose, he would not bow to them, would need no technology, would not need to resort to machines to make his position felt. But as it went on and on into the week, then stretched past the end of the month, then into the odorous spring, the dampest stink of spring he had ever known, his voice began to fail and they gave him the microphones. In full-throated whisper he explained his position, took them through all of it again and again, hating his weakness, his dependence. Their attention was fixed; not even at the Reichstag had he had a crowd held in such thrall. Yet he could tell that the situation had been poised against him, he was not getting through. He was not making his position clear. They did not believe him. If they had accepted what he had to say, then the full monstrousness of their own deeds would have reared up against them and they would have known that they were worse than he. So from the start it was necessary to target him, make him the assassin at the center of the state. Himmler, Streicher, Goering, and all of the rest of them, and now the Allies, were in their palm. I was not responsible, he said in open court. It was the manufacture of bitter and disloyal aides, Jew-haters and gypsy killers. Regiments of the feeble-minded fell before them like wheat. I was preoccupied with the international situation. I was concerned with great matters of state. What did I care, what do I care about your bunch of Jews and what would you have me do for any of them? He raises his hand in bitter salute in the dank cell of his inquisition and hears the engines of history clattering dimly for him, the voices of the guards riotous in the hall.

He is a small man but filled with self-confidence, dapper and precise, clean and organized. Here in these quarters he holds on to his dignity, gives them a head of state who they will see has not crumbled to circumstance. The thousand-year Reich was not to be, but the Fuehrer remains. In the courtyard when Goering and Himmler approach him, he moves away quickly, making gestures of dismissal. He will not talk to them, not now, not ever again. They have secret microphones on their persons and will broadcast his words to the Allied interrogator, he knows that. They will do anything now to protect themselves, to make a stab at salvation, they will deliver the Fuehrer to these conquerors as if they were gods. Only Streicher has access to him, old Julius who speaks the language of the people and has always had an amusing, peasant insight. "I hear rumors," Julius has said to him, "our armies are still in the field. They are under cover. They are preparing themselves for a final assault. They will storm this place and we will be free. That is what I hear," Julius says. "We must have courage and we must be patient. In the meantime, we eat pork and tell them whatever they want to hear and wait for better times."

Julius is an idiot. His intelligence is borderline at best, worse than that, but he has had his virtues of loyalty, and here in his ragged uniform and ridiculous cap he seems to have been stripped down by the captors and the situation to the schoolboy he once was, the bully with terror lurking at the corners of his being. It is possible to feel pity for Julius if not for his situation. The man is a fool, they are all fools. They should not be here.

In the rooms when Dunetz had brought word of the final assault Eva had said, "Take the poison. I am ready to take the poison," and as he had promised he ha counted out the capsules, one, two, three, four for her, the other six for him, he had estimated that he was one and a half times stronger than she and so had saved the larger amount, but after she had downed her share, he found that *he was not able to take them,* something powerful within him denied the capsules and, terrified, he had flung them against the wall. Eva had stared and screamed, staggered to her feet filled with rage at his betrayal, and had made desperate retching motions to try to disgorge her own share, but the retching acted only to weaken a frame already caved in and she had fallen, rolling then into a dull state of inanition and alone in the bunker then he had waited. He could not take the poison, after all. He had had it all planned; the poison surely was the proper fashion, the proper rebuke for these sinister enemies who had infiltrated what he thought were his last loyal troops and had destroyed him, but suicide was a sin, it was an evil, and unlike Hess he would die defiant, would resist them to the end.

So that was the way they had found him then, clutched in the corner, arms in a cross over his chest, hands on his throat, shouting at them, "I will not yield, I will not yield," as they dragged him away. Or was that what he had shouted? He could not remember. Another voice, one from a distance, might have cried "I surrender, I surrender," or "don't kill me," but he is not sure of this. He is not sure of anything, the old certainties seem to have departed. He paces the courtyard, shrugs at the guards, spits at his associates, waves away Julius. "No," he says, "not even you. I do not want to talk to you." In his mind he goes over the testimony again and again. Tomorrow once more he must attempt to explain himself, make clear to them why it could have been no other way and why he had in those last years been turned into the figurehead in whose name mad generals did unspeakable things, but he knows that they will not believe him. None of them will ever believe him again. It is enough to make him weep.

I sent Hess. I detailed Hess to England, I could tell that early how out of control the situation was. They were killing Jews in my name, advancing toward Stalingrad in the worst of winters with orders to sack the capital, and I knew nothing of it until much later. They had sealed me off by then, put me in Berechtesgarden with false information and the dogs running wild and free in the mountains. The dogs, always the dogs, sniffing, poking, ramming their way into everything. "Hess," I said, "sue for peace. Tell them what the situation has become. I would go with you but they watch me every moment. They follow me with their eyes and with their guns. I am a prisoner here. Take the plane and the documents. Tell them that we will capitulate. Tell them that we will admit their entry into Berlin and turn over control if they will allow us a just and generous and honest surrender." His eyes gleamed with assent. Hess was a weak man, but his weakness was all that I could trust. "You have my full and confidential support," I said. "Go on your way."

I detailed Hess. It was all my doing, he went up into the plane, up in the air, over the border, and then into the bizarre, pathetic aftermath. Of which I learned only later. I was always afraid of Eichmann. I knew there was a craziness, an evil in the man. "Jews do not have to be killed," I said to him. "Do not kill the Jews. Intern them if you must and use them as pressure for munitions and cooperation, release them piecemeal for quarter from Roosevelt and Churchill, but do not kill them. The Jews are valuable capital, not to be expended."

"I never had extermination camps in mind," he said to the prosecutor. "*Arbeit machen frei,* they were work camps." Jackson laughed at me, opened his mouth and roared with laughter while the court quaked. I could see then that there was no chance, no chance for me while I was there to act as scapegoat. If I had been dead, if I had taken the poison, they would have said that it was all my orders, that they were just following orders, and even though I had not taken the poison, my presence was only a small inconvenience. "We were just following orders," Goering said. That fat fool sat in court day after day, facing me, his eyes locked to mine as he explained this, and then one by one these men who had seized the government in my name said that they were following orders. If Eichmann had been there, he would have said that it was for the love of Jews that he had taken the job and that he had used the camps as exterminating devices only because I insisted. Eichmann would have said that he was a clerk who went home to his quarters night after night, wretched from a day of following orders, but he had fled. I knew from the start, could not have known otherwise, that it was all fictitious, a dumb show, and that they would destroy me to save themselves. But then such is the obligation of the head of state. I had seen that clearly in '33 and taken upon myself that risk and obligation. I do not complain.

I complain no more, I will resist but not seek pity. It is their dock, their lies, their option. Goering and Himmler will be next, but I will go first with the sat-

isfaction of knowing that hanging me means *nothing.*
They have the wrong man, they have the wrong understanding. They cannot hang a country, they cannot
hang the world, but only this poor and necessary symbol. I know this. I know that it could not have been
otherwise. I am clear and determined, I meet the enemy on his own terms and my own declaration.

Permitted the courtyard no longer after the verdict,
he says that he does not mind the confinement in the
cell. He monitors the time carefully and listens to the
birds in the trees in this damp season. Goering is
brought under guard to express his condolences, but he
will not listen. Himmler arrives, but he turns away.
Streicher comes in sackcloth, the sheen of alcohol on
his face and they embrace and he feels the palpating
waves of sweat and event coming from Streicher's
glands. Good-bye, Julius, he says. Of all of them you
were the only one I could trust. Because you were so
stupid, he does not add. Julius is taken away. Now,
erect in his camouflage, neatly dressed and waiting for
the guards, he sits calmly in his cell, thinking of Eva
and the long nights now in Berechtesgarden, the dogs
clamoring in the hills, the two of them clamoring further, the smell and necessity of the century all around.
He had plans, great plans, but they were destroyed by
those he trusted and there is nothing to do now but
wait for the full and final verdict which he hopes will
be somewhat more generous than this. *"Coward,"* Eva
had shrieked at him, dying. *"You coward!"* No, not exactly. There was something larger at issue. The century
knifes through him, the lightning bolt carrying him toward the millennium. The rope is light and amazingly
soothing as it is yanked into place. It could have been
any of you, any of you.
  Any of you.

# ELVIS INVICTUS

## by Judith Tarr

*In my anthology* Alternate Kennedys, *best-selling author Judy Tarr wrote of an alternate universe in which the four Kennedy brothers were a rock band and Elvis Presley was the President of the United States.*

*It proved so popular and received so much fan mail that I was able to persuade Judy to write a sequel, this time concentrating on President Presley.*

### I. *Pater Patriae*

### Elvis Presley, The First Four Years
### A Presidential Album

1. *From a Jack to a King: After the Inaugural.* There they are, posed on the steps of the Ritchie Valens Center for the Performing Arts, the President magisterial in white tie and tails, the First Lady floating in a sea of white tulle. No hint in this official portrait of the tragedy that struck the Inaugural Ball: Secretary of State Lennon gunned down by terrorists, Vice President King narrowly escaped from a similar fate, the President's life saved by the lead singer of the Kennedy Brothers musical combo. The show must go on, the President's expression declares. All's quiet on the Potomac front. No bad omens for the new, young, radical Administration.

2. *Kissin' Cousins: Swearing In the New Secretary of State.* The freshly minted Secretary has a new set of hornrims for the occasion. Grave responsibilities await him in the international arena—and like rot, as the late, lamented Mr. Lennon would have said. Secretary Holly

keeps a diplomatic distance from President Presley, but their wives, arm in arm, proclaim the close relations between the two families.

3. *For the Good Times: At Home in the White House.* A rare opportunity for the public eye to examine the private life of the First Family. Matriarch Dolly oversees a Rose Garden outing. Elvis, Jr. gives little Mary Lee a riding lesson on the Presidential pony, Heartbreak. Verne and Jeff David romp with two of the family's black-and-tan hounds. The bitch, Nancy, will drop her litter two days after the photograph is taken: ten prime puppies. Sale of the litter will benefit Dolly's favored cause, the Butterflies-Aren't-Free Foundation.

4. *Treat Me Nice: With King Vladimir III of Russia.* The major diplomatic triumph of the President's first Administration: the Congress of Vienna (that's the Opera House behind the dignitaries). King Vladimir, having agreed to open diplomatic relations with the Cossack Republics and the Grand Khanate of Tartary, appears rarely pleased to be in the President's company. Secretary of State Holly tries to efface himself in the background. Note Elvis, Jr.—he has his father's looks—with the lovely young lady in red. A celebrated romance is about to begin between the First Son of the Grand Republic and the Tsaritsa of All The Russias.

5. *Trouble: The Banana Boat Crisis.* Next to the greatest triumph, the greatest frustration. The President, in fatigues, views the wreckage of the American embassy in Costa Chiquita. The first all-female unit in Marine history stands guard. Two Medals of Honor and many Purple Hearts later, the Fighting Amazons will be forced to withdraw to Grenada, leaving the field—or rather the banana plantation—to the People's Army. President Presley vows, "I shall return."

6. *The Wonder of You: Gala in Graceland.* Home at last for a splendid occasion: the reception in honor of the year's American Nobel Prize winners. The President and the First Lady stand proudly with the three laureates: Asimov—onetime chemist, world-renowned roboticist,

cited for his work in artificial intelligence and the Laws
of Robotics. Clarke—astronomer, cosmologist, explorer
of the bizarre magnetic anomaly on the Moon. And
Heinlein, author and admiral, winner of the Nobel Prize
for Literature. The gala is an unqualified success. When
it winds down, the laureates and the President will de-
camp to the Ritz Graceland and celebrate till dawn in a
mob of well-wishers, fellow dignitaries, and science-
fiction fans. The Secret Service will cope.

7. *Good Rockin' Tonight: Jamming in the White House
Studio.* The President unbuttons for an old-time hoedown.
Mad Jack Kennedy shares the mike in a rendition of
"Graceland on My Mind." Dolly adds her voice to the
chorus. The backup band is a stellar gathering: Secretary
of State Holly, Attorney General Ellington, Vice President
King, and Prime Minister Starr of United Britain at the
drums. Kennedy will refuse appointment to the Cabinet
as Secretary of Defense. His brother, Teddy, will take his
place, signaling the entry into politics of a famous musical family.

8. *It's Now or Never: At the Mars Shot.* A dream fulfilled: the first expedition to Mars blasts off from Cape
Lennon. Inset shows the President with the crew. The
President seems as elated as the astronauts—but is that a
suggestion of sadness? Envy, maybe? "If I have to be remembered for only one thing," the President says, "I
want to be remembered for this." Protesters pack the
gates, demanding the lifting of the banana embargo.

9. *Suspicious Minds: Running for Reelection—
Debating the Hollywood Faction.* President Presley faces
off against candidates Ronald Reagan (Democrat) and
Woodrow "Woody" Allen (Independent). Reagan's Let-It-
All-Hang-Out Economics vies with Allen's Government-
as-Yenta. Sharp attacks on the President's Banana
Republic policy, his handling of the People's War in
Berkeley, and his rockabilly adaptation of "Rock of
Ages." He counters with copious examples of his policies
of moderation, modernization, and world unity. The con-
clusion is foregone. Even in this blurred newspaper shot,

we see the President looking ahead to his second term, with its new triumphs, its new defeats, and its ever-new promise of photo opportunities.

## II. *Rex Gloriosus*

### "What I did on My Summer Vacation"

What I did on my summer vacation was, I went to see the King.

Momma collects kings. We saw King Ronnie in California del Sud last year, and the year before that we went all the way to All the Russias (actually, there's just one, but they like to make it look like a lot) and saw Tsarina Tatiana and her husband, Prince Elvis. Momma said Prince Elvis looks just like his daddy did when he was his age, so I sort of knew what to expect when we went to see the King—the *real* King—in Graceland.

He used to be President. We studied that in Social Studies last year, and I got an A on the test. I wrote an essay about how Presidents got worn out and President Danforth's government went to pieces and we ended up with kings and dictators and anarchs and presidents-for-life and queens-for-a-day. It's hard to collect queens-for-a-day, they really add up and you have to get there before the midnight execution, which is tough if you just found out this morning and all the flights are booked, but kings stay around for a while.

So we went to see the King. Momma saw him a long time ago, when he first got elected King, after he stopped being President and Junior married the Princess of All the Russias and little Mary Lee went to be Dictator-for-the-Revolution of Mars Colony. He was the first King in her collection. Now she's got six dozen, less one, and she decided she'd collect him again. Besides, Aunt Hattie's something important in Graceland Palace, and she said she could get us in and actually *meet* him.

We never met a king momma's collected before. We met Prince Charles in London, but he doesn't really count, and King Billy in Plains wasn't really a king, he just said he was. Momma actually thought about leaving me at home with Daddy and Grandma and Graciebot and the babies, but I said she'd been collecting kings with me since I was a fetus, it wasn't fair if she stopped just when it was starting to get good.

Momma cares about fair, but she doesn't sell it cheap. I had to wear a dress—a *real* dress, no cheating with wide-bottom pants—and I had to promise not to speak unless spoken to. That almost decided me into staying home, but I'm as stubborn as momma is. I put on the dress and buttoned my lip, and off we went to Graceland.

Graceland's kind of like Buckingham Palace, and kind of like Versailles (we collected King Louis XXVII there), but not as tacky. The Royal Guard wears white sequins and long sideburns and carries pearl-handled pistols. One of them met us when we drove up in the taxi. He checked momma's papers and acted like we were some kind of royalty, bowing and ma'aming and calling me Miz Rollins.

"Actually," I was all set to say, "Bille Sue Rollins is just my nom de plum. I'm really Lady Gloriana Alexandra von Roehling. You can call me Your Ladyship." But momma gave me a Look and I didn't say it.

When I'm eighteen, you bet I get my name changed.

Meanwhile I'm just twelve—well, eleven and a half—and momma wasn't having any of what she called nonsense. So I kept quiet and followed along after the guard in the sequins, and kept half an eye on momma. Momma was looking like she got escorted into Graceland Palace every day, nice and calm, with her best dress on, the one with the blue suede skirt and shoes to match, and her jacket with the sequins and the fringe, and her hair in a Dolly do, platinum curls all over and puffs out to here. I wanted one, too, but momma said no. So I was stuck with my boring old red curlytop.

We must have walked forever. We kept getting

passed on to different people. Each one was fancier
than the last one, but they all called momma ma'am.

I know we're supposed to do a lot of description,
and I should write all about the mirrors and glass and
fancy tassels and pretty-colored carpets, but I was too
busy looking around to really *see* much of anything,
and it's a lie to make it up, isn't it? Even if I do get
points off my grade. Anyway, it was mostly just lots of
things. Lots of doors. Lots of stairs. Lots of shiny
floors. They were all so slippery I had to creep along
on my slick new shoe-soles. I wondered how the people who lived there did it. Maybe they skated when
people weren't looking.

"Sticky tape," momma whispered when I asked. She
wasn't missing a step in her high, high heels. Just after
she said that, the guard opened a door, and there we
were.

I was kind of disappointed. You know all the pictures, how they show the King on his throne that they
made out of a white Cadillac, in white fur and blue
suede and of course sequins, with his crown on his
head dazzling fit to make you blind. I'd brought my
sunglasses just in case, had them right in my little bag,
and I was all set for the long, long hall with the white
carpet, and all the bows you had to make in the movies, and lords and ladies bowing back, and trumpets,
and everybody's name called out when they came in.

What we got was a room. It was ordinary, kind of. I
mean it was big and everything, and it had a white carpet, but it wasn't the throne room. The furniture in it
was just furniture, chairs and things, and people were
standing around, like when daddy does his real-estate
cocktail parties at the Dewdrop Inn.

I got my name called out, sure enough. *"Billie Sue!"*
in a honk like a foghorn, and there was Aunt Hattie
bearing down on us, all set to hug me to death. I could
lip-synch the script, she's been on it since momma was
a baby, practically. "Billie Sue! Oh, you've *grown!*
Hasn't she grown, Linda Mae? Why, she's almost as
big as you are!"

I wanted to crawl right down between the floorboards, if there'd been any, which there weren't, this being Graceland. It was marble clear down to China.

Momma looked kind of put out herself. She wore her company smile, the one she puts on when daddy's had too many extra cocktails and it's time to get home. "Harriet. How wonderful to see you. Thank you so much for inviting us."

"Oh, don't thank me," said Aunt Hattie. "Thank his majesty here."

And there he was. I looked right past him the first time, looking for somebody who looked like Prince Elvis. Prince Elvis is *old*—he must be almost thirty— but he's got these swoony eyes and all that black hair, and he looks at you just right, and—

Well, anyway. We're all sorry Prince Elvis is married. So I was looking for him, you know, but older.

Good thing momma made me button my lip. The King didn't look *anything* like his pictures. He was fat, for one thing. He had a suit like daddy's friend Joe Bob wears, it tried to make him look thin, but it didn't work. There weren't any sequins on the suit. At all. And he wasn't wearing his crown.

You collect kings as long as momma and I have, you get so you know kings are people, too. But if you're going to meet them in person, right there to talk to, you'd think they'd dress up a little, put a crown on, play it up.

He did have a nice voice. He said hello to momma and hello to me. He said momma was looking right pretty, and he said he was sorry Dolly couldn't be there but she was out saving the butterflies or something. Momma said thank you and that's too bad and yes isn't it a nice day.

I didn't say anything. I guess I mumbled something when he said hello, but that was it. Everybody says I should have asked him things, like had Nancy the Tenth had her puppies yet and was he going to visit Mary Lee on Mars and did he really write the words to the Banana Boat Song. But come right down to it, I was tonguetied. He looked at me, see. He gave me that little smile he has, that all the boys try to do but they only look stupid. And I couldn't say a word. Boring old suit and no throne and big gut and all, he was the *King*. Even if he didn't wear his blue suede shoes.

He had to go away and do something important, but before he did, he told Aunt Hattie to take us around. So we saw the throne, and I even sat in the back seat for a minute. It felt weird, sitting up there in a car that runs and everything, with a gold key in the ignition all ready to turn and the gas tank reading *Full* in diamond letters. So people would know the state was running smooth, Aunt Hattie said. So he could make a fast get-away if a terrorist came along, *I* thought.

We saw the throne, like I said, and we saw where the lords and ladies all meet and have dances and jam sessions and parliaments, and we got to see a bit of the place where the royal family lives, just the living room and a little bedroom that wasn't much bigger than mine at home. We got to see the kennels, too, but not Nancy the Tenth, who was still waiting to have her puppies. I asked momma if we could get a puppy when we got home. Momma gave me a Look.

Then Aunt Hattie took us out to the Heartbreak Hotel for dinner, and momma had lobster but I had steak, I didn't like the way the lobster was looking at me. We were ma'amed there, too, and they gave us champagne on the house. Momma looked real happy at that. I thought it was icky, so they gave me ginger ale instead.

Then we stayed the night in Graceland, right there in the palace, and in the morning we went home. Momma and I decided that she had prettier kings in her collection, and younger ones, and even a few who were kingier, if you know what I mean. But when we came right down to it, for a real, solid, all-around King, there isn't anybody to beat Elvis.

### III. *Divus Elvis*
#### *Rex quondam, rexque futurus*

The pope was dying in Memphis. The cardinals stood in attendance, a circle of blue and glistening white, intoning the prayers for the all-but-departed. The Sisters of Saint Marilyn knelt in their red habits; the Brothers of Saint John Lennon bent their heads, obscuring the gleam of their wire-rimmed spectacles. Acolytes stood waiting with censers and lumelights. One proud, trembling child held the Keys to the Cadillac, which she must pass to the pope's successor in the moment of the pope's death.

Her holiness lay deep in a coma. She wore the full regalia of her office, the white sequined jumpsuit hanging slack on her wasted bones, the wig with its pompadour fallen askew on her shaven skull, her hands folded over the platinum-plated mike with its crusting of sequins and sacred symbols. Before she lost consciousness she had refused the ritual drug overdose. She would die under her own power, she had said. Those were her last words.

Her successor should have been seated by the bed, watching the rising and falling of the sunken breast, waiting for it to stop. But he had excused himself. Fled, one might have said, from the light and the music and the faint, advancing reek of death.

The election was past, her holiness' will affirmed. He would inherit the Mike and the Wig and the Keys. He would serve the Servants of God in Song, prince of the Church of Elvis Transcendent. There was no appeal of that judgment, and no escape from it but the one his predecessor was taking.

He walked softly into the cathedral. The Cadillac, once mere earthly throne, now seat of the Divine King, shone blinding under the spotlights. There was the usual mob round the Tomb, streaming past it on the rolling runway, with guards to keep them from stopping or backpedaling. They were silent except for the shuffle of feet, the catch of a sob.

Beyond the altar and the Tomb, the cathedral was nearly dark. Lumelights and the occasional lava lamp dispelled the shadows in side chapels. He made his way with sure steps, evading pews and praying devotees, walking patrol as he liked to think of it.

His destination was near the farthest corner, a chapel to which few people went. Its lumelight was almost dead. He plugged in the lava lamp, reverently, and knelt in its glow. The altar here was plain, a chrome table spread with a white cloth, no image on it, no vessels, only the table, the quiet, the emptiness.

But here more than anywhere, he felt the presence of the King. In this plain place, this silence without disruption, he heard best the Voice above all voices.

"Lord," he whispered, "I am not worthy."

He received no answer, unless silence itself was a response.

"I was a simple man," he said, "a keeper of hounds in your kennel. What have I done to deserve your favor?"

Silence. Outside the chapel, a figure passed. Sister of the Sacred Spouse—his eye caught the gleam of silver fringes, the sheen of lavalight on the platinum wig.

"Your yoke is heavy, your burden too great. How am I to speak for you in these worlds? Mars Ultima has seceded from Mars Proxima. Titan Station has turned apostate and embraced the Unfaith of Unholy Marx. Earth wages its wars as it has since time began. Who will listen to my poor voice?"

"Who else among the cardinals can carry a tune?"

He did not start or turn. Cardinal Archbishop Rollins sat beside him in a whisper of blue suede. She was the oldest of the College, but she had a bent for the unusual; she had tried one of the new rejuvenation treatments. It had been, as far as he could see, a remarkable success. He doubted that she had been so Dollyesque in contour even as a young woman.

"So you need me to sing the masses," he said. "Wouldn't any backstage crooner have done as well?"

"Any backstage crooner isn't Cardinal Bishop John Elvis Lennon."

"So," he said with bitterness that he did not need to feign. "It's nepotism, no more."

She shrugged. "Why not? We need a solid figure-head. Martha was good, mind you, but she wasn't holy family. She had to work that much harder to make her authority stick. You've got it from the start. It's bred in."

He tapped his forehead. "Not up here."

"Who cares what's up there? You'll think for yourself, or we'll do your thinking for you. We've got to get Titan back, and Disunited Europe is getting worse by the day, and Venus Dome is trying to renege on its contract. You're young, you're holy family, you look vigorous enough to last. Even Titan might be willing to pay attention when you put them under anathema."

"Anathema won't mean a thing to the Unfaithful," he said.

"It will if you put the fear of the King in them."

He sat on his heels and fixed his eyes on the empty altar. It wavered and blurred. "I don't want to be pope. I didn't even want to be a cardinal. I'm not *worthy!*"

"Bullpuckey," said the Cardinal Archbishop. "Pull up your socks and stop sniffling. You'll be pope and that's that."

His fists hurt with clenching. "Why don't *you* do it?"

"Because I can serve the Church better where I am," she said. "Now get up. Martha's hanging on by a thread, and you're going to be there when she takes that last breath."

"No," he said.

For too brief a moment he thought he had won. Cardinal Archbishop Rollins was a little thing, no higher than his shoulder; he could dig in his heels, and she could never move him.

Then she got a grip on his ear. "Are you walking or am I dragging you?"

"I'll cry murder," he said.

"Go right ahead," she said. "I'll yell louder. Off key."

He flinched.

She did not let go his ear, but neither did she twist
it. "Look here," she said more softly. "We really do
need you. *You,* not somebody else. Because of who you
are, yes. Because you can sing—which, really, was
more than the King could do. He always sang flat."

He sucked in his breath, horrified; but a small, vile
part of him whispered that she was right.

She went on as if she had not uttered heresy. "And,
my dear, because you honestly do believe the cant you
sing. Martha was too dry a wit. She lost converts because she challenged their brand-new faith. She asked
them to think about what they believed in. Which you
don't do if you're building a church."

He clapped his hand over the ear that was still free
of her deathgrip. Her voice came unimpeded through
the other. "You're going to be our evangelical pope,
young John. You'll rock and sing your way across the
worlds, and you'll make us triumphant."

"I will not!"

She let him go. His ear ached and burned. But he did
not move to comfort it. She smiled a she-devil's smile.
"You won't advance the faith? You won't help the
church to prosper? You'll let it fall because you don't
want to get involved?"

Cardinal sins, all of those. And yet what she asked
of him, vile, venal, cynical—

She shook her head. "You've been a cardinal this
long, and you never caught on? Maybe you are as
brainless as you think."

"I close my eyes to foulness, my ears to temptation." As he spoke, he did both. The dark was blessed,
the quiet less than absolute.

"They'll love you in Titan City," she said, sharp and
clear. "Sulk for a while, then. But not too long. When
they blow the horn, it's going to be you behind the
wheel, and your Key in the ignition. Like it or not."

Alive, he wondered, or dead?

That was despair. Despair was a sin. "Is there no escape?"

"Not a one," she said.

He huddled on the cold hard floor. "You are all devils."

"We serve the King," she said.

His head came up. Even as far down as he was in desperation, her tone astonished him. "You do believe that."

She did not answer. She had the face of the rejuvenated, smooth but not young; ageless. Like a dark angel's.

Temptation, he thought. Corruption.

And yet . . .

"If I take what you force on me," he said, "and I cry anathema on you all, what will you do?"

"Accept," she said, "and pray that you find good guidance."

"Guidance controlled by you?"

"You could kill us," she pointed out.

He shuddered. But he said, "I might."

She neither flinched nor laughed. She waited. For what, he could well guess.

He did not give her what she wanted: either threats or pleading. He folded his hands, bowed his head.

There was no Voice in this place, with her presence throbbing in it. He had no guidance but his heart, and that thudded and stuttered. He had never had a choice. This cup was his, no matter where he turned.

But what he did with it—there was all the power he had.

She thought she knew what he would do. So did they all. And maybe they were right. Maybe, Elvis willing, they were not.

He felt the brush of wings as soft as sleep, but stronger than sleep could ever be. Death had come for the pope. And yet, maybe, it waited; it watched him, not to claim him, nor to compel him, but simply to see how he would move.

Still he remained on his knees. The cold weight of the Keys seemed already to fill his hands. In his strong sweet voice he began to pray. He prayed long, and he prayed hard, and he prayed alone.

Until he had come almost to the end. Then at last her

voice wound in with his; and the horn sounded beneath it, the clarion call of the Cadillac, marking the passing of the Keeper of the Keys.

*Holy Elvis, father of songs, pray for us singers, now and to the end of our dance. Amen.*

# Science Fiction Anthologies

☐ **FUTURE EARTHS: UNDER AFRICAN SKIES**  UE2544—$4.99
*Mike Resnick & Gardner Dozois, editors*
From a utopian space colony modeled on the society of ancient Kenya,
to a shocking future discovery of a "long-lost" civilization, to an ingenious cure for one of humankind's oldest woes—a cure that might cost
too much—here are 15 provocative tales about Africa in the future and
African culture transplanted to different worlds.

☐ **FUTURE EARTHS: UNDER SOUTH AMERICAN SKIES**
*Mike Resnick & Gardner Dozois, editors*  UE2581—$4.99
From a plane crash that lands its passengers in a survival situation
completely alien to anything they've ever experienced, to a close encounter of the insect kind, to a woman who has journeyed unimaginably
far from home—here are stories from the rich culture of South America,
with its mysteriously vanished ancient civilizations and magnificent
artifacts, its modern-day contrasts between sophisticated city dwellers
and impoverished villagers.

☐ **MICROCOSMIC TALES**  UE2532—$4.99
*Isaac Asimov, Martin H. Greenberg, & Joseph D. Olander, eds.*
Here are 100 wondrous science fiction short-short stories, including
contributions by such acclaimed writers as Arthur C. Clarke, Robert
Silverberg, Isaac Asimov, and Larry Niven. Discover a superman who
lives in a *real* world of nuclear threat . . . an android who dreams of
electric love . . . and a host of other tales that will take you instantly
out of this world.

☐ **WHATDUNITS**  UE2533—$4.99
☐ **MORE WHATDUNITS**  UE2557—$5.50
*Mike Resnick, editor*
In these unique volumes of all-original stories, Mike Resnick has created a series of science fiction mystery scenarios and set such inventive sleuths as Pat Cadigan, Judith Tarr, Katharine Kerr, Jack Haldeman,
and Esther Friesner to solving them. Can you match wits with the
masters to make the perpetrators fit the crimes?

---

## *Welcome to DAW's Gallery of Ghoulish Delights!*

☐ **DRACULA: PRINCE OF DARKNESS**
  *Martin H. Greenberg, editor*
A blood-draining collection of all-original Dracula stories. From Dracula's traditional stalking grounds to the heart of modern-day cities, the Prince of Darkness casts his spell over his prey in a private blood drive from which there is no escape!
UE2531—$4.99

☐ **FRANKENSTEIN: THE MONSTER WAKES**
  *Martin H. Greenberg, editor*
Powerful visions of a man and monster cursed by destiny to be eternally at odds. Here are all-original stories by such well-known writers as: Rex Miller, Max Allan Collins, Brian Hodge, Rick Hautala, and Daniel Ransom.     UE2584—$4.99

☐ **JOURNEYS TO THE TWILIGHT ZONE**
  *Carol Serling, editor*
From a dog given a transfusion of werewolf blood, to a cocktail party hypnosis session that went a step too far, here are 16 journeys—to that most unique of dimensions—*The Twilight Zone.*—by such masters of the fantastic as Alan Dean Foster, William F. Nolan, Charles de Lint, and Kristine Katherine Rusch.
UE2525—$4.99

☐ **URBAN HORRORS**
  *William F. Nolan and Martin H. Greenberg, editors*
Here are 18 powerful nightmare visions of the horrors that stalk the dark streets of the cities and the lonely, echoing hallways of our urban dwellings in this harrowing collection of modern-day terrors, stories by Ray Bradbury, Richard Matheson, John Cheever, Shirley Jackson and their fellow fright-mastern
UE2548—$5.50

☐ **THE YEAR'S BEST HORROR STORIES: XXI**
  *Karl Edward Wagner, editor*
More provocative tales of terror, including: a photographer whose obsession with images may bring to life trouble beyond his wildest fantasies . . . a couple caught up in an ancient ritual that offers the promise of health, but at a price that may prove far too high . . . and a woman whose memory may be failing her with the passing years—or for a far more unnatural reason.     UE2572—$5.50

---

# FANTASY ANTHOLOGIES

Coming in HARDCOVER in January 1994:

# THE BLACK GRYPHON
## Book One of the Mage Wars
## by Mercedes Lackey
## and Larry Dixon

A grand excursion into the prehistory of the best-selling Valdemar series, THE BLACK GRYPHON takes place more than a thousand years before the action of Mercedes Lackey's other novels. It is an age when Valdemar is yet unfounded, its organization of Heralds yet unformed, and magic is still a wild and uncontrolled force. Skandranon Rashkae is perhaps the finest specimen of his race, with gleaming ebony feathers, majestic wingspan, keen magesight, and sharp intelligence. Courageous, bold, and crafty, Skan is everything a gryphon should be. He is the fulfillment of everything that the Mage of Silence, the human sorcerer called Urtho, intended to achieve when he created these magical beings to be the defenders of his realm—a verdant plain long coveted by the evil mage Maar. Now Maar is once again advancing on Urtho's Keep, this time with a huge force spearheaded by magical constructs of his own—cruel birds of prey ready to perform any evil their creator may demand of them. And when one of Urtho's Seers wakes from a horrifying vision in which she sees a devastating magical weapon being placed in the hands of Maar's common soldiers, Skandranon is sent to spy across enemy lines, cloaked in the protection of Urtho's powerful Spell of Silence. As days pass and Skandranon doesn't show up, all in Urtho's camp wait anxiously, fearing that this prince of gryphons will never return. . . .

☐ **Hardcover Edition**                                    UE2577—$22.00

---